Seduced by His Touch

SEDUCED BY HIS TOUCH

TRACY ANNE WARREN

THORNDIKE
CHIVERS

This Large Print edition is published by Thorndike Press, Waterville, Maine, USA and by BBC Audiobooks Ltd, Bath, England.
Thorndike Press, a part of Gale, Cengage Learning.

The text of this Large Print edition is unabridged.
Other aspects of the book may vary from the original edition.
Set in 16 pt. Plantin.

LIBRARY OF CONGRESS CATALOGING-IN-PUBLICATION DATA

Warren, Tracy Anne.
Seduced by his touch / by Tracy Anne Warren. — Large print ed.
p. cm. — (Thorndike Press large print romance)
ISBN-13: 978-1-4104-2700-7
ISBN-10: 1-4104-2700-5
1. Nobility—England—Fiction. 2. Arranged marriage—Fiction. 3. London (England)—Social life and customs—19th century—Fiction. 4. Large type books. I. Title.
PS3623.A8665S43 2010
813'.6—dc22 2010008744

BRITISH LIBRARY CATALOGUING-IN-PUBLICATION DATA AVAILABLE

Published in 2010 in the U.S. by arrangement with Avon, an imprint of HarperCollins Publishers.
Published in 2010 in the U.K. by arrangement with HarperCollins Publishers.

U.K. Hardcover: 978 1 408 49160 7 (Chivers Large Print)
U.K. Softcover: 978 1 408 49161 4 (Camden Large Print)

Printed in the United States of America
1 2 3 4 5 6 7 14 13 12 11 10

Seduced by His Touch

Chapter 1

London, England
Early August 1809

"Dearly beloved, we are gathered together here in the sight of God, and in the face of this congregation, to join together this man and this woman in holy matrimony . . ."

Lord John Byron — or "Jack" as he was known to his family and friends — fought the urge to give a good, hard tug to his starched, white cravat. Ever since he'd walked into St. George's Church this morning and taken his place at the altar, his breath had grown increasingly shallow, his throat constricting, as though an invisible hand were squeezing in a vise grip.

His reaction might have been understandable except for one small fact — he was only the best man!

But just watching his brother, Cade, take the irrevocable, final step into matrimonial bondage was enough to send Jack's usually cool composure straight to the devil. That and the realization that in a few months' time — if matters progressed as they seemed likely to — he would be following in his brother's footsteps.

Blast, Jack cursed in his head, barely aware of the continuing ceremony, *I've gotten myself into a real fix this time.* If only he'd never gone to that accursed gambling hell last Wednesday night. If only he hadn't sat down across the gaming table with that unremarkable-looking, middle-aged Cit and the lure of his irresistibly deep pockets.

The play had gone well at first — Jack winning enough hands to slowly and steadily build his earnings, just as he'd expected. The assumption that he was an excellent player was no idle boast; he'd spent enough years supplementing his meager inheritance by working the card tables to know he possessed more than average skill. And unlike many of his fellow aristocrats, who were willing to bet entire fortunes on a single hand, he never took wild risks. He was always careful, playing with premeditated calculation and a healthy respect for the odds.

Until last week, that is.

He remembered relaxing back in his chair, certain he owned the game. After all, he had an unbeatable hand. There was only one card that could best it, one card that stood between him and a hundred thousand pounds! The chance of the other man having it was astronomical. Studying the rich Cit on the other side of the baize-covered table, he'd waited, eager to experience the thrill and satisfaction of becoming a very wealthy man himself. With that kind of money, he'd found himself thinking, he would never have to gamble again.

Then the merchant had revealed his cards and sent Jack's world reeling.

Ironic, he mused now, as the ceremony droned on, *that a red jack was the cause of my downfall.* One wicked little card that had stabbed him through the heart and given his opponent a once-in-a-lifetime win.

And now that opponent wanted his pound of flesh — only not in cash but in trade. All Jack had to do was marry the merchant's spinster daughter and his debt would be erased. In exchange for the sacrifice of his freedom and his happiness, he could be as rich as he'd dreamed.

"I'm not an unreasonable man," the Cit, Ezra Danvers, told him during their private meeting two days later. "I want my Gracie well-cared for, which is why she'll come to you with her dowry intact. Sixty thousand pounds. I'll kick in another sixty when the ring is on her finger and the marriage consummated. I want grandchildren, mind you. *Aristocratic* grandchildren, who will move with kings and princes, and who will never know what it is to be shunned by your kind of Society."

"Why me?" Jack ground out when he could manage the question. "Why not a titled peer? Surely there must be one willing to take your daughter to wife."

"Probably so, but I don't want some damned fortune hunter. I won't have her abused."

"What makes you think I will treat her well?"

The other man raised a grizzled brow and stared at Jack over his large beak of a nose, his eyes shrewd with intelligence. "Oh, I know a great deal about you, my lord. You have a way with the ladies, and although you don't stay long with any of them, you're never cruel when you leave. You'll see to it my girl's pleasured in bed and treated with the proper respect. If you don't, of course, I'll have your head."

Gauging Danvers, Jack had no trouble believing the threat.

"I cannot promise a lifetime of fidelity," Jack stated, hoping such an admission might dissuade the merchant.

Instead, Danvers shrugged. "What man can? Keep her pregnant and contented, and seek your occasional comfort elsewhere. Discreetly, of course. I understand you nobs are good at that. Having hush-hush affairs outside the sanctity of marriage."

Danvers was right. Most aristocratic marriages were based on practicalities, such as the accumulation of wealth, land or social position. Love, even liking, was a matter of scant consideration, expected to be found with someone other than one's spouse.

In general, Jack considered himself a cynic. But perhaps there was more of the romantic in him than he cared to admit, since he didn't fancy the idea of wedding for money, or without affection. As for love . . . well, he would leave such sentimental folderol to the poets. Perhaps that fellow Lord Byron, who shared nothing in common with Jack and his family save a name, might enjoy trying his hand at the subject.

"You do realize I am a third son and will never inherit anything of significance, certainly not the title," Jack offered, feeling the noose growing tighter around his neck by the second. "Your grandchildren will never be more than ordinary misters and misses."

"Not ordinary at all. They'll be the nieces and nephews of a duke, and for that they'll marry well when the time comes. In the meanwhile, my girl will be a lady. Lady John Byron, sister-in-law to the Duke of Clybourne — one of the most powerful men in the realm. I like the sound of that, and she will, too, once you convince her to marry you."

"What do you mean? *Convince?*"

Danvers waved a dismissive hand. "Grace has these notions in her head, but never mind that. She'll come around. All you've got to do is make her fall in love with you. That and persuade her you return the feeling."

"That might not be so simple."

The older man's face hardened. "Make it simple. You're good at seducing women, so seduce her. Otherwise, there's a little matter of one hundred thousand pounds outstanding. I presume, my lord, that you are not in possession of such a sum."

No, by God, Jack had thought, silently grinding his teeth. *I most certainly am not.*

One hundred and twenty thousand pounds, plus his debt cleared. For that kind of money, one might expect that Miss Grace Danvers would have married long ago. Perhaps it was simply a matter of her father protecting her from unscrupulous predators, but he sensed there was more.

What if there's something amiss with her? he considered with a queasy swallow. According to her father, she was five and twenty years of age. No dewy-eyed ingénue but instead a woman full-grown, who was close to earning a permanent place on the shelf.

But no matter Miss Danvers's potential faults, what real choice did he have? If he didn't agree to marry her, he faced the unenviable option of going to debtor's prison. Or worse, applying to his brother Edward for the funds.

Frankly, he'd rather take his chances in Fleet!

"Oh, and one more thing," Danvers had warned. "Grace must never learn of our arrangement. In fact, I'd advise against her even knowing you and I have met. If she ever gets wind of the truth, well, the whole plan will go up like a cannon blast. See you take care to remember that."

And so, here he now stood, caught firmly beneath the sword of Damocles. He supposed there were worse things than marriage, although right now he couldn't seem to think of any. *Cade looks happy enough,* Jack reasoned, as his attention returned to the ceremony. *Why wouldn't he though, when he is marrying an angel?*

His brother's bride, Meg, certainly looked the part, dressed all in white, with her blond hair swept upward in soft waves beneath her lace veil, her lake blue eyes aglow with unconcealed joy. Her love for Cade was clear, as was her gentle sweetness and caring ways. *Cade is a fortunate man,* he thought. *I should be half so lucky.*

"And now for the ring," the bishop intoned.

Jack waited, along with the nearly one hundred other guests gathered to witness the marriage. Someone coughed, the sound echoing through the church, followed by a faint rustling as people shifted in the pews.

Suddenly, he began to notice the stares, especially those of the rest of the bridal party. Edward, who had given the bride away, furrowed his dark brows from his front-row seat next to their mother. His sister Mallory and the other bridesmaids started nodding and mouthing things at him from the bride's side opposite, while his brother Drake nudged him none too gently in the ribs. Even Cade and Meg turned their heads to see what was the matter.

Abruptly Jack's mind cleared. "Oh, the ring!"

Light laughter floated through the hall as he patted his pockets, disremembering in which one he'd placed the engraved gold band. His irreverent seventeen-year-old twin brothers, Leo and Lawrence, began to snicker from their places in the line of groomsmen.

Seconds later, Jack located the ring, his fingers brushing briefly against a note tucked next to it. Ignoring the missive, he extracted the jewelry. "Exactly where I left it," he announced with a smile. "Thought I'd give everyone a little extra excitement." With an apologetic glance at Cade, he handed over the ring. Cade, however, was far too ebullient to do more than shake his head with good humor and turn back to his bride.

As the vows proceeded, Jack couldn't help but think of the note his fingers had brushed against, the paper suddenly burning a hole in his breast pocket.

If you want to see Grace, go to Hatchard's this afternoon at four. She'll be the tall one with red hair. Knowing my girl, she'll most likely have on her spectacles. Don't be late.

Yours,
E. G. Danvers

A tall redhead with spectacles, Jack groaned in his head. *At least it ought to make her easy to spot! Please God,* he prayed, as he watched his brother join his life with his new bride's, *just don't let her be a gorgon.*

The sense of being watched prickled over Grace Lilah Danvers's nerve endings as she stood in the stacks at Hatchard's Bookshop. She swung her head around sharply but found no one there.

I am being silly, she admonished herself, looking away. *After all, who could possibly be watching me?*

Long ago, she'd resigned herself to the knowledge that she was not the sort of woman who received looks — at least not of the admiring variety. Although she had often been told that she had a pleasant — some might even say pretty — countenance, with lovely translucent skin and straight, white teeth, she was what the vernacular of the day called "a long Meg."

Standing five feet ten inches tall in her stockings, she supposed they had good reason for applying the term. She towered over all the women of her acquaintance, and a great many of the men as well. To make matters worse, she wasn't the delicate, ethereal sort with slight bones and a wispy shape. Instead she was what her father liked to call "sensibly built," neither fat nor thin but "as robust and seaworthy as one of his fleet of shipping vessels." Not that she was without her share of feminine curves, but thanks to the current fashion for empire-waisted gowns, that fact wasn't always so easy to discern. Then, too, there was her need for reading spectacles, unfortunate but unavoidable.

Glancing around once more, she shook her head and resumed her inspection of the book in her hands. She turned a page and skimmed a passage or two, then carefully placed the volume back onto the shelf before selecting another.

As she did, she caught sight of a pair of shoes just visible in the aisle beyond. Men's shoes. Startled despite her best intentions, she spun the opposite way and, in doing so, lost hold of her book. The leather-bound tome hit the waxed wooden floor with a resounding thud and skidded several feet distant.

At that same moment, another gentleman appeared around the corner, the book coming to a halt beside the toe of his neatly polished Hessians. Stopping, he bent to retrieve the wayward volume. He straightened, then strolled toward her.

"Yours, I presume?" he said in a deep, richly modulated voice that put her in mind of hot buttered rum on a cold winter day and the sensual luxury of lying amid warm silken sheets. Inwardly, she quivered. Her reply, whatever it might be, stuck like a stone in her throat; the incapacity only worsened when she lifted her gaze to his.

Bold and intelligent, his eyes shone like a set of imperial jewels, their shade an improbably pure blue that lay somewhere between sapphire and lapis lazuli. He was sinfully handsome, with a refined jaw, a long, straight nose and a mouth that seemed the very embodiment of temptation. His mahogany-dark hair was cut short, the severe style unable to tame a rebellious wave that lent the ends just the faintest hint of curl.

But most enticing of all was his height — his large, muscular, impressive height. She guessed he must be six feet three or four at least, his build broad and powerful enough to make even her feel small.

Drawing a shivery breath, she dropped her gaze to the floor. *What am I doing?* she chided herself. *Acting like some giddy schoolgirl, that's what. Men like him are out of my reach. As distant to me as the stars. Men like him are also dangerous, and I would do well never to forget that fact.*

"Dr. Johnson, hmm?" he mused aloud, inspecting the title. "Personally, I prefer someone with a really cutting tongue. Swift, for instance."

She waited until she could trust herself to speak with calm self-possession. "Both are fine authors in their own way, each with his faults and merits, to be sure. I thank you, sir, for retrieving the volume for me."

There, she thought, *that should be the end of that.* He would hand her the book, offer some polite comment, and be on his way again.

Instead he made her a bow. A very elegant, very urbane bow that, she imagined, charmed ladies wherever he went. In fact, his every word and movement bespoke the fact that he was a gentleman, an aristocrat. Further reason why their encounter should have a quick resolution.

"Pray allow me to introduce myself," he said, much to her surprise. "I am Lord John Byron. 'Jack' to my acquaintance. And you are . . . ?"

A tiny frown settled between her brows, her spectacles inching slightly lower on her nose. "Miss Grace Danvers. Now, if you will excuse me, my lord, I must be on my way."

"Surely not so soon. There is your choice

of reading material yet to be decided."

"I have books aplenty already waiting with the clerk, and at home as well. I count myself well satisfied."

He paused. "If you are certain. I shall bid you good-day then. A pleasure, Miss Danvers."

"Hmm, yes. Good-day, my lord." Turning, she forced herself to walk away. As she did, she began the process of putting him from her mind, knowing she would never have cause to encounter the likes of Lord Jack Byron again.

Careful to maintain his distance, Jack followed Grace out of the stacks. He stopped and folded his arms across his chest, then leaned a shoulder against an end post as he watched her stroll into the open common area where patrons congregated to read and talk. Clerks buzzed hither and thither as they strove to be of assistance. It was to one of them that she applied, the young man moving to retrieve her selections and see them properly wrapped. Accepting a seat and a cup of tea in the meantime, she waited.

So that, he mused, *is Ezra Danvers's daughter.*

As he'd expected, she had not been difficult to locate — her height, more than her red hair, giving her identity away. When Danvers said she was tall, Jack hadn't realized just how true that would be. Of all the women Jack had come to know over the course of his eight-and-twenty years — and that was a great many indeed — Grace was far and away the tallest.

During their brief conversation, he'd found himself struck by the novelty of not having to crane his neck or stoop downward in order to accommodate a shorter female companion. With Grace he'd been able to remain at his full height, needing to do nothing more than lower his gaze a few scant inches to meet her own.

And while she was clearly not the most beautiful woman he'd ever met, she was far from the gorgon he'd initially feared. Her features were . . . amiable. Her skin was clear, her cheekbones nicely rounded, her nose neither too long nor too short, with a full lower lip and a chin that reminded him a bit of a button.

Of all her rather unremarkable features, her eyes were her strong point, despite being partially hidden behind a pair of spectacles. A gentle blue-grey, their color shifted in the most interesting manner from gentian to pewter depending upon the light. He supposed most people never noticed such subtle variations, thinking her irises to be either plain grey or ordinary blue, but he'd found himself intrigued; more so than he might have expected after such a brief encounter.

As for her figure, she had all the right feminine parts. Her breasts appeared more than adequately sized — enough to give a man a good handful to fondle and kiss. Her waist, hips and legs — concealed as they were beneath the drape of her petticoats and gown — hinted at all manner of shapely possibilities. What would it be like, he wondered, to lie atop such a long, agile body? To have legs that must go on forever wrapped around his waist or hooked over his shoulders? How low down his back would her heels touch? And what tricks might he be able to teach her using those lovely hands and feet?

His groin swelled with unmistakable arousal, leaving him surprised. At least bedding her, he realized, was not going to be a problem.

Abruptly he blinked. *Lord above, am I really planning to go through with this? Am I really going to make her my wife?*

He swallowed, his erection partially subsiding at the thought. Just because he didn't mind the idea of tupping her didn't mean he was eager to slip a ring on her finger. But try as he might, he could conceive of no other way out. Danvers had him trapped like a fox in a covert, hounds poised at the ready to make the kill. His only salvation was marriage — to Grace Danvers.

There were other heiresses, he supposed, with finer pedigrees and more beautiful faces. But none of them possessed the kind of dowry necessary to pay off his vowels — not and still leave enough funds for him to support a wife. Besides, if Danvers got wind he was trying to marry some girl other than his daughter, the crafty old man would call in the debt so fast that Jack might as well step into a prison cell right now.

No, it was Miss Danvers or no one.

And so, assuming he was truly determined on this course — and it would seem that he was — he would do well to begin.

First, he would need to woo her. Luckily, he had no doubt as to his abilities in that quarter. He'd been seducing women since he was a green lad, not even old enough to shave. He could have her on her back with her skirts up around her waist before she even knew what he was about. But getting her to trust him, to love him . . . ah, now that would be the real trick.

With most women he would use flattery and flirtation, appealing to both their vanity and their pleasure. But Grace was no ordinary woman. With her, he knew he would have to take a more subtle approach. Less than half a minute into their acquaintance, he'd sensed her reserve, as well as her insecurity. He surmised she wasn't used to being boldly pursued by men, so any sudden, overt interest on his part would only provoke her suspicions and put her on the alert.

Instead, his approach would require a deft touch and gentle, patient persuasion. A shy doe required proper coaxing, after all. The key was to figure out what kind of inducement she liked best and be there to offer it.

He watched as she raised her teacup to her lips — unaware of his observation this time. He realized now that he'd been careless before, that despite his efforts at stealth, she had sensed his presence as she wandered among the books. If not for that other man, she would likely have fled from him. Instead, the stranger had inadvertently sent her in his direction, casting him in the guise of savior. Really, he owed the fellow his thanks. Otherwise, securing an introduction would have required a great deal more effort on his part, particularly since he and Miss

Danvers didn't ordinarily run in the same social circles. But she knew him now, and very soon she would come to know him a great deal better.

He was about to depart, when he saw a man approach Grace. It was obvious from her reaction that she knew him, a friendly smile curving her mouth as she stood to greet the newcomer.

Nearly a match for Grace in height, the man topped her by no more than an inch. His hair was sandy blond, his build rangy and loose-limbed, with features designed to neither excite admiration nor draw disdain. Judging by his attire, he was likely in trade of some sort. Or possibly in one of the professions. A solicitor, maybe, or a physician?

Who is he? Jack wondered. *More importantly, who is he to Grace?* Danvers hadn't mentioned any beaux. Of course the fellow could be a relative of some variety, but he didn't think so. No, the other man had designs on her. What kind, however, remained to be seen.

Well, no matter, Jack told himself. His sandy-haired rival wouldn't be competition for long. And once he was eliminated from the field, Miss Grace Danvers would be free and ready to step straight into Jack's waiting arms.

Chapter 2

"My thanks for seeing me home," Grace told Terrence Cooke a half hour later as she walked through the front door of her father's house in St. Martin's Lane.

A frequent visitor to the residence, Terrence strolled inside with her. After exchanging familiar greetings with the housekeeper, who took his hat to set on the hall credenza, he and Grace went into the parlor.

"Will you stay for tea?" she asked, laying her brown-paper-wrapped parcel of books on the sofa before taking a seat beside it. "You know Martha will be here, as soon as the kettle can be set to boil. She'll bring a tray of sandwiches and sweets, then make you up a big plate, all the while fussing about how thin you are, and why don't you eat better at home."

"She forgets sometimes that I have a mother of my own."

"Who lives by the seashore in Lyme. An

excuse such as that will never do, not in Martha's estimation at least."

He smiled and took a chair opposite. "I'll stay long enough to appease her, but then I ought to be going."

Grace paused, well aware of his preference for not tarrying. "Papa won't be home until after seven. You know he meets with his investors every Thursday night."

"True. Still, it's easier not to chance an unexpected encounter. I'm not high on your father's list of favorites, you know."

Sadly, on that point, Terrence was correct. For reasons Grace had never understood, her father did not approve of her friendship with Cooke and barely tolerated her continued association with him. She assumed his dislike stemmed from the fact that Terrence was the publisher of a small press — successful in his way, but nothing to compare with the immense achievements and ambition of her father.

She should surround herself with a better class of people, Papa liked to complain. Do everything in her power to move up in the world by marrying a man of wealth and rank, instead of dabbling in the silly, nonsensical pursuits in which she insisted upon squandering her time. *"I didn't send you to that fancy ladies' academy so you could rub shoulders with the likes of paper-inkers and wood-cutters!"* he would rail every so often after one of Terrence's visits. If he could have bullied Grace into severing the connection, she was sure he would have banned Terrence from the house long ago.

"You may not be on Papa's list of favorites," she admitted, "but you are on mine. Therefore you have every right to stay as my guest. In fact, why do you not remain for dinner? Martha would relish the chance to stuff you full of turtle soup, roast chicken and peach tart; all selections on tonight's menu, if I remember correctly."

His brown eyes warmed. "It sounds delectable. However, I really do need to be leaving shortly. A prior engagement, you see."

"An engagement, hmm?" she teased in a soft voice. "This wouldn't happen to involve a lady, now would it?"

His expression grew serious. "No, not at all. Besides, you know you're the only woman for me."

"I most certainly hope not," she said, trying to laugh off the remark.

But he leaned forward in his chair and stretched out a hand. "Just say the word, Grace, and I'll set matters in motion. You're of age, so there's no impediment to obtaining a special license. Tell me yes, and we can be married in less than a week."

Her smile dropped away. "Terrence, don't, please. We've been through this before and you know my feelings —"

"And you know mine," he interrupted. "I won't ever be as rich as your father, but I have money, enough to keep you in a nice house and fine gowns. I would see to it you never wanted for anything."

Just so, she thought, lowering her gaze to the floor. *With Terrence, I would be comfortable, contented even. With him, I would have everything. Everything, that is, except love.*

How often she'd wished things might be different, that she could wake up one morning and find herself in love with him. How simple everything would be, then. For despite her father's certain displeasure, she would have weathered the storm for Terrence if she truly loved him. But she did not, and to her great sorrow, she knew she never would.

She sighed. "Please, let us speak no more of this. Can it not be enough that we are friends?"

"Yes, of course," he said, acceding to her wishes. "For now anyway. But I reserve the right to hope that someday you'll change your mind. When you do, I will be waiting."

Desperate to move on and put their conversation back on its earlier, easier footing, she rose and crossed the room. Taking a small key from her pocket, she unlocked a drawer in her satinwood writing desk. "I . . . um . . . I nearly forgot. I have these finished for you." Reaching inside, she withdrew a leather-bound folio, which she carried across to him.

Silently, he accepted the case, untying the strings that held the sides closed. One by one, he studied the illustrations inside, careful as he turned the large paper sheets with their fine watercolor renderings of birds. "These are your best yet," he pronounced. "Stunning, Grace. Absolutely stunning."

Her cheeks warmed with pleasure. "The chimney swallow turned out best, I think. I would like to have added a bit more green to the mallard, but I suppose he'll do."

Terrence smiled. "He'll more than do. It was my lucky day when we met at that ornithology lecture four summers ago. If not for that fateful introduction, I would likely never have thought of producing a series of illustrated nature books. I have no doubt this new one is going to make us a nice little profit."

Pin money, Grace thought. At least that's what Papa liked to call it, since her earnings never amounted to much more than her quarterly allowance. Nonetheless, the money she received from the publication of her "little watercolors" provided a small reserve for her use. More importantly, the money was hers. All hers. Derived by means of her own skills and efforts.

"We're receiving advanced orders already," Terrence confided as he carefully straightened the group of drawings inside the folio, then retied the strings. "Lord Astbury is taking two dozen this time. Told me he plans to give them out as gifts to his hunting friends."

Her lips parted as the implication sank in. "Why, that's dreadful. This book is supposed to be an ornithological reference guide."

"Apparently he and his toff friends don't care about such niceties. They like to study the birds, then go out and shoot them. Of course, what is it you said your cook is serving for dinner tonight? Roast chicken, I believe."

She glared at him for a moment, then released a laugh. "Point taken. Are you certain you won't stay to enjoy the carnage?"

Smiling, he shook his head. "No, but it is tempting. Look now, here is Martha with our tea." Setting the folio aside, he stood and helped the housekeeper with the heavy tray.

A crumpet and a slice of meat pie later, Terrence wiped his mouth on his napkin, then laid his plate aside. "So will I see you next Tuesday at the theater? They're doing Midsummer, I think."

Grace returned her teacup to its saucer. "Oh, did I not tell you? I am to go to my aunt Jane's in Bath for a few weeks. Apparently she wrote to Papa asking if I could stay with her. She wants to take the waters and hates the idea of being in the city alone, despite her wide circle of friends. I didn't see any way I could refuse."

"No, nor should you," he agreed, a slight frown on his brows.

"Not to worry," she assured him. "I shall take everything I need to begin work on the flower illustrations. You needn't have any concern that I shall be late in completing the new renderings."

"I know you won't. If there is anyone upon whom I can count, it is you. I will only miss you, that's all."

"Ah." She knew she should not encourage him. Still, he was her friend. "And I you," she said with sincerity. "And I you."

Late the following evening, Jack claimed his

release, his body shuddering, as he lay locked inside his mistress's arms. She glided her hands over him, her satisfaction plain. He'd taken care to make sure she peaked first, her cries of satisfaction loud enough to awaken the entire household. Luckily her servants were far too well-trained to react, even if they had noticed.

Striving to recover his breath, he rolled onto his back in the wide, satin-covered bed, unabashedly naked, the sheets and counterpane kicked to the floor long ago.

"Heavens, darling, you do that so-o-o-o-o well," she cooed, reaching out a delicate hand to smooth over his chest. "How soon do you imagine we can do it again?"

He chuckled. "Give me a minute and we'll see."

She smiled, her fingers drifting downward with the obvious intent of helping him along. For a moment, he allowed her to play, his interest only mildly reawakened. Then with a gentle touch, he captured her hand and folded it inside his own. "Philipa," he began, "about the country party next week . . ."

"Yes?" she said, leaning up so that he had an unobstructed view of her bare breasts and the tendrils of long, dark hair that cascaded over her shoulders in a most enticing way. "Just think of all the fun we're going to have. I can't wait to sneak into your room. Or would you rather sneak into mine?"

"I am sorry, but there isn't going to be any sneaking at all. At least not with me."

"What do you mean? Of course it will be with you."

He shook his head. "Not this time. I am afraid something else has occurred. I won't be attending the party."

Her smile fell away. "But I don't understand. You always go into the country this time of year."

"This year is different."

Sitting up, he propped himself against the pillows. As he did, he thought about the message he'd received this morning from Danvers advising him about Grace's plans for the remainder of the summer and fall. Considering all the implications, he set another few inches between himself and Philipa.

"I am going to Bath," he stated on a solemn rumble.

A hearty laugh rolled from her bow-shaped, cherry-pink lips. "*Bath!* As in the city? Oh, you're joshing me. Jack Byron in Bath, that will be the day. I suppose next you're going to tell me you are journeying there for the waters."

He lowered his gaze. "Actually, I'm going there for a bride."

Philipa's green eyes grew wide. "What! You're getting married?"

"So it would appear." Careful to make no mention of names or share the specific details of the agreement he'd struck with Danvers, he confided the basics of his situation to her.

"As you see," he concluded, "it's the only viable solution. I wish I could have found an easier way to tell you this, but the unvarnished truth seemed best."

Sliding from the bed, she retrieved her cream, flowered silk dressing gown from the floor and slipped into it. Tying the fastening at her waist, she turned back. "I can't say I am glad of the news, but I understand. Obviously, it is the prudent choice. I just never envisioned you entering into a marriage of convenience. This girl. What is she like?"

"She's . . ." He broke off, finding himself oddly reluctant to talk about Grace Danvers. *She's interesting,* he thought. And unusual, not at all like the women he knew. She was . . . complex.

Realizing the direction of his thoughts, he brought himself back to the topic at hand.

"What does it matter what she's like?" he said in a cool tone. "I am marrying her because it's what I must do. Anything else is irrelevant."

"Poor creature," Philipa remarked, strolling around to his side of the bed. "But knowing you, she'll probably fall instantly under your spell and count herself lucky to be your wife, whatever the circumstances. And I am sure, in your way, you'll be kind, even generous, to her."

Shifting her hip, she sat down next to him. "As for me, I know how to be patient. After all, I waited ten long, dreadful years for the death of that lecher my father forced me to wed. At least this girl will be getting a virile man in his prime rather than some dried-up goat, old enough to be her grandfather. Knowing what a fine lover you are, she is fortunate indeed. No woman would object to giving up her maidenhead to you. Would that I could have done so myself."

"Philipa —"

"Shh," she murmured, reaching up to feather her fingers through his hair. "Not to worry. When a suitable amount of time has passed, and you find yourself weary of playing husband, come back to me. You will always be welcome in my bed."

Catching her hand, he brought her palm

to his lips for a kiss. "You are too good, do you know that?"

She smiled and shook her head. "Good? There is nothing good about me. Unless you are talking about my abilities in the boudoir. Now, at that, I more than excel." Divesting herself of her dressing gown again, she moved to sit astride his hips. "What do you say to one last tumble before you go? Something to tide you over in the coming days, since Bath is one of the deadliest dull spots on earth."

He smiled and slid his arms around her small, willowy body. As he did, a memory of rich, red hair — Grace's hair — flashed in his mind for reasons he couldn't even begin to fathom.

Banishing the thought, he arched Philipa closer and took her up on her very generous offer.

CHAPTER 3

A little over a week later, Grace made her way into a small assembly room not far from Bath's Sydney Gardens, where an afternoon lecture on perennial floriculture was scheduled to take place.

So as not to let either her height or that of her bonnet brim impede anyone's view, she took a seat in the last row of chairs set up for the event. Withdrawing a small notebook and pencil from her reticule, she prepared to wait.

She'd arrived in the company of her maid, who was currently taking her ease with a group of other servants in an anteroom beyond. Grace had invited Aunt Jane to join her, but the older woman declined. Her aunt might love the fragrance and beauty of fresh flowers, but she had no patience for learning about their cultivation.

"That's what I keep Perkins for," Aunt Jane had told her this morning over tea, toast, and sausages. "I let him grub around in the garden dirt and tend the plants so I don't have to."

Given that Grace was no longer in her first flush of youth, her aunt had deemed it acceptable for her to attend the lecture with only a servant accompanying her. Aunt Jane had promised, however, to come by with the carriage at the end of the lecture so they could drive home together.

She checked the delicate gold and pearl watch pinned to her bodice and saw that another ten minutes remained before the talk was scheduled to begin. Glancing around, she studied the small, but growing, crowd, which was made up of mostly older, academically minded men and a trio of middle-aged bluestocking females.

Gazing idly along the length of her own row of chairs, she noticed a man seated at the far end. Dark-haired and attractive, he put her in mind of a panther who'd mistakenly wandered into a room full of ordinary grey cats. A curious little tingle sizzled along her spine as she stared, her pulse giving a rabbity hop.

Surely it can't be, she thought, but he reminded her of the man she'd met that day at Hatchard's. *The gorgeous, sophisticated, dangerously appealing Lord Jack Byron!*

After all, what would a man of Byron's obviously cosmopolitan tastes be doing in Bath? More particularly, why would he be attending a lecture about flowers?

Aristocrats went to their country estates this time of year to shoot grouse and visit with their lofty friends. They didn't come to the ancient, barely fashionable environs of Bath — not unless they were ill and in need of taking the waters. And no one looking at this man would ever believe him in anything but robust good health.

But it isn't him and I'm only misremembering, she told herself as she studied the dynamic angles of his profile, completely unable to look away.

Suddenly she had to know, aching for him to turn his head and let her see his entire face. One fleeting glance — just a glimpse of his eyes — and she would have her answer. After all, how many nights had it been now that she had dreamt of him, conjuring up images of the man and his unforgettable eyes?

Only every one since that first brief encounter.

How many moments had she spent woolgathering about him during the day?

Enough that I feel like a simpleton for being so weak and foolish.

She was scolding herself for acting the pea goose again when he turned his head and gazed straight at her. Her heart jumped; his eyes were even more sensuous and vividly blue than she recalled, his face more strikingly handsome than the warmest of her recollections. Air wheezed from her chest, the impact hitting her with the force of a quick, one-two punch. Glancing downward, she stared blindly at her shoes.

Stars above, it is Jack Byron!

Desperately she struggled to compose herself, forcing her heartbeat to slow and her breath to come at less erratic intervals.

Did he see me? Recognize me? Do I want him to?

Slowly, after a long, long minute, she glanced up and over, peering out from beneath her lashes.

Disappointment crashed through her. Not only was he *not* looking at her but he wasn't even in his chair anymore! In fact, it seemed he'd left the room.

She was still collecting herself and her thoughts when the guest speaker stepped up to the podium. A full five minutes passed, though, before she was able to pay him any mind, and another two after that before she opened her sketch pad and began to draw the floral samples arranged for illustration and display.

She was drawing with steady intent when she sensed someone ease into the chair to her right. At first she took little notice, her pencil moving with deliberation over the paper. Then, out of the corner of her eye, she glimpsed a pair of large, elegant black leather shoes. Slowly, her gaze roved higher to find powerful male legs clad in fawn-colored pantaloons positioned barely inches from her own.

A shiver tingled over her skin, along with an odd feeling of familiarity, as if she'd experienced a similar situation in the past. Abruptly, she realized she had.

Her pencil fell still.

"Your pardon," murmured the rich, masculine voice she'd heard that day at Hatchard's, "but haven't we met before? Miss Daniels, is it not?"

Even though she had no doubt as to his identity, her gaze slid upward. The action itself was noteworthy, considering she rarely had the need to look *up* to meet anyone's gaze. A quick glimpse of vivid azure irises sent fresh shivers racing through her. "Danvers," she whispered, correcting his error. "It is Danvers."

He inclined his head. "Ah, of course. My sincerest apologies, Miss Danvers."

The lecturer's voice faded into the background, her attention focused completely on the man at her side.

"Jack Byron," he introduced himself in a controlled sotto voce, apparently assuming that she would not have remembered his name.

As if any woman could forget.

Laying a hand on the back of her chair, he leaned closer. "London, was it not?"

She couldn't help but stare, startled to find him so close that she could trace the faint grain of dark bristles on his smooth-shaven cheeks. And near enough to catch the clean scents of fine-milled soap, lemon water, and starch, which lingered on his skin and clothing. For an instant, she leaned nearer, drawn by the elusive fragrances. But then she remembered herself and pulled away.

"Gunter's, wasn't it? For ices?" he inquired.

She paused and took a moment to recover. "No. Hatchard's. For books."

"Quite right. Dr. Johnson. I remember now. So, how is the good doctor?"

"Still deceased, as far as I know."

He barked out a short laugh.

Several heads turned in their direction. Finding herself the sudden focus of more than one disapproving set of eyes, she came rapidly to her senses. Straightening, she drew away from Lord Jack. He did the same, removing his hand from the back of her chair.

For the span of an entire minute, the pair of them listened solemnly to the presentation.

He tipped his head toward her and whispered, "What brings you to Bath?"

She stared straight ahead, aware she shouldn't respond. "I am visiting my aunt for a few weeks."

"A pleasant time of year for seeing family. And where is the esteemed lady? Surely you are not here alone?"

She cast him a glance. "No, my maid is with me. My aunt will be arriving later." She paused, trying to pay attention to the lecture and failing dismally. "What of you, my lord? Why are you in the city?"

He grew silent, his gaze directed ahead. Curiously, she wondered if he was going to answer.

"Personal business," he said at length. "Such that will keep me here for a few weeks as well. So, you enjoy flowers, do you?" he observed in a smooth redirection of the conversation.

She nodded. "As do the majority of my

sex. Although technical lectures like this one don't generally hold much appeal for the average female." She settled her small notebook more comfortably on her lap, the pencil on top. "Actually, I'm a bit surprised to find a man like you here either."

He arched an imperious brow. " *'A man like me'?* Now, what is that supposed to mean?"

A slight flush rose in her cheeks as she realized she'd let her tongue run wild again. "Pray take no offense. It is only that most people, even those who like plants, have scant patience for the study of botany and horticulture."

Shifting in his chair, he bent nearer. "You think me a brainless fribble then, do you?"

"Not at all. I . . ." Her words drifted away as she caught the shrewd gleam dancing in his eyes.

"Yes, you were saying?" he drawled.

"I just would not have expected you to be at an event of such an academic nature . . ."

His lips twitched, but he refrained from further comment.

Inwardly she cringed, knowing she was digging herself deeper yet somehow unable to stop. "I mean that robust men such as yourself usually prefer other, more physical pursuits."

The color of his irises intensified. "Physical, hmm? And just what sort of 'physical pursuits' did you have in mind?"

Her cheeks grew warm, subtly aware that she had stumbled into dangerous territory. For some unfathomable reason, images of secluded, romantic rendezvouses and stolen kisses leapt into her head — subjects about which she was sure Jack Byron was an expert.

"Hunting and angling and riding, for instance," she said in a hushed tumble of words.

"Well, I must admit I enjoy a round of hunting and angling every now and again. As for riding . . ." His gaze lowered to her lips. "I'm always up for a good ride."

Her throat became too tight to swallow. *Why,* she wondered, *do I have the impression that he isn't talking about horses?*

Flustered, Grace lowered her gaze. Only then did she realize that the speaker had finished his lecture and was busy answering a last few questions from the audience.

"As for your assertion that a man such as myself cannot take an interest in serious academic subjects like botany, I must protest," Lord Jack continued. "Floriculture may not be my main area of interest, nevertheless it's worth an odd hour here and there. I had hoped our lecturer might have something new to offer on the use of hybrid cultivars and the grafting potential for *Rosa centifolia* and other highly fragrant varietals. Unfortunately, he seems only moderately well-versed on the topic, though I would never wish to cast aspersions."

Grace stared. "Y-your pardon, my lord. I stand corrected."

His mouth curved in a devastating smile, white teeth flashing. "That's quite all right. It is usually easier to see what lies on the surface of a person rather than taking the time and attention to delve deeper."

"Yes, exactly so," she whispered, her lips parting in surprise at his candor and perception.

How many times had she thought that very thing herself? Wishing that people were capable of looking past the surface to discover a person's true worth. Shame rolled through her, that she, of all people, would so shallowly underestimate him. She would be careful not to do so again — assuming they had occasion to meet in the future.

Only then did she become aware that the other attendees were beginning to make their way out of the room.

"It would appear the presentation has

concluded," he observed. "I scarcely noticed, given our conversation. Did you say your aunt is arriving to accompany you home?"

"She should be here quite soon."

He stood and offered a hand to assist her to her feet. Accepting, she couldn't help but be aware of the way his large gloved palm fit so firmly around her own. Flutters danced like tiny wings in her stomach.

"Allow me to thank you for a pleasant diversion, Miss Danvers. I sincerely enjoyed our talk. Ordinarily I would remain, but the hour grows more advanced than I anticipated and I find I must take my leave. Shall we locate your maidservant?"

Grace shook off her sense of disappointment, wondering suddenly if he had only been amusing himself and now wished to be quit of her as soon as he could.

"There is no need," she told him, her tone cooler. "She is only in the adjoining room."

"Even so, I insist."

Having no alternative, she walked from the room at his side. Far too soon, her maid was found.

As they strolled back into the main corridor, he turned and made her an agile, elegant bow. "I shall not say goodbye but rather *au revoir.*"

Grace curtseyed. "Good day, your lordship."

An enigmatic expression shone in his gaze, as if he might say more. Instead, he inclined his head, then turned and strode away.

"Gor, who was that?" her maid cooed in a low voice as Lord Jack departed. " 'e's a looker, 'e is, miss, and make no mistake of it. Handsome, and a gentleman, too."

"Be that as it may, I doubt we shall see him again," Grace said, suppressing a wistful sigh. "He merely came to hear the lecture."

Slipping her notebook into her reticule, she moved toward the entry, relieved to see her aunt's coach arrive.

From a sheltered area several yards distant, Jack watched Grace step into a black barouche and drive away, her aunt presumably inside.

All in all, he thought the afternoon had gone well. He and Grace had met again and talked, establishing the beginnings of what he planned to be a fairly rapid, thoroughly satisfactory courtship — assuming one could call what he was doing a "courtship." *Conquest* was a far more appropriate term considering the cold-blooded nature of his arrangement with her father. Still, "Campaign Grace" was proving far less of a chore than he'd originally imagined.

As with their first encounter, he'd found her intelligent and engaging, with a quick wit and a clever tongue. Of course, it was only a matter of time before he grew bored, but for now, she was proving unexpectedly fascinating.

He would have to take care, though. She'd almost caught him out with her inquiries about his attendance at the lecture. She was right that he wasn't the sort of man to take an interest in such a dry topic. Good thing he'd taken the precaution of skimming a few botany books.

Years ago, as a boy longing to be outside on clear spring and summer days, he'd developed a gift for memorization. His father had chosen a strict, serious-minded man to serve as tutor to him and his brothers. The only way to escape the schoolroom had been to recite that day's lesson without flaw. After a bit of practice, Jack had taught himself how to quickly visualize anything. It was a skill he'd put to good use ever since — including his years at Eton and Oxford, where he'd moved effortlessly through his studies, leaving him more time to indulge in a variety of pleasurable pursuits. This afternoon, the ability had once again come in handy with Grace.

He smiled, thinking about her, marveling at his response.

And he was definitely having a response!

Many might find her ordinary, but the more he saw of her, the more he liked. In fact, he'd had a hard time keeping his hands off her during their hushed tête-à-tête, wanting to draw her outside into the gardens so he could steal a kiss. But he supposed it was just as well they'd been inside a lecture hall, since it was far too soon for kisses.

Which is why he'd excused himself so abruptly and left. Had he stayed, he might have pushed matters too far, too fast, and risked alarming her. He'd already gone beyond what he'd planned for their first true meeting, forgetting himself long enough to trade innuendos a more experienced woman would have recognized for what they were. Instead, Grace Danvers had blushed and looked unsure, of both herself and her reactions.

In those moments, he'd found her adorable.

And kissable.

And far too innocent.

The time would come for intimacy. And when it did, he promised she would find exquisite pleasure. He might be taking her as his wife because he must. But he would be taking her to his bed because he wanted her.

Considering his next move, Jack strode toward his lodgings, deciding a walk would do him good.

CHAPTER 4

Three days later, Grace accompanied her aunt to Bath's finest perfume shop. Drawing her spectacles from her reticule, she set them on her nose and began perusing the array of glass bottles lined up for display. Beside each one stood a small white card with a description of the scent penned in crisp black ink.

Oil of Bergamot
Eau de Neroli
Essence of Frangipani

As a rule, she didn't often wear perfume. On the rare occasions when she did, she preferred simpler, lighter scents, such as violet water or a few drops of plain vanilla rubbed on her wrists or behind her ears.

Aunt Jane, however, adored perfume. The polished walnut dressing table in her bedchamber was completely obscured by a mass of perfume bottles, skin creams and powders. She had so many, in fact, that she needed a separate cabinet to house her hair combs, brushes, feathers, and jewelry.

"What do you think of this one?" her aunt asked, drawing near with an open bottle in hand.

Leaning dutifully forward, Grace gave a delicate sniff. She wrinkled her nose and pulled away, fighting the urge to sneeze. "Too heavy for my taste," she murmured. "What is it? Cloves, if I'm not mistaken, and cinnamon perhaps. But there's another scent . . . something I cannot place."

"Civet oil," Aunt Jane said. "Apparently the Empress Josephine wears a similar fragrance, though from what I've read rumors are swirling that she may not be Boney's wife for long. They say he's going to cast her aside because she's barren, or so the story goes."

Grace nodded, having read the same news stories herself. "Yes, well, those rumors have been swirling for a while. But perhaps you would do well to steer clear of perfumes favored by wives of the enemy, even ones in danger of being divorced."

Aunt Jane waved a dismissive hand. "*Pish-tosh.* If we did away with everything French, we'd have nothing decent to drink or wear.

Still, I think you're right about this particular perfume."

Replacing the stopper, her aunt gave a contemplative nod. "Mayhap I should discuss a custom-made scent with the owner, a fragrance created exclusively for me. I suppose the price might be a bit dear, but what's the point of a widow's portion if you can't spend it on an indulgence or two?" Visibly excited, she hurried off to find the head perfumer.

Grace watched with a smile before resuming her inspection of the merchandise.

Seconds later, the tiny brass bell that hung above the door gave a tinkling chime as a new patron stepped inside. Instead of another woman come to join the all-female throng, however, the newcomer was a man. But not just any man.

Jack Byron.

From the moment of his arrival, he dominated his surroundings, tall and commanding in a superfine coat of rich dark, Spanish fly green that was all the rage that year. He wore a pair of close-fitting navy blue pantaloons that hugged the muscular contours of his long, powerful legs, with polished black boots on his feet. On another man, the outfit could easily have appeared as ostentatious as a peacock. But on Lord Jack, the effect was nothing short of divine.

As he strolled further into the shop, Grace noticed that hers wasn't the only pair of female eyes to turn his way, nor the only ones to linger in clear appreciation.

Annoyed by her weakness, she turned away.

What is he doing here? she wondered, since the shop catered almost exclusively to feminine tastes.

And where has he been? she wanted to ask, since she hadn't managed to catch so much as a glimpse of him lately.

Not that I care, of course.

She hadn't long to ponder either question before she sensed him at her side.

"Miss Danvers," he greeted in a throaty rumble that caused tingles to chase over her skin. "We meet again."

Turning slightly, she looked up as though she had only just then noticed his arrival. "Your lordship. How do you do?"

"Quite well, thank you," he replied. "Particularly now that I have the pleasure of such lovely company."

Aware that flirtation must come as naturally to him as breathing, she did her best to ignore his remark. "So, what brings you here, of all places? This hardly seems like your sort of diversion."

One mahogany brow arched skyward, an amused glint sparkling in his eyes. "Ah, Miss Danvers, there you go again, deciding what does and does not suit me. Whenever shall you learn?"

She flushed slightly at his amused rebuke.

"I am here to make a purchase," he offered in a gentle tone.

Of course he is, she realized. *Undoubtedly he's buying a gift for a female acquaintance, maybe even a lover. Surely he isn't shopping for his mistress,* she thought, the notion settling like a lump of undercooked potato at the bottom of her stomach.

"Perhaps you might be so good as to assist me," he continued.

Help him buy perfume for his paramour? Most certainly not!

"I am looking for a present for my sister. Or at least for one of my sisters, since the other is far too young yet for such adornments. I thought there might be something here to please her."

"Your sister!" she exclaimed, relief rushing through her. "Well, of course. What a thoughtful idea."

His azure eyes twinkled again. "I am glad you think so. Although you seem a bit surprised to discover I have a sister. To whom else had you imagined I might be giving such an intimate gift?"

"N-no one," she denied, hoping he would let her gloss over the answer. "So, what kind of fragrance does your sister prefer?"

For a brief moment, his face went blank. "Actually, I have no idea."

"Does she like flowers, or are herbs and spices more to her taste?"

He considered her query. "Flowers, I believe. Mallory loves anything with petals and a scent."

She smiled. "That should make it easier then. Mallory, hmm? What a pretty name."

His gaze met hers. "Indeed. Though not as lyrical as your own." Almost imperceptibly, he moved closer, the warmth of his body radiating outward, together with his own mesmerizing scent — clean and male and uniquely him. "What fragrance are you wearing?" he asked.

"Nothing. I don't wear perfume, at least not often."

He inched nearer still, his voice lowering to a murmur. "You're just naturally sweet then, are you? Exactly as I suspected."

Her legs turned weak. Surreptitiously, she gripped the wooden counter in front of her, glad of its support. She was relieved as well that she didn't send any bottles toppling over to crash in a noisy splash of scent on the floor.

"She . . . um . . . she might like jasmine or hyacinth." Grace broke eye contact, striving to collect herself. "Is she older or younger than yourself?"

"Younger. She's nineteen."

"Something more youthful, then. Orange blossom water. It's light and frivolous, like a warm spring day."

He placed a hand on the counter next to hers, so close that their gloved fingers were all but touching. Although her hands were appropriately proportioned for her height, she'd always considered them far too large, even ungainly. But his hands dwarfed hers, big and wide and so clearly strong beneath the dark fabric covering them. She stared, noting their differences, wishing suddenly that he would lift his hand to cover her own.

Her pulse sped faster. *What am I doing? Thinking? More to the point, what is he thinking?* Very likely nothing, she decided. He probably wasn't even aware of her response, and if he were, he'd be appalled. Or, worse, amused.

Abruptly she drew away. Taking a step back, she straightened her shoulders and deliberately, almost defiantly, stood at her full height. "Your sister might also enjoy lilacs. Always a delightful scent."

He lowered his hand to his side. "I'm sure it is, but the orange blossom water sounds just the thing."

Signaling a clerk, he placed his order, then waited while the man moved away to box and wrap the purchase.

"I am in your debt," he said. "My thanks for your aid. Perhaps you might suggest something for my other sister as well."

Grace swallowed, deliberately meeting his gaze as she forced aside any lingering awareness of him. "How old is she?"

"Ten. And she likes to draw. Art is quite her favorite pastime."

At the mention of something so completely familiar, Grace relaxed. "There is a fine store only a block distant on Bond Street. Ask for George and he'll find you anything you need. A paper block never goes amiss with an artist. Nor paints or crayons."

"George, hmm? You must be a frequent visitor to know the clerks by name. I assume you paint?"

"I watercolor a bit."

"Ah," he said, though without the usual note of male condescension.

A brief silence fell between them. He was just opening his mouth to say something further when her aunt appeared suddenly at her side.

"My new fragrance is created!" Aunt Jane announced. "Carnation with a delicate hint of lime. Delicious." She paused, her keen gaze fixing on Lord Jack. "But pardon me for so rudely interrupting. Perhaps you might make the introductions, Grace, since it is obvious from the way you two have been conversing that you are acquainted with this gentleman."

Grace traded a brief glance with Lord Jack before turning to her aunt. "Yes, his lordship and I met a few days ago at the botanical lecture near Sydney Gardens."

"Did you now?" Aunt Jane's grey-haired head bobbed with interest.

"And briefly in London before that," Lord Jack offered in a smooth aside. "Miss Danvers and I frequent the same bookseller, you see."

Grace shot him a look for divulging such unnecessary information, then hurried on before anything further could be added. "My lord, pray allow me to make you known to my aunt, Mrs. Jane Grant. Aunt Jane, Lord John Byron."

Her aunt's eyes grew round. "Byron? No relation to the poet, I suppose?"

"No, ma'am. That particular gentleman and I share no familial ties, nor do I claim to have so much as an inkling of talent in the art of penning sonnets and odes. Let me say, however, that it is a distinct pleasure to make your acquaintance." He bowed with a practiced flair that made her aunt's cheeks pink like a schoolgirl's despite her nearly sixty years.

Apparently age was no barrier to succumbing to Lord Jack's undeniable charm. Grace was sure women routinely fell at his feet, especially since he was obviously one of those men who simply liked women — no matter their age, looks, size, or marital status. He could, she suspected, have his pick of any woman in the world.

So why is he troubling with me? Then again, he really wasn't, since their encounters were no more than mere happenstance and coincidence.

Her aunt recovered enough to recall her manners and sink into a respectful curtsey. "Oh, the pleasure is all mine, your lordship," she said, straightening to a height that only brought her up as far as Grace's shoulder.

"Byron, did you say?" Aunt Jane continued, tapping a finger against her chin. "There is another family, quite illustrious and noble, who holds that surname. I have read accounts in the guidebooks of the

Duke of Clybourne's principle estate. It is said that Braebourne is even more elegant than Chatsworth or Blenheim, and that the duke's grounds and gardens rival those of the royals themselves. I don't suppose you are at all acquainted with *those* Byrons, are you?"

"Aunt Jane, really," Grace admonished in a hushed tone.

Lord Jack, however, seemed to take her aunt's inquisitive nature in his stride. His face remained composed, although Grace thought she detected a glimmer of amusement in his eyes.

"As it happens, ma'am," he answered, "I do know that family. Quite intimately, in fact. The duke is my brother, you see."

Grace's eyes were the ones to widen this time. Surely she had misheard him? Surely he hadn't just said his brother was the Duke of Clybourne! But it would seem he had said exactly that, since her aunt was, at that very moment, fluttering her small hands in front of her chest, as a flurry of "oh my's" bubbled from her lips.

Lord Jack smiled with sympathetic amusement at her dismay.

Lord Jack.

Of course, Grace thought, she should have realized long ago that he was the son of some high-ranking noble, since only the children of dukes, marquises, and earls were granted the use of an elevated courtesy title such as his.

Nevertheless, a duke's son. A duke's brother.

Good heavens, if she'd thought him out of her reach before, he was so far away now that an ocean might as well be standing between them.

Maybe two oceans!

Her aunt recovered quickly, her tongue in as fine shape as ever. "Oh, your lordship," she said, "I never dreamt you might be the duke's brother. How extraordinary. And to think I am standing here in a little shop in Bath speaking to one of the most distinguished men in the land."

"Fear not, dear lady. There is nothing much distinguished about me. I am only a third son and of little use for much more than conversation and making up an occasional fourth at cards."

"Oh, do go on," Aunt Jane scolded with a teasing smile. "I am sure you are only being modest. Particularly if you like such serious pastimes as botany lectures and books. I can't see the point to either, but dear Grace loves anything that exercises her mind."

Lord Jack turned his head, his jewel-colored eyes meeting Grace's over the top of her aunt's bonnet. "Nothing wrong with a bit of exercise for the mind. Or the body."

Warmth swirled abruptly to life within her. Anxious to extinguish the flame, Grace looked away.

"Well, I vastly prefer entertainment," her aunt said. "Nothing better in my estimation than a good party. Oh, heavens, what a superb idea I've just had."

Grace frowned, suddenly sure of her aunt's next words. "Aunt Jane, I am certain he doesn't wish —"

"Of course he does," she said, waving aside Grace's objections. "You mentioned cards, my lord, so you must like to play."

"I enjoy a game every now and again," he conceded.

"Then you must join us this Friday eve. I am hosting a card party with a bite of supper afterwards. I would be ever so honored if you would come. Do say you will and I shall send 'round a card with all the particulars."

Inwardly Grace cringed. Bad enough that her aunt had interrogated him over his lineage. But now to invite him to a party that was so clearly beneath him socially — well, it went beyond the bounds of proper decorum.

Grace's late uncle might have been a well-respected solicitor in his day, and of genteel heritage, but his background was nothing compared to the son of a duke — even a younger one.

As for Grace herself, her father was one of the most brilliant men in England, at least when it came to finance. But he was of humble origins, having clawed his way up from poverty as the child of a village blacksmith. As a young man, he'd run off to London to make his fortune, and he'd succeeded. He'd married her mother, whose own father had been a physician.

But no matter Ezra Danvers's immense wealth, he would always be the son of a blacksmith, and Grace the granddaughter of one. Her time at the ladies' academy had taught her that much. Her years since had only reinforced that lesson.

Duke's sons and tradesmen's daughters did not mix. Nor did aristocrats come to card parties hosted by audacious middle-class matrons who clearly did not know when to hold their tongues.

Grace waited for Lord Jack to think up an excuse and refuse.

He smiled at her aunt. "You are all kindness, ma'am. Cards on Friday, hmm? I shall be delighted to attend so long as you promise to partner me for at least one hand."

Grace stared, her lips parting in surprise.

"Oh, your lordship," Aunt Jane tittered, her smile as wide as the street outside. "I cannot wait for the days to pass between now and then. Not to worry, you will have a fine time and make no mistake. Grace will see to it as well, will you not, dear? You won't let our dear Lord John grow bored."

"Dear Lord John" met Grace's gaze again, one eyebrow sweeping upward like a dark, silky wing. For a second, she thought she saw a spark of pure devilment and delight in his eyes.

Suddenly the clerk arrived behind the counter, the wrapped bottle of perfume in hand.

"Your gift for your sister, my lord," Grace said, grateful for the interruption. "I hope the scent is to her liking."

"I am sure it shall be," he drawled, accepting the parcel. "Until Friday, then."

"Until Friday."

CHAPTER 5

He won't come.

That was the phrase Grace had been silently repeating to herself over the past four days, ever since she and Jack Byron had happened upon each other in the perfume shop — and Aunt Jane had invited him to the card party.

Any minute now, a footman would arrive at the front door bearing Lord Jack's note of regret — some politely worded excuse written in a fine hand on heavy white vellum. Undoubtedly, her aunt would be cast into the boughs over the news, particularly given how she'd been telling the entirety of her acquaintance that the Duke of Clybourne's brother was promised to attend her party! But Aunt Jane was a resilient sort and would recover apace.

As for herself — well, she would have nothing to recover from, she told herself. No disappointment to assuage, since she'd known all along that he would bow out of the engagement. Ill-founded generosity had prompted him to accept. Clearheaded rationality would lead him to refuse.

It's not as though I care if he attends tonight's party, she assured herself from her seat at her bedchamber dressing table. *The man is nothing but trouble disguised in a pleasing package.* A truly gorgeous, heart-stopping, mouthwateringly delectable package that would send even a blind woman into a swoon — but trouble just the same. The less she saw of him the better off she would be.

She sighed aloud, her shoulders sinking beneath the amber satin of her short-sleeved, empire-waisted evening gown.

" 'old still, miss, or I'll never get these pins set right," her maid chided from where she stood behind her.

The girl worked to arrange the burnished mass into a pleasing style, combing and re-combing a few strands of Grace's long, thick hair. Grace held steady and forced herself not to fidget, as the last of her willful tresses were tamed into place.

With her coiffure finished, she fastened a simple gold locket around her throat, the piece a favorite that had once belonged to her mother. Next, Grace drew on a pair of long, white gloves, then stood and crossed to the door.

He won't come, she thought once again before she moved into the hallway and down the stairs.

An hour later, she was more convinced than ever of the correctness of her assumption, for the house was noisy with guests — everyone save Lord Jack. Still, she couldn't help but glance toward the parlor doors every few minutes to check for signs of his non-arrival.

She was conversing with a round-faced, former legal associate of her uncle's when a tingling sense of awareness traveled down her spine. Without quite realizing what she was doing, she stopped talking and turned around.

And there he stood — Jack Byron, in the flesh.

He was large and dynamic, and so handsome in stark black and white evening attire that, for a moment, all she could do was stare. Framed in the doorway, he eclipsed every other person in the room. In an earlier era, she was sure they would all have fallen to their knees in obeisance to beseech his indulgence. Instead, guests began to fall silent as his presence was noticed and acknowledged.

Yet it wasn't the admiring crowd he was surveying. Instead, his gaze was focused on her, his vivid blue eyes locked upon her as though she were the only woman in the room worth noticing.

Her lips parted on a soundless inhalation, and she was unable to look away as he sauntered toward her with a sinuous, tiger-like stride.

Grace.

Her name whispered through Jack's mind like the silken stroke of a hand.

He'd never seen her look as pretty as she did tonight, the vibrant bronze hue of her gown lending her skin a creamy luminosity, her hair gleaming a rich, fiery red that reminded him of living flame.

And passion.

He wondered if that same intense fire lay hidden inside her, and he relished the idea of finding out. This evening, however, he would have to restrain himself, exactly as he'd been doing these many long days.

What an excellent stroke of luck to have happened upon Grace at the perfume shop. He'd been waiting for the right moment to meet her again, when there she'd been, visible through the store window. In need of a small gift for his sisters, he'd known the task would give him the perfect excuse to further their acquaintance. And when her aunt had issued her invitation for tonight, he'd nearly kissed her, delighted to gain such easy entree into Grace's inner circle.

Now, here the both of them stood with barely half a room between them. He was starting toward her, when his hostess stepped into his path.

"Oh, your lordship, you have arrived," Grace's aunt gushed, her aging features alive with pleasure. "Welcome to my home. I am honored."

"The honor is mine, ma'am," he said, turning his attention to Mrs. Grant.

"So gallant, just as I have been telling everyone."

He gave an indulgent smile. "And what else have you been telling them?"

"Why, everything, of course," she confided with a laugh before taking hold of his arm. "Come, you must let me introduce you."

Having no other recourse, he allowed himself to be drawn forward.

Nearly an hour passed before the niceties were satisfied and he had an opportunity to seek out Grace. To his consternation, he discovered her already at play — one of four partnered for whist. He supposed he could have joined another game, but it wasn't the game that interested him. Rather, it was one particular player.

Smiling inwardly, he strolled her way.

Grace sensed, rather than saw, Lord Jack appear at her elbow, his presence disrupting her decision about whether to lay down a diamond or a spade. Her partner groaned when she played the wrong card, allowing the other couple to win the trick.

"I believe a diamond would have been the better choice," Lord Jack murmured in a voice meant for her ears alone.

She tossed him a fulminating glance. "Thank you for that sage bit of wisdom, my lord," she retorted in an equally quiet tone.

Rather than take umbrage, he laughed.

Drawing up a chair, he sat down, positioning himself just slightly behind and to her right. "I trust no one objects if I stay to watch the game," he asked the group.

The others — two older women and a slender, rather mousy-looking man — readily gave their ascent. Grace said nothing and the game quickly resumed. As a result of her prior distraction over Lord Jack's arrival and her resulting misplay, she and her partner lost nearly every hand as they finished out the round. Finally, the slaughter was over and the cards gathered for a fresh shuffle.

"My apologies for not greeting you properly before," Lord Jack told her, while the others shared their own conversational asides. "Your aunt kept me rather busy."

"My aunt is good at such things," she replied in a low voice. "And we spoke. I distinctly recall saying hello as you made your rounds."

And they had, exchanging how-do-you-do's and a few innocuous remarks about the weather before Aunt Jane dragged him on to the next group of guests eager to make his acquaintance.

"But we had no time for more personal conversation."

"Nor do we now," she retorted, taking up her cards, "since the play is ready to resume."

Grinning, he leaned back in his chair.

Despite his casual stance, however, she felt as though she were seated next to a great jungle cat. He might appear relaxed, his eyelids lowered in an inattentive, almost sleepy way, but she sensed the exact opposite was true. Underneath his seemingly bored façade, he was alert, watchful and ready to pounce at a moment's notice.

Arranging the cards in her hand by suit and number, she did her best to keep them hidden. However, his superior height and the angle at which he sat gave him easy means to peek.

Well, no matter, she thought. *It's not as though he's playing.*

But as the round got underway, she realized that Lord Jack *was* playing, shifting subtly in his chair or rubbing the edge of his nose each time she was about to make a wrong move. She tried holding her cards closer to her chest, but it did no good. He knew each correct play before it was made, leaving her to wonder if he possessed some sort of extrasensory sight that allowed him to see through everyone's cards. As a result of his silent assistance, she and her partner won the round, as well as the small pile of winnings that came with it.

Soon, the others stood to stretch their legs and get a refreshment. Grace remained seated, however, waiting until she and Lord Jack were alone before she turned to him. "What do you think you're doing?" she said on a hiss.

"What do you mean?" he asked, his expression all innocence.

"You know *exactly* what I mean. You were helping me, feeding me little signals throughout the game. I'm surprised none of the others said anything, particularly after you rubbed your nose for the fifth time."

He flashed a white-toothed grin. "None of the others had any idea what I was doing. As for my signals, you looked like you could use the help."

"I would have done just fine on my own."

He raised a clearly skeptical brow.

"I feel like a cheat," she bemoaned.

He sent her a sternly mocking look. "Of the most vile sort, to be sure. You ought to be banned from card play forever for 'stealing' all eight pence in that pot."

"The amount is not the point."

"No, and neither were our actions a crime. At worst, we played as a team. I mean it's not as if I could see their cards."

Despite the uncanny accuracy of his hints, he was right about that. From his vantage point, she knew he couldn't have seen anyone's cards but her own.

She studied him for a thoughtful moment. "How *did* you know which cards to play?"

He shrugged and stretched his legs out before him. "It's simply a matter of watching what is being played and taking care not to forget. Once a few opening cards are established, the rest becomes easy."

She paused, digesting the information. "Remind me *never* to play cards against you."

He chuckled. “I shall look forward to the occasion and the opportunity to change your mind. Now, if I am not mistaken, I believe your aunt is about to announce supper. Pray agree to dine with me.”

“I am not sure I can, since the place cards may require otherwise.”

“Then we shall simply have to switch them so they’re arranged to our liking,” he said, adding a naughty wink that sent tingles whirling through her system like maddened fireflies.

He stood and offered his arm.

“You wouldn’t really switch them, would you?” she asked as she gained her feet.

“What do you think?”

She studied him, his azure eyes unreadable. “I think,” she said, “that you are the wickedest man I’ve ever met.”

He choked out a laugh, then leaned over so that his lips were a mere inch from her ear. “You had best take care to avoid me, then, else I cease being a gentleman and decide to lead you astray.”

Which was precisely what made him so dangerous — because unlike other men, she just might let him tempt her if ever he should ask. But he was only teasing, she was sure.

With that dismal reassurance in mind, she

laid her palm atop his sleeve and let him lead her in to supper.

As she'd suspected, her aunt had arranged the table so that specific guests were — and were not — seated next to each other. To her surprise, however, she found herself placed next to Lord Jack.

"Once more, I find myself indebted to your aunt," he said as he read the names inked on the cards.

To her left sat an elderly man, who needed a brass ear trumpet to hear. After an exchange of greetings that had to be repeated more than once, he nodded and smiled, then applied himself to his soup, apparently content to eat in silence.

With the woman to Lord Jack's right happily conversing with the man on her other side, Grace found herself the sole focus of his attention. She expected him to continue his earlier flirtatious teasing. However, what he said next surprised her.

"So, Miss Danvers," he began as he dipped a spoon into his bowl of mushroom bisque. "What is your opinion of Descartes?"

Her own spoon wavered over her bowl. *"Excuse me?"*

"Descartes. You know, 'I think, therefore, I am.' Surely you are familiar with his writings."

Descartes? He wants to talk about Descartes? A frown settled over her brows. "Why would you think that?"

"Because we both know you like to read, and since you are familiar with Swift and Johnson, it follows you might have an interest in other men of thought, even a few French ones."

"But Swift and Johnson were essayists, not philosophers."

"So you *do* know Descartes." He smiled and ate a mouthful of soup.

"My father says I should not. Our society believes a woman ought to plead ignorance about any matter more mentally taxing than stitchery, housekeeping and child-rearing. Politics and philosophy should be left to men."

"But you do not agree?" he prompted in a measured tone.

"Apparently not, since you are correct that I have read Descartes. I told Papa that he, Voltaire and Rousseau were part of my French language lessons when I was in school."

Lord Jack laughed.

They each ate a spoonful of soup before continuing.

"Voltaire and Rousseau, hmm?" he mused. "Do not tell me you believe in the rights of the common man, the will of the people, and other such radical notions?"

She paused, gauging him. "I'm not in favor of abolishing the monarchy, if that is what you are alluding to. But neither do I think it wrong to allow ordinary people more of a say in their existence. The right to vote, for instance."

"Ah, so you would give the vote to everyone regardless of education or income, then. Even women, I suppose?"

She fell silent, struggling to decide whether or not to answer him. "Yes. Even women."

He ate another spoonful of soup, then patted his mouth with his napkin. Leaning near, he lowered his voice. "Don't tell anyone I said this, but I agree."

"You do?" Astonished warmth spread through her.

He nodded. "Shameful, is it not? A duke's son who wants to give the commoners their say. As for women, well, they have more intelligence than men like to admit. That's why so many of my sex want to keep their females ignorant and pregnant. Just imagine the competition if we gave them equal footing."

She smiled, marveling at his sentiments. "Yes, just think."

Their conversation continued on throughout the meal, roving from one subject to the next — some topics serious, some fanciful, even funny. By the time dessert was served, Grace realized she had no real idea what she had eaten, having been too enraptured by Jack Byron to pay attention to anything else.

Never one to stand on ceremony, Aunt Jane didn't ask the women to withdraw in order to allow the men to enjoy their port and cigars in solitary splendor. Instead, everyone rose from the dining table to make their way back to the card room together. To Grace's secret delight, Lord Jack took her arm, neither of them in a hurry as they strolled toward the parlor.

Rather than join one of the games, however, the two of them settled onto a padded window seat. While she sipped tea and he nursed a brandy, they continued their discussion, delving for a time into the subjects of art, music and favorite plays and playwrights.

Then, without quite realizing where the time had gone, the evening was over.

"Until next we meet, Miss Danvers," he said in his rumbling baritone as he bowed over her hand. "I had a most enjoyable evening."

"As did I, your lordship."

And she had, she realized. So enjoyable she couldn't remember a pleasanter time. She'd relaxed and been at ease in his company in a way she rarely was with anyone — man or woman.

Curtseying, she bid him *adieu,* then stood watching from the doorway as he climbed into his carriage and drove away.

Once the last guest had gone and the door was closed and locked for the night, she and her aunt turned toward the stairs.

"A fine time, was it not?" Aunt Jane said with a sleepy smile.

"Yes. Very fine," Grace agreed.

"I should imagine so, considering the way a certain handsome lord could not be torn from your side. You've made a conquest there, my girl."

She stopped. "Conquest? Oh no, you mistake the matter."

Her aunt gave a disbelieving snort. "I mistake nothing. Men have a look about them when they're pursuing a particular woman, and when it comes to you, Lord Jack has that look written all over him. He's certainly a bold one, singling you out the way he did, then keeping you all to himself for the whole of the evening."

"It wasn't the *whole* of the evening,"

Grace defended. "And he did not single me out. We were merely talking and the time got away."

"Talking, hmm?" Aunt Jane patted her shoulder as they reached the upstairs landing. "Call it what you like, but that man wants you."

Wants me? No, she thought, *he doesn't want me, at least not in the way Aunt Jane thinks.* He'd come tonight out of gentlemanly politeness, then spent time with her because she was the youngest woman in the room. His attentions were nothing special, nothing she should take seriously. Likely he was bored and she amused him for some unfathomable reason. Once his personal business here in Bath was concluded, he would leave, forgetting he had ever known a young woman named Grace Danvers.

"We are merely friendly acquaintances, who share a few interests in common," she stated. "He has no deeper regard for me, I assure you."

"Time will tell," her aunt said, a smug expression in her eyes. "For now, I am off to bed. Good-night, dear, and sweet dreams. If Lord Jack is in yours, I know you'll sleep well." With a little laugh, she walked down the hallway to her room.

A moment later, Grace went to her own

bedchamber, certain that on that last score her aunt was right.

Chapter 6

Over the next two weeks, Lord Jack Byron gave Grace's aunt plenty of ammunition to bolster her argument that he was courting Grace. Everywhere she and her aunt went, there was Lord Jack.

He happened upon them while they were taking the air strolling along The Circus, and another time while they were shopping on Bond Street.

They crossed paths on the Royal Crescent, where Lord Jack had taken a lease on one of the area's luxurious town houses.

Grace encountered him at public assemblies and at one or two private parties, as well.

She even met him at the Pump Room, agreeing to walk along the room's perimeter to share the latest news from London and abroad, while her aunt sat with friends and took the waters.

Yet despite Aunt Jane's certainty that she

was being pursued, Grace saw nothing particularly lover-like in his attentions to her. He flirted, yes, but she discounted that as a case of Jack Byron simply being Jack Byron. As for his seeking her out when they were in company, well, they talked easily and had developed a rapport of sorts — one that led them both to gravitate toward each other for a measure of easy talk and undemanding companionship.

She was certain he viewed her only as a friend. For in spite of his roguish promises, he never made any effort to lead her down temptation's path. Nor did he try to hold her hand or draw her away for a private stroll or a stolen kiss.

Not that I want him to, she assured herself. She was content with his friendship. Quite content. She needed and expected nothing more. Still, the platonic nature of his attentions proved that Aunt Jane was mistaken about his interest in her. Clearly, he saw her as a sister, which meant she had no reason to guard her emotions against him.

The third week in September dawned warm and sunny, the sky a clear, pristine blue after two nights of heavy rain. Deciding the weather was just right for an excursion to Sydney Gardens to do some drawing, Grace collected her paper and pencils and prepared to set off with her maid in tow. Aunt Jane told Grace to have a good time, informing her that she planned to spend the day with several friends — scouring the shops for bargains — before adjourning to Mollands for tea and sweets.

After a pleasant walk to the gardens, Grace located a bench near some likely blossoms and took a seat. Reading the wistful expression on her maid's face, she let the girl go off to visit a footman who worked at the nearby hotel, making her promise not to be away too long.

Content, Grace settled into her drawing, losing herself as she began sketching a colorful patch of late-blooming hollyhocks. She was only vaguely aware of the crunch of footfalls approaching on the shell path.

"You look a picture, perched there on that bench," remarked a deep, familiar voice. "Every bit as lovely as one of the flowers."

Glancing up, she met Jack Byron's rich blue gaze. "My lord," she said, sending him a warm smile. Her pencil fell still while she studied him, his handsome features never failing to steal a bit of her breath. Impeccable as ever, he wore a tobacco brown coat and fawn pantaloons, the gold watch fob on his waistcoat winking in the sunlight.

"Where did you come from?" she asked,

her fingers curling reflexively against her pencil.

"Along the main path," he said in a wry drawl. "You really ought to pay more attention to your surroundings, you know."

"I am drawing."

"Yes, so I see." Crossing, he sank down onto the stone seat next to her. "I met your aunt on the high street. She told me you were here."

"Was that before or after she finished raiding all the stores?"

"*After,* I would say, based on the armload of packages her footman was carrying. Although I might be wrong, considering the militant gleam in her eye. As I recall, there was some mention of ribbon at a ten percent discount just as I was departing."

Grace grinned, then returned to her drawing.

Silence descended, comfortable and undemanding, as Lord Jack lounged on the bench at her side.

"What are you drawing? Those stalky, puffy-headed flowers over there?" he asked.

Pausing, she tossed him a curious glance. With his knowledge of botany, he had to know a hollyhock when he saw one, since it was a common enough variety. *He's teasing me,* she realized. "Yes, the hollyhocks, of course. You're very amusing, you know. Stalky, puffy-headed flowers indeed." She chuckled.

For a brief moment, an odd, almost alarmed expression passed over his face. Then, just as abruptly, it vanished. "No point in always being precisely accurate, is there? Sometimes a description says it best."

Smiling, she shook her head at his antics.

"May I see?" he queried.

She hesitated for an instant, then turned the drawing his way.

He contemplated her work, long enough that the faintest flutter of nerves jiggled over her skin. "It's only a preliminary study," she defended. "I'll do a far more refined sketch later, then another in color."

"It's wonderful," he stated, his tone clearly sincere. "When you said you do some drawing, I assumed you dabbled like most young women. But this is a far cry from dabbling. You have true talent."

Pleasure spread through her, radiant as the sun shining overhead. *When did his opinion come to mean so much to me?* she wondered. *Why do I care that he approves?* But she did, she realized, wanting him to like her work, even admire it. Admire her.

Tiny lines formed on his brow. "There is an artist who does similar watercolor renderings of natural subjects. I have one of his folios in my own book collection. Danvers is the name . . . G. L. Danvers." His eyes widened. "Good Lord, it's you, isn't it? Grace L. Danvers."

"Lilah," she murmured, her pleasure increasing. "The *L* is for Lilah. And yes, I've done a few little books."

"There's nothing *little* about those books, either in size or content. Grace, you are an extraordinary artist. Why does no one know the truth of your identity?"

He has one of my books. The thought made her a little giddy.

"*I* know," she told him. "And that is enough. I would have no use for fame anyway. It's better that people believe I am a man, that way my work is taken seriously. Otherwise, many would say my watercolors are good — for a young woman who dabbles."

For a moment, he looked as if he might argue the point. "Sadly, I suppose you're right. I'm glad, though, that I have uncovered your secret."

"As am I, your lordship."

His gaze met hers. "I shall demand a private showing of anything you have in process, you know."

Her heart beat with excitement. "That

might be permissible."

"And your autograph as well."

She smiled. "I would be honored." Although she didn't know when she would have such an occasion.

"I suppose I should go and leave you to your work."

She shook her head. "Actually, I would rather you didn't. My drawing will keep for a bit."

His mouth turned up in a slow smile. "Good. If that is the case, then perhaps I might persuade you to take a stroll."

"Here in the gardens, you mean?"

"Of course in the gardens. Maybe you will see some new plant that inspires your muse."

A small voice whispered that she should remain where she was and keep drawing. A far louder one urged her to accept.

"Yes. All right," she agreed. Rising to her feet, she secured her sketchbook and pencils inside a small satchel.

"Allow me," he said, reaching out a hand to take the cloth bag.

Passing it to him, she took his arm and they began to walk.

"Where is your maid, by the way?" he asked a few moments later. "I assume you didn't walk here by yourself."

"No. I let her go visit a friend for a few minutes."

"A friend? You are too generous by half, since she should not have left you at all. But I am here now, so there is no harm done."

Actually, he thought, *leaving me to stand guard is rather like asking a wolf to oversee the sheep.* But why quibble when it gave him a chance to be alone with her?

The past few weeks had been wearing on him, to say the least. As the days crept by, he'd been forced to place strict controls upon himself, trying to act as though he wanted nothing physical from her at all.

But denying himself had only increased his appetite for her — together with his enforced abstinence. He hadn't had a woman since he'd left London. He supposed he could have sought out a convenient female, but the idea held no appeal. Once he'd met Grace, she was the only one he desired.

From the first, he'd known he would need to get past Grace's barriers and win her trust. What he hadn't counted on, though, was earning her friendship as well. Nor had he expected to like her.

But he did. A lot.

Guilt raked through him like a sharp set

of claws. *Lord knows, I hate the necessity of lying to her.* But the wheels had already been set in motion, and there was no stopping them from spinning. His fate was fixed now and hers along with it.

He took care to be as honest with her as he could, however, not simply because it made things easier, but also because he wanted there to be as much truthfulness between them as possible. After all, she was going to be his wife.

When he'd discovered she was *the* G. L. Danvers, his surprise and admiration had in no way been feigned. He really did own one of her folios, and his esteem of her artistic talent was genuine. His motives and methods in pursuing her might not be strictly honorable, but that didn't mean the whole of their dealings were false. Of course, Grace might not see it that way should she ever learn about his bargain with her father, he thought with an inner wince.

But she won't find out, he promised himself. He would make certain of it. And so he had nothing to worry about. Nothing whatsoever.

"I understand there is a labyrinth here," he said, cutting off his own uncomfortable thoughts. "Do you like mazes?"

She nodded, her eyes appearing more blue

than grey today in the brilliant sunlight, her red hair gleaming like fire-colored silk beneath her bonnet. His hands itched suddenly to slip the little hat free of its moorings and send it sailing so he could spear his fingers deep into her tresses. And then he would kiss her, taking her mouth in a zealous joining that would soon have her aching for more. He nearly reached for her, but stayed himself. He'd waited this long; he could wait a while more.

Quietly, he cleared his throat. "Shall we go inside, then?" he asked, directing their footsteps along the path that led to the labyrinth. "I'll even give you the advantage of going in before me. We can make a game of it and see which one of us reaches the center first."

"I haven't been inside a maze since I was a little girl," she confided.

"Then it would seem a repeat of the experience is long overdue."

They soon arrived at the maze entrance, the precisely trimmed boxwood hedge rising upward in a seemingly impenetrable wall of thick, leafy green. The warm, ripe scent of vegetation hung in the air, birds chirping in nearby tree branches, while a pair of butterflies danced on the light breeze.

Yet Jack was barely aware of anything

except the woman at his side and his anticipation of the mock hunt to come.

"I'll give you to the count of ten," he declared, tucking her satchel into a sheltered spot just inside the entrance where he felt certain it would be safe. "Hurry along now, else I catch you." Crossing his arms over his chest, he turned his back to the maze opening. "One!"

Grace sprinted away.

"Two!" he called in a carrying voice. "I can still hear you."

She giggled, bushes rustling as she clearly ran into her first obstacle.

"Three!"

The sound of her passing grew more distant, the accelerating beat of his heart taking its place.

"Four!"

He heard an "oh drat" and smiled, trying to estimate how far into the maze she had likely traveled.

"Five!"

Her footfalls faded into silence, as he fought the urge to turn in search of a lingering view.

"Six!"

I shouldn't have given her so much time.

"Seven!"

What if she eludes me?

"Eight!"

What if she doesn't?

"Nine!"

Almost there.

"Ten! Ready or not, here I come!"

Turning sharply on his heel, he headed inside.

Grace bit her lip and forced herself not to giggle, her feet flying as she hurried along a narrow corridor of greenery that towered far above her head.

A few moments later, Lord Jack finished his count of ten and started after her. Soon, a distant rustling sounded, making her wonder if he'd blundered into the same trap in which she'd also been temporarily ensnared. But he was smart and resourceful and would soon find his way free.

Knowing she dare not waste a second, she continued on. Yet each turn looked frustratingly like the one before, every angle leading to a potential trap. Coming to a new break in the foliage, she stopped and looked right, then left, wondering which choice led in the correct direction.

Behind her, she couldn't hear Jack at all now, his progress silent despite his large physique. He might be tall, but he was agile, quick and stealthy on his feet. She knew how a doe must feel being pursued by an experienced hunter. Her heart thudded beneath her breasts, her breath issuing in soft gusts — though with excitement, she realized, not fear.

Making a random choice, she turned and dashed forward, the pale blue skirt of her India muslin gown floating around her as she ran. The move led her deeper into the labyrinth, drawing her in ever-tightening circles, each one more bewildering than the last.

Twice, she had to double back, worried every time that she would stumble upon Lord Jack, or he upon her. But as the minutes ticked past, she realized that he must be as mired in confusion as she. She also became aware of the fact that the two of them were completely alone — no hint of other human voices or movement anywhere in the vicinity.

Finally she sensed she was nearing the center of the maze, her goal barely feet away. But being close to the middle and actually finding it were two different things.

Turning again, she glided forward, her steps bringing her into a square-shaped section of hedge that functioned as a box. An inescapable box from which there was no exit save the one through which she had come. Trapped, she raced back toward the break in the vegetation.

She was just passing through when a long male arm emerged seemingly from out of nowhere, coiling like steel around her waist.

She squealed, the sound reverberating in the air, as she twisted for a moment in Lord Jack's grasp.

"Got you!" he exclaimed, triumph plain in his voice.

"Oh, you scared me!" she said, breathless as she met his gaze. "You're as silent as a breeze."

"And you're as lithe as a gazelle, slipping from row to row as though you were made of fog. For a few moments, I thought I'd lost track of you."

"This is a tricky maze. The center is nearby, though. Shall we both dash to find it?"

A gleam came into his eyes, along with an expression she'd never seen him wear before. He shook his head, his gaze roaming over her face before lowering to her lips.

"No," he murmured in a tone as rough as gravel. "I have what I came to find."

She trembled, abruptly aware that he was still holding her against him. Her heart leapt when he reached up and began untying the bow that anchored her bonnet in place.

"What are you doing, my lord?"

He smiled. "Claiming a forfeit. I caught you. I believe I deserve a reward."

"B-but the game isn't finished."

"You're right about that," he mused aloud, lifting her hat from her head. "The game has only just begun."

Without giving her time to consider, he tossed her bonnet to the ground, angled his head and kissed her.

She froze, completely unprepared for the heady sensation of his lips moving against her own. His mouth was surprisingly warm and luxuriously soft; his kiss demanding and persuasive in ways that made gooseflesh pop out all over her skin in spite of the late summer heat.

On a quivering gulp, she forced herself to break away. "M-my lord, what are you doing?"

"I believe you asked me that once already," he remarked. Reaching up, he traced the curve of her ear with his thumb and forefinger. "I should think the answer is obvious."

Catching her earlobe between his fingers, he rubbed the nubbin of flesh in a circular motion, then bent to scatter kisses along the column of her neck. Her eyelids fluttered, her toes curling like petals inside her shoes.

"Y-yes, but I don't understand why," she

said on a half-gasp. "You d-don't think of me that way."

"Do I not?" he said in a silky tone. "Are you sure?" Moving to her other side, he fanned a line of kisses over her throat.

"You see me . . . as a sister."

He stopped and lifted his head to meet her gaze. "I assure you, I do not." His arm tightened around her waist, yanking her flush against the long length of his body. "Now, I ask, does this feel at all brotherly to you?"

Locked hip to hip, she became aware of an insistent bulge pressing against the lower portion of her stomach, just slightly above the juncture of her thighs.

Is that him? she thought. *Is that hard jut wedged against me — his sex? Mercy, surely he isn't aroused? For me?*

Having never felt an erection before, even through the barrier of clothing, she wasn't certain. But a glance at the fixed set of his jaw and the intense gleam in his azure eyes made her realize she must be right.

"But I'm so plain and tall," she cried, unwilling to let herself believe that this man — this big, virile, gorgeous specimen of masculinity — could possibly want her. *Her.* Grace Danvers — unremarkable spinster — who had never so much as tempted a man to kiss her in all her twenty-five years. Not even Terrence had tried. Despite having asked her on repeated occasions to be his wife, he had never once attempted to take liberties.

Yet here was Jack Byron, sophisticated libertine and lady-killer — a man who could have any woman of his choosing no matter how beautiful or well-born — demonstrating his attraction for *her.*

"You don't want me," she whispered.

"Don't I?" He dropped a lingering kiss on her lips, then another on her cheek, and a third on her temple. "You continue to be mistaken in your estimation of my opinions, and in your own as well."

Her brows drew tight. "My own?"

"You are *not* plain," he told her, his words low and husky.

When she made a sound of disagreement, he hushed her. "You may not be beautiful in the traditional sense, but that doesn't mean you aren't lovely all the same. Uniquely lovely, with an inner radiance that far transcends what passes for pretty these days. Take your eyes, for example."

"My eyes?"

"Hmm. Have you ever noticed how they change color with your moods?"

She shook her head.

"Well, they do. When you're happy, they're a pure pristine blue, like twin brushstrokes of sky. And when you're displeased or lost in serious thought, they shift to grey. Silvery, sensual grey, the sort that ripples like dawn mist over a lake. I can think of no other woman with eyes like yours. Magnificent, soul-deep eyes in which a man could drown if he weren't careful."

He laid a hand against her face and touched his lips to hers. She quivered, blood throbbing in her temples, her skin turning hot beneath his touch.

"As for being tall . . . ," he went on, stroking his thumb in an arc over her cheek as he scattered random kisses along her brow and chin and neck, ". . . I am tall myself. I like that you're tall, too. I like that I can hold you and gaze with ease upon your face. I like it that I can do this" — he captured her lips for a slow, soft kiss — "without having to stoop or crouch or dip in order to make you fit against me. You are a perfect complement, Grace. The feminine half that makes me whole."

He bumped his hips gently into hers and drew a ragged gasp from her throat. "See what you do to me?" He cupped a hand over one breast. "See what I do to you?"

Of its own volition, her nipple peaked, the

stiffened bud rising traitorously against his palm. Her breath soughed fast between her lips. Her knees grew weak, making her thankful he was holding her, since she was sure she would have crumpled to the ground in a heap otherwise.

"Put your arms around my neck," he told her.

Trembling, she did as he asked, bringing their bodies even closer together.

His thumb stroked over her breast, back and forth across the hardened tip, then back and forth again.

"Shall I stop?" he whispered, changing his caress to a circular glide. An ache rose between her legs, a yearning that drew an involuntary whimper from her throat.

"What did you say?" he asked, his breath warm against her ear.

She shook her head. "No, don't stop, your lordship."

"Jack," he said, tugging her even tighter. "From now on, you are to call me Jack."

"Yes, my lord. Yes, Jack."

And then, as if the sound of his name on her lips broke through some self-imposed restraint, he crushed his mouth to hers, kissing her with a fierce possession that scattered every sensible thought in her brain.

She jolted as his hand slid lower, his wide

palm stroking over the full curve of her bottom to knead her through her gown and petticoats.

"Open your mouth," he muttered against her lips. "Let me in, Grace. Let me have you."

Blindly, she obeyed, his tongue sweeping inside the instant she parted her lips. Her heart hammered against a flood of new sensations, nerve endings sizzling in places she hadn't known she had nerves. Her body grew hot, but not from the sun shining overhead. Instead the source was an inner heat that threatened to burn her up from the inside out. She groaned, surrendering to the dark, wet, delicious slide of his flesh tangling with hers.

Ravenous, he showed her how to respond, how to follow his lead and mimic everything he did. He seemed to approve of her fledgling attempts, coaxing her to try, then try again.

When she felt his fingers working open the buttons at the back of her gown, she made no demur, too abandoned to object to anything he might do.

Jack shifted his stance, using his legs to spread hers apart so he could step between. Kissing her harder, he quaked as she tentatively used what he'd been teaching her to draw circles inside his mouth with her tongue. Her taste was intoxicating — like fresh strawberries and champagne — the sweet, light flavor tingling in his mouth and buzzing in his brain.

He knew he needed to slow things down, to put a halt to what he'd originally intended to be no more than a few simple kisses. But the moment he'd touched her, he'd been lost, unable to keep himself from wanting more, taking more. The keen ache riding him wasn't helping matters either. He was so hard it was a wonder his straining member didn't pop the buttons right off his falls.

He considered laying her down, finding some small patch of grass where he could take her. She would let him. He could tell she was as far gone as he. Without further preamble he could have her beneath him, her skirts tumbled upward as he thrust himself deep into her tight, wet depths.

But despite his powerful longing, some niggling spark of conscience still remained, reminding him that she was a virgin and that a hard plot of earth was no place for her first time.

And it would be her first time.

Based on her untutored responses alone, he knew she'd never even been kissed. A fierce rush of possessiveness roared through him, an atavistic satisfaction that was totally at odds with his usual relaxed attitude concerning sex and female chastity. Never before had he cared whether a woman was innocent. Rather, in the past, he'd always chosen experienced partners, women who knew what to expect and relished the opportunity to explore the boundaries of their sensuality. Virgins, on the other hand, were nothing but a bother.

Yet he thrilled now to the knowledge that he would be Grace's first. Grace's only. The one man with the privilege of touching her and teaching her everything she needed to know regarding the depths of sexual satisfaction and human desire.

Ah, the pleasure we shall find together when I get her in my bed.

He shuddered at the idea, ravishing her mouth while he tugged open the buttons on the back of her gown. He wouldn't take her today, he swore to himself, no matter how much his body screamed for release. But he had to have a little more, a last drink of ambrosia before he tore himself away.

Yanking down her bodice, he unlaced her stays, loosening the stiffened cloth enough to free one of her breasts. She cried out as he fastened his mouth over her, shuddering with a clear mixture of surprise and delight as he drew upon her tender flesh. Nestling the fulsome curve in his palm, he kneaded her with gentle finesse, licking her in gradually diminishing circles before pausing to press his tongue and teeth against her sensitized peak.

Her body jerked, her fingers sliding into his hair to cradle him closer and urge him on. With a groan, he freed her other breast and repeated his ministrations — licking and suckling and claiming her utterly. She swayed, trembling and all but insensate, when somehow he found the Herculean strength to stop and pull away.

Ragged breaths bellowed from his lungs, one fist clenched against his thigh in an agony of longing.

He nearly dropped to his knees, seriously tempted to lift her skirts and bury his face between her thighs. Given her innocence, he could likely bring her to completion and have her well on the way to a second release before she even knew what he was doing. But he supposed such diversions would have to wait for later. Closing his eyes, he fought for control.

When he opened them again a few moments later, he found her flushed pink from breast to forehead, visibly trembling as she plucked futilely at her disheveled clothes.

"Shh," he murmured, brushing a comforting kiss over her lips. "I see I've shocked you, and for that I'm sorry. Here, let's get you righted again."

With a minimum of fuss, he had her laced and dressed, her gown smoothed into place with nary a wrinkle. Anyone seeing her would assume she had merely taken a little too much sun. Unless they looked into her eyes. She wore an overly bright, slightly dazed expression — obviously still trying to adjust to everything that had just transpired between them.

Moving a few steps away, he leaned down to retrieve her bonnet. After brushing a speck of dust off the brim, he turned and gently fit it over her head.

"A shame to cover up your glorious hair," he remarked, "but you know what they say about fair-skinned redheads burning, and I believe you've had more than enough sun for today." He tied the blue grosgrain ribbon beneath her chin. "Let us retrieve your sketchbook and find your maid, then I shall escort you home." Taking her hand, he laid it over his arm.

Only then did she speak. "Jack."

"Yes?" He met her gaze.

"Did you mean it?"

He tipped his head to one side. "Mean what?"

"What you said? You know . . . about wanting me."

A guffaw escaped him. "After everything that just passed between us, you still have doubts?" He sobered, reading the uncertainty in her eyes. "Yes, Grace, I want you. Quite badly, in fact."

"And will I see you again? You aren't leaving town?"

"No, I'm not leaving, and you will most definitely see me again. Why do you imagine otherwise?" He paused, as a new thought suddenly struck him. "Did someone else leave you?"

She shook her head and looked away. "It is nothing. I should not have said."

"But you did say. Now tell me, what is this about? Did a man hurt you? Leave you?" At her renewed flush, he knew he was right. "Who is he?"

And how can I kill him?

"He is no one," she said. "And it happened long ago. I was eighteen, too young to know better than to put my trust in a scoundrel. He wanted my money, you see, and I was too foolish to realize what he was really after."

A muscle twitched in his jaw. "And you

think I'm the same?"

Christ, he realized, *I am the same.*

Reaching up, she laid a hand on his shoulder and hastened to assure him. "No, not at all. You are nothing alike."

"So, what happened between you and this man?" he asked, a raw flare of emotion blazing in his chest.

She shrugged. "He courted me for a few weeks. We shared some dances, a carriage ride or two. It was nothing serious, not really."

But he could tell it had been serious — at least for her.

"My father found out," she continued, "and that was the end of that. He left one day without so much as a word. No note. No good-bye."

"Have you ever seen him again?"

"No. Once my dowry was out of reach, so was he."

"And you think I will go away too?"

"I don't believe you will pack your valise and disappear one morning. It is only that I know you are here temporarily and I just wondered how much time we have . . . rather, how much longer you mean to stay in Bath. Don't be angry, my lord. I know you don't need nor want my money."

No, I just need your father to forgive my

gaming debt, he thought, his stomach rolling in a slick wave.

"Are you certain?" he challenged in a quiet tone. "Maybe I do just want your dowry."

She shook her head. "If you did, you'd never be so foolish as to mention that fact. Please, forget I ever said a word about such matters and walk me home."

I should tell her now. End this charade, these lies. But he couldn't take the chance of admitting the truth and losing her — and no longer just because of the money. She wasn't some means to an end for him anymore. He knew her now. Wanted her now. And the only way to have her was by way of holy matrimony.

Strangely, the idea no longer repelled him as it once had. He would still prefer not to get married, but he was sure when they were wed that he and Grace would rub along well together through the years.

He would ask her to marry him now — except for one thing. She didn't love him. Not yet.

But she was close. And once she said the words, once he knew for certain that he'd won her heart, then she would be his — to have and to hold forever.

Leaning close, he took her lips again — a

full, leisurely kiss that was as much about possession as it was pleasure. "If I ever decide to leave," he whispered, "I shall make sure you're the first to know."

CHAPTER 7

Over the next several days, Grace discovered that she need not have worried about seeing less of Jack Byron. Quite the contrary — beginning the very next afternoon, when he called on her at her aunt's town house.

To Aunt Jane's clear delight, he stayed to take tea and biscuits before asking Grace to accompany him on a walk to Sion Hill. Forty minutes later, she found herself concealed within the shelter of a great mulberry tree being kissed senseless.

The following evening, they met at a dance. After standing up together for a set, he suggested they adjourn for refreshments. But she quickly realized he wasn't referring to drinking glasses of punch. Instead he led her to a secluded alcove, where he proceeded to take all manner of knee-weakening liberties — his roving hands and passionate kisses leaving her so dazed that she was nearly incapable of returning to the entertainment afterward.

And then there was the carriage drive to the Avon Valley. Stopping his curricle in a sheltered vale, he kissed her until she feared she might explode with pent-up longing. Jack seemed even more affected, releasing a harsh, pained groan as he forced himself to set her aside. If not for their out-of-doors location, she suspected she might have lost her virginity then and there.

In spite of his obvious desire for her, though, he always ended their embraces before they went too far, careful to bring her pleasure without taking her innocence.

Aunt Jane was certain he meant to propose and kept dropping not-too-subtle hints about the best linen-drapers for wedding clothes and where the most fashionable newlyweds were spending their honeymoons.

Yet Grace wasn't so sure he had marriage in mind.

Jack Byron, third in line to a dukedom, moved in the highest circles of English Society. Ordinary Miss Grace Danvers, on the other hand, did not. *Why then,* she found herself wondering, *would he have any interest in marrying me?* True, she had a sizeable dowry, but he quite obviously lived well and had no need of her wealth. As for love . . . he never said a word on the subject, telling her instead how much he admired her, desired her. Which led to a rather discomfiting conclusion — that what he really wanted was to make her his mistress.

She knew she ought to be appalled, even angry, at the idea that Jack might be intending to offer her a carte blanche. Instead, she found herself curiously intrigued by the idea, and more tempted than a young woman raised to be a virtuous lady had any right to be.

What would it be like to belong to him? she mused now as she lay in bed with the dawn light rising in the sky. How would it feel to sleep at his side and let him claim her body? To experience the culmination of the passion that raged like white-hot embers between them?

If his kisses and caresses were any indication, she knew she would find exquisite pleasure in his arms. And joyous delight in his company as well. But what of her heart? Could she give herself to him knowing that someday their affair would end? That he would turn his back and desert her, leaving her even more alone than she was now? And worse — brokenhearted with love? For him.

The last thought stopped her, forcing her to shake off any further contemplation of an idea she should find alarming at best. Instead she put it all from her mind as she tossed back the covers and climbed from bed to bathe and dress for the day. She would make no decisions for now, she decided. Rather she would let the hours pass as they pleased, without plan or expectation.

"My brown cambric," she told her maid. "Lord Jack and I are going watercoloring this morning, and I don't want to risk getting paint stains on my skirt." As to whether or not there would be a repeat of their kisses inside the labyrinth, she did not know.

Tingling with anticipation, she let the servant help her into her gown.

Later that afternoon, they turned onto the street that led to Grace's residence, her hand cradled securely over his arm.

"Behave yourself, my lord," she murmured in response to a remark he'd just made, "or I shall be forced to administer a punishment."

Leaning closer, he brushed his lips against her ear. "Is that a promise, my dear Grace? If so, I'll be sure to be even naughtier than before. I suspect I might like being punished by you."

Warmth stole into her cheeks, an unrepentant laugh bursting from his lips at her bemused expression. Taking pity, he schooled his features into a more serious mien, repressing the urge to drag her into his arms and kiss her. But they'd done enough of that for one afternoon. Touching her without the promise of consummating the act was like playing with fire, and he didn't think he could take more right now — not without suffering a serious burn.

Not too much longer, though, he told himself. Winning her love was part of the bargain he'd made with her father, and he was confident he would make good on that pledge. Soon, she would admit she loved him, and once that happened, he would ask her to be his wife.

Then he would wait no more.

Smiling, he escorted her up the front steps and into the house. A footman came forward to take Grace's painting supplies, while she removed her bonnet and gloves.

She gazed at Jack. "Will you stay for tea?"

"Actually, I have some business I should attend to this afternoon. But I thought I would return tonight to escort you and your aunt to the theater, if that would be agreeable."

"Most agreeable," she murmured. "Then I shall see you in a few hours?"

"You may count upon it."

"Pardon the interruption," said the butler. "But I thought I should let you know there is a visitor waiting in the parlor."

"Someone to see my aunt?" she asked.

"No, miss. The caller asked most specifically for you. He said his name is Cooke."

A wide smile lit her face. "Terrence is here? Oh, why did you not say so sooner?"

Who the devil is Terrence, Jack thought, *and what has he to do with Grace?*

Without preamble, she hurried across the foyer and disappeared through the painted parlor doors. Seconds later, voluble exclamations of delight issued from the room. Jack followed, his brows drawn tight. He walked inside just in time to see her taken inside a man's embrace as she accepted a pair of enthusiastic kisses on her cheeks.

Willpower alone kept him from striding across the room and dragging her bodily out of the other man's embrace. Instead he stopped inside the entrance and crossed his arms over his chest.

"Well, this is a wonderful surprise. What are you doing here?" she asked the man, one of her hands still caught in his. "You made no mention of coming to Bath."

"I had business in the area and thought I'd stop by," the interloper replied.

"Well, I'm glad you are here," she said. "I had your last letter, but that was over two weeks ago at least."

Letter? She writes him letters!

Jack was still contemplating that bit of information when Grace and her companion turned around. The instant they did, recognition kicked in. It was the sandy-haired fellow from Hatchard's! The one who had escorted Grace from the bookshop that day.

Obviously becoming aware of his regard, she moved forward. "Jack . . . my lord, please forgive me for not introducing you right away. Lord John Byron, pray meet Mr. Terrence Cooke. Terrence is my publisher from London."

Her publisher? Well, at least that answers a few questions.

"My lord, a pleasure," Cooke said, offering his hand.

For a moment, Jack stared at the square palm, with its blunt nails and calloused fingers. "Cooke," he said. They exchanged handshakes, his own confidently firm, while the other man's was surprisingly weak and indecisive.

"So you print Grace's artwork?" Jack stated after drawing away. "She is extremely talented."

"She is indeed," Cooke agreed.

"You're lucky to have her. I hope you're paying her well."

Grace's eyes widened, while Cooke let out a laugh that sounded just a bit nervous. "Well enough, I trust."

"His lordship's sentiments are flattering, but as you know, I don't paint for the money," she said. "Lord Jack has one of my folios, Terrence."

"A fan of the natural world, are you?" Cooke commented.

"At times. However, in this instance, I am more a fan of Grace's."

Cooke met his gaze straight on in a kind of silent challenge. "As are we all."

Grace gave a brief laugh. "Well, before you two make my head swell to twice its normal size, I suggest we adjourn to the sofa and have some tea." She paused, turning to Jack. "Oh, except I forgot. You said you were needed elsewhere. Business, I believe."

At her reminder, Jack recalled that he did indeed have business to conduct. Or rather what constituted business for him, since this afternoon he was promised to play cards at a gentlemen's club, where there were always men eager to be parted from their cash.

Considering Jack's present situation and the debt he owed Grace's father, some might have advised him to refrain from further gaming. However, his ill luck with Danvers had been a fluke. He'd walked away a winner on the pair of occasions when he'd played since. He knew he would do so again, so long as he paid attention to the cards, abided the odds, and held the wagers in reasonable check.

He hesitated, reluctant to leave Grace and her visitor alone. However, given the rent coming due on the elegant town house he'd leased here in Bath, he decided he had better depart as planned.

Were he worried that Grace was in any way attracted to Cooke, he would have stayed regardless of his prior commitment. But despite her obvious friendship with him, he could tell that her affection went no deeper. Oh, Cooke wished it did, Jack realized, sensing again that he had a rival in the man. But if Grace were interested in him that way, she would surely have acted on her emotions long ago.

It certainly hasn't taken her long to respond to her attraction to me.

"Unfortunately you are right and I cannot remain," Jack told her, lowering his voice to a confidential tone. Taking her hand, he lifted it to his lips and pressed a warm kiss onto her palm. "Have a most excellent afternoon, and I shall see you this evening."

Pink stole into her cheeks. "I look forward to it, my lord."

"Jack," he whispered against her ear.

Straightening, he turned to the other man and exchanged farewells. With a last glance at Grace, he departed.

"So, that was the infamous Lord Jack Byron, was it?" Terrence remarked not long after Jack left.

Grace finished pouring the tea that had arrived and passed Terrence a cup. "What do you mean by that?"

"Nothing." He gave a negligent shrug, then took a drink of the gently steaming beverage. "Only that the man has a reputation, and not all to the good."

"Well, I am sure no man is perfect, and I am not surprised to hear as much about Jack — Lord Jack, that is."

"So you're aware he's a womanizer."

A plum-sized fist squeezed beneath her ribs. "No, but again, I am not surprised. He is a very handsome man. Women must naturally flock his way."

Terrence gave a derisive snort. "If you like the type, I suppose." Leaning over, he reached for a wafer-thin slice of shortbread. After dipping it into his tea, he took a bite and swallowed. "You've heard he gambles then, too, have you?"

"All gentlemen gamble. It is practically a social requirement of the breed."

"Yes, but do most make a habit of using the tables to fatten their incomes? I understand he is quite the sharp."

Her brows drew together, the heat of the cup warming her suddenly chill fingers. Having sat beside Jack watching him anticipate every card played in an entire game of whist, she could well believe Terrence's assertions. Jack did have a rare aptitude for games, but that only meant he was clever. Many people liked to play cards. There was no reason to think ill of him for it.

"I suppose next you will say he drinks too much," she charged.

Terrence frowned. "He drinks, but not to excess. Compared to many aristocratic lords, he's practically temperate."

"Well, at least he is spared that criticism." She set her cup down on the table with a snap. "What is this? Why the interest in Lord Jack? I don't understand how it is you even come to know of him."

"Do you not? Perhaps it is because I've heard talk all the way to London about the pair of you."

"What talk?"

"About how you've taken up with him. How you're being squired all over Bath by him."

"I find it highly unlikely that I am being mentioned in the gossip pages. So where are you getting your information?"

He glanced to one side. "From an acquaintance here in the city, who keeps an eye on such things."

Her lips tightened as a suspicion rose within her. "On *things?* Or on *me?*"

He had the humility to flush. "I care about you, Grace. I want to make sure you are all right. That's why I came to see you, to intervene before it's too late."

"Too late for what? As you can tell, I am perfectly well."

"You are now, but what of later? What do you think you are doing, consorting with that man?"

"What do you mean, *'consorting'?*"

"Letting him dance attendance on you, flattering and fawning over you? He wants something from you."

"Well, it isn't my money, if that is what you are insinuating."

"Having met him, I tend to agree. No, what he wants is something worse. He wants *you,* Grace, and he doesn't mean to offer you a ring in exchange for your favors."

She stared at her clasped hands. "Yes, I am already aware of that."

"What?"

Glancing up, she met his gaze. "I know he wants me. He's told me that himself. And I realize he very likely doesn't have matrimony in mind."

"And you are still seeing him?" Terrence said, his voice rising to a near shout.

She nodded. "For now. I am trying to decide."

Leaping to his feet, Terrence took a few pacing steps. "Decide what? Whether or not to accept? Don't be insane. You will say no, of course. My God, how could you even consider anything else?"

Knowing he might not appreciate her answer, she held her tongue.

"He's bewitched you."

"He has not."

"He's seducing you, urging you to go against your nature."

"And what is my nature?"

Is it to be five and twenty and alone? A perennial spinster who will never know real passion or the full measure of a man's touch?

Striding back, he dropped down on the sofa at her side. "It isn't to be used and cast aside. It isn't to be dishonored. And that is what he'll do. He'll take you and enjoy you, and when he grows tired, he'll abandon you and forget you ever met. He's had dozens of women. It's what he does. You'll be just one more. And when it's over, what then? What will become of you, since I am sure your family will not approve."

She closed her eyes, having had those very thoughts herself. Was Terrence right? Was she being a fool to cast aside her virtue and her pride for a fleeting love affair with Jack Byron?

"He's an aristocrat, Grace. You deserve the world, but facts are facts. Men of his class don't marry women from yours."

No, she conceded. *They don't.*

"I'm aware this isn't the best time to ask, but I will again regardless."

"No, Terrence — ," she said, suspecting what he was about to say.

"Marry me, Grace. Marry me and let me make you happy. I'll shower you with love, enough that you'll forget all about him. Say yes and let me show you how grand our life can be together."

She opened her mouth to refuse, prepared to let him down gently, just as she had all the times before. But suddenly, the words did not come. Suddenly she was unsure — not only of her answer but of herself as well.

"I . . . ," she began, studying his earnest-eyed face. "I . . ." Her heart beat in a slow, heavy cadence. "I will think about it."

"But Grace . . .," he said, starting to argue out of habit. Abruptly he stopped. "What? What did you say?"

"I said I shall consider your proposal."

His features lit with happy surprise. "You will?"

"Yes. In the meantime, why do we not talk of other matters? The latest goings-on in Town, for instance. Here, I'll pour us more tea while you regale me."

Several hours later, Jack leaned back in his chair and listened to the actors on the stage. But the play wasn't what held his real interest — that belonged to the woman at his side.

Entrancing in a gown of vibrant green silk, Grace radiated femininity, but not the frail, tepid sort borne by so many of her sex. She was bold and colorful — her lush red hair providing a perfect foil for the crisp apple green of her dress. Looking over at her, his mouth watered at the thought of taking a big juicy bite.

But sadly, even he knew a crowded theater was no place for the kind of things running through his mind. He would have to content himself with a far more innocent touch instead, particularly since her aunt was seated in the row ahead of them. The deep shadows inside the box worked to his advantage, though, providing concealment as he reached for Grace's hand. Lifting it gently, he settled her palm against his thigh.

She sent him a sideways look, her hand lying lax beneath his own. When a line in the play drew applause, she eased her palm away and softly joined in.

His brows drew fractionally closer before he tipped his head near. "Is anything the matter?" he whispered.

"No, of course not." Giving him a quick smile, she redirected her eyes toward the stage.

Leaning back again, he watched the actor portraying Petruchio hoist his Kate onto his shoulders. The audience laughed at the ribald, fast-paced dialogue delivered with unerring skill by the performers.

Gazing at Grace's profile, he skimmed his fingertips along the side of her neck.

She shivered and gave a small shrug to discourage his touch.

With a smile, he paused before moving to toy with a curl at her nape.

"Jack, stop," she said on a hushed undertone.

"Why?" he teased.

"You know why. Now stop."

His lips twitched. Reaching higher, he traced the shell-like edge of her ear, drawing a quiver from her this time.

"Please."

He smiled, slow and intimate. "Please what?"

"We're in a theater."

"Yes, but in this dark corner no one can see."

"What about Aunt Jane?"

"She is busy watching the play." Angling his head, he caught her earlobe between his teeth and gave a light, playful nip.

Her eyelashes fluttered and she bit her own lip to hold back a sigh.

"I could do more," he promised in a low, suggestive tone.

Her eyes turned to his, heavy-lidded and beseeching. "Don't."

"Are you sure?"

She stared, the play forgotten. "Yes."

He met her gaze for a long moment before taking pity and easing away. As he did, he reached for her hand again, causing her to tense. "Just relax," he told her softly. "It's only your hand."

With a slight nod, she relented, allowing him to cradle her palm inside his.

They sat just so for the next two minutes,

watching the performance with their hands clasped.

Unable to resist another foray, he eased open one of the pearl buttons on her glove, then a second. Ever so gently, he stroked the warm, translucent skin on the inner curve of her wrist, moving his fingers in a seductive, circular glide.

Her hand trembled, quickened breath soughing from between her lips. Suddenly he was glad for the noisy action of the play.

For some little while, he continued touching her in that way, learning the feel of her delicate veins and sinew. Then, needing more, he opened another button.

Her breath caught as he inserted his forefinger, sliding it in a silky caress over the sensitive length of her palm.

She shuddered, her eyes falling closed.

Forward and back he went, then forward and back again. And again.

The symbolic imagery worked its spell on him as well, his groin stiffening painfully beneath his evening breeches. Hard and throbbing with need, he knew he had reached his limit. With one last wandering caress, he withdrew, taking time to patiently rebutton her glove.

Glancing over at her, he saw the flags of color in her cheeks and the bright glaze of desire visible in her eyes. It took every ounce of his control not to pull her into his arms and claim her mouth for a hot, wet kiss. Fighting the urge to draw her to him rather than away, he carefully returned her hand to her lap.

Gulping down an unsteady breath, Grace curled the fingers he'd freed into a fist and strove to calm the sensations whizzing like fireworks through her system.

All evening she'd been trying to place some much needed distance between herself and Jack — emotionally, anyway, considering the fact that she'd had no choice but to accompany him and Aunt Jane to the theater tonight as promised. Because ever since Terrence had taken his leave, their conversation had been replaying itself in her mind with distressing frequency.

Clearly, Terrence was right about Jack's affinity for women — he had only to snap his fingers and a multitude would come running. Nor did she doubt he was the gamester Terrence claimed, given his remarkable talent with cards. And as for his intentions toward her . . . if his ardent kisses were anything to judge by, he wasn't planning to lead her down the paths of virtue and self-restraint anytime soon.

He was a rake doing what rakes did best.

Sadly, her meager efforts to erect some mental barriers against him were proving worthless. One touch and she'd turned as malleable as clay. A single caress and she'd been his willing supplicant — longing for more.

And he didn't even have to kiss me!

What she needed, she realized, was time to think. Time that did not include Jack Byron's company.

To her relief, he made no further romantic overtures for the remainder of the play, conducting himself like a perfect gentleman rather than the rogue he truly was.

When the performance ended, her aunt excused herself for a few moments to go speak with a friend — leaving Grace and Jack alone.

"I thought I would stop by tomorrow afternoon," he said as both of them rose from their seats. "What do you say to ices at Ford's, then a walk to Beechen Cliff? I hear there are no finer views of the city than from that location."

"It sounds delightful."

And truly it did, she thought. But she needed an opportunity to consider her choices — and some distance from him while she did so. What better solution than a journey out of the city?

"I am afraid, however," she continued, "that we shall have to postpone the outing. I haven't had an opportunity to tell you, but Aunt Jane is traveling to Bristol tomorrow. I am to go with her."

Originally she had planned to remain at the town house, one of her aunt's female acquaintances happily agreeing to keep her company for a couple of nights. But Grace knew her aunt would be thrilled by her change of plans, as well as with her companionship on the journey west.

"Bristol." His dark brows shot straight. "How long are you going to be in Bristol?"

"Only a couple of days. Likely little more than the weekend. Aunt Jane is visiting an old school friend who just moved north. I am certain we shall not remain long." But long enough, she hoped, to enable her to make some decisions.

Jack looked completely nonplussed, as though news of her departure had thrown him off balance. Moments later, however, he recovered his usual affability. "Well, I wish you a good journey and shall count on seeing you upon your return."

"Yes. I shall send you a note the moment I am in town again."

His expression eased at her assurance. "Good. And not a moment later, mind, else

I too find myself with a sudden need for a trip to Bristol. Four days at most and I shall expect you back."

"Four days," she agreed. She only hoped that four days proved to be enough.

Chapter 8

"Are you certain you don't wish to remain a couple days longer?" her aunt asked as they stood together in the bedchamber where Grace had slept the last three nights.

Grace handed a pair of books to the maidservant, who was helping her pack. "I have had a lovely time here with you and Mrs. Duggin, but I would rather return to Bath today as planned. You stay and visit a while more. Truly, I do not mind in the least."

Aunt Jane's lips firmed with clear indecision. "Yes, but you will be all alone at the town house. What will you do, rattling around by yourself?"

"I am sure I shall find ways to occupy my time. And I will hardly be alone, not with eight of your servants in residence," she countered. "I assure you they shall keep me well-fed and eminently comfortable."

"Just so. But I fear your father would not

approve."

"Then let us not tell him, and that way he won't be displeased."

Her aunt's eyes glittered with surprised enthusiasm at the suggestion. "I suppose you are right in that."

"Besides," Grace continued, "it is not as if I am a girl any longer. At five and twenty I am quite capable of looking after myself."

A soft smile lightened her aunt's face. "From my perspective, five and twenty is plenty young. But I am forgetting that you can still send for Mrs. Twine to come visit. She won't mind in the least. Promise you will send for her the moment you arrive."

Seeing that her valise was packed, Grace reached for her spencer of lightweight fawn sarcenet. Slipping it on, she fastened the short row of buttons, then turned to dust a kiss over her aunt's cheek. "I shall be sure to let her know I am returned."

"I will only be another day or two."

"Stay as long as you like. I shall be fine."

Yet an hour later as she sat in the coach traveling back to Bath, Grace wasn't sure how "fine" she actually was. Despite the time away, she was no closer to making a decision about her situation than she had been when she'd left.

She'd told Terrence she would consider

his offer of marriage, but each time she started to do so, her thoughts seemed to shy away and before she knew it, she would find herself occupied by some other activity.

As for Jack, she couldn't think of him without her pulse picking up speed, her body tingling with heated memories of his touch. She missed him, her dreams and daydreams leaving her with a deep, yearning ache only he could assuage.

Even so, she still didn't know what to do.

Terrence was a good and loyal friend — safe, steady, and dependable. With him she would enjoy the benefits of companionship and shared interests. As his wife, she would have few worries, her life a pleasant, even easy one. If only she loved him, her choice would be simple. But as much as she might wish it, Terrence ignited no fires inside her. He didn't make her burn with a passionate intensity she hadn't even realized she was capable of feeling.

But Jack Byron did.

Like a warrior laying siege, he'd taken her unawares, turning her suppositions about herself and her needs completely on their head. A part of her wanted him desperately. Another part of her was afraid of those very desires. He would bring her pleasure and excitement, making her heart and body soar. But what of the crash to follow? What of the scandal and shame?

Terrence might never excite her heart, but neither would he break it.

Then again, she could refuse them both, return to London, and continue on as she had been doing. Only a few weeks ago, she hadn't minded the idea of spending her life as a spinster. So why did it no longer seem sufficient? Why did the idea leave her dissatisfied and oddly incomplete?

No more at ease with her thoughts than before, she glanced out of the coach window and watched as Bath came into view. Arriving at her aunt's town house, she went up to her room to change out of her traveling clothes and bathe.

An hour later, attired now in a fresh gown of sprigged lilac muslin, she sat down to a light meal of cold sliced beef and crisp, late summer vegetables and fruits. Afterward, she went to her writing desk to pen a note to Mrs. Twine.

But as she lifted her quill above the parchment, she hesitated. As amiable a companion as the older woman was, Grace didn't want or need her company — at least not at present. What she wanted was some resolution to her situation. What she needed was to make up her mind and find some peace.

Maybe if I talk to Terrence, I'll be able to decide once and for all?

It was late afternoon, but not too late for a social call between friends. Surely he would be at his hotel, where they could talk the matter through. If she listened to his counsel, maybe it would give her the strength to do what she knew she ought.

She might not be a lady born, but she had been educated as one. And ladies did not toss their virtue away on handsome aristocrats bent on leading them into a life of sin — however wonderfully pleasurable and decadent that life might promise to be. Clearly, the rational choice was to break things off with Jack.

Perhaps a talk with Terrence would convince her of that wisdom. And then she would be free to decide whether or not to say yes to marrying him.

Setting down her pen, she rose and went downstairs. Without giving herself further time to consider, she gathered her spencer and reticule and made her way from the house.

"You've the devil's own luck, my lord," complained one of the men across from Jack, as he flung down his hand in grudging defeat. "Never seen anyone have such a deuced smooth way with the cards."

Jack scraped the stack of winnings off the baize-covered table and fed them into his coin purse, the additional weight making the leather sag. "Comes from careful play, my good sir. Luck, on the other hand, is a fickle mistress, one over which I have no greater advantage than any other man." Sliding back his chair, he stood. "My thanks for an excellent game."

"But you can't leave now!" the man protested. "I haven't had a chance to recoup my losses."

Jack gave him a cautionary look. "I rather thought you might appreciate leaving here with a few quid in your pocket. Personally, I'd use it on a nice dinner and a visit to the theater. But if you insist on continuing to play, there's a game starting just across the way. Now, I have other business. Good day, gentlemen."

Actually, he had no other business — at least nothing pressing. But he'd already taken plenty of blunt off these three new arrivals to the city, and there was no need to strip them bare. Added to that, he was eager to return to his town house and see if he'd received a message from Grace. Four days and not so much as a word. The silence was driving him mad.

I should never have let her go to Bristol.

Short of chasing after her, though, he'd had no choice in the matter. One minute he'd been planning their next excursion, the next he was listening to her say she was leaving town for a few days.

Well, her few days were over. If he didn't hear from her by tomorrow, he would go after her regardless of how it might look. Who knows, perhaps she would be touched by his apparent devotion, fling her arms around his neck and confess her love — admitting that she'd been utterly bereft without him.

For his part, he could honestly say that he missed their outings. Even — dare he say it — missed her. He certainly hadn't expected to, assuming he would think little of her while she was gone. Yet as each new day arrived, his thoughts turned often to Grace. Wondering how she was faring and what she was doing. And most importantly, how soon she would return.

But such musings meant nothing. He was merely anxious to get on with his plans, that's all. What he wanted most was to be done with this game, put his ring on her finger and be free of the debt teetering like a five-ton boulder over his head.

That and bed her.

Yes, he was definitely looking forward to bedding Grace. Since that first kiss, his hunger for her had only increased, leaving him frustrated and impatient for the day when he would claim her fully. So far he'd been careful not to let their interludes go beyond kissing and a few harmless touches. But his restraint was wearing thin — very thin.

When, he thought as he strode toward the door, *is she coming back?*

Terrence's hotel was quiet when Grace walked inside, with only a couple of men lounging idly in the lobby. As for the clerk's desk, it stood deserted, no one available to answer inquiries or to provide assistance. Luckily, Terrence had mentioned his room number in passing, commenting on how comfortable he found the second-floor accommodations.

Number twenty, she recalled.

Moving swiftly, she ascended the stairs, turning at the top to make her way down a long, narrow hall. Another turn led past number nineteen, then onward to the final room at the end of the corridor. Late-afternoon sunshine poured through a single window, creating a nimbus of light whose reflection would mask from observation anyone standing within its rays.

Giving a gentle rap on the door, she took a step back to wait.

Half a minute passed without an answer.

Maybe he hadn't heard her knock? Or perhaps he wasn't there at all? She supposed she could leave him a note, but she disliked the notion of having to wait to speak to him later. For all she knew, he might not return until after midnight, which would be far too late for him to call on her at home.

Moving close to the door again, she was raising her fist to knock once more when she heard a faint creaking noise from inside the room.

So he is here.

Without thinking, she reached for the handle and opened the door a few silent inches.

"Terrence?" she called in a soft voice before moving into the room. She knew she shouldn't barge in unannounced, but surely he wouldn't mind. They were good friends, too comfortable with each other to stand on formality.

Finding herself in a small unoccupied sitting room, she walked forward. A second door stood on the far side — one that led to the bedchamber, she surmised. She hesitated before approaching, noting that the door was half open.

She would just give a quick tap and call out to him, she decided, then wait for him to join her in the parlor. But as she stepped up to the door, she heard noises again. A creaking sound like shifting bed ropes, followed by a low, guttural moan.

Was he asleep and dreaming?

Then she heard something else — a murmured voice that sounded nothing at all like Terrence. She nearly turned around, but it was too late, her gaze having already traveled past the opening into the chamber beyond.

Suddenly she couldn't move, her limbs locked in place as though she were buried in sand. Her heart hammered, as a strange buzzing started in her head.

Terrence lay naked on the bed. As if that sight weren't astonishing enough, he was leaning over another man in an equal state of undress. The pair were touching, big hands sliding over each other, their strong male faces locked in rapt concentration as they pleasured one another. Reaching up, the other man slid his fingers into Terrence's hair and brought him close for a wide, open-mouthed kiss that was as passionate as it was shocking. As he did, Terrence reached down and took hold of the man's jutting erection, earning a ragged groan as he began to stroke him in a firm, hard clasp.

She must have made a noise, since the stranger suddenly opened his eyes and looked straight at her.

"Who's that?" he asked, breaking off the kiss. "She here to join us? I thought you understood I only like men."

"What?" Terrence mumbled, his voice slurred with desire. "Who?"

Slowly, he turned his head and met her gaze. His eyes widened, jaw falling slack as recognition set in. *"Grace?"*

As though the sound of her name freed some internal bond, she let out a strangled cry and spun on her heel. Behind her came a series of thumps and an exchange of raised voices, making her flee all the faster.

"Grace!" Terrence called. "Grace, stop!"

Her palm slipped on the knob as she tried to wrench open the door. She tried again, but before she could pull it wide, Terrence's palm came down on the wood near her head.

"Grace, don't," he entreated. "Don't leave. Please, give me a chance to explain."

"Let me out!"

"No, not like this." Slipping between her and the door, he blocked her path.

She stepped back, relieved to note that at

least he wasn't naked anymore. Somehow, despite his quick sprint after her, he'd managed to grab a dressing gown along the way.

With shaking hands, he drew the robe's edges tighter and tied the belt with a firm tug. "Good Lord, what are you doing here?"

"I came to talk. I guess I didn't think that you might be . . . that you would . . . that someone else . . ." She broke off, her cheeks flaming so hot that she was sure her hair looked pale in comparison. "I-I should go."

"No," he told her as he walked forward. "Sit."

But she couldn't sit. Instead, she curled her arms over her stomach and took another step back.

Just then the other man walked out of the bedroom, fully dressed in trousers, shirt and a coat. "I'll be at the tavern later if you want to share a pint." He tossed her a glance. "She's not your wife, is she?"

"No!" she and Terrence both said together.

The man gave a wry laugh and let himself out the door.

A heavy silence fell between them, the thud of the stranger's footsteps echoing in the hall before fading away.

Terrence paced a few steps, dragging his fingers through his tousled hair. The gesture reminded her of what she'd seen — of him lying with that man, kissing and touching him as a lover. Of the two of them embracing with an intimacy she'd never imagined two men might share.

Suddenly she couldn't breathe.

"I'm sorry," he said, turning to face her. "You were never meant to know about this —"

"I'm sure I wasn't. But really, you don't have to explain —"

"But I do. I must." He waved a hand toward the bedroom. "This . . . well, what you saw, it doesn't mean anything." He paused as she shot him an incredulous look. "Or at least it doesn't need to mean anything when it comes to you and me. It's a compulsion of mine. Something I'm trying to stop. But I swear that once we're married, I'll never do it again. You won't ever have to worry —"

Her lips parted on a silent gasp. "*Married?* How can you even think —"

"Because I love you," he said, his gaze beseeching as he reached for her hand. "Honestly, I do. Just because I was with some fellow doesn't mean my feelings have changed toward you."

" *'Some fellow'?* You sound as if you don't even know him."

Ruddy smudges formed across his cheekbones. "We only met recently, but that isn't important. I know you're upset now, and I don't blame you. But everything can be as it was before. Just say you forgive me and we'll start again."

She stared at him, her chest tight with emotion and grief. "Oh, Terrence, can't you see that nothing will ever be the same again? How can it after today?"

An expression of panic darkened his eyes. "But —"

"You deceived me and would have kept on deceiving me. If I agreed to marry you, our union would be based on a falsehood."

"I told you, I'll give it up. I'll never do it again."

"I know you mean that now, but what of later? What if you can't stop? What if deep down this 'compulsion,' as you call it, is simply part of who you are?" She shook her head and cast off his touch, curling her hand against her skirt. "It wouldn't be fair to either of us. I can't live a lie, and I care about you too much to let you live one either."

"Please," he begged, reaching for her again. "We share so much in common. We're such good friends. Don't let this be the end."

Evading him, she hurried to the door. This time she succeeded in opening it.

"Don't," he pleaded. "Don't go."

"I have to," she said, feeling suddenly as if her world was crumbling around her. Knowing she was on the verge of tears, she fled down the hallway, Terrence still calling after her as she ran.

Chapter 9

Jack flicked the reins, controlling his roan gelding as he maneuvered his curricle through the late-afternoon traffic. Compared to London, the thoroughfare was barely crowded. Nonetheless, with Bath's more relaxed pace, there was no driving fast — since anything above a moderate walk was considered recklessly inconsiderate.

Taking his time, he drove toward his town house, directing an occasional glance over the passersby ambling up and down the sidewalks. He was passing a wagon that had stopped to unload its cargo when a flash of red hair caught his eye.

A flash of red hair that reminded him of Grace.

The woman was walking straight ahead, her head bowed, her attention apparently too fixed upon her own thoughts to pay much heed to her surroundings. He drew closer, and as he did, he realized the woman didn't just remind him of Grace — she was Grace.

He pulled his curricle toward the curb. "Grace!" he called.

She kept walking, in no way acknowledging that she heard his greeting.

"Hello, Grace!" he called again, louder this time as he walked his horse and carriage along the street at her side. "Miss Danvers!"

She made no response.

Stopping his curricle along the curb, he tied off the reins with a quick twist, then jumped to the ground. Striding toward her, he soon caught up and reached for her arm.

She startled visibly at his touch, glancing up in alarm to see who was accosting her. "Jack?" she said, clearly relieved to find a familiar face.

"Did you not hear me? I called out several times."

She shook her head. "No, I . . . I'm sorry."

"No matter. When did you arrive back?"

"Back?" Lines puckered the smooth skin of her forehead.

"Yes, when did you return from your trip? From Bristol?"

"Oh, Bristol. I came back today. Earlier today. This afternoon."

His brows drew together. *Something is*

amiss, he realized, noticing the distracted expression in her eyes — eyes turned a deep, troubled shade of grey.

"What's wrong? I can see something has overset you."

Her lower lip trembled, her face turning vivid pink. "Nothing. It's nothing."

"Yes, it is. What has occurred?"

She shook her head, her lips sealed tight.

He captured her hand and tucked it over his arm, wishing he could pull her into his embrace instead. But such intimacy was impossible given their very public location. "I can see you are distressed. Did your aunt come out with you? Is she in one of the shops? Let me find her for you."

"She isn't here. She stayed in Bristol."

"You mean you're alone? Do you even have your maid with you?"

He could see by her reaction that she did not.

"What has happened?" he asked. "And don't bother to deny that something of note has occurred, since I know it would be an untruth."

She trembled but would not say.

Briefly, he considered his options. "Come, I shall drive you home."

After another agitated look, she nodded, then let him assist her into his carriage.

She spoke not so much as a word as he set his horse in motion, but merely folded her hands in her lap and cast her gaze low. Only when he drew the curricle to a halt did she glance up again.

"This isn't my aunt's house," she said with surprise.

"No, it's mine. I thought it might be easier for us to talk here."

He also thought it might give him some advantage. With her on his territory, she would be far less likely to slough off his questions. Nor would she tell him to "go away" and let her aunt's butler show him out.

For a moment, she looked as though she was going to protest and insist he drive her home, after all. Instead, she gave a small shrug of acceptance, then waited while he helped her alight from the carriage.

Inside, he exchanged a murmured greeting with his own butler — one of the handful of servants he'd brought with him from London. He trusted his staff implicitly — both for their excellent service, as well as their unassailable discretion. He knew without question that no mention of Grace's presence would ever pass any of their lips.

Turning, he directed her across the white marble entry hall toward the stairs. She followed but stopped at the base.

"The family drawing room is upstairs," he explained. "It's far more comfortable than the one on this level, though we can use it if you prefer."

She hesitated only a few seconds more. "No, the one above is fine."

Leading the way, he ascended the stairs, almost viscerally aware of her as she followed — pleasure coiling in satisfying tendrils at the knowledge that she was here in his house.

Her thin muslin skirts whispered around her ankles as she crossed after him into the drawing room, then again when she settled onto the long, comfortably upholstered sofa.

With a few quick movements, he poured drinks, balancing the snifters as he returned to her side. "Here," he said, holding out the glass with its inch of amber liquid inside. "Drink this."

She sent him an inquiring glance. "What is it?"

"Brandy." Taking a seat next to her, he set his own glass onto a nearby side table before turning to press the second snifter into her palms. "Drink."

"No, I can't." She shook her head and tried to refuse the libation.

"Yes, you can. It's obvious you've suffered

some kind of shock. This will take the edge off. Now, no more arguing. Drink."

"But Jack —"

"Drink." Cupping a hand around the base of her glass, he urged it upward. Finally giving in, she raised the snifter to her lips and took a tentative sip.

"Ugh!" She gasped, sputtering and coughing against the strong taste.

"Have another," he told her as soon as her paroxysm died down.

"No. One was bad enough."

"The next will be easier. Go on."

Shooting him a skeptical look, she obeyed, cradling the glass in both hands as she swallowed another small mouthful. This time she didn't cough.

"One more."

"You'll get me drunk."

"Exactly." He flashed his teeth in a devilish smile.

She laughed and drank more.

Beneath his watchful gaze, tension drained visibly from her shoulders. Reaching over, he picked up his own glass and took a swallow. "So, tell me what has happened to distress you?"

Her gaze dropped to the floor. "Nothing."

Slowly, he turned the snifter in his hand. "Let's try again. Where were you before we met on the street?"

She cast him a glance before raising her glass to quaff another sip of brandy. Her eyelids lowered as the alcohol slid down her throat. On an inhale, she opened them once more. "I went to see Terrence."

A small frown pinched between his brows as he worked to place the name. "Cooke, you mean?"

She nodded. "There were things I wanted to talk to him about."

His frown increased. "What sort of *things?*"

"Personal matters. The details are of no import."

"If that is true," he said in a smooth tone, "then you won't mind sharing."

Her gaze darted to his again, then shifted away.

As it did, a fresh thought dawned on him. "Was it about me?"

"No. Well, not specifically," she hastily amended. "Not today anyway."

"But earlier. So what did Cooke have to say? I assume it wasn't flattering."

"My lord, it isn't —"

"Of any import," he interrupted. "Yes, I know. Indulge me regardless. I assure you my feelings will in no way be hurt."

She hesitated. "For one, he says you're a

gamester."

Does he now? Jack mused, realizing the man must have been inquiring after him. But so long as Cooke knew nothing about his arrangement with Grace's father — and Jack didn't see how he could — everything would be fine.

"He's right," Jack admitted. "I do enjoy games, including ones that have nothing at all to do with cards. Go on, what else?"

"He . . . um . . . he may have mentioned that you have a keen admiration for women."

" *'Admiration'?"* Jack smiled. "Is that how he put it? I confess he's correct again. I do hold the feminine half of society in great esteem. But then I believe you are already aware that I like women." Reaching out, he traced his fingertips along the sleek line of her jaw, eliciting a delicate quiver. "Some women more than others."

He caught her earlobe between his thumb and forefinger and gently rubbed the nub of flesh. "I suppose he suggested you and I part company?"

Breath sighed from between her lips. "He did say he thought you weren't a good influence."

And yet here she sits, alone in my house. The knowledge warmed him yet again.

"I've never claimed to be a saint," he agreed again. "So is that all?"

She shook her head, a little tendril of hair coming loose from its moorings. Drawn to it like a hawk to flight, he twined his finger around the strand.

"He also asked me to marry him."

He jerked, his knuckle inadvertently snagging in her hair.

"Ouch!" she cried.

Immediately he untangled himself. "Sorry. Did you say marriage? You didn't accept, did you?" He forced down the wave of panic that caught him like a blow to the belly. *My God, if that is the case, then I've badly mishandled the situation, as well as underestimated my rival.*

"No, I didn't accept."

Relief poured through him.

She sipped her brandy. "But that's why I went to see him at his hotel this afternoon. To talk."

"His hotel?" Jack's hand tightened at his side, wondering what other revelations she was going to tell him next.

Draining her glass, she held it out. "May I have more?"

For a moment, he stared, then tossed back the contents of his snifter in a single gulp. "I could do with a refill myself."

Taking her glass, he stood and went to the sideboard. Removing the stopper from the crystal decanter, he added a splash to hers and a heartier measure to his own.

Resuming his seat, he placed her glass into her hands. "Go on. What happened at the hotel?"

Her cheeks flashed a brilliant red, a color that had nothing whatsoever to do with the spirits she had imbibed, he realized.

"He didn't make advances, did he?"

I am the only man allowed to do that, he thought, his jaw clenching. *So help me, if Cooke touched her, I'll hunt him down and rip him limb from limb.*

A peculiar look crossed her features. "No, he didn't make advances. Not to me."

Thank heaven for that!

She drank again.

A new thought struck him. "If not to you, then . . . Lord, you didn't walk in on him, did you? Did you catch him with another woman?"

Improbably, her skin flushed an even deeper red, so vivid it looked as if she was standing mere inches from a bonfire.

"Not a woman, no," she whispered. "He . . . he . . ."

"He what?" he asked, a sudden speculation beginning to form.

"He was with . . . a . . . a man. And they were naked!" She downed more brandy, coughing when she took too hasty a swallow.

Reaching out, he patted her on the back, leaving his hand there to rub in slow, reassuring circles. "Better?"

Nodding, she drew in a deep breath and released a long exhale.

"I'm sure you were shocked," he said.

"Never more in my life."

That I can well believe. Poor girl must have gotten an eyeful.

Still, Jack couldn't help but be relieved to know his rival wasn't really a rival. Then again, from what she'd said, the bounder had proposed marriage to her in spite of his sexual preference.

At least in the essentials, I'm not that much of a fraud, he thought.

Perhaps his motives weren't wholly pure, but with him she would have a real marriage. In his bed, she would be well pleasured and know the full extent of what it meant to be a woman fulfilled. Her father had told him to keep her happy and pregnant, and he vowed suddenly that he would do his best to make good on that promise.

"Well, I am sorry for your distress," he told her, continuing to stroke her back in easy circles. "But I cannot say I regret the outcome. If not for your unexpected discovery, you would not be here with me now." He slid closer. "And I am very glad you are here. I've missed you these last few days."

She met his gaze, her irises looking very blue. "You have?"

"Hmm hmm. What about you?" Lifting his other hand, he traced a finger over one fire-colored eyebrow, then down her cheek and over to her lips. "Did you miss me. Even a little?"

Her eyelids trembled. "Yes. I did miss you. But I–I oughtn't to have. I should go."

"Should you? Why?"

Tiny frown lines appeared. "Because . . . because . . ." She paused as though she were searching for a reason and having a hard time finding one. "Because it's getting late and I ought to be returning to the house."

"It's scarcely dinnertime." He skimmed his knuckles over her jaw before roaming lower to the satiny column of her neck, then back up again. "Surely you could stay for dinner? You said yourself your aunt is away. I can't believe you would prefer eating alone."

Her frown increased. "No, but —"

"Then stay. My cook sets an excellent table. Delicious fare designed to tempt any palate. Tell me your favorites and I'll send word to her to make them especially for you."

Sliding his arm around her back, he bent and pressed his mouth to the base of her throat. "Do you like roast beef?"

"Ahh, I . . ."

"Too heavy, you're right," he stated, dropping kisses against her skin in a leisurely pattern. "What about venison? Unless you are worried it might be gamey. Hmm, I agree."

Her eyelids fluttered, one hand coming up to catch in the fabric of his coat.

Working his way up, he paused and breathed a gentle gust of warm, brandy-scented air into her ear. She shuddered, a tiny moan escaping her lips.

"Partridge, perhaps? In a sweet vermouth with plump raisins and orange peel. How does that sound?"

"Delightful."

He smiled, wondering if she was referring to the food or his kisses. He definitely hoped the latter.

"Or I know," he whispered, brushing his mouth ever so lightly against hers. "Lobster and oysters. Light and delicate, with a taste as fresh as the sea. Shall we try that? I could feed them to you bite by delectable bite."

Before she had a chance to answer, he traced the shape of her mouth with his tongue, then slid inside, as her lips parted to receive him. Leaning her back against the sofa pillows, he plundered the sweet, velvety depths of her mouth, exploring with sudden purpose, as well as with undeniable pleasure.

Maybe it was wrong of him, but he sensed he could not afford to let her leave tonight — not without forging a deeper bond between them. And what better way than to complete her seduction? His methods might be a tad unfair given the amount of brandy he'd let her consume, but she was destined to be his, whether she knew it or not.

So why not now?

Why not tonight?

His hand moved to her breast, fingers seeking the sensitive flesh inside her bodice. But as he began to delve beneath, she stiffened slightly and reached to deny him. "I . . . I thought you said dinner."

"I did. And we'll eat — after a while. We have plenty of time." *All night,* he thought, taking her mouth with demanding persuasion.

Moments slipped past as she surrendered, responding enthusiastically to his kiss. Then just as suddenly, she groaned and tore herself away. "N-no, stop. I should go. I told you, I have to go."

Pushing against him, she levered herself up and off the sofa. But after no more than a couple of steps, she faltered, weaving in a most alarming way.

Springing up, he hurried forward and reached her just in time to prevent a fall. Wrapping his arms around her, he pulled her tightly against him.

"Stars," she cried, lifting a hand to her head. "I feel so dizzy. It'sh that brandy," she accused in what she obviously wanted to be a stern rebuke. Instead her words came out slurred.

And adorable. She was definitely adorable.

"You've gotten me fosked."

"Foxed, do you mean?" he repeated.

"Yes, fosked. All your fault."

"Not *all* my fault, since I believe you are the one who insisted on that second glass, if you will recall."

Her brows furrowed in clear confusion. "Oh, you're right. I d-did, d-din't I?"

"Hmm, and so you did."

"I should go home."

He shook his head. "You're in no condition to go home, not right now. I suggest a lie-down for a few hours." *Or perhaps the entire night.*

"M-maybe just a tiny while," she agreed, trying to pinch her fingers together for illustration, and missing. "In a guest room."

"There are several." But he had no intention of taking her to any of them. *She'll sleep in my room. In my bed.*

Bending slightly, he slid his arms around her knees and back and lifted her high against him.

Instinctively, her arms curved around his neck. "Are you carrying me?" she asked, her voice holding a note of amazement.

"You appear to be in need of assistance."

"But I must be too heavy. What if you drop me?"

He met the surprised blue of her eyes. "Impossible. You're as light as a feather. You feel just perfect to me, Grace. You are just perfect *for* me."

And oddly enough, in that moment, he knew that she was. He might not love her, but she would make him a splendid wife. With her, he knew he would always be challenged and would never grow bored. They would make a fine family together, producing strapping dark-haired boys and pretty, long-legged, redheaded girls.

But, he reminded himself, *first things first.*

Cradling her tighter, he gazed into her eyes. "Ready?"

With a tremulous smile, she nodded, then leaned her head against his shoulder with a contented sigh.

Pleased, he turned and strode from the room.

CHAPTER 10

She sank into an ocean of feathers and satiny dark blue brocade, floating as the room spun slowly around her.

Or perhaps I am the one spinning? Now there was a funny notion. She giggled a little to herself and closed her eyes while she waited for the world to settle back on its proper axis.

A gentle hand stroked her hair, the feathery ocean rolling slightly as someone joined her on the satin counterpane. "Jack?"

"Hmm hmm?" he said in a rich, deep rumble.

She stretched, as comfortable as a cat and half inclined to purr, as his fingers glided over, then into, her hair. He massaged her scalp with the lightest of touches, her tresses coming loose as the pins popped free.

"Are you taking down my hair?" she mused aloud, feeling the long, heavy mass flow across the pillows.

"Just making you more comfortable."

A faint metallic ping rang out as he set a handful of pins on the night table. Then his fingers were back, combing through the strands to smooth out any tangles. She couldn't help but sigh with enjoyment, tingles dancing over her body in little electrical skips and pings.

"It's even more beautiful than I imagined," he said in a throaty voice. Wrapping a long strand around his fist, he lifted her hair to his face. "Glorious."

"Aunt Jane says it looks like a forest fire."

"On this particular topic, your aunt is singularly misinformed. The gods themselves would kill for hair like yours."

Smiling, she let herself float as her eyelids drifted downward.

The touch of his lips against her temple and cheek brought her back to her surroundings. Opening her eyes, she gazed up at the ornate ceiling, then across to the richly carved bedposts, with their elegant hangings. "D'you always keep sush big, fancy beds for guests?"

His lips moved into a smile, pausing as he kissed her neck. "I'm a tall man. I like a long mattress."

She frowned, knowing something wasn't quite right about his answer, although at the moment she couldn't figure out exactly what it was. But being a tall woman, she had no complaint with large beds.

My feet don't even come close to the bottom in this one, she noted, stretching out her toes just to double-check. To her delight, she discovered nothing but more bed.

His fingers moved again, busy this time unfastening the buttons on the back of her gown. He was as efficient as a lady's maid, she found, the fastenings already open before she half realized what he was doing. She blinked again and felt him loosen the laces of her stays.

She drew a deep, refreshing inhalation, her bodice sagging downward in a rather alarming manner. Only she was too relaxed at the moment to really be all that alarmed. Still, she decided she couldn't let the matter go without offering some remark. "Why'd you do that?"

"Just making you more comfortable, remember?" he drawled in a voice that was as smooth and heady as the brandy she'd drunk. "Are you not more comfortable?"

She mulled over the question and realized that she was.

Deliciously, deliriously comfortable.

Except for my sleeves, she thought. She just had to get her arms free of the nagging confinement of her sleeves.

Without considering the ramifications of her next move, she worked her arms out of the garment. Glowing from her successful liberation, she followed her instincts further and stretched her arms over her head.

Out popped her bare breasts, her bodice and stays slipping down her torso. "Oops!" she said, giggling even as her skin flushed pink with embarrassment.

Instantly, her nipples tightened, both from the cool air in the room and the heat of Jack's gaze — his eyes fastening like a beam of light on her exposed flesh.

She didn't know what came over her next — or where her earlier inhibitions and misgivings went — but instead of attempting to cover herself, she lay still. Brazenly, she let him look his fill.

And look he did.

Abruptly, he swallowed, his Adam's apple shifting up, then down, beneath the skin of his throat. A rueful gleam came into his gaze, one that seemed tinged with guilt. "You really are tipsy, aren't you?"

After a moment's thought, she nodded in agreement.

"Two small brandies and you're as drunk as a lord."

She smiled. "No, you're the lord, milord.

Milord Jack. Gorgeous, mouthwatering, lovely Lord Jack."

"Lovely, am I?" he remarked with a chuckle. The sound soon turned to a groan. "Bloody hell," he muttered under his breath. "I'm going to regret this, but it would just be wrong."

"What would be wrong?"

Taking hold of her bodice, he gently covered up her exposed breasts. "This." Leaning over, he combed his fingers through her hair again. "You should rest."

"I am resting."

"Sleep then."

"But I'm not sleepy. Not anymore."

"You will be soon enough. Close your eyes and relax."

"Where will you be?"

He swallowed again, as though his decision was tearing him in two. "Close by. You have only to ring when you awaken."

Her frown returned. "But I don't want you to go. Don't go, Jack. Stay with me."

Suddenly she knew she meant every word. She didn't want him to leave, and no matter what might happen, she would have no regrets. For in spite of all the warnings against him and the knowledge that his motives were undoubtedly dishonorable, she didn't care. She'd trusted Terrence, and look where that had gotten her? For good or bad, she felt safe with Jack. She could count on him not to deceive her. With him, she knew who she was and where she stood — with no lies between them.

Unmindful of her loosened bodice, she sat up and wrapped her arms around his neck. "Stay." Emboldened as she had never been before, she kissed his cheek, then his jaw.

"That's the spirits talking," he said in a strained voice.

She shook her head. "No. The spirits may have freed my tongue, but they haven't put words in my mouth. I know what I'm saying."

He pulled her away so she was forced to meet his gaze. "And do you know what you're doing? What will happen if I stay? I'll strip the rest of these clothes off you and lay you beneath me in this bed. I'll take you the way a man takes a woman, and I won't stop."

"I don't want you to stop."

"Do you also realize this is my bedchamber and that I brought you here to seduce you? That I still plan to seduce you. Later. But right now, you're foxed and I —"

She put her hand over his mouth. "Want this. Want you. I love you and that's all that matters."

She wasn't sure which of them was the more surprised, but the instant she said the words, she knew they were true. She did love him — fully and deeply. Her indecisiveness this past week and her impromptu trip to Bristol had been nothing more than excuses to deny her real feelings. Even Terrence and her contemplation of marriage to him had been based on fear. Fear of herself. Fear of letting herself love Jack. Fear of letting herself take what she wanted most. But suddenly she wasn't afraid any more.

"You love me," he repeated in a measured tone.

She nodded. "You probably wish I hadn't said it," she continued, "but it's how I feel. Please don't think I expect anything in return."

His jaw tightened, a fierce look in his eyes. "You should."

"Just tell me you want me."

"Of course, I want you. Considering these last couple weeks, how could you still be in doubt?"

"Then you'll stay?"

He hesitated. "I shouldn't, but how can I refuse now?"

Reassured, she lay back against the pillows. When she moved to unclothe herself for him again, he stopped her.

"Don't," he said in a throaty growl, catching her hand inside his own. "Let me."

With his gaze holding hers prisoner, he peeled down her bodice, then reached out to touch one breast. His fingers circled, sliding rhythmically around a single taut peak. Ever so lightly, he pinched the sensitive nub, then released it, before beginning the leisurely progression all over again.

She couldn't breathe as he toyed with her, her senses spinning wildly around her again. But her reaction had nothing to do with the alcohol this time. Trembling, she let him do whatever he wished, confident he would bring her nothing but exquisite pleasure. An acute ache rose between her thighs, a longing to be possessed that made her restless and needy.

Clasping a hand behind his head, she drew him down for a kiss. She expected him to meet her demand with wild, ravishing passion. Instead, his touch was unhurried, his moves tempered with a care that bordered on the reverent.

Slow and easy. Soft and gentle. His every caress made her melt, turning her insides as warm and slick as candle wax left out too long in the sun. His kisses were magical, weaving a spell around her — around them both — that left her no hope of escape.

Not that she had any wish to escape. Quite the opposite, since she was unable to keep herself from writhing beneath his caresses as he continued to shape and stroke her breasts, moving from one to the other with a thoroughness that verged on torment.

Swallowing a moan, she pressed herself more deeply against his palm, seeking more. He complied, breaking off their kiss so that he could slide down to take one of her breasts in his mouth.

Hot, wet heat engulfed her, his tongue like satin against her sensitive peak. Answering moisture gathered between her thighs as he suckled with an intensity that reached to her very core. Raking her with his teeth, he paused to suckle again, feasting upon her with long, slow licks that were punctuated by intense, mind-spinning draws. She quivered and threaded her fingers into his hair to cradle him closer.

She felt his lips curve into a smile as he transferred his ministrations to her other breast. Not stinting in the least, he lavished her willing flesh with the same degree of blissful attention. At length, he slowed, drawing upon her with a last, lingering pull before levering himself away.

Instantly, she was bereft and reached to bring him back.

But she needn't have worried, his broad, skillful hands moving to peel away her gown, stays, and petticoats with calm, simple efficiency. Once he was done, her stockings and lacy garters were all that remained to shield her from his view — leaving her with absolutely no protection at all.

His azure eyes gleamed, turning an even more intense shade of blue, as he raked her with his gaze. Surveying her body in a leisurely downward sweep, he studied every inch of her form. When he reached the spot where her fiery triangle of curls met the apex of her thighs, he paused before continuing his amorous perusal all the way down to her feet.

Abruptly, she became self-conscious, lowering her arms across her body and bending her knees in a concealing half-curl.

"Ah, sweetheart, don't turn shy on me now," he admonished in a mild tone. "I assure you, you have absolutely nothing to hide. Quite the contrary, in point of fact."

Laying a palm on her stocking-clad ankle, he roved upward with a light, tensile glide. "I can't tell you the number of times I've dreamed of seeing these legs."

Her eyes widened. "You have?"

"Oh, yes. I've fantasized endlessly, dying

to know just how shapely they are and exactly how far up they go." Reaching the bare strip of skin above her silken garter, he stopped and smiled. "I am overjoyed to note that they do go up — way, way up. You are gorgeous, even more so than I expected."

Her lips quivered on a tremulous breath. "So, you're pleased?"

Something darkened in his gaze. "Yes, very much. Now let me please you in return."

She didn't know precisely what he intended, but he moved quickly to demonstrate by sliding his hand sideways. Warm as toast, and darker-hued than her own pale white skin, his strong fingers spread outward against the delicate flesh of her inner thighs. The sight of him touching her there was dramatic — a powerful contrast of male to female. But because she still had her legs locked together, he could go no farther. Ever so gently, he traced the seam between her thighs.

"Open up," he murmured.

Her pulse sprang into a frantic rhythm.

"Open your legs, Grace. I promise you won't be sorry."

She hesitated, her heart pounding like a relentless fist beneath her breasts. Slowly, aware she was literally laying herself bare to him, she did as he asked.

His lips curved with approval. "God, you're lovely. Now, just a little more."

More?

She didn't think she could manage. But somehow she found the courage. Emboldened once again by the carnal appreciation she saw in his gaze, she spread her legs wider.

And then he touched her there.

She gasped, her eyes falling shut at the devastating sensation of his fingertips teasing her nether curls. Stroking her with light, glancing touches, he delved beyond, gliding along her sleek folds as he gradually explored.

She grew wet in a way that ought to have mortified her. But Jack appeared to find nothing amiss, so why should she? If anything, her body seemed eager to aid him, his fingers rubbing with a slippery friction that made her thoughts scatter to the four winds.

Then she couldn't speak or think at all, her hands bunching in the fabric of the counterpane, as pleasure wove through her like the tendrils of a wild, rapacious vine. He speared a single finger into her, making her shudder and arch.

She bit her lip to keep from crying out,

but he wouldn't let her stay silent.

"Do you like this. Yes?" he coaxed.

"Y-yes."

"Tell me where to touch you next."

But she couldn't speak, rolling her head on the pillows instead.

"Here?" His thumb circled in a lazy glide. "Or perhaps you prefer this spot?"

"Oohh," she gasped aloud, perspiration breaking out over her skin.

"What about now?" He added a second finger, filling her more than she thought she could stand. Yet it felt right. Exactly right. She groaned, craving more.

"Maybe this."

He slid higher to caress some hidden nub of flesh. Need swamped her, burning like a raging fire.

Relentless, he scissored his fingers inside her. Open, then closed, then open again. "Shall I stop?"

"No!" she sobbed, abandoning all caution or control.

Then suddenly he did everything at once — circling and scissoring and rubbing. The combination proved too much, bliss crashing over her in a dark, merciless wave.

Her senses went flying, whirling as thoughts and emotions tumbled through her with an intensity that made her earlier intoxication seem as nothing. She felt drunk. Drunk and delirious, glowing from a surfeit of delight that was humming like bottled lightning in her system.

Good God, she thought, *no wonder women beg to be in his bed. No wonder they're willing to risk everything for even a taste of this. Of him.*

She barely had a chance to catch her breath before he began again, caressing her with a deep, intimate massage that instantly ignited her desire. Need swamped her, building so fast it was all she could do to hang on and hope she didn't shatter before he brought her to release again. She was poised on the edge, held in the grip of a hunger so strong she was shaking from the force of it.

Then, with no warning at all, he stopped and moved away. For a second, his withdrawal made no sense, her body throbbing with a savage intensity that demanded satisfaction. "Jack?" she called, rising up slightly on her elbows. "What are you doing?"

"Disrobing," he told her as he climbed from the bed. "Not to worry. I will be back to pleasure you in a trice."

"You'd better be," she said without considering her words.

He chuckled at her candor, his nimble fingers moving to open the buttons on his waistcoat, shirt and pantaloons.

She watched him with brazen interest, reclining against the pillows as he revealed inch by delicious inch of hard masculine flesh. The sight of him made her giddy. He was better than any Grecian sculpture she'd ever seen — long and tall where he should be, broad across the shoulders, but equally narrow at the hips. Muscles flexed beneath his superb physique, powerful bone and sinew covered by taut, supple skin. A dusting of short dark hair grew on his powerful legs and across his elegant forearms. His chest was covered by a heavier thatch of nearly black hair. A line of it tapered downward across his flat stomach, then all but disappeared, before flaring out again around his groin.

It was this last part of him that fixed her attention most completely. From the instant he stripped off his pantaloons and drawers, she couldn't look away. Without conscious awareness, she riveted her gaze on his swollen shaft, taking note of its rampant length and girth. He paused for a few moments — hands on his hips as if he were letting her study him.

"You don't look anything like Terrence,"

she said, not realizing she'd said the words aloud until they were already out of her mouth.

He quirked a brow. "I believe I shall take that as a compliment."

She nodded in agreement, marveling at the fact that until today she had never even seen a naked man — much less three of them. But then she had no more time to ponder such matters as Jack padded forward on bare feet.

Her nipples stiffened to hard points, need throbbing inside her with a wrenching ache as he bent a knee upon the bed and came down beside her. He took her in his arms, making her tremble at the hot slide of his naked skin against hers.

"You'll have to show me what to do," she whispered, shy once more as she met his gaze.

"Don't worry." His lips brushed lightly across hers. "We'll take everything as slowly as you need."

Reassured, she curved her arms around his neck and gladly gave herself up to his kiss. He claimed her mouth in a languid joining that was as sultry as it was sublime, her nerve endings igniting like kindling set to a flame once again.

His hands resumed their earlier wandering, each caress heightening her passion, every stroke leaving her hungering for more. Something hard and insistent pressed against her stomach. With surprise, she realized it must be his erection.

Stroking a palm over his shoulder and back, she slid gradually downward, growing bold enough to roam as far as his waist. But she couldn't muster the courage to go lower, her fingers flexing ineffectually against his hip.

"You can touch me if you like," he said, breaking off their kiss to nuzzle the underside of her ear. His tongue darted out, lapping at a spot that sent quivers whizzing through her system like champagne bubbles gone out of control. "Touch me anywhere, Grace," he encouraged in a husky tone. "Let those hands of yours run wild."

Emboldened, she skimmed her fingers across his buttocks, feeling the muscles clench in response, then onward to the top of his thigh, finding it just a bit rough with hair. Then, before she had time to talk herself out of the impulse, she reached for his shaft and encircled him with her fingers.

A harsh groan issued from his throat.

She stiffened and began to withdraw, but he stopped her with a hand, forcing her fingers to stay where they were. "Stroke me," he said. "Please."

Trembling, she hesitated just a moment more, then did as he wished.

The feel of him was astonishing, hard and thick, yet covered with a skin as sleek and smooth as velvet. She glided up his length, then down, pausing at the last to brush a curious thumb across the tip. His shaft jumped in her palm, Jack releasing another throaty moan.

"Harder," he said. "Stroke me harder."

And she did, caressing him with increasing confidence while he massaged her breasts and took her mouth in a savage kiss. As she opened her lips wide, he slid his tongue inside, licking and lapping, then thrusting in and out in time to the movements of her hand.

He kissed her until she was dizzy, her grip gradually weakening on him as he drowned her in a tide of pleasure. Rolling her to her back, he used his knees to spread her legs apart and fit himself between. Crushing her lips to his, he moved her hand away, then positioned himself and thrust inside her body.

She tensed against the intrusion, his size stretching her to the point of pain. Her cry reverberated against his mouth, and he stopped, his chest rising and falling against hers as he rested on top of her.

"Give it a few moments. It'll get easier," he murmured.

Will it? she wondered, rather doubting his words. He was large, her body gripping him like a too-tight glove.

Then he began to move again.

Her panic increased when she realized he was barely inside her, despite the agonizing sensation of fullness. She remained motionless, her pain intensifying as he forced himself deeper inside.

Finally, he was all the way in.

Only then did she sense the tension in him, his muscles quivering from the strain of holding himself back. A hand on the back of her thigh urged her to lift her legs and wrap them around his waist. She did, the shift in position lodging him even deeper. Yet oddly enough, her discomfort lessened, the pain receding as her body adjusted to his penetration.

How peculiar, she thought, to have that part of him inside her. How incredibly close. Intimate in a way she had never truly imagined two people could be.

Slowly, he began to thrust, and her thoughts drifted away like tufts of dandelion fluff caught in a rough wind.

"Better?" he questioned in a gravelly voice.

Reaching up, she captured his mouth in a fervid kiss and gave him all the answer he needed.

In and out he went. In and out, over and over again until sparks of her earlier desire began to rekindle. He kissed her — long, wet, open-mouthed kisses that stole her breath, even as the vigorous movements of his hips turned her liquid and wanton with need.

She cried out, only this time not in pain, but in longing. Digging her heels into his buttocks, she urged him onward, clasping him to her with a sudden desperation she was helpless to resist.

Arching, she bounded upward to meet him, to take him as far and fast as her body would allow. Keening sounds came from her mouth, moans she barely recognized as her own as she gripped him harder. She remembered him saying something once about liking to ride, and suddenly she knew what he'd meant.

He was riding her — and it was sheer heaven.

Opening herself fully to him, she surrendered everything that she was, giving him her body and her mind. As for her heart, he possessed that already, love swelling within her as she clasped him tight and waited for all the pleasures yet to come.

She wasn't prepared when the crisis claimed her not long after, ecstasy rippling through her bones and blood and flesh until all that remained was a sensation of pure, unadulterated bliss. She glowed — beyond rapture, beyond speech. Then, she was spinning once again, with Jack her only lifeline.

Barely coherent, she continued to float as he thrust inside her — pumping harder and deeper and faster. Abruptly he grew rigid, his body quaking violently as he claimed his release with an echoing groan of satisfaction.

For long moments, they lay locked in each other's arms, neither seemingly capable of movement. With breath and sanity finally returning, he shifted, rolling onto his back before drawing her once more into his arms.

Snuggling against him, she let her eyes drift closed. "It's still early yet, is it not?" she mumbled. "We never had our dinner."

"Dinner will wait," he said, soothing her with a hand. "For now, you should sleep."

With her eyelids like leaden weights, she took his advice and let herself sink into oblivion.

Chapter 11

Grace squinted against the light and raised a hand to shield her eyes as she burrowed deeper into the pillows.

"Oww," she groaned, before grimacing in pain, even that slight amount of sound too much for her already aching head.

Lie still, she warned herself in a silent whisper. *Don't move and maybe the agony will go away.*

But even thinking seemed to hurt, her head throbbing in violent beats between her ears.

"Here. Drink this," said a quiet voice.

Drink what? Is that Jack speaking? What is Jack doing in my bedroom?

"Do you think you can sit up?" he asked.

No! Absolutely not. Couldn't he tell how miserable she was, unable to even lift her head off the pillow, much less sit up and drink something. Besides, she'd already drunk far too much last night. Her stomach lurched at the notion. The tom-toms in her head beat harder.

"Come on, sweetheart," he said. "Here, let me help you."

He set something down on the night table with a clink that reverberated as loudly as a blacksmith's hammer striking an anvil. She held back a groan, knowing she dare not react for fear of jarring loose some vital organ — her brain, for instance. Before she could prevent him, Jack slipped an arm around her recumbent form and levered her upright.

"Aaagh!" she cried, gripping her head with both hands to keep it from rolling off her neck.

"Shh," he crooned. "You'll feel better once you get this in you."

Squinting, she peered at the glass that had appeared again inside his hand. The concoction looked revolting, with a color somewhere between yellow and grey. "What is it?" she whispered.

"Hair of the dog."

"Dog!" Fresh pain jarred the inside of her skull.

He laughed.

"Oooh, don't." She waved a hand to hush him.

"Sorry," he said, lowering his voice again.

"None for me," she whispered. "I'll just lie down again."

"Oh no, you don't," he admonished, holding her against him. "First, you have to drink."

"Not if it has dog hair in it." Her stomach did a somersault.

"It's only an expression. Drink."

"That's what you said last night, and look where it's gotten me." The drums beat harder again.

"So now I'm here with the cure."

"I don't want —"

"The sooner you get it down, the sooner you'll be better."

Better? How can that disgusting concoction possibly make me feel better? Though at the moment, she felt so dreadful she supposed anything would be an improvement.

Letting him press the cool glass into her hand, she gave the beverage another skeptical look. Losing her courage, she tried to pass it back. "I can't."

He pressed it toward her again. "Down fast. Drink and don't think."

"Did you make that up?"

"Friend of mine. Go on."

Grimacing, she drew a steadying breath and took a swallow. "Ugh," she said, breaking off on a near gag. "That's vile."

"All of it."

"No."

"Do it, Grace. Drink and don't think."

She sent him a nasty look. "I hate you."

He smiled and stroked her hair. "Last night you said you loved me."

And so she had, she realized, bits of the evening flashing in her mind. Pushing the memories aside for now, she raised the glass again. *Drink and don't think.*

She gulped the brew as quickly as possible, her stomach bucking and lurching with each and every swallow. When she was done, she shoved the glass at him and gasped for breath. "Oh, my God, I think I'm going to be sick."

"Give it a minute."

Leaning back against the mound of pillows he'd somehow found time to stack behind her when she wasn't looking, she closed her eyes and prayed for death. Her stomach churned again, her head throbbing as if an orchestra were playing a symphony inside.

Jack left but quickly returned, his weight depressing the feather mattress as he sat down next to her.

Opening her eyes a sliver, she saw he had an empty porcelain washbasin in his lap. "Just in case," he said.

Groaning once more, she turned her head away and waited to see how long it would be before she disgraced herself by being violently ill in front of him.

But one minute lapsed into two, then two more passed, as her stomach began to settle from a series of fearsome dips and flips into a gentle, gradually ebbing tide. The hammering receded in her brain as well, diminishing to a mildly uncomfortable pang. She relaxed with a sigh, a delicate belch escaping her lips before she could prevent it.

Flushing, she covered her mouth with her hand.

Jack chuckled and set the washbowl aside. "Better?"

Meeting his twinkling blue eyes, she nodded. "Yes, much better. Thank you."

"Wonderful. Now we can proceed on to breakfast."

"Breakfast!" She shook her head, a lingering twinge of pain shooting between her eyes. "No food, please."

"But food is precisely what you need, especially since you didn't eat dinner last night."

Heat washed over her cheeks again. He was right. After tumbling into bed together, they never had managed to get out again, too busy slaking their mutual passion to even think about food. Her memories were slightly hazy, but she recalled Jack making love to her again after that first time, rousing her from a heavy sleep in order to satiate his needs and hers once more.

Now, it was morning and she had spent the night in his house. In his bed. *Oh my, I still am in his bed.*

Clutching the sheet, she drew it higher, becoming excruciatingly aware that she was naked. She never slept naked. Then again, she'd never slept with a man before either.

"What time is it?" she ventured, half-afraid to hear the answer.

"A little after ten, I believe." Crossing to a table set beneath one of the room's many windows, he picked up a red-and-gold patterned Sevres coffeepot.

"Ten! Oh, good Lord. They'll have missed me for sure. What if the servants have already sent word to Aunt Jane? What if she is even now cutting short her stay in Bristol and returning to the city?"

"Coffee?" he said, strolling toward her bearing a cup filled with the dark, steaming beverage.

"No, no coffee." Ignoring any lingering malaise, she swung her legs over the side of the bed and scanned the room for her clothes. "I need to get home. I need to see who the servants have told, then figure out how I am going to explain."

"What you need to do is get back in bed and sip some of this. Once it stays down, you can try a few bites of toast and eggs." Without asking permission, he set the coffee onto the night table, then reached out to swing her legs back onto the mattress.

"But Jack, you know I can't stay —"

"Of course you can. Relax, my sweet. I have already taken care of the matter."

She froze. "What do you mean, 'taken care' of it?"

"I awakened earlier and penned a note to your aunt. I also sent a boy around to her house to inform her staff that you are quite unharmed and visiting a friend for the day."

"B-but Jack, I —"

"Spent the night. A few hours more will make little difference now." Resuming his seat on the side of the bed, he reached for the cup and saucer. "I thought coffee would do best this morning rather than tea. Careful you don't burn yourself."

With numb resignation, she accepted the offering. She even managed to take a sip without scalding her tongue. Feeling her stomach quiet, she sipped some more.

What had he told her aunt? she wondered. The truth, she suspected, as well as the fact that she was now his mistress. And considering the way she'd given herself to him last night, she couldn't blame him for drawing that conclusion. Drunk or not, there was no pretending she hadn't known what she was doing when she'd agreed to make love. She just hadn't thought all the consequences through, or the enormity of the changes she would be facing in her life from this point forward.

She drank more coffee, glad he'd left it black, since it was more bracing that way. "I'm rather new to this, so will you be sending for my belongings today?"

"A change of clothes, you mean? I had one of the maids freshen your gown. It's ironed and waiting for you over there on the wardrobe."

And so it was, she noticed, her gaze shifting to the large walnut armoire on the far side of the room, where the lilac-sprigged muslin dress hung neatly on its half-open door.

"As for a hairbrush and such," he continued, "I thought you could use mine."

Use his brush? Despite all the intimacies they'd shared in the past several hours, the notion of using his grooming implements seemed almost too personal somehow. Silly, considering she'd let him inside her body last night. What could be too intimate after that?

"Thank you, that is most kind," she said. "But what of later?"

He arched a brow. "Later?"

"Well, yes. I am simply wondering what you expect."

"In what regard?"

She stared at him for a long moment before lowering her gaze. *What is he about with this cat-and-mouse game? Should he not be the one informing me of his intentions, rather than the other way around?*

Resisting the urge to blush and wishing she wasn't quite so naked under the sheets, she forced herself to meet his gaze. "Now that we are . . . well, closer than before, I suppose I wish to know where I shall be residing? Here in Bath or in some other establishment?"

Would he be procuring a separate town house for her, she wondered, as many gentlemen did with their light o' loves?

"Are you planning to remove from Bath altogether?" she continued in a rush. "Or return to London perhaps and take a town house there?"

She hoped he didn't say he wished to live permanently in London. Papa lived in London, and he would not be at all pleased by her descent into the realm of the demimonde. Although she supposed Papa would not be pleased wherever she decided to live, given her new status as Jack Byron's *chere amie.*

He gave her an inquiring look. "At the expense of appearing dull-witted, what exactly is it you are saying?"

Her brows gathered in an impatient scowl. *Surely he doesn't expect me to spell it out?* But it would seem, she realized, that he did. "Since I'm your mistress now, where am I going to live? Is that plain enough for you?"

"My mistress!"

"Well, yes. After last night, I assumed . . . that is, I thought . . ." She broke off as she realized her error. "So I'm not to be your mistress?"

"No."

The cup and saucer shook inside her hand at the implications.

Jack relieved her of her half-finished coffee before she could spill it, then set the china aside.

"Did it never occur to you that I might want something else?" he asked.

Her brows scrunched together again. Beyond words, she shook her head.

"Well, I do," he stated. "I was planning to ask you later, since you aren't feeling your best at present, and this is hardly the most romantic of settings. But I suppose it will have to do."

She stared at him, puzzled.

"Then again," he said, pausing to run his gaze slowly over her, his eyes heating along the way, "maybe this *is* the perfect time and place. What could be better, after all, than having you alone and naked in my bed?"

Now she was the one who could be accused of being dim-witted. What was he saying? What did he mean? She was pondering the alternatives — and truly could conceive of none — when he took her hand in his own.

"Grace Lilah Danvers," he said in a solemn tone. "Will you marry me?"

Her mouth dropped open.

Quiet descended over the room.

"Well," he said with a self-deprecating smile, "this isn't quite the reaction I hoped for. Either you're so happy you've been stunned into silence, or else you're trying desperately to think of a good way to refuse."

"But you can't marry me," she blurted.

"Can I not? Why, pray tell?"

"For one thing, because your brother is a *duke!*"

"Quite true, although I believe you are

the only woman in England who would consider that a drawback."

"Be that as it may, you are an aristocrat and I am not. By that measure alone, I am entirely beneath you."

A sensuous smile turned up the edges of his mouth. "I must admit," he drawled, "that I did enjoy having you *beneath me* last night. Why don't you scoot down and we can try it again."

Ignoring him, she pressed on. "And, of course, there is your family. What will they think of you marrying a girl whose station in life is so decidedly below your own?"

One of his dark brows arched upward. "I had no idea, my dear, that you were such a snob."

She flushed. "I am not a *snob,* I am a *realist,* and I know all about such things."

"Do you?" he challenged softly. "And where did you learn such lessons? At school, with mean-spirited girls who thought themselves better than you simply by virtue of their birth?"

She swallowed, memories of those years rising in her head. "Yes. And the teachers and parents as well. I may have been sent to a ladies academy, but I was reminded each day that I was nothing of the sort."

"Then they were fools, the lot of them. I

assure you, in all the ways that count, you are every inch a lady. In intellect and speech, manner and style, there is no one superior to you."

"Jack —"

"And for the record, my family will adore you. Despite Ned being a proper toff, we Byrons aren't snobs."

"Ned?" she ventured.

"My brother Edward, the duke. He'll love you too as his newest sister."

She studied him, unable to believe he was saying all these things. Doing his utmost to convince her to be his bride.

"So?" he asked. "Any other objections?"

Other objections? No. But she did have one last question.

"Why?" she murmured, asking the most pressing question on her mind. "Why me?"

His expression turned serious, an enigmatic glint that she couldn't entirely read forming in his deep blue eyes. Reaching out, he cupped her cheek inside his palm and met her gaze.

"Because I've come to realize over these past few weeks that I can't do without you." He stroked a thumb over her lower lip in a way that made her quiver. "I want you too much, need you too desperately, not to have you for my own. Say yes, sweetheart. Say yes and tell me you will be my wife."

Leaning forward, he dusted a kiss over her lips, his touch light and sensuous. Her eyes closed, wonder and delight shimmering through her like faerie dust — dreams wrapping her in their silken hold.

"You love me, Grace." His mouth brushed against hers. "That's what you said last night. You meant it, did you not?"

Her eyes opened, locking on his. "Yes, I meant it," she said in a hushed tone. "Of course, I love you."

"Then don't let any of these so-called problems stand in our way. They're insignificant distractions and of no consequence at all. Say yes and let me make you happy. Be my bride and we can spend our lives together for now and always."

Grace trembled, knowing she'd never wanted anything so much in her life. A single word and Jack Byron could be hers. He would be her husband — hers to have and to hold for the rest of their days.

So why was she hesitating? Why was she questioning his sincerity when everything she desired most was right there within her grasp? All she had to do was reach out and take it.

So do it! Take it! whispered a little voice in her head. *Stop thinking so much and for once just let your heart rule your head!*

"Yes!" she exclaimed, a joyous smile breaking over her face. "Yes, I will marry you."

Flinging her arms around his shoulders, she kissed him, laughing against his lips as happiness welled up inside her like an overflowing dam. Laughing too, he kissed her harder, plundering her mouth with an intensity that soon made her forget everything but him.

The clocks in the house struck noon by the time they remembered breakfast. Too happy to mind cold eggs and toast, they feasted in bed, then once again on each other.

Chapter 12

"You have made me the happiest woman in England!" Aunt Jane declared the following morning, as she sat with Grace and Jack in the drawing room of her Bath town house. "It is just as I knew it would be. As soon as I laid eyes on our dear Lord Jack, I knew he was the one for you, Grace." She clasped her hands and beamed, her gaze going from one to the other and back again.

Grace smiled in return, wishing a bit ruefully that she might have been equally as certain about the outcome of Jack's courtship as her aunt. *Only think of all the anxiety I could have spared myself these past few weeks,* she mused. But as the great Bard so aptly said, "All's well that ends well." So any travail she may have suffered was well worth the temporary distress.

As for Aunt Jane's assertion that she was the happiest woman in England, Grace knew her aunt was mistaken. *No one could possibly be happier than I am,* she thought, having spent every minute since Jack's proposal yesterday feeling as though she were floating at least a foot off the ground.

When she'd awakened in her own bed this morning, she'd wondered for a few long moments if she'd imagined the whole thing.

Was it only a dream?

Then she'd caught sight of the sparkling square-cut diamond ring on the third finger of her left hand and knew the engagement was as real as the exquisite gemstone itself.

Catching sight of the ring now, her lips curved into a secret little smile. Apparently not secret enough, though, Jack angling his head to meet her gaze with a knowing look of his own.

"The instant I read Lord Jack's note telling me he planned to ask for your hand in marriage, I couldn't stay put a moment longer. I had to come home as quickly as may be to share in your good news," her aunt continued. "Edna is ecstatic and waved me on my way, despite my having to cut short our visit. She says she cannot wait to hear all the exciting details, and mayhap have the opportunity to make Lord Jack's acquaintance one of these times."

"I shall look forward to the occasion," he said. "But please, Mrs. Grant, you must call me Jack now that we are to be relations."

Her smile grew even wider, if that were possible. "Oh, you are such a dear — is he not a dear, Grace?"

Grace met his gaze again. "Indeed he is."

"Jack it is, then, if you insist," the older woman giggled. "And you are not to stand on ceremony a moment longer; you must call me Aunt Jane. Or simply Jane, if you prefer. I will accept nothing less."

Jack smiled. "As you wish, Aunt Jane."

She let out a merry laugh and drank a sip of tea.

"Now, about wedding preparations," Aunt Jane went on. "We must consider your trousseau."

Grace paused, realizing she hadn't even thought of such a thing, having been far too wrapped up in Jack and the newness of their intimate relationship to consider practicalities. There was another far more pressing matter awaiting her as well — the necessity of informing her father that she was to be wed.

"Yes," Grace agreed. "But first Jack and I must go to London and see Papa, and meet Jack's family as well. We have decided it would be best to ask both their blessings in person rather than attempting to share the news by letter. Seeing that time is of the essence, we thought it wise to depart in the morning."

Her aunt nodded. "Well, of course, you are right. Certainly you must go without delay. I would accompany you, but as much as I love your father, you know how he and I get when we're living in the same house — worse than a pair of wet cats in a bag. And I positively refuse to stay in a hotel. Pray send my love to him and write as often as you are able."

Grace rose and gave her aunt an exuberant hug, knowing she would miss the older woman. "On that you may rest assured, dearest Aunt Jane. I shall write every day and leave nothing untold."

The journey to London took less than a day, the two of them departing early the next morning as planned. Seated beside Jack in his coach, Grace looked happy, pretty and increasingly nervous the closer they got to the city. She chattered on about a variety of topics for the first forty miles, then fell nearly silent for the rest.

Although he managed to conceal his own reaction with a veneer of relaxed anticipation, Jack couldn't help but experience a measure of anxiety over his upcoming "introduction" to Ezra Danvers. Each time he thought about what was to come, his stomach muscles drew tight. Oh, he was sure he could pull off the required act and play the part of prospective bridegroom meeting his father-in-law for the first time, but he felt every inch the fraud.

Damnation, I am such a bounder, he thought.

The slip knot in his gut turned greasy with guilt. To assuage the feeling, he sent Grace a warm smile, then reached out to tuck a stray wisp of her hair back in place. "Have I told you how lovely you look today?"

Her eyes shone a deep blue. "You have, but you may tell me again. Although I can't say I agree, not with the new pair of freckles I discovered on my nose this morning. But you have told me I am not allowed to argue with you on the subject of my appearance, so I shall not."

"Very wise. And I like your new freckles. They're absolutely adorable, just like you." Leaning forward, he took her lips in a sweet kiss that lingered far longer, and became far more intense, than he intended.

With a reluctant sigh, he forced himself away, wishing he could pull her onto his lap instead. If they weren't in his coach on the way to see her father, he would have done exactly that. But now was not the time to start something amorous, since they were due to arrive in the city in a short while.

Leaning back into the corner, he crossed his arms. "I sent a note to my mother and Edward at Braebourne asking if they could travel to Town for a few days," he said. "I didn't mention why, just said I had some happy news I wanted to share in person."

"I did the same last night with Papa. He knows I'm coming home, but not the particulars."

Danvers was smart; Jack was sure the crafty old man knew precisely why. However, if Grace hadn't mentioned him in her letter to her father, perhaps the suspense was killing Danvers even now and he was wondering if Jack had been successful in his courtship. Jack just hoped Danvers didn't turn too conspicuously smug at his victory once he learned for sure that Jack was the reason for her return home.

Grace deserved better. At the very least, she ought to be spared the knowledge that she was being used as her father's unsuspecting pawn. And his own as well. *I will do my damnedest to make sure she never learns the truth,* he pledged, *for both our sakes.*

Not long after, the city rose around them, streets teeming with noise and life as people went about their daily business. Before long, they arrived in St. Martin's Lane, Jack jumping down to assist Grace from the coach.

"Ready?" he asked, offering his arm.

She glanced first at the town house, then at him, smiling as she met his gaze. "Never more."

The front door was opened by a servant, and in they walked.

The house feels different, Grace mused, as she took off her gloves and hat and exchanged greetings with the butler. *Or maybe I'm the one who's different?* Not surprising, she supposed, considering how much her life had changed in the few short weeks since she'd been away.

Casting another sideways glance at Jack, she wondered at his unusually solemn mien. But then there was no more time for further speculation, as he took her arm and quietly suggested she lead the way to her father.

At this time of day, she knew she would find Papa in his study, likely bent over his ledgers and reports. She stopped just outside the closed door and turned to Jack. "Perhaps I should go in first."

One mahogany brow arched upward. "You aren't expecting him to object, are you?"

"No," she said, though she honestly didn't

know what to expect, given Papa's sometimes irascible humor. He might be delighted. Then again, he might not.

"Good. Then we'll go in together," he stated in a determined, almost protective tone. "You're mine now, with or without your father's blessing."

Her pulse fluttered, a warm glow spreading through her that made her want to bury herself in his arms. Instead, she drew a breath, then rapped her knuckles in a quick one-two on the door.

"Come," called her father in his usual gruff rumble.

"Papa, it's me. I'm home," she announced, as she walked inside.

Ezra Danvers looked up from where he sat at his heavy oak desk, piled high with ledgers and correspondence. His grey brows furrowed over the rims of his wire-framed reading glasses. "Gracie? Is that ye, girl?" Tossing aside his quill pen, he sprang to his feet and hurried around. Catching her close, he gave her an exuberant hug and a kiss on both cheeks. "If you'd told me what time to expect you, I'd have been waiting at the front door."

She laughed and hugged him in return. Stepping back, she found herself next to Jack, who cupped a steadying hand around her elbow. As he did, her father shifted his gaze toward him. "And who might this be, Gracie? I didn't know we had company."

The two men exchanged looks, their expressions curiously enigmatic in a way she couldn't quite define. Perhaps they were taking each other's measure, as men were sometimes wont to do. Likely Jack was considering his first impression of his future father-in-law, while her father was speculating about the identity of this stranger she'd invited into his home. But Jack wouldn't be a stranger for long. Soon he would be family.

"Papa, allow me to introduce Lord John Byron to you. Jack and I met in Bath and have spent the past few weeks becoming acquainted. We are . . . that is . . . we are here today with happy news we wish to share."

Her father glowered. "What sort of *happy* news? Just who are you, sir, to have so obviously ingratiated yourself with my daughter?"

"Papa!"

He ignored her, his gazed fixed on Jack. "Well, what have you to say for yourself, young man?"

Jack's mouth curled with sardonic amusement. "Good day, I suppose, for a start.

That and to express my wish that you relieve Grace's mind by granting your consent for our nuptials. You see, your daughter has recently done me the honor of agreeing to be my wife, and I am most determined to have her."

"Are you now?" Her father crossed his arms over his chest. "And what makes you think I would entrust my only child to your care?"

Jack sent him a piercing look. "Because I'm amply equipped to provide for her comfort and safety. But even more, I'll do my utmost to make her happy. What else can you require?"

Her father stared for a long moment before turning again to her. "And what have you to say about this? You've told me plenty of times in the past that you weren't interested in trading your independence for a fancy title. Has the word *lord* before his name given you a new set of ideals?"

She flushed. "No, not at all. His title matters not — well, not to me — although given your opinions, I should think you'd be pleased to know that a duke's son wishes to take me to wife."

"A duke's son, eh? But not a duke's heir, is he?"

"No, and thank heavens. I have no desire

to live such an elevated existence. Being a lord's wife will be difficult enough."

"Nothing could ever be too far above you." Something intense gleamed in his gaze. "Is he truly what you want?"

Her chest squeezed, her eyes lifting to meet Jack's vivid azure gaze. "Yes. With all my heart," she declared, reaching out for his hand. "I love him, and nothing would make me happier than to spend my life at his side." She looked again at her father. "And although I would much prefer receiving your blessing, I will have him regardless of your approval. So what say you, Papa? Will you wish us well or not?"

He stared for another long moment before his glower vanished, a hearty smile taking its place. "Of course, I'll wish you well! Come, come, give me a hug, both of you. That's what children and parents are meant to do."

Laughing, Grace hurried into his arms for another long, strong embrace. He and Jack ended up shaking hands, which was a good enough beginning, she supposed.

The three of them talked for several minutes, Grace recounting the highlights of her trip to Bath — or at least the ones that didn't make reference to any of her and Jack's intimate interludes. She also passed along well-wishes and news from Aunt Jane.

After a while, her father stood and gently ushered her to the door. "Now, why don't you go on upstairs to your room? You must be fatigued from your journey."

"Not terribly, though I could do with a repast. Why don't I ring for tea for all of us?"

"Tea would be wonderful. Later. First, however, I should like a private word with Byron here."

She frowned. "A private word about what?"

Her father laughed. "Always the inquiring mouse, aren't you? We're just going to discuss the basics of your settlement, that's all. Not to worry, I'll have him back to you in a trice."

"Yes, but —"

"Surely you don't wish to listen in on such tedious matters?"

Actually, settlement negotiations did sound boring in the extreme. Nevertheless, for reasons she couldn't quite fathom, she didn't feel entirely comfortable leaving the two men alone. Knowing she was being ridiculous, though, she shrugged the sensation away. Considering her and Jack's upcoming marriage, she was sure the two men would have many private discussions, maybe even ones of a father-son nature. She certainly hoped as much.

"Very well, Papa. An hour then? Will that do?"

"An hour sounds perfect."

She cast a last look toward Jack, who gave her a reassuring smile, then she turned and left the room.

"Was all of that really necessary?" Jack demanded as soon as Grace was upstairs and safely out of earshot.

Danvers crossed to a small cabinet in one corner. "Of course it was necessary. I had to put on a bit of a show or else she would never have believed our 'introduction.' Whiskey?"

"No."

"Ah, now, don't be ungracious." Taking down two glasses, he unstoppered a bottle and poured them both a draught. "You deserve to celebrate. When I devised my plan, I knew you were the perfect man to win over my girl, and now I see just how right I was."

Danvers held out one of the glasses, leaving Jack little choice but to accept, else he would appear as ungracious as he'd been accused of being. He didn't raise the libation to his lips, however.

"Besides," Danvers continued in a conversational tone, "I needed to see how Gracie really feels about you. I must say that you've exceeded even my own high expectations. Masterfully done, Byron." Raising his glass, he drank a swallow.

Jack ground his teeth. "She's not a marionette to be manipulated at will, you know."

Danvers shot him a hard look. "No, she's my daughter, for whom I want only the best. She just required a push in the right direction to find what she's really needed all along. A husband, and the babies you're going to give her. Children I suspect you're already well on your way to providing."

Jack held his tongue, deciding not to satisfy the old man's curiosity about whether he'd taken Grace to his bed yet — even if both of them knew the answer.

"I'm pleased she loves you," Danvers said. "I can tell you make her happy. See to it you keep her that way." The older man swallowed a mouthful of whiskey, then set down his glass. "Now, about the money."

Bloody hell, the money, Jack thought. *I'd almost forgotten that particular detail. Almost.*

"Sixty thousand pounds will be deposited into the account of your choice as soon as notice of your engagement appears in all the appropriate papers," Danvers stated.

"The other sixty thousand will be yours the day of the wedding, along with the erasure of your gaming debt to me, of course. I assume that will be satisfactory, my lord?"

Jack's fingers tightened around the glass in his hand. How he wished he could toss the offer back in Danvers's face. Tell him he didn't need, or want, his damned money. But both of them would know his words to be nothing but an empty lie. Jack might wish to rely on pride, but like it or not, he did need that money — to say nothing of the necessity of being freed of the hundred thousand pounds he owed Danvers.

His future father-in-law certainly knew how to keep him under his thumb until the marriage vows were taken. Obviously Danvers was worried Jack might bolt unless he maintained a certain amount of leverage against him. But in spite of the undeniable lure of keeping his bachelor's freedom, Jack knew it was already too late. He couldn't run, not without hurting Grace. And that he would not do. He'd taken her innocence, and she was his responsibility now. He wouldn't abandon her, nor did he wish to do so, even if he could.

Glancing down, he stared at the whiskey glass in his hand. *Maybe I could do with a drink, after all?* He tossed the draught down in a single gulp, grateful for the resulting sting in his throat and the burn in his belly.

"Yes," he said, his words sounding faintly numb even to his own ears. "That will be more than satisfactory."

Chapter 13

The following afternoon, Grace tucked a hand against her hip to keep it from trembling as she sat next to Jack on the sofa in the Clybourne House drawing room. His voice was low and smooth as he spoke to his mother, the Dowager Duchess of Clybourne, his sister Lady Mallory, and his eldest brother Edward, the Duke of Clybourne.

Try as she might not to be intimidated, she was finding the task far from easy. While it was true she'd attended school with the daughters of several aristocrats, none of them had possessed anything close to the ancient lineage and innate nobility of the Byrons. The members of Jack's family were quite simply some of the most elegant, naturally refined people she'd ever met. How on earth would she ever be able to fit in with them?

Surely they'll revile me for my inferior birth

and wonder at Jack for bringing me into their midst? Worse, what would they think when he told them the news of their engagement? Suddenly she realized that while she'd been woolgathering, he'd been busy doing exactly that.

"Married!" Ava Byron declared, the dowager's still beautiful features alighting with clear pleasure. "I knew when we had your letter that something momentous was afoot, and I see I was right. But still, I never expected an engagement. Only think, I will have gained two new daughters in the same year."

"Not to mention another sister for me," Mallory chimed with a happy smile. "Just wait until you meet Meg. And everyone else, of course."

Everyone else? Just how many Byrons are there? She knew Jack had another sister, but were there more siblings than the ones presently in the room? "I shall look forward to making their acquaintance," she murmured, deciding she'd wait and ask Jack for further explanation when they were alone.

As for the duke, he wore a frown, his gaze fixed on his brother with a look of speculative appraisal, as though he couldn't quite believe what he'd just heard. But moments later, he turned to her and his expression cleared, replaced by one of warmth and kindness.

"Allow me to welcome you to the family, Miss Danvers," he said in rich, rounded tones that instantly caused her to relax. "I always knew it would take an exceptional woman to bring Jack to heel, and I see I was not mistaken. He's made a wise choice in you. But are you sure you're prepared to put up with him? I fear you might yet decide you've made a bad bargain taking on such an unrepentant rogue."

Her eyes widened at what she took to be his teasing candor, a half-nervous laugh escaping her throat. "Oh, he's not a rogue. Or at least not too much of one." She sent Jack a sideways look and caught a dangerous gleam in his eyes. "And I'm quite prepared for whatever may come, since I love him and cannot wait to be his wife. Most couples don't start out with even that much, so what further assurances could I possibly require?"

"What indeed," the dowager said. "Now quit baiting your little brother, Edward, and wish him well."

The duke's teeth flashed a wicked grin that reminded Grace forcefully of Jack. "Congratulations on your forthcoming nuptials," he said. "I hope you know what a lucky man you are."

Jack's face sobered. "I do, Ned. More and more each day." His gaze shifted to hers and lingered.

For a moment, she lost herself in the compelling depths of his azure eyes, swaying ever so slightly toward him as he took her hand and enfolded it in his own. Her pulse quickened as the seconds stretched onward, her surroundings dimming as she sank deeper beneath his spell. In silent anticipation, her lips parted, ready and waiting for his kiss.

Suddenly his mother cleared her throat.

Grace jumped, heat flowering in her cheeks like a field of scarlet poppies. She fought the urge to cover her face with her hands, knowing it would only draw further attention to her lapse. Surreptitiously, she tried to free her palm from Jack's clasp, but brazen, irreverent devil that he was, he wouldn't let her go. Tightening his hold instead, he leaned back against the comfortably upholstered sofa cushions, as though nothing whatsoever had occurred.

The dowager — bless her heart — took up the tea urn and refreshed the contents of everyone's cup with an easy charm. "So," his mother inquired with faultless timing, as she set the delicate china pot aside. "Have you decided on a wedding date?"

With their engagement only a few days old, Grace realized she hadn't even considered the question. "We received my father's blessing just yesterday, so I'm afraid there hasn't been time yet to settle on the details."

Ava Byron nodded with understanding. "Jack mentioned that you have lately been residing in Bath with your aunt. Will she be helping you with the preparations?"

Grace's brows furrowed. "I'm not certain. She'll be happy to aid me in selecting a few new gowns, I'm sure, but otherwise I imagine most of the tasks will fall to me."

"To you! But no, you cannot be expected to shoulder such a weighty obligation all on your own. I realize your mother passed on some years ago when you were no more than a child, but surely there is another female relation who can aid you? A sister or cousin, mayhap?"

"No, ma'am, there is just my father and myself. I am quite self-reliant, however, so I'm sure I shall find my way in this as well."

Creases gathered on the dowager's forehead. "But you shouldn't *have* to find your way. After all, you are the bride, and this should be your special time. I hope you will not take it amiss, but if I might, I would like to offer you my assistance."

"Your assistance?" Grace repeated, her lips parting in surprise.

"Yes, if you would like."

For a long moment Grace made no reply, taken completely off guard by the notion that Jack's mother was not only warmly welcoming her into the family but was offering to help her with the wedding arrangements as well. A lump swelled in her throat.

"Well, child?" the dowager prompted gently.

"Y-yes. Oh, yes, Your Grace, I should like that above anything." A fulsome smile spread across her face. "Thank you. That would be wonderful. You are so kind."

Ava Byron beamed with pleasure. "Not at all. I adore planning weddings. And Mallory can help."

Lady Mallory nodded in eager agreement. "Of course I shall. I love nothing so much as a good shopping expedition, and we shall have many."

"To that fact, I can safely attest," the duke remarked in a wry tone. "What was it this month that caused you to exceed your allowance? The ermine arm shawl you bought, or the engraved gold and pearl etui you had sent over from Rundell and Bridge?"

Mallory sent her brother a narrow-eyed glare. "Neither. It was the extra pairs of dancing slippers I ordered. Of which I was in dire need, I'll have you know, since I've quite worn through my others."

Edward gave an amused snort. "All dozen of them, hmm? Unless I'm misremembering the details of the shoemaker's latest bill, of course."

Mallory glared again and stuck out her tongue, clearly uncowed by her older sibling. "And I shall need that arm shawl this winter," she defended. "The almanac says it's going to be frightfully cold."

Edward shook his head, while Jack let out a quiet guffaw.

"If we're done with shawls and slippers, perhaps we might return to the topic at hand?" the dowager stated in a soft, yet firm, voice. "Now about the wedding, summer is always a lovely time of year for a ceremony. Or next fall, with its cooler temperatures and all of the leaves turning color."

"Next summer or fall?" Jack set down his empty teacup. "But that's months away. Grace and I aren't waiting that long."

His mother's frown returned. "A year for an engagement is an excellent length of time, what with the trousseau to be designed and the church to be arranged. Not to mention deciding on the guest list and where everyone shall lodge and dine."

"You ladies have my leave to make whatever plans you like, but I'm not waiting a year. Three months, that's my limit."

"Three months!" The dowager looked aghast. "Oh, not you too. I've barely recovered from Cade and Meg's whirlwind wedding."

"But only think what an expert you now are on the intricacies of hasty nuptials," Jack said with warm persuasion. "And compared with Cade, you have plenty of time. As I recall, he only gave you six weeks."

"Six frantic, exhausting weeks."

"And yet you pulled off a spectacular ceremony and a reception that won you nothing but praise. Just imagine what you'll be able to achieve with twice that amount of time."

His mother's lips tightened. "I ought to box your ears for such impertinence and imposition, John Richard Byron."

Jack gave her a perfect, angelic smile. "But you won't, will you, Mama? Not for your favorite son."

She gave a snort that would have been indelicate had she been anything less than a duchess. "I love all my sons with equal affection, as you well know. But were I to have a favorite, it would most certainly not be *you* at the moment, given your unreasonable impatience and willful stubbornness."

Rather than being chastened, Jack's smile only widened.

"However," she conceded, with a regal dip of her head, "I shall put aside my irritation for your fiancée's sake." Her gaze shifted, alighting on Grace. "What would you like to do, dear? You are the bride, after all."

Grace fought hard not to squirm as every eye in the room turned her way.

Yes, she mused, *what would I like to do?* Then she looked at Jack and didn't need to consider a moment more.

"I'm sorry, Your Grace, but I'd rather not wait long either. Maybe we could have a simple ceremony. Something that wouldn't require a great deal of work."

"If I procured a special license, we could be married here in the drawing room one evening," Jack remarked.

Grace sent him a chastening sideways glance. "Yes, well, perhaps not quite *that* simple. I would prefer a church, or even a chapel."

"A chapel? We have a lovely one at Braebourne." The dowager paused and tapped a finger against her chin. "Oh, that gives me a wonderful idea. What would you say to being married at Braebourne?"

At Braebourne? Be married at one of the most beautiful, illustrious estates in the whole of England? She would never have even considered such a notion. But oh, how idyllic, how romantic!

"Unless you would rather remain here in the city," Ava continued. "We could inquire about St. George's, though it's doubtful we'll find an available date given our time limitations." She paused to send Jack a reproving look. "We were only able to secure the church on such short notice for Cade and Meg because it was in the hottest part of August and most of the Ton had already departed for their estates."

"No, no," Grace hastened to assure. "Braebourne would be lovely. If you are quite sure you and the duke wouldn't mind, that is."

"Mind? Of course we do not mind. Edward would be delighted to act the host, would you not, dear?"

He smiled with affable agreement. "Certainly. What's several dozen more people come to stay when the family hordes are preparing to descend for the holidays anyway."

The dowager clasped her hands together and let out a little chortle. "Oh, but that's exactly the answer! The holidays. Yes, yes, it's perfect."

"What's perfect?" Jack stated in an echo of Grace's thoughts.

"Why, the timing for the wedding. Everyone will be at Braebourne, so half the guest list is done before we start. Grace can invite her father and aunt, of course, and anyone else she would like. The food and lodging arrangements will be no difficulty whatsoever with the staff already in full fettle. And I'm sure the bishop won't turn down an invitation to spend Christmas with us. So what say you both to a holiday wedding? We could even hold the ceremony during the New Year just before Twelfth Night."

A New Year's wedding to usher in the start of my new life with Jack. Grace liked the sound of that. A smile spread over her mouth, excitement burgeoning inside her. "I believe it's a most excellent plan, Your Grace." Angling her gaze, she fixed her eyes on Jack. "What do you think?"

"That I am hopelessly outnumbered." Raising her hand to his lips, he pressed a kiss to her knuckles. "But if it makes you happy, then New Year's at Braebourne it shall be."

CHAPTER 14

With the date and location of the wedding decided, Grace found herself thrust into an immediate flurry of preparations.

Beginning the very next day, the dowager duchess and Mallory whisked her away for the first of a multitude of shopping expeditions. They took her to the most fashionable stores in London, arranging for everything from engraved, hot-pressed stationery to exotic foodstuffs and a set of special crystal wine goblets that would be used exclusively for the wedding toast.

Then there were the clothes, whose vast excess seemed to know no limits. From hats, shoes and gloves to pelisses, petticoats and gowns, she ordered so many new garments that she didn't see how she could possibly ever wear them all. But Jack's mother and sister assured her that she would need each and every one in the months to come, including the dozen silk nightgowns that were so sheer they made her blush.

She ordered such a large wardrobe, in fact, that she feared incurring a sharp scold from her father for her overindulgence. But he said not a word, apparently happy to pay the continual stream of bills that arrived in the post and by messenger each morning.

When she wasn't shopping, she stayed busy with invitations to Clybourne House and visits to and from friends. She even had a pair of her old schoolmates drop by — surprising, since neither lady had been particularly friendly toward her during those long-ago years, much less since then.

Peppering their conversation with frequent smiles and fawning flattery, they made several poorly disguised attempts at soliciting an invitation to the wedding. Yet with a skill that surprised even her, she managed to elude their ploys, seeing the visit through to its polite conclusion before escorting them to the door — all without granting them their much hoped-for prize.

The visit was noteworthy enough that she decided to share the highlights with Aunt Jane. Despite her promise to write often, she'd been a lamentably poor correspondent, so busy she'd only managed to pen a single letter during the past month.

Determined now to resolve her lapse, she sat down at her writing desk in the drawing room, selected a piece of paper, took up her quill pen and opened the silver filigreed jar of black ink to begin.

Half an hour later, she was adding a few last lines to the missive when she heard the deep rumble of Jack's voice in the front hall. Her father's servants didn't hold to the custom of announcing visitors, so she wasn't surprised when Jack strode into the room alone. Supremely handsome in a close-fitting jacket and pantaloons made of tan superfine wool, he brought an instant energy with him, together with a lingering touch of the brisk, late October air outside.

"Get your things," he told her without preamble. "You and I are going house hunting."

She laid down her pen. "We are? Your mother didn't say anything about it."

"That's because she doesn't know."

"Really? What of Mallory. Will she be joining us?"

He shook his head. "As much as I adore my family and enjoy their company, I thought we could tackle this particular project on our own. After all, this will be our new home, so it only makes sense that we should be the ones doing the choosing."

She mulled over his statement, a smile coming to her lips. "So, we're going alone, then?"

Jack sent her a wink. "Exactly. Except for the estate agent, it will be just us two."

Her pulse leapt at the notion. Since arriving in London, she and Jack were hardly ever alone, and then only for the occasional carriage ride or stroll through the park. She supposed they wouldn't be completely alone today either — not with the estate agent there to escort them in and out of prospective town houses. But still, it would be the closest thing to privacy she and Jack were likely to enjoy before their wedding in January.

"Just let me tell Papa I'm going out and we'll be on our way." Taking a moment to blot the undried ink on her letter, she tucked it into her desk drawer, then leapt to her feet and hurried from the room.

Five minutes later, she returned clad in a soft, pearl grey kerseymere pelisse that complemented the pale blue of her gown. "I'm ready," she declared in happy tones.

Taking Jack's arm, she let him lead her outside to his carriage.

They were met at the first house by the estate agent, a short, barrel-chested man with an obvious taste for flamboyant waistcoats. The one he wore today was a rich, purplish puce with silver buttons fashioned in the shape of owls. Yet in spite of his dramatic appearance, he soon proved himself knowledgeable and attentive, with a manner that was neither too insistent nor too obsequious.

He showed them three town houses before they found one they liked — a lovely residence on a quiet section of Upper Brook Street not far from Grosvenor Square. Jack pronounced it near enough to Clybourne House for convenience without being so close as to invite a constant round of impromptu, unannounced morning calls.

After touring the spacious rooms, with their high ceilings, wide windows, crown molding and cheerfully painted walls, Grace knew it was the one. Both beautiful and elegant, there was a delicacy to the place far beyond anything she'd ever known — excepting Clybourne House itself, of course. Still, she hesitated, wondering if it might be a touch too grand.

In spite of her father's immense wealth, they'd never lived in high style, as many of the newly rich were eager to do. Rather than build an ostentatious mansion designed to display his success, Ezra Danvers had been content to live in the same modest house he'd bought for her and her mother when Grace was only a toddler. The house was tidy and comfortable, located in a pleasant, if not terribly fashionable, part of London.

Like her father, she'd never minded, happy to live where she'd always lived without any real wish for more. Yet here she now stood, contemplating a property the likes of which she'd only ever read about in the Society column of the *Morning Post.*

Of course I'm engaged to a man the likes of whom I'd only ever read about in the Society columns as well, so why am I worrying over a mere house?

"Well?" Jack asked in a quiet tone. "Do you like it?"

She strove to keep her features calm, even as qualms rose inside her again. "How can I not? It's absolutely lovely." *And truly, it is,* she mused. "Still, do you think it might be a bit too large?" she ventured. "Maybe something of a more moderate size would suit us better for now?"

Jack studied the dimensions of the morning room with obvious consideration. "Really? The house seems a most agreeable size to me. Plenty of space to relax and not feel crowded when we have visitors."

Visitors? *Does he mean guests?* she

thought in sudden dismay. *As in party guests?*

She hadn't considered it before, but she supposed it was only natural that he'd expect her to entertain once they were wed. She was used to arranging dinners for her father's business partners, so small gatherings presented no difficulty. But hosting large Society fêtes for the Ton — well, she had about as much experience with that as she did shooting lead balls out of a cannon, and nearly as much trepidation too. Hopefully, the dowager duchess and Lady Mallory would help her when the time arrived; otherwise, she feared the potential results.

Deciding to shelve that particular worry for later, she returned her attention to the topic at hand. "It would hold a great many people, I suppose."

"More than that, it will give us room to grow. Once we start our family and the nursery's bursting at the seams with babies, I imagine you'll be glad of the extra room."

She lost her breath at the idea. "Bursting at the seams! Just how many children are you expecting us to have?"

His blue eyes twinkled. "As many as we can manage, and as soon as may be," he said, lowering his voice so she was the only one able to hear. "I look forward to keeping you very busy making them."

"Jack!" she hushed. "In case you've forgotten, we aren't alone."

And she was right. The estate agent was still in the room, loitering on the far side with his hands tucked in his pockets as he stared out a window, pretending not to eavesdrop.

"So, other than the house being too big, have you any objection to it?" Jack asked quietly.

"No. It's one of the prettiest places I've ever seen." And truly it was. In spite of her reservations, she loved the house and knew she would be happy living in it.

Something about the tenor of her thoughts must have shown, since moments later Jack turned toward the other man. "We'll take it," he declared.

A big smile appeared on the estate agent's face. "Excellent, my lord. This is as fine a town house as I've ever seen. I knew from the start that it would please you and your bride-to-be."

Jack nodded, a sudden impatience radiating from him. "Why don't you go downstairs and draw up the necessary papers. Miss Danvers and I wish to look around a little bit more. We'll find you when we're ready."

The agent raised a pair of brows at the

request, but he was clearly too excited at the prospect of a sale to offer any sort of protest. "Of course, my lord. Take all the time you need." With a bow, the little man hurried away.

As soon as he'd gone, Jack strode across the room and pulled the door closed. Turning back, he crossed to her and pulled her into his arms.

She gave a surprised laugh.

"Now, what was I saying?" he mused aloud. "Something about babies and the delightful ways they're made."

Her heart beat so hard that she felt it in her shoes. "Jack! I thought you said you wanted to look around some more."

He shook his head. "All I want to look at is you. Now, give me a kiss."

"Here?" she gasped.

"Yes, here. In case you hadn't realized, it's been thirty-three days, twelve hours and forty-one minutes since I last had you in my bed."

"You know how many hours it's been?" she said, awed by the knowledge that he'd been keeping count.

"Close enough to make a fair guess," he admitted. "Now, let's stop talking. We're wasting precious time." Capturing her mouth, he gave her a kiss that sent hot rivulets of need surging through her veins.

Fighting her own desire, she soon broke away. "W-we can't. Not with the estate agent waiting downstairs. What if he comes to check on us?"

"He won't." His lips moved in a silky glide over her neck. "But should he be so foolish, he'll no doubt get an eyeful."

Her own eyes widened, enough to draw a laugh from him.

"Don't worry. I'm only teasing," he said. "He won't see a thing. Not with the door locked."

He'd locked the door? She didn't remember seeing a key. But if Jack said he'd locked it, then he must have done exactly that.

Relaxing, she leaned farther into the circle of his arms. "Well, maybe we could stay in here for a couple of minutes. If he asks, we'll tell him we were measuring for drapes."

Jack's eyes were the ones to widen this time. He barked out a laugh before sliding his hands down to cup her bottom. "Come closer, minx, and let me measure *you.*"

Then his lips were on hers again, stealing her breath and making her mind grow hazy with a rush of staggering delight.

Jack kissed her long and deep, with a driving need that radiated all the way to his bones. Pausing, he took an extra moment to breathe in the honeyed fragrance of her skin, to taste the sweet flavor of her tongue as it slid like hot, damp silk against his own.

He shuddered from the pleasure, relishing the sensations as though they were manna from heaven. After more than a month of sexual deprivation, his need was sharp — his recitation of precisely how many days had passed since their last coupling, and of his intense desire for her, no exaggeration.

Another man would likely have taken his ease elsewhere by now; there were certainly plenty of willing women to be had here in the city. But the act would have felt wrong, serving as yet another betrayal of Grace's trust. Even more significant was his personal reluctance to avail himself of another woman. He didn't want anyone else. He wanted Grace.

Unfortunately, with her residing in her father's house, and with members of his own family in almost constant attendance, there weren't many opportunities to be alone. Actually, until today, there'd been absolutely none, since the only time they'd been together unchaperoned was for carriage rides and walks in the park.

But she was in his arms now and he meant to make the most of it. He knew he couldn't take matters to their ultimate conclusion, but he could certainly indulge himself. Indulge her, as well.

Sliding his hands more fully over the supple curves of her delicious derriere, he fit her closer, settling his erection against the V of her thighs as he claimed her mouth for an even deeper kiss. Her hands came up to clutch his shoulders, her breasts pressing in soft mounds against his chest.

Lifting his hand, he cupped one, savoring the shape and fullness of her feminine form. Even through the barrier of her shift and stays, he felt her body's response, her nipple drawing into a hard bud that begged to be lavished with attention and praise.

He obliged as much as he could, given his limitations, strumming her flesh with firm strokes of his fingers. Little whimpers hummed in her throat, sounds he'd come to crave the way he did food or water. And yet there was something he wanted even more. Something he knew he had no right to covet or demand. Still, even as he tried to shunt aside the desire, it came upon him again.

Leaving her mouth, he traced a path across her cheek to her ear, catching the lobe between his teeth for a half-playful, half-savage nip. "Tell me, Grace," he demanded, his voice husky and a bit raw.

"Tell you what?" she repeated, dreamy and low.

"Tell me how you feel. Do you love me?"

"Yes. You know I do," she said without hesitation.

His lips glided over hers, making quick, plucking forays. "Then say it. Tell me what I want to hear."

She met his gaze, eyelids heavy with passion, her mouth swollen and red from his kisses. "I love you," she whispered.

He drank in the words, needing them for reasons he couldn't fathom, yet requiring the warmth they left behind. "Again. Tell me again."

"I love you." Her arms wound around his neck. "I've never loved a man the way I love you, and I never will. Kiss me, Jack. There's nothing better in the world."

And he did, taking her mouth in a fervid joining that left them both shaking. Hunger roared inside him like a beast, tearing apart the restraints he'd placed upon himself.

Without really even knowing what he was doing, he danced her backward toward the wall. When they reached it, he pressed her gently against the smooth painted plaster, her hair a fiery slash of color against the pale cream surface. She looked beautiful, her skin flushed, her eyes a pure, vibrant blue.

Reaching out, he began gathering the material of her skirt into his hands.

"Jack?"

"Shh," he hushed, kissing her again with deep, drugging need.

She made another throaty hum — a sound that shot straight to his groin this time. Yielding to the persuasion of his kiss, she leaned her head against the wall, pliant as his hands curved around the bare skin of her thighs just above her ribboned garters. He touched her there for a few long moments before gliding higher.

Up he went, bunching the silk of her gown so that it collected around her waist and over his forearms. Coaxing open her thighs, he slid a pair of fingers inside her, the action drawing a convulsive shiver from her more than willing body. Moisture gathered against his hand, easing his way as he pleasured her further, her moans muffled against his open mouth.

Curving his other hand around her naked buttocks, he lifted her a couple inches higher so that she was balanced on the very tips of her toes. Clinging, she wrapped her arms tighter around his shoulders and held on as he worked his fingers in and out of her hot, moist folds.

He knew when she was on the edge, knew by the subtle tightening of her inner muscles against his hand that she was nearing her peak. Wanting her throbbing and desperate for his possession, he stopped just short of letting her claim her bliss.

Her eyes popped open at his withdrawal, her fingernails curling like talons into the material of his coat. "W-why are you stopping?"

"I'm not," he assured her as he yanked open the buttons on his falls. "Just finding another method of satisfying you."

"B-but surely you don't mean to . . . to . . ."

"Take you here against the wall, even though the estate agent is waiting for us downstairs? I most certainly do."

She stiffened at the reminder that they weren't alone in the house. But he didn't give her time for further consideration, as he spread her thighs wide and stepped between, lifting her as he did so that her toes were no longer touching the floor.

"Wrap your legs around my waist," he ordered.

She complied, trembling against him in a clear combination of astonishment over their unusual position and her own raging need. He met her gaze, liking the fact that their faces were on the same level. Because of her height, he'd only had to raise her a few inches to find the proper angle. A perfect fit. Using their complementary heights to his advantage, he positioned himself again and thrust inside.

A moan puffed from her lips at his powerful penetration, her flesh clasping around his own like a hot, velvety glove. Since she was no longer a virgin, there was no pain this time. Still, her passage was narrow, her body taking a few long moments to accommodate his substantial size.

He swelled even more, lengthening, as his shaft set up a fierce, throbbing ache that demanded appeasement. Kissing her with rapacious hunger, he pumped inside, driving himself deep, then deeper still. Fast, then even faster.

Her eyes closed, and he felt her tighten her hold, clinging to him with complete trust as she gave him total control over her body. Adjusting her again for maximum pleasure, he thrust harder, finding exactly the right angle to bring her to peak.

She didn't last long, quaking violently in his grasp as the crisis came upon her. He swallowed her cries in his mouth, her inner muscles squeezing him with a sleek, milking pressure that drove him wild.

Beyond control, he plunged inside her, thrusting several times with a force that made him want to shout. Instead, he bit his lip as he reached his own peak, quaking as he poured himself violently inside her.

Resting his face against her own, he kissed her. Slowly, he let her legs slide downward, holding her steady while she once again found her feet. Curving an arm against the wall above her head, he kept her nestled in the lee of his body.

"I can't say I quite intended to do that, but neither am I sorry," he murmured. "Are you all right?"

"F-fine. Wonderful, in fact." She gave him a tremulous smile.

He smiled back, bending to kiss her again. "Good."

Reaching out, he helped her straighten her dress. "You know something, Grace?"

"What?"

"I almost wish we hadn't already settled on this house."

"Why? Don't you like it? Have you changed your mind?"

"No, it's not that. It's just that I like house hunting with you. I'll be sorry not to do it again."

A becoming shade of pink spread into her cheeks.

He laughed. "Maybe we can come back again, though, to measure another room for drapes."

A light frost coated the windows of the Danverses' drawing room on St. Martin's Lane. During the six weeks that had passed since Grace and Jack's memorable house hunting expedition, fall had ceded dominion to winter and the advent of cold December days.

Cozy inside near the cheerfully burning fireplace, Grace reached for the Meissen shepherdess on the mantel. Taking particular care, she turned to wrap the delicate piece in tissue paper. Over the last several days, the servants had been busy packing her belongings for the move to Upper Brook Street, but there were a few special items she wanted to handle herself. This figurine was one of them, greatly cherished because it had once belonged to her mother.

She'd been surprised and deeply touched when Papa had suggested she take it with her, especially since she knew how much her mother's remaining possessions meant to him.

"She'd want you to have it," he'd told her

in a hoarse tone. "To bring you peace and happiness in your new home. You're to take her best silver service too. What use does an old widower like me have for such fancy bits and pieces?"

She smiled as she thought of his words, bending to lay the securely wrapped figurine into a small packing crate. Catching sight of a few books on a nearby shelf, she moved to retrieve them, knowing they would get far more use by her than by her father. She was placing them into the crate when a brief tap came at the door.

"Hallo, Grace," said a voice she hadn't heard in weeks.

Glancing up, she discovered Terrence Cooke standing in the doorway, a large folio in his hands. "I hope I'm not intruding," he said, looking distinctly uncomfortable in a way she'd never seen him before. Then again, considering what had transpired between them the last time they'd been in the same room, his reticence was understandable.

His brows furrowed at her silence. "I can see you're busy. I ought to have sent 'round a note. Forgive me." Looking away, he began to turn.

"No. Oh, please don't go," she called out.

He stopped and met her gaze.

"I was only surprised to see you, that's all." She motioned toward a chair. "Come in and tell me how you've been and what you've been doing. Sit and I'll have Martha bring us some tea and cream biscuits. You were always partial to Martha's cream biscuits, as I recall."

"Thank you, but no biscuits or tea," he said, stopping her before she could cross to the bell pull. "I don't intend to stay long. I only wanted to bring you these."

Opening the folio, he drew out a thin leather sheath. "It's your original watercolor drawings for the bird volume, or rather your bird volume, I should say. Production is underway and I wanted to return these to you now, so they don't get lost."

She clasped her hands at her waist, sadly aware of the tension that stood between them like a wall. "That is very kind of you to bring them yourself. Thank you."

He nodded, directing his gaze off to one side. "I-I'll just leave them here then, shall I?" Striding over to her writing desk, he placed the sheath on top. "Well, I . . . um . . . suppose I ought to go. Lots of work, you know."

Was he really going to leave, just like that, with nothing more to be said between them?

"I intend to finish the flower folio," she

blurted. "Assuming you haven't decided to cancel the contract and give the job to someone else."

His sandy brows rose as he shook his head. "Of course I haven't cancelled the contract."

"I wouldn't blame you if you had. I've been quite remiss about my painting lately. What with the wedding arrangements and the packing and the plans to go to Braebourne soon, there simply hasn't been time. I ought to have written to let you know my intentions. My apologies, but I just wasn't sure . . ."

"Wasn't sure of what?"

"If you would want to hear from me again."

Something shattered on his face. "But you're the one who shouldn't want to hear from *me.* After . . . well, after what happened in Bath I assumed I was the last person you would wish to see again. I'm sorry, Grace. Truly."

"No, I'm the one who is sorry. I had no right to intrude on your privacy that day. I've felt dreadful ever since."

One side of his mouth turned up in a rueful smile. "Believe me, I've felt worse. You don't know how many times I've thought of coming here, of talking to you, or at least sending you a letter. I tried, but I always ended up tossing my attempts into the fire. I've missed you."

She smiled. "I've missed you too. We were always such good friends."

"We were," he said with a nod. "I should like to be friends again. But I suppose that's impossible now, what with your upcoming marriage." His gaze dropped to his shoes. "Only think, you'll be a lady soon. Lady John Byron. The papers are buzzing with news about your exclusive Society wedding to be held at the Duke of Clybourne's principal estate."

"You should come."

He looked shocked. "To your wedding? No, I couldn't come to your wedding."

"Why not?" she countered, warming suddenly to the idea. "I haven't seen Braebourne yet, but Jack tells me the house is nearly as large as a royal palace. There's plenty of room, and you would be most welcome. I was told to invite anyone I like, so I shall advise the dowager duchess to add you to the guest list."

"No, I couldn't."

"But —"

"I wouldn't fit in, not in a room full of nobs."

"You'd like them if you met them. They're

very nice nobs."

He chuckled. "I'm sure they are. But it's impossible, for too many reasons to count." The smile fell from his face. "I thank you for the invitation, but I don't want to sit and watch you get married. You may not believe it, but I do love you, even if it's not in the conventional sense. I would have taken good care of you."

"I know." She glanced away, unable to stand the regret shimmering in his eyes.

"Are you happy, Grace? Is he really what you want?"

"Yes," she replied, her voice growing soft with emotion. "I've never been so happy. Some days I wonder if it's all a dream, and then I see him again and I know it's not."

"Then I'm glad," he said. "For your sake, I'm glad."

She met his gaze, knowing this was another ending between them. A silent acknowledgement that they were both moving on to a new phase of their lives.

"Well, I really ought to go," he told her. "I have a business to run, you know."

"Of course you do. Write to me, Terrence. I should like to hear what you're doing."

He gave her a genuine smile. "You may count upon it. And you are to take all the time you require with your painting. The flower folio will be waiting whenever you are ready to return to it."

"You are too kind."

"Not at all." He strode to the doorway. When he reached the threshold, he paused and turned back. "Grace?"

"Yes?" She arched a brow.

"I meant it about being your friend. If there is ever anything you need, you have only to say."

"You as well." Going to him, she kissed his cheek. "I wish you every happiness."

"I wish you more. Godspeed, dear Grace."

Chapter 15

When Aunt Jane had long ago described Braebourne as one of the most elegant homes in all of England, with grounds and gardens beautiful enough to rival those held by the royal family itself, she hadn't exaggerated in the least.

From Grace's first glimpse of the estate, she'd been alternately enchanted and intimidated. *Lord have mercy, what have I gotten myself into?* she'd thought, as the house had come into view at the end of a magnificent, two-mile-long, tree-lined drive.

Nestled in the northern part of the Cotswold hills, the Byrons' majestic ancestral home was perched atop a gently sloping rise. Fashioned from the rich, honey-colored limestone so plentiful in the area, the grand edifice rose like a gleaming jewel set amid a vast forest of ancient trees, whose branches were now bared for winter.

Before the trip, she'd fleetingly wondered

if there would be enough room for all the guests the dowager duchess was inviting. But now she saw her error. Braebourne wasn't merely grand; it was, for all intents and purposes, a palace.

Nerves were jumping in her stomach when the coach-and-four rolled to a stop. But then Jack climbed out, reaching back to lift her down. The moment his arms closed around her, she knew everything would be all right.

And so it continued to be, the ten days before Christmas passing by in a flurry of merrymaking and excitement. Each day brought a fresh influx of family and friends, the big house filling with so many aunts, uncles and cousins that they soon reached the proportions of a horde — just as the duke had once predicted.

But they were a happy horde, everyone full of good spirits and holiday cheer. She met the rest of Jack's siblings — brainy mathematician and inventor Drake; war hero Cade; irrepressible twins Leo and Lawrence; and precociously artistic ten-year-old Esme, for whom she had once suggested the purchase of watercolor paper and paints.

Lord Cade's new bride, Meg, was a welcoming presence, her face aglow with happiness from what she reported to have been a most satisfactory honeymoon sojourn. Grace took an immediate liking to her soon-to-be sister-in-law — bonding with her not only because of their similar ages but even more so because of their shared backgrounds. As commoners, they both knew what it was like being drawn into the glittering, whirlwind existence of the Byrons' aristocratic fold.

As for her own family, Papa and Aunt Jane arrived two days before Christmas, her aunt pausing to whisper her thanks in Grace's ear for giving her "the most spectacular adventure of my life."

During the day, Grace helped the dowager duchess with the last of the wedding preparations. In the evenings everyone relaxed, gathering to dance and sing songs, or play charades and raucous games of hoodman's bluff.

But the best treat by far was her Christmas Eve sleigh ride with Jack. A slick coating of snow had fallen the night before, turning everything shimmering and white — perfect for a cold-weather outing. With twilight upon them, she'd ridden snuggled close against his side, his hands steady on the reins as he'd urged their horse to run as fast as it could manage.

Seated now on the drawing room sofa, she smiled at the memory, the room abuzz with Christmas morning noise and laughter as everyone opened their presents. She'd already received a pair of lavender leather driving gloves from Mallory, a book of poetry from her aunt and the softest green cashmere shawl she'd ever touched from the dowager duchess — or Mama, as she kept gently reminding Grace to call her.

Placing the wrap around her shoulders, she reached for another present.

"I was starting to think you'd never open that one," murmured a husky voice near her ear.

Glancing up, she met Jack's twinkling azure gaze. "I hope it's not anise seed cookies," she teased. "You know they make me sneeze."

He laughed and slipped into a narrow bit of space between the sofa arm and her right hip. "Not to worry. Considering the spectacle you put on a couple nights ago after dinner, I've had all the anise seed in the house locked away until after our departure. I want there to be no further mishaps."

"My thanks for interceding with the kitchen, my lord."

"Oh, it's no trouble. I wander down there every once in a while to visit with Cook.

She's been with the family since I was about this high." He held a hand three feet above the ground.

"I suppose she stuffs you full of cream cakes and biscuits during these visits?"

A grin spread over his face. "Can I help it if she wants new recipes tested? Now, are you going to open that present or not?"

Glancing at the box, she studied its small size and square shape. Without further hesitation, she tugged open the green silk ribbon and pulled off the lid. A sparkling flash of purple and gold winked boldly back.

Nestled into a bed of shiny cream satin lay a heart-shaped pendant on a simple gold chain. The heart itself was created from over a dozen delicate round amethyst stones, while the center held a miniature painted on porcelain. Done in a series of fine, delicate strokes, the artist's rendering depicted a tiny garden, alive with masses of yellow and white hollyhocks.

Right away, they reminded her of the flowers she'd been drawing that long-ago day in Bath. The day of her and Jack's very first kiss.

Her gaze went to his, breath stilled in her chest. "Oh, Jack. It's Sydney Gardens, isn't it?"

"That's right, with those stalky, puffy-headed flowers." He gave her a gentle smile. "Do you like it?"

"I love it."

"I chose amethyst, since you said it's your favorite stone. I hope I remembered right?"

"You did. It's so lovely. Thank you. I'll wear it each and every day," she promised. "Your heart tucked against my own."

A peculiar shadow flickered momentarily across his eyes before he reached for the necklace. "Here, let me help you put it on."

"Yes. Please," she said, relieved he'd offered. Her hands were trembling with so much emotion that she doubted she could have managed the task on her own.

Turning slightly, she angled herself so he could place the chain around her neck and fasten the clasp. The slight weight of the gold and stones grew instantly warm against her skin. "There. How does it look?" she asked as she moved to face him again.

"Beautiful," he said.

But when she glanced up, she realized he wasn't looking at the pendant. Instead, he was looking at her.

Her lips parted on a silent exhalation, the room and all its guests fading away. His eyelids dipped in a way she'd come to recognize, then his head did the same, his mouth seeking out her own. The quiet majesty of his kiss rocked her down to her toes.

"Here now, none of that, you two," called her father in a sternly indulgent voice. "There are children present, if you'll recall, not to mention a few adults who'd rather not be witness to such goings-on. You'll be married soon enough. Have patience."

Slowly, Jack broke their kiss and raised his head to address the legion of onlookers. "Patience, as everyone in this room well knows, has never been my strong suit. Has it, Grace?" Then he winked and grinned, utterly unapologetic.

The others laughed, good-natured over a chaste kiss between an engaged couple on Christmas Day. Grace joined in, but she soon stopped, lowering her gaze to her lap in an effort to will away her need to blush.

She was actually winning the battle, when Jack put his lips against her ear. "We'll continue this tonight. Be sure not to lock your door."

Hot roses blossomed across her cheeks, while barely repressed anticipation sparked in her blood.

Despite the danger of being caught, tonight's promised rendezvous wouldn't be the first time Jack had stolen into her room. Both of them knew they were supposed to wait for their wedding night, but the days still remaining before the ceremony were simply too long for either of them to bear.

Last night, in fact, had been particularly passionate, with Jack bringing her awake sometime well after midnight. She'd roused to find herself naked, Jack having slipped off her nightgown without her even being aware. But she'd barely thought anything of it at the time, desire burning in white-hot pulses through her aching body. Nearing desperate, she'd been thankful to let him put out the flames.

Her cheeks grew hotter now as she shifted on the sofa with a sudden, highly inappropriate discomfort. Thankfully no one was watching them anymore; they were too busy tearing open the last of their presents and indulging in the myriad conversations taking place throughout the room.

"Shall I bring you a hot milk punch?" Jack asked with a gentle, surprisingly knowing smile. "Or would you rather have something cool?"

"Cool. And nonalcoholic, please. You're causing me enough trouble without my being tipsy."

Chuckling, he stroked a cool finger over her warm cheek, then rose to obtain her drink.

Barely a minute passed before Mallory appeared, sliding into the spot so recently inhabited by her brother. "So," Mallory said without preamble. "What did he give you? I saw something sparkle from three seats down."

Smiling, Grace showed off her pendant.

"Oh, how exquisite. I didn't know my brother had such good taste. May I?" Mallory lifted her hand, clearly wanting to touch the piece in order to get a better view of the tiny miniature inside. But as she reached out, something shiny glittered on her left hand.

"What is that!" Without stopping to think, Grace grabbed her friend's hand and yanked it down to eye level. "Is that what I think it is? Mallory, are you engaged?"

Mallory's eyes brightened, her skin pinking a bit as she gave a little nod. "Yes. He asked last night."

"Oh, how wonderful! I knew the major wouldn't make it through the holiday without a proposal."

"You're right. He didn't. But I promised we'd wait until later to say anything, since he has yet to speak to Edward. Drat, I know I shouldn't have this on, but I couldn't resist."

"Shouldn't have what on?" interrupted

Jack's deep voice, a pair of filled glasses balanced in his hands. "What the devil's that rock doing on your finger, Pell-Mell?"

Quickly, Mallory buried her palm against her skirt. "Nothing. Mind your own business, Jack Byron."

"A stone like that on my little sister's finger sounds exactly like my business. Good Lord, Hargreaves did it, didn't he?" Jack set down the drinks on a nearby table.

"Who did what?" inquired India Byron.

Lithe and dark, she was one of the many cousins come to visit for the holiday. She held a small wrapped gift in her hand, the attached tag flipped around to display Grace's name. "Did I hear something about an engagement? Oh, Mallory, are you getting married too?" India, who was only recently engaged herself, let out an excited whoop.

Eyes turned her way from all corners of the room.

The dowager duchess rose to her feet, her interest now obviously piqued. While not far distant stood the Duke of Weybridge — India's tall, dark, enigmatic fiancé. Unconcealed amusement shown on his compelling face, as though he were well-used to such exuberant outbursts from his new betrothed.

This situation, Grace realized, *is rapidly getting out of control.*

Suddenly Major Hargreaves appeared at Mallory's side. Reaching down a hand, he helped her to her feet. "I knew you wouldn't be able to keep this to yourself," Grace heard him whisper.

"I'm sorry, Michael," she said. "I know I shouldn't have worn the ring, but I simply couldn't resist."

"Not to worry. I just finished talking to your brother. All is well."

"You didn't talk to *this* brother," Jack said.

Hargreaves met his gaze with a startled one of his own. "I didn't realize I needed to."

Jack crossed his arms and stared.

"However, in the interest of maintaining good family relations," the major continued, "I shall be perfectly happy to oblige. My lord, may I have the honor of your sister's hand in marriage?"

"Do you love her?"

Hargreaves cast a glance at Mallory. "Yes. Very much."

"And what if I said no? What would you do then?"

The major's blond brows furrowed, his jaw tightening. "I'd be sorry for it, but I'd marry her regardless."

Moments passed, the two men locked in a silent battle of wills.

Abruptly, Jack grinned. "If you'd said anything else, I'd have refused and told Edward to take back his consent as well." He offered a hand. "Welcome to the family. I hope you know what you're in for."

Hargreaves grinned back. "I believe I have a reasonable idea."

As though they'd been friends forever, the major slapped his palm into Jack's for a hearty, good-natured handshake.

Mallory rolled her eyes. "Men."

Grace met her gaze and gave a nod of agreement.

Soon after, Ava Byron joined the fray, Edward arriving not long after.

"Now, what is going on over here?" the dowager demanded, clearly determined to be let in on the secret. Once she was, Ava let out a cry of gladness at the news and hugged her daughter. "Well, it's about time, young man," she told the major once she eased away from Mallory. "I was beginning to wonder if you were just toying with my girl."

"Not at all, ma'am," Hargreaves assured her. "No toying whatsoever."

Quickly realizing that everyone else in the room was curious as well, silence was called for so that the major and Mallory could publicly announce their happy news. The instant they did, the engaged couple found themselves surrounded by well-wishers.

And Grace found herself squeezed out, forced to abandon her formally cozy seat rather than battle the sudden onslaught. Jack, she realized, had been forced out as well, and was lost somewhere in the mass of family and friends.

From the safety of a less crowded section of the room, she was searching for Jack when she caught sight of Adam Gresham instead. Standing alone near the doorway, Gresham was watching the ongoing tableau. She'd had a chance to speak to him at length the other night at dinner and had found him immensely charming and cheerful. But there was nothing cheerful in his expression now. His face was solemn and a shade too pale, his eyes stark with desolation.

Glancing back, she looked to see which of the ladies he was watching, telling herself he must be observing someone other than Mallory. She was considering and discarding possibilities when Jack came up behind her and slid an arm around her waist.

"There you are," he declared in a throaty murmur. "For a moment I thought you'd disappeared."

She shook her head. "No. Just needed a bit more breathing room."

His lips turned up in a seductive grin. "It has grown impossibly crowded in here. What would you think if we went looking for even more breathing room somewhere else in the house. Unless you still want that milk punch, that is?"

A pleasant shiver traced over her skin. "But what if someone notices we're gone?"

"In this crowd? I think we're safe until luncheon, which is a good three hours away."

"But it's still morning. What if my maid comes in?"

"Ah, sweetheart, you should have a bit more faith in my inventive nature. I grew up in this house, remember? I know all sorts of places where we will most definitely not be disturbed."

She gave him a severe look, even though her insides were turning to mush at the notion of trysting someplace besides the bedroom. "As I said once before, Jack Byron, you are a very wicked man."

A laugh rumbled in his throat, his eyes gleaming like a sunlit sea. "But you wouldn't have me any other way."

To her consternation, she realized he was

right. Offering not the slightest resistance, she let him lead her to the door.

Chapter 16

Five evenings later, Grace hummed a little tune under her breath as she slipped into a robe and tied the belt at her waist. She'd dismissed her maid a few minutes ago, sending the girl on her way with a pleasant goodnight. Then she'd waited, counting the minutes until she figured it was safe to proceed with her plan.

Or rather her surprise.

Usually she climbed into bed to lie warm and snug beneath the covers while she waited for Jack to sneak down the hall and join her. But today was his birthday and she wanted to do something extra special to celebrate. What better way, she decided, than to be waiting for him in his room when he came up to bed?

Mercy, what a wanton I've become, she decided, wondering what had become of the shy young woman she'd once been. No doubt the poor thing had expired, killed by an excess of carnal bliss at the hands of a thoroughly libidinous scoundrel. A scoundrel she now loved to distraction and couldn't wait to marry.

Only six more days and she would be his bride. Just six more days and they would be free to share a marriage bed with no further necessity for subterfuge. But for now she would need to content herself with stolen kisses and secret late-night rendezvouses. And really she didn't mind the intrigue — so long as they didn't get caught.

When she'd left Jack downstairs forty-five minutes ago, he'd been on his way to play billiards and share a bottle of vintage Scotch with his brothers and a few of the other men. She hoped they didn't keep him up all night, or else she was in for a very disappointing evening. Then again, Jack had to sleep sometime, so with enough patience, her surprise would still work fine.

Buoyed by the knowledge, she crossed to her door and cracked it open to make sure the corridor was clear. Praying she wouldn't bump into anyone along the way, she hurried down the hall.

To her relief, she made it inside Jack's bedchamber without incident. She was even more relieved to find the room empty, his valet nowhere in sight. She'd been prepared to offer the servant some excuse about needing to talk to Jack regarding the wedding, but she was glad to find the precaution unnecessary.

Realizing Jack must have sent the man to his quarters for the evening, she relaxed and strolled deeper into the room. A fire was burning cheerfully in the grate, a few lighted candles illuminating the appealing décor that was done in rich, masculine shades of cream and brown.

Casting about for a place to wait, she stared at the bed.

The big, wide, luxuriously comfortable-looking bed with its plump feather pillows and cocoa-hued satin counterpane.

Obviously, it was the most logical location to wait. Yet even with her newfound confidence, she couldn't bring herself to walk over and climb in.

Where else then?

There was always the sofa, but that seemed too staid, as though she'd simply come to chat.

By the window then? But no, what if someone glimpsed her shadow through the drapes?

The fireplace? Men were always leaning against one mantelpiece or another, and given her height, she was certainly tall enough to pull off the trick. Yet even thinking about taking up such a pose made her laugh. Then too, she risked being left standing for what might turn from minutes into hours.

No, she needed someplace where she could sit.

His writing desk.

Of course! Why hadn't she thought of that from the start? Waiting there would be simple, even elegant. And perhaps, if she timed it right, Jack would discover her posing like one of the sensuously clad Grecian goddesses that were so popular these days on vases and urns.

Smirking at her own folly, she strolled over to the desk. As she rounded the corner to pull out the chair, the skirt of her robe flapped open and caught on a slim leather folder resting on top of the desk. Off it flew, the sides fluttering open to unleash a flurry of paperwork into the air.

Oh, stars! she thought, shaking her head at her carelessness. Rushing forward, she bent to gather the documents. She'd collected nearly all of them and was about to tuck them neatly back into place when the sight of her name on one of the pages caught her eye.

. . . marriage to Grace Lilah Danvers. In exchange, the following terms shall be agreed upon . . .

It was the settlement, she realized.

Papa told her he'd negotiated the weighty legal document a few weeks ago, assuring her that it more than amply provided for her welfare, and that of any future children she might have. He'd said her interests were safe and secure, and that she had nothing over which to be concerned.

Not that she was in any way concerned. Quite the contrary, since she knew Jack wished only for her happiness.

Once again she was about to slip the page back inside the folder when her gaze caught on something else — a phrase that seemed wholly out of place.

. . . forgiveness of accrued gambling debts . . .

Gambling debts?

Scanning backward to locate the beginning of the paragraph, she began to read. Once she was done with that, she forced herself to read more, to read it all, no matter how much each word might hurt.

By the time she finished, her entire body

was numb. Dropping to her knees, she closed her eyes and wondered how she was ever going to survive.

The clock chimed two as Jack rounded the landing at the top of the stairs. Covering a yawn with his fist, he made his way down the corridor to his room. He would be glad to climb into bed and get some rest. Then again, he'd be even gladder to climb into Grace's bed and take his ease with her. But maybe he should let her sleep. Considering the late hour, she must surely have drifted off by now.

Despite his constant desire for her, he supposed a night apart wouldn't do either of them any harm. In fact, were he any sort of gentleman, he would have left her alone these past few weeks, rather than tempting the fates by taking her to bed as frequently as he could manage.

So far, she hadn't conceived a child. But every time he was with her was another new chance. Then again, only six days remained until the wedding, so even if he did get her pregnant, who was to know?

Six days, he mused. *Six final days of bachelorhood.*

Given his previous opinion on the topic of marriage, the idea ought to terrify him. Or at the very least leave him queasy and on the verge of making a wild dash for freedom.

But curiously he felt no such urges. He was . . . content . . . even eager for the coming union. He genuinely liked Grace, and, as amazing as it was to admit, he wanted to marry her. Of course, it didn't hurt knowing their marriage would give him complete access to her body, allowing him to take her whenever, wherever, and as often as he wished to exercise his husbandly prerogatives.

His shaft stirred at the thought, aching in violent anticipation of their approaching honeymoon. He couldn't wait to get her to himself inside the secluded little cottage he'd chosen for their wedding trip. By the time they left the place, she would be well and thoroughly satisfied, so much so that she would have long ago forgotten what it was like not having him in her several times a day.

Biting back a groan, he shoved open the door to his bedchamber and stalked inside. A quick change into his robe, he decided, and then he was going to her room, where both of them could enjoy the delicious pleasure of having him wake her up.

But as he walked farther into the room, he stopped, his pulse leaping to discover her seated at his desk. "Grace. You're here."

"Yes. So I am," she murmured.

"How long have you been waiting?"

"A while." She didn't look at him, nor did she move, not even by so much as the twitch of a finger.

Something's wrong, he realized, though he couldn't for the life of him imagine what could have occurred to upset her in the few short hours since dinner. Well, he'd soon find out and have her smiling again. "I must say I'm glad you're here." He glanced at the bed, wondering how quickly he could get her in it.

"Are you?" Her voice sounded odd, almost hollow.

"Of course." He strolled closer. "I can't think of anything better than an unexpected late-night visit from my beautiful bride-to-be."

She flinched. "Can you not?"

He stopped and studied her, noting the ashen cast to her cheeks.

"Grace —"

"I did some reading while you were downstairs," she said, as though he hadn't spoken.

"Oh?"

"The document was quite . . . illuminating."

Document?

Only then did he notice the leather folder lying on the desk a few inches from her hands. Only in that instant did he remember exactly what it contained.

Double hell and damnation! The settlement!

Danvers had given him a copy of the final executed agreement yesterday with the change he'd requested. Unsatisfied with the terms should he predecease her, Jack had insisted on a larger widow's portion than was generally customary. The original sum had been generous and more than sufficient to see to her comfort and needs. The new amount, however, would ensure that she could continue to live as she had during his lifetime, with no necessary alterations to her existence except those she chose herself. He'd done it to protect her. Why hadn't he thought to protect her again by locking the papers away where she would never see them?

Careless, stupid fool, he cursed himself. But then he'd had no reason to conceal them, since he'd never once imagined she would be here in this room. At least not until after they were married. Generally, single young women weren't given to visiting their fiancés' rooms prior to the wedding. On the other hand, Grace was not most single young women, as she continued proving to him each and every day.

"I came to surprise you," she said in that same hauntingly empty tone. "I wanted to give you one more *gift* for your birthday. But it seems I'm the one who ended up surprised."

His stomach churned, aching as though he'd swallowed a handful of rocks. "It's not what you think —"

Her gaze shot upward, meeting his own for the first time since he'd entered the room. "Is it not? The agreement appeared rather straightforward to me. But then I am only a woman and not privy to the superior machinations of men. Perhaps I don't have a full understanding of such worldly matters."

He stifled a groan, giving her full marks for her sarcastic condemnation of himself and her father.

"The one thing I don't understand, however, is why?" she mused aloud.

"Why?" he repeated with a frown.

"Oh, not why you did it. That much is patently obvious. Clearly you became indebted to my father — at cards, I presume — and as repayment you agreed to take me off his hands. No, what I want to know is why the pretense? Why this . . . elaborate charade these past few months to make me think there was something more between us than base commerce?"

"It's not like that, Grace," he defended. "I . . . it's complicated."

"*Complicated?* Yes, I'm sure lying constantly would become complicated."

"That isn't what I meant," he said through clenched teeth. "And I haven't been lying constantly."

"Only part of the time, then? Was that before or after you met my father? And by that I mean when you *first* met my father, not that day at the house when we came to ask his blessing on our marriage and you both pretended not to know one another."

This time, he was the one to flinch. "Fine. I won't deny it. Your father and I crossed paths one evening over the gaming table, many days before I met you. As for my subsequent pursuit of you, what else would have served?"

"The truth, perhaps?"

"Oh? So if I'd come to you from the start, lain myself bare, and asked you to marry me, you would have said yes?"

She gave him a long, impenetrable stare before lowering her gaze. "No. Of course not."

"Exactly. Which is why seduction was the only way to win you."

Closing her eyes, she turned her face away. A small silence fell. "So, did you propose the . . . arrangement, or did he?" she asked.

Jack clenched his fists at his side and tried to think of some way to explain the bargain he'd made with her father in a manner that wouldn't just make things worse.

"But of course it was him," she continued, as she opened her eyes again on a sigh. "You might be an unprincipled libertine, but you're not a fortune hunter. At least not the common variety, or you'd have been married to some other woman years ago. I've seen you play cards, though, my lord. How is it a man of your exceptional talents lost to an amateur like Papa?"

"Bad luck, that's all." As soon as the words were out, he wished he could take them back.

She cringed and wrapped her arms around herself.

"Grace, I didn't mean —"

"No, it's quite all right. I'm sure it must have killed you to agree to this. It must be killing you still. But Papa's always wanted me to marry well. What better way than to buy me a bona fide lord?"

His jaw tightened as he found himself unable to dispute her claim.

"But I forget," she continued. "You're getting a fortune out of it, aren't you? My dowry, plus another sixty thousand pounds when we wed. And your gaming debt expunged. Just how much do you owe him, anyway?"

For a fleeting moment, he considered refusing to tell her. But the damage was done. What did it matter now? "A hundred thousand pounds."

She sucked in an astonished breath. "Good God! No wonder you agreed. I'm sure that much money makes even a redheaded giantess like me look attractive."

"You aren't unattractive. Quite the contrary. I never lied to you about that. And I like your height. There's nothing wrong with being tall."

She looked away again, so he couldn't tell if she believed him or not.

"Grace, I know you're upset and angry, and you have every right to be. But let's talk about this."

"I think we've *talked* enough already."

He walked around the desk. "But we haven't. We can work this out. It's true, I admit, that I agreed to marry you in order to pay the debt I owe your father. It was unforgivably wrong, and for that I'm sorry. But since I've known you, things have changed."

"What things?"

His voice deepened. "Everything. You weren't at all what I expected. I liked you, for one."

"*Liked* me?" she repeated on a skeptical note. "You *liked* me so much you were willing to lie, to manipulate and use me for your own gain?"

His gut tightened, her accusation hitting him like a roundhouse punch. "As I said before, I only lied when it was necessary, in order to keep you from knowing about the bargain with your father. Nothing else between us has been false."

"Nothing else, hmm? So, you honestly enjoy attending lectures about flowers and plants, do you?"

Her question caught him off-stride. "What?"

"Flowers. Remember how you happened upon me that day at the botany lecture in Bath? Did you attend the seminar simply because you wanted to learn more about plants, or were you there to ingratiate yourself to me as part of your plan? Tell me our meeting that day was nothing more than a pure coincidence."

He ran a hand through his hair.

"That's what I thought," she said, jumping to her feet. "Do you even know the names of any flowers?"

"Of course I do."

"Then tell me. Name some. Name one."

He opened his mouth to reply.

"And not the common name," she insisted. "I want the genus and species." Trembling, she reached a hand into her robe and drew out the pendant around her neck. "What about this one? What about these h-hollyhocks?"

He frowned and said nothing. Because he didn't know. *Damn, why don't I know?*

A single tear slid over her cheek as she yanked hard at the chain. The thin gold links bit into her neck and held. But she gave a second vicious tug and it broke free. "Here, take it! I don't want it! I don't want to see it ever again!"

When his hands remained at his sides, she flung the pendant onto the desk.

Whirling away, she hurried forward. Her foot twisted beneath her, though, and she stumbled. Instinctively he reached out and caught her. She pulled back as though his hands were made of fire.

"Don't!" she hissed, wrenching herself out of his hold. "Don't you ever touch me again."

"Grace, please —"

But she was gone, running to the door and

out into the corridor. He could have followed, but he knew it was no use. She was beyond consoling. And what could he offer her, when he was the cause of her grief?

Hours later, Grace lay awake on her bed, staring into the darkness. Mellow orange embers were all that remained of the fire in the grate, while the pair of candles her maid had lighted earlier had sputtered out in squat pools of melted wax.

She hadn't slept, nor would she that night. How could she rest when her entire world had just come crashing down around her? When everything she'd believed had been violently torn apart?

Sweet Lord, how had everything gone so horribly wrong?

Until a few hours ago, she'd been so happy, so full of joy and anticipation, as she counted the last few days until her wedding.

Wedding, ha! Bondage more like, as she was bartered in trade by the two men she had trusted most. But there was no trust now — her faith, her love, was breached beyond redemption.

As for her father, she wasn't really surprised by his scheming. He'd never taken pains to conceal his dearest wish that she marry into the ranks of the Ton and, by doing so, further the dynasty he'd worked so long and hard to build. Despite his recent silence on the subject, she ought to have known he would never have given up on his quest. Once her father wanted a thing, he always found a way to make it happen.

Of course, he wanted her "happy" as well, and what better way to see to her comfort and contentment than to find her a man she would like? Someone designed to please her in all ways, whom she could love if she let herself. When he'd chosen Jack Byron, he'd chosen well, finding her a strong man — but more, a gentleman — one he'd instinctively known she would not be able to resist.

And then there was Jack.

A harsh shudder went through her, her eyes squeezing tight against the pain that threatened to slice her in two. Curling on her side, she waited for the worst to pass. Waited until she thought she could keep from crying aloud and shaming herself should someone happen to hear. But thankfully, the household was asleep, so her agony was hers to bear alone.

How amused he must have been all these weeks, watching her fall so easily beneath his spell, she thought. The towering, twenty-five-year-old spinster, who'd toppled into his waiting hands like a ripe piece of fruit. But then any woman would topple into his hands; he had only to beckon the one he desired most.

In her case, however, his interest was feigned, calculating. He didn't really want her, she was simply the means to an end. Deep in her heart, she'd always known it wasn't right, that it made no logical sense for a man as handsome and sophisticated as Jack Byron to desire a plain, ordinary mouse like her. And now she had proof that she was right.

The knowledge gave her no satisfaction, however; the truth lay cold and hollow in her heart. Part of her wished she could take back the past few hours, erase everything that had happened tonight so she could live happily again inside her delusions. But doing so would merely have put off the inevitable. Eventually — months or even years from now — she would have come to realize her folly, awakening one bleak day to the reality of her empty, one-sided love.

He *liked* her, did he? She noticed there'd been no mention of any deeper emotion. Because in that, he hadn't been able to lie. When she thought back, she realized he'd never spoken of love — only need and desire. How had he phrased it the morning he'd proposed?

I've come to realize . . . that I can't do without you.

Considering her father's hold over him, she could see now just how accurate that statement had been. As for letting her assume he loved her . . . well, she was sure he'd figured it only made his task that much easier. He said he'd set out to seduce her, and he'd done exactly that. She'd been utterly besotted, giving him not just her body but her heart as well.

She cringed now to think of the ways she'd exposed herself, openly professing her love in the mistaken belief that he returned her sentiments.

Worse still was the manner in which he'd played on her vulnerabilities. How he'd urged her, even demanding at times, that she tell him she loved him, aware all the while that he was perpetrating a sham of the most heinous kind.

Bastard.

She squeezed her hands into fists and pressed them hard against her aching chest. The fact that he'd used her, she could understand, even if she might not condone his actions. The fact that he'd made a mockery of her in the process — well, that she would never forgive.

So, what to do next?

The wedding would have to be called off, of course. She couldn't possibly marry him now, not knowing the things she did. Their breakup would cause a huge scandal, resulting in a public humiliation he quite richly deserved.

Once she left Braebourne, though, she would have no choice but to return to her father's house — a fact about which neither she nor her father would be pleased.

And afterward? She lay there, staring blindly, while her future stretched outward as dark and impenetrable as the room around her.

If only she had money, she could choose her own path.

If only she had independence, she could forge a destiny free of the dictates and manipulations of men.

And yet, maybe I can, she realized several moments later.

Wiping away the last of her tears, she began to plan.

Chapter 17

Jack groaned and rolled onto his back, the empty crystal tumbler in his hand dropping to the carpeted floor with a muffled thud. The small sound was enough to bring him awake, his eyes popping open as though a gun had just been fired.

Sitting upright, he looked around and immediately wished he hadn't when the room took a sickening spin around him.

Clutching his head, he waited for the dizzying stab of pain to subside. As he did, he became aware of two things. He'd slept on the sofa instead of his bed. And Grace hated him.

Grace.

He winced as the memories swept through him.

After she'd left last night, he'd gone over to his desk, taken out his pocketknife, and proceeded to slice the settlement into tiny little pieces. While he was at it, he'd hacked the leather folder apart as well. His desk and the floor beneath were still littered with the remains.

The impulse had been childish, he knew, but at the time he'd been so angry, so frustrated with himself, that he'd needed some means of relieving his seething emotions. It was either that or start punching something. But even then, he'd known better than to put a hole in one of the walls. Although, under the circumstances, the misery of the broken hand he would surely have sustained might well have been worth it for a measure of satisfaction — however fleeting.

Ten minutes later, he'd located a brandy decanter and started drinking. At some point, he remembered getting sleepy. Rather than make the short trip over to the bed, he'd stretched out on the sofa and passed out.

Despite all wishes to the contrary, however, nothing could change what had occurred last night. Grace had found the settlement. She'd read it. And everything between them was over.

If he hadn't already destroyed the blasted thing, he might try again now. Of course, Danvers and both their solicitors still had copies. But that wouldn't matter for long.

At any moment, he was sure someone would be knocking at his door, demanding to know why Grace had just ordered the coach to take her back to London.

On a sigh, he scrubbed a hand through his tousled hair.

Suddenly a knock came at the door, startling him despite his anticipatory musings. Climbing to his feet, he made a half-hearted attempt to straighten his shirt and trousers, then gave his permission for whoever was there to enter.

He expected it to be Ezra Danvers. But it wasn't. Instead, one of the maids walked inside, bearing a small note card on a silver salver. She was Grace's lady's maid, if he wasn't mistaken.

"Your pardon for the interruption, your lordship," she said. "But Miss Danvers asked me to give this to you without delay."

For a long moment he hesitated before reaching out for the note. Dismissing the woman with a nod of thanks, he waited until she'd gone, then broke open the seal.

> There are things we must discuss. Meet me outside in the rose garden after breakfast. Assuming you know what a rose bramble looks like.
>
> Grace

He winced, then refolded the note. So she wasn't leaving yet, after all. Surprising. Although perhaps she simply wanted to end their engagement in person. Dragging in a deep breath, he rang the bell for his valet.

Grace's half-boots crunched against the shell pathway, her long green cloak eddying in a slow swirl around her ankles, as she paced in the center of the rose garden. Her breath frosted on the air, but she barely noticed the chill, too numb inside to be disturbed by a little cold. A second set of footsteps soon joined her own, and she turned to see Jack strolling toward her.

An ache rose inside her chest as she watched him draw near. Defiantly, she chose to blame her reaction on the freezing air, rather than the shock of seeing him again for the first time since their confrontation last night.

He looks tired, she thought. Despite his neat appearance and close-shaven face, his eyes were slightly bloodshot, as though he hadn't slept well.

I hope he had a terrible night. Heaven knows, I certainly did.

"Good morning," he said.

She ignored the greeting. "I see you found the right section of the garden."

"Yes. Even I know where the roses grow." A hard gust of wind blew, ruffling her cloak and the short woolen capes on the shoulder of his greatcoat. "Though perhaps we'd both be more comfortable inside," he suggested. "It's freezing out here."

She suppressed a shiver. "This will do. What I have to say won't take long, and I don't want anyone to overhear us."

He gave a nod. "As you wish."

Despite having spent half the night rehearsing what she planned to say, the words didn't come instantly to the fore. She buried her hands inside her pockets and took several pacing steps. "I've given this situation a great deal of thought, and I've come to a number of decisions. First of all, I wish to reiterate how strongly I disapprove of what you and my father have done. I am not some object to be bartered back and forth. I find your actions reprehensible and wholly unworthy of a gentleman."

She waited to see if he would try to defend himself.

He didn't.

"Secondly, and I tell you this with complete candor, I would like nothing better than to pack my bags, leave this house, and never set eyes on you again. What you did was unforgivably cruel, and any regard I may once have felt toward you is now at an end. The f-feelings I harbored were for a man I believed I knew. You are not that man."

A scowl settled on his forehead. "Grace, I —"

"No," she said, cutting him off. "Pray allow me to finish."

His jaw tightened as he closed his mouth.

After a few moments of silence, she continued. "In spite of all that, however, the fact remains that I am a single woman with limited sources of support. I have a small amount of money laid aside from the publication of my artwork, but it is by no means enough to live on were I to leave my father's residence. And given his involvement in this . . . this scheme, I refuse to ever live in his house again. Which is why I have decided that you and I shall marry as planned in five days' time."

"What!" His blue eyes widened in clear astonishment. "You aren't calling off the wedding?"

"No. However, I do have conditions."

"What sort of *conditions?*"

"Nonnegotiable ones." Resuming her pacing, she rubbed her gloved hands over her arms, her heart picking up speed. "I want half of the settlement money deposited into an account established in my name only, and to which you, as my husband, agree to relinquish all current and future rights."

He lifted a dark brow but said nothing.

"The profit from my painting remains mine, as well. And should I accept any additional commissions in years to come, those funds will be mine too, to earn and spend as I choose."

"Interesting," he remarked, crossing his arms. "What else? I assume you're not finished."

She shook her head, refusing to meet his gaze for fear of losing her nerve before she'd laid out all her demands. "I want a house in the countryside, deeded in my name alone."

When he remained silent, she continued. "Something comfortable, though it need not be extravagant, in the location of my choosing. I'm thinking Kent perhaps, or maybe Essex, I haven't decided which. Some place near the coast where the winters aren't too long or harsh."

"And what do you plan to do with this house?"

Stopping, she glanced up. "Live in it, of course."

Lines of puzzlement formed on his forehead. "You want us to live in a country house near the coast?"

"No. *I* want to live in a country house near the coast. You may take up residence in London or wherever you please. It shall make no difference to me."

A muscle ticked in his cheek. "So, just to be clear. We will marry, but not live together?"

She linked her hands together in front of her. "That's right."

"Do you not think people might notice if you desert me the moment we say our vows? Your father, for instance? Knowing Danvers, he'll probably refuse to pay the rest of the settlement, if we separate."

She nodded. "I did consider that, and you're right. Papa will know something is amiss if we part immediately after the wedding. And if he does, he may attempt to interfere again by having our marriage annulled. Should that happen, it's doubtful I would receive my half of the money. He might also insist you pay him back the full amount of your gaming debt, after all."

"You certainly seem to have an excellent grasp of the situation," he said in a wry tone.

"I do. Therefore, I will consent to live under the same roof as you for the first few months of our marriage. I imagine the end of the Season should be long enough to allay anyone's suspicions. When the Ton leaves the city at summer's end, I will quietly retire to my new house in the country, while you can go . . . wherever you prefer to go."

"To the devil, perhaps?" he suggested.

"If that's what you'd like," she replied with studied nonchalance.

He shot her a piercing look. "There will be talk, you know."

"Not a great deal, I imagine. From what I am given to understand, most aristocratic couples spend the majority of their time apart. You and I shall be no different."

"You realize if we marry, it's for life. We may separate, but there will be no divorce."

Her heart squeezed to hear him speak so coldly. And yet this whole matter between them was cold, as frigid and grey as the winter day around them. "Even if a divorce were possible, I have no interest in marrying again. A permanent separation is fine."

An unfathomable expression passed over his face. Pausing, he took a moment to gaze into the distance. "You're sure this is what you want?"

"Quite sure. I have been manipulated and maltreated quite enough, thank you. I want my independence, and I can think of no better way of achieving it than by means of this arrangement."

Linking her fingers together, she squeezed them tight, using the discomfort to hold down the rising tide of emotions churning inside her. With only the tiniest provocation on his part, she feared she would be lost, a torrent of tears — or worse — breaking loose. As he continued to gaze out across the manicured grounds, she studied his profile, tracing the planes and angles of his beautiful face. His once beloved face that concealed the cold heart of a liar.

Her resolve hardened at the reminder.

"Really," she remarked in a deliberately casual voice. "I should think you'd be relieved. If I call off the wedding, you'll just be back at the beginning, and up to your ears in debt to my father. Agree to my conditions, and you'll not only have your freedom but a fortune to boot — even if it is slightly less than you'd been planning on."

He shifted his gaze, regarding her for a long, silent time. "Very well, Grace. It shall be as you wish."

Air rushed from her lungs. "Can your solicitor be here to draw up the agreement before the wedding, do you think? I want no misunderstandings between us."

Sudden anger flared in his eyes. "Oh, there won't be. And neither is there any need for a solicitor. You may no longer consider me much of a gentleman, but my word as a man is still good. You shall have your money and your house, without strings, exactly as agreed. If that isn't sufficient, perhaps we should go see your father right now and call the whole thing off."

Her gaze swept down, realizing she'd pushed him too far. "No. Your promise is satisfactory."

"Good. And one more thing while we're having this tête-à-tête. You may detest me now, but you're going to have to pretend otherwise for the duration of the holiday. Until we're wed and off on our own, everyone will be watching us, expecting to see a happy couple. Do you think you can manage to show a measure of affection toward me for the next few days? Otherwise, there's not much point to this plan of yours."

Her chin came up. "I can play the moony-eyed romantic if you can."

He showed his teeth in a feral smile before offering his arm. "Let us return inside then. I don't want you to take a chill."

But a chill was exactly what went through her as she laid her hand on his sleeve, shivering as she wondered just what she'd done.

CHAPTER 18

Grace walked up the aisle on her father's arm, so numb she was barely aware of the exquisite beauty of the chapel around her. Neither did she pay heed to the multitude of family and friends seated in the rows of glossy mahogany pews, focusing her concentration almost entirely on the simple act of moving her feet across the gleaming white marble floor.

On the domed ceiling above lay a masterpiece of angels, their seraphic faces gazing downward from a heaven of brilliant cerulean blue skies and peerless pale clouds. But the ceiling might as well have been blank for all the impression it made on her. Neither did she see the profusion of lush pink roses gathered in several tall, elegant urns, nor smell their scent, which turned the air perfume sweet.

All she knew was the reality of that moment, and the fact that today was her wedding day — the most miserable day of her life. How ironic, since not long ago she had dreamed of it being the happiest.

Arriving at the altar, her father drew them to a halt. She swayed and took a moment to steady herself.

"You all right, Gracie?" he asked in a hushed tone, his brows puckered with concern.

"Fine," she whispered.

Then, as she had at least a hundred other times over the past five days, she forced a smile. Her lips felt false and waxen, but her response seemed to satisfy him. Exactly as all her responses had appeared to convince everyone of her supposed happiness in this charade that lately had become her life.

Suddenly, Jack was there to take her father's place. Gently, he reached out and laid her palm on top of his dark blue sleeve.

"Your hands are like ice," he said in a low undertone.

When she made no reply, he sighed and signaled the bishop to proceed.

She trembled despite the warmth of her white satin gown, with its matching, long-sleeved spencer trimmed at the collar and cuffs with soft, snowy ermine. When she'd selected the simple, yet elegant, dress, she'd been brimming with excitement over the prospect of wearing it. Now, she no longer cared, chilled through to her toes.

Somehow she managed to say the right words at the appropriate times, remaining calm and steady when Jack slid a wide gold band onto her finger next to the diamond engagement ring already there. For a long moment, she stared at the rings and everything they represented. Or rather everything they were supposed to represent — and did not.

Amid cheers and congratulations, they walked from the chapel. But instead of finding relief at the end of the ceremony, she realized the ordeal had only just begun.

Inside the ballroom at Braebourne, she and the wedding party formed a receiving line. The tradition quickly devolved into an act of endurance, where she was forced to talk and laugh and behave as if she were the happiest woman in the world. Pasting a smile on her face, she did her best, even though her heart beat with the slow pace of someone dying inside.

Finally, that particular misery ended and she was on to the next.

With her hand on Jack's arm, he escorted her into the formal dining room, where an elaborate wedding breakfast had been arranged. Taking a seat in the place of honor designated for her and Jack, she let him prepare her a plate heaped with an array of mouthwatering delicacies.

She might have been able to find some contentment in the delicious food. Unfortunately, she had no appetite. Unable to do more than pick at the meal, she slid little bits around here and there, so no one would suspect she was barely touching her food.

Jack noticed, however, his mouth disapproving as he glanced over at her plate. "Why aren't you eating?"

"I'm not hungry."

He shared a smile with one of his cousins, who raised his glass in a silent cheer. Then he bent his head toward her. "I find that hard to believe. Particularly since I understand you didn't take so much as a cup of tea this morning before the ceremony."

"I wasn't hungry then either."

"Have a few bites anyway. You're pale enough already. We don't need you fainting as well."

She sent him an insincere smile. "Not to worry, my lord. I won't do anything to embarrass you."

"This has nothing to do with embarrassing me. I don't want you ill."

"I'm quite well," she lied.

He ate a forkful of kipper. She couldn't

help but grimace as he chewed the delicate fish. Washing it down with a draught of wine, he patted his mouth dry on his napkin. "You aren't with child, are you?" he asked in an offhand tone, low enough that no one else could hear.

"No!" she shot back, her startled gaze flashing to his. "Most certainly not."

How dare he ask me something like that, here in front of all our friends and family!

He studied her with probing azure eyes. "You're sure? It's only been a few days since —"

"Quite sure." Blood pumped swiftly in her veins. Smiling sweetly for anyone who might be watching, she reached for her own glass of wine, then drank, hoping the spirits would ease some of her irritation. Steadier, she set down the glass.

"At least that put some color in your cheeks," Jack remarked. "I think you could use a little more, though."

Without giving her time to consider what he meant, Jack leaned across and kissed her, taking her lips with a familiar, sultry demand that sent sparks of pleasure whizzing through her system.

At first, she sat motionless, too stunned to react. Breathing in the intoxicating scent of his skin, her eyelids fluttered downward, and for a few brief moments, she kissed him back. But suddenly memories of the divide between them came rushing back. Eyes popping wide, she broke their kiss.

Reaching up, he smoothed the edge of his finger over one burning cheek. "That's better," he murmured softly. "Healthy and pink. Now, why don't you eat a few bites of your meal and prove to me that you don't have morning sickness after all?"

Only the knowledge that everyone in the room must be sending them looks kept her from giving him a good hard box to his ears.

Apparently aware of the violent direction of her thoughts, he arched a warning eyebrow. Forced to restrain herself, she curved her fingers into a fist on the arm of her chair.

Leaning back in his seat, he lifted his wineglass again and drank. Some of the male guests tossed out a few ribald comments. Nodding, Jack sent them a good-natured grin.

Her throat tight, she stared at her plate, wishing she could toss her napkin onto the table and storm out of the room. But that option was denied her today. Only a few hours more, she reminded herself, and she would be able to stop this playacting. Until then, there was no choice but to keep pretending she was a blissfully happy new bride. Tipping her head at an intimate angle, she leaned toward him. "You are detestable," she whispered.

"Eat your breakfast, Grace."

"Or what?"

He gave her a long look that dared her to find out.

Lowering her lashes to conceal a glare, she stabbed a small piece of ham, put it in her mouth and chewed.

"Have another," he suggested, when she was done.

Her fingers clenched against her fork, but at length, she obeyed.

"The almond biscuit with the cream on top is quite good," he remarked in a gentle tone. "I'd try it next, if I were you."

She was about to refuse when her stomach gave a very distinct, yet luckily inaudible, growl. To her consternation, she realized she was hungry. Ravenous, in fact.

Nonetheless, the idea of giving in to his tyranny went against every instinct inside her. Better to go hungry, she thought, than to give him even an iota's worth of satisfaction.

And yet, by refusing to eat, whom was she really hurting?

A full minute passed while a battle raged inside her. Staring down at the suddenly appetizing fare on her plate, she abruptly decided that hunger trumped pride. Let him gloat if he wished. What did it matter?

Still, she started with a tiny orange cake instead of the almond, the pastry melting like ambrosia against her tongue.

Out of the corner of her eye, she saw him smile.

"I hate you, you know," she whispered.

His smile faded. "Enjoy your meal. It's going to be a long day yet before we can depart."

Knowing he was right, she dug into her food.

Hours later, cheers and congratulations rang out from the crowd of well-wishers gathered to see Jack and Grace off on their journey.

After assisting his new wife into the coach, he climbed in and took a seat next to her. A footman put up the coach steps and closed the door. Less than a minute later, they were on their way, both he and Grace leaning forward to call out a last good-bye. Through the window, he watched his mother wipe a tear from the corner of her eye before she waved her handkerchief, her face wreathed in smiles.

The house disappeared swiftly from view.

The instant it was out of sight, Grace stood and moved to the seat opposite. Settling herself as far away from him as possible, she turned her head and gazed out the window.

He sighed.

This is going to be a delightful honeymoon. One month of newly wedded hell.

Deciding there was no point trying to coax her out of her sulks for now, he gazed out his own window. Good thing he'd packed a few books. Based on present circumstances, he would be enjoying lots of quiet time alone.

He knew she had a right to be angry, and he would give her some latitude in venting her disappointment and distress. But angry or not, they were married now, and they would have to find a way to deal with each other.

In the meantime, perhaps he should catch up on his sleep. Crossing his arms over his chest, he closed his eyes.

How dare he sleep, Grace thought ten minutes later. Shooting him a fulminating glare, she considered scooting close enough to kick him, but decided the act was unworthy.

Everything about this situation is unworthy.

Of both him and me.

She knew her anger was doing neither of them any good, but she couldn't let it go. Not now. Not yet. Because deep inside she knew that if she stopped hating him for what he'd done, there would be nothing left between them at all.

Wiping away a tear, she gazed out the window at the passing landscape, the late-afternoon sun winking off the snow-covered fields like hidden diamonds. She stared at them until her eyes hurt. Squeezing her eyelids tight, she tucked her face against the luxurious upholstery and wished for oblivion.

A few minutes later, the rhythmic movement of the coach did its work and sent her to sleep.

Burying her face against his shoulder, she snuggled closer. Warm and relaxed, she was content in a way she hadn't been in days.

"Jack," she sighed, still caught inside her dreams.

"Hmm hmm," he murmured in the low, rich tone she loved. "Keep sleeping. I'll carry you inside."

How nice. But why was Jack carrying her? Scowling, she came partially awake.

What had he said about going inside? Inside where?

Just as his arms began to slide beneath her knees, she roused, jerking against him. "What are you doing? Where are we?"

"We're at the cottage. I'm helping you out of the coach."

Remembering everything, she smacked at his hands. "I don't need your help. Let me go."

He sighed. "Grace. Don't be like this."

"Like what?" Awake now, as if he'd dumped a bucket of snow over her head, she stiffened and struggled against him. "I told you not to touch me. What part of that do you not understand?"

His gaze met hers for a long moment, his jaw rigid. Abruptly, he set her back down on the seat and climbed out of the coach.

She took a minute to collect herself before following, allowing the footman to help her down, since Jack was no longer in sight. Standing cold and stiff with residual sleepiness, she gazed at the night-shrouded cottage. Even in the darkness, she was able to make out its quaint shape and size. Ordinarily, she would have found it charming. Tonight, it only made her sad. Sighing, she walked inside.

The house was warm, courtesy of the cozy

fire burning in a large stone fireplace in the main room. On the opposite side of the central hallway stood a small study, with a dining room and kitchen taking up the rear.

It was from the kitchen that the housekeeper emerged. After greeting Grace with a voluble smile, she led the way upstairs, her ample hips swaying beneath the plain brown cloth of her skirts.

"Here ye are," she declared, as she showed her into one of the two large rooms upstairs. "I hope you'll be comfortable. There's hot water and towels on the stand, and your supper will be on the table as soon as ye and his lordship are ready."

"Actually," Grace said, stopping the woman as she turned to leave. "I'm rather tired after the journey. Would it be possible to have a tray sent up?"

The housekeeper stared for a moment but recovered quickly. "Of course, milady. Whatever ye wish."

Milady.

For a moment Grace didn't realize that the housekeeper was referring to her. But then the remembrance sank in that she was married now, with a new name and a title that would likely feel strange for some time to come. Except she didn't feel married. Instead, she felt lost and very much alone

— bound to a man who didn't love her and never would.

After asking the housekeeper to send up her maid, she went to the washstand and poured water into the pretty china basin so she could rinse her face and hands.

The rest of the evening passed slowly, her nerves stretched thin, while she waited to see if Jack would appear and demand she join him downstairs. But he didn't. Not as she ate dinner alone in her room, nor later when she drew the pins from her hair and chatted about inconsequential matters with her maid as she prepared for bed.

Actually, if not for the occasional sound of his deep voice carrying through the house as he spoke to one of the servants, she wouldn't have even known he was there.

Dressed now in one of the utilitarian, white wool nightgowns she'd insisted on having packed, she carried a lighted candle to her end table, set it down, and climbed beneath the sheets. Tucking the covers under her chin, she closed her eyes and willed herself to relax.

He won't be in, she told herself. *He has what he wants now — and it isn't me.* Not that she had any desire for him to join her in bed, since she didn't. Not now. Not knowing the truth as she did.

Even so, a wistful sigh slid past her lips, a tear rolling over her cheek before plopping onto the cool linen pillowcase beneath. Scrubbing a hand over her eyes, she forced aside her maudlin thoughts and set herself to the task of falling asleep.

She was dreaming many minutes later when the bed sank on the empty side, the mattress bouncing slightly as someone sat down.

Her dream stopped abruptly, her eyes popping wide. "Jack?"

He peered at her through the dim light. "Expecting someone else?" he asked in a faintly mocking tone.

Grabbing the covers, she pulled them to her chin. "I wasn't expecting *you!* What are you doing here?"

One dark brow arched toward the ceiling. "I should think that must be obvious. I'm going to bed."

Keeping hold of the sheets, she scooted upright and faced him in a defensive pose. "Oh no, you're not. You're not sleeping here."

Unfastening the buttons at the wrists of his shirt, he drew the garment over his head and tossed it onto a nearby chair. "Who said anything about sleeping?"

Air puffed out of her lungs. "You're not

doing *that* either!"

She assumed he would argue. Instead, he heaved a sigh, then stood to toe off his shoes and remove his trousers. Bare-chested and clad in nothing but his drawers, he turned. "Don't worry. I won't touch you, so you can stop worrying over your virtue. I'm just going to sleep."

"If you're just going to sleep, then do it somewhere else. The other bedroom, for instance."

"The *other bedroom,* if you'd taken the time to notice, is an upstairs library. This is the only bed in the house."

Her fingers quivered on the sheets. "Then sleep on the sofa in the front room. It looked long enough, even for you."

"I'm not sleeping on the sofa." Lifting the covers on his side of the bed, he slid inside.

As soon as the mattress depressed again beneath his weight, she tossed back the bedclothes. "Fine. Then *I'll* sleep on the sofa."

Moving more quickly than she could have imagined, he reached over and caught her wrist. "No, you're not. No one is sleeping on the damned sofa. Now come back here and get in bed."

Leaning back on her heels, she tugged against his hold. "Let me go."

"I will. As soon as you stop being ridiculous. It's not as if we haven't shared a bed before."

No, it wasn't. But her reaction had nothing to do with modesty and everything to do with emotion. When she'd slept with him before, she'd done so out of love, letting him inside both her body and her heart out of the mistaken belief that he returned her affection. But sleeping with him now would be like inviting a stranger into her bed. A stranger who might have the same face and form as the man she'd loved, but not the same spirit.

She was about to refuse him again when he leaned up on his knees and used his other hand to catch her around the waist. Ignoring her struggles, he tumbled her down, settling her beneath him.

For a few seconds, she couldn't breathe, her heart threatening to beat out of her chest. Jack surrounded her, his body covering hers like a living blanket — warm, strong and so vitally male that she didn't want to move. Forgetting herself for a moment, she savored the sensations, relishing his familiar scent and the ripe heat of his skin.

"We can stay like this all night," he said. "Or you can have one side of the bed and

I'll have the other. It's your choice."

Remembering herself again, she bucked against him, only then becoming aware of the arousal riding heavily between his legs.

"Keep that up," he warned, "and I'll be sleeping *in* you, not just on you. Again, it's entirely your choice."

But she knew his desire wasn't for her — not truly. He was a healthy man and would react that way to any woman lying half naked beneath him. He wanted sex. He didn't want her.

Throat tight with unshed tears, she shoved against his chest with both palms. "Get off me. I'll sleep here in the bed."

The slightest hint of disappointment seemed to flicker in his azure gaze, as if he'd hoped she would put up more of a fight and push matters further between them. But then the look was gone, likely nothing more than a trick of the candlelight, she decided.

"You're going to stay put?" he questioned.

"Yes," she panted. "I told you to get off me. You weigh a ton."

The edge of his mouth turned up in an unapologetic grin before he levered himself away.

Rolling onto her side, she turned her back to him and crossed her arms over her breasts. Closing her eyes, she did her best to ignore the yearning ache between her legs, hating herself for desiring him despite everything between them.

Meanwhile, he straightened the bedclothes, tossing them over both himself and her. Then he settled back, beating a fist into his pillow to get the proper shape.

"Good-night, Grace."

She said nothing, refusing to give him the satisfaction of an answer. Biting her lip to keep from crying, she willed herself to sleep.

Damn and blast, how can she sleep? Jack thought half an hour later. Worse, why had he insisted on sharing a bed with her when he was in absolute agony as a result? If he'd had any sense, he would have let her have her way and gone downstairs to sleep on the sofa. No matter how uncomfortable the furniture might be, at least he could have gotten a few minutes' rest. Instead, he was consigned to spending the night lying beside Grace, hard as a pikestaff and aching for release.

Not exactly the wedding night I'd planned. But then nothing about this marriage has turned out as I planned.

Slinging an arm across his face, he groaned, half hoping the sound would wake her. A look through his lashes confirmed it had not. Lowering his arm again, he gazed at her through the darkness and caught the subtle shimmer of her red hair, visible even in the low light.

Reaching out, he gathered up a waist-length strand and rubbed the silky ends between his fingers in a slow, measuring glide. Without giving himself time to think, he raised the tress to his nose and inhaled, closing his eyes as Grace's sweet rose-and-honey scent flooded his senses. He groaned again, wanting to slide closer and spoon in tight. Once there, he would slowly kiss her awake, listening to her throaty little sounds of pleasure as he roused her passions to a shattering peak.

But he'd told himself he would give her a few days to adjust to their changed circumstances. She might not like him very much at the moment, but she was still his wife. He was hoping that if he gave her a bit of space, she would come to terms with that fact and try to make their marriage work despite all her talk of separation.

And if she didn't?

Well, he would deal with that later. Who knows, maybe he would be relieved by an amicable split a few months from now. In the past, he'd always tired of his lovers, no matter how beautiful or adept in bed they might be. So why should Grace be any different?

She won't, he realized with an odd sense of sadness. *It's simply a matter of time until this hunger for her fades.* But until it did, he wanted her. And he meant to have her again. All he needed to do was let time and desire weave its spell, and she would be back in his arms.

I seduced her once. I can seduce her again.

Only this time there would be no lies between them and nothing to hide, no need for pretense or artifice of any kind. When they made love again, they would come together out of naked desire — and find pure, sizzling ecstasy along the way.

Until then, however, he was in for some very long, very frustrating nights.

Releasing her long strand of hair, he gazed at her recumbent form for a few moments more. Jaw clenched and groin aching in abject misery, he turned his back on her and closed his eyes.

CHAPTER 19

Jack was gone when she awakened the next morning.

Apparently he'd been telling the truth when he'd said that all he'd wanted to do was sleep and nothing else. Honestly, she should be grateful for his lack of interest, and for the fact that he'd obviously had no difficulty forgoing the exercise of his husbandly rights with his new bride on their wedding night.

Not that she would have let him exercise those rights, but still, he might have tried a little harder.

Knowing that he hadn't, merely demonstrated that she'd been right about his calculating motivations. Nevertheless, the knowledge came as cold comfort. It was one thing to suspect he cared for nothing but her money. It was quite another to know for sure. With her chest tight, she tossed back the covers and rang for her maid.

An hour later, she descended the stairs dressed in a warm cerise kerseymere day dress that ought to have clashed with her hair but amazingly enough did not. The gown had been a suggestion of her new mother-in-law, who had an eye for such daring fashion choices.

With a newspaper folded open beside his nearly empty plate, Jack glanced up from his seat at the dining table when she entered the room. "Good morning," he said in an even tone.

Unable to bring herself to return the greeting verbally, she gave a brief nod, then moved to the sideboard, where a pair of silver chafing dishes were arranged.

While she helped herself to a slice of toast and a single, coddled egg, Jack returned to reading his paper. He looked up again when she took a seat at the far end of the table.

"Is that all you're having?" he asked, his blue eyes looking critically at her selection.

Taking up her fork, she thrust the tines into her egg with a defiant stab, letting the warm, orange yolk run over the bread. "It is. Yes."

He stared for another moment, then turned a page of his paper.

A maid entered the room with a fresh pot of tea. After pouring a cup for Grace and refreshing Jack's, the girl left the pot on the table, then departed once more.

Silence descended.

Jack sipped his tea and read his paper, while she applied herself to her breakfast.

"Is there anything you'd like to do today?" he inquired after she ate the last bite.

With him, does he mean? A little frown creased the skin between her brows. "No."

He met her gaze for a few seconds. "Fine. I'll be in the library, then. Reading." Draining the last of the tea from his cup, he stood and walked from the room.

Her shoulders sank the instant he was gone, misery sweeping through her like a cold wind. And cold was certainly right, she decided. The atmosphere between them was as frosty as the January day outside. How would she ever bear living with him like this for the next four weeks?

With halfhearted enthusiasm, she went upstairs to retrieve a few sheets of sketch paper, then quickly returned back downstairs again. Inside the parlor, she took a seat in front of the window and attempted a pencil rendering of the winter-shrouded grounds and attractive outbuildings. The results were so dismal, however, that she ended up tossing them all into the fireplace, where the flames turned the evidence to ash.

Returning to the bedroom, she tried next to take a nap but managed no more than a fitful, unsatisfying doze. Ringing for her maid, she bathed, then dressed in another of the new gowns from her trousseau — a watered peach satin that made a sibilant whispering sound as she moved.

Since they were keeping country hours, dinner was served early. Taking a seat across from Jack in the dining room, they ate in near silence, neither of them making more than a few attempts at conversation. Once the meal was over, he withdrew again to the library.

Then it was time for bed.

Her maid helped her into her nightgown and robe before withdrawing for the evening. Briefly, Grace considered taking a blanket and pillow and going downstairs to sleep on the sofa. But knowing Jack, he would probably just make her return upstairs as soon as he realized she was missing.

Still, something inside her rebelled at the notion of climbing meekly into bed while she waited for him to join her — even if all he wanted to do was sleep! Taking a book to keep herself entertained, she padded across to the large armchair positioned near the fireplace and settled inside.

She roused a long while later to the sensation of his arms coming around her, the fire burned so low the room was cast in heavy, nearly black shadows.

"Hush," he murmured in his deep, divine voice. "I'm just going to carry you over to the bed."

". . . sleep here in the chair," she mumbled.

"Sleep in this chair and you'll wake up with a sore neck."

Too tired to protest further, she let him gather her into his strong arms. Moments later, cool sheets and downy soft feathers enveloped her as she sank onto the mattress. Covers were pulled up around her, his big hands tucking her in tight so that warmth spread through her body with a toasty bliss.

She was floating on the edge of sleep when his fingers brushed her cheek and combed the hair away from her face. She sighed in contentment, vaguely aware as his lips pressed lightly against her own. And then she knew nothing else.

Again, he was gone when she awakened, early morning light creeping gently beneath the curtains. If not for the rumpled bedclothes and the imprint of his head on his pillow, she wouldn't have thought he'd slept next to her at all.

She questioned her assumption again when she descended for breakfast and found him as quiet and reserved as he'd been the day before. And yet she knew she'd fallen asleep in the armchair, so it couldn't have been a dream. Could it? Touching her fingers to her lips, she wondered which parts were real and which ones were not.

The day continued much as the one before, with Jack disappearing into the library for hours, while she occupied herself alone — first embroidering and then reading. They met for dinner, their conversation confined to casual small talk and observations about the meal.

Then bedtime arrived once more.

Stubbornly, she sought out the armchair again, where she sat reading until her fingers grew limp on the pages and her eyelids too heavy to remain open. She dreamed of him carrying her to bed and kissing her as he settled her between the sheets.

But exactly as before, he was gone come morning.

And so it went for the next three days, each one slower and more tedious than the last.

Pouring himself a brandy, Jack paced inside

the night-darkened library and wondered how much more waiting he could take.

After nearly a week, he'd hoped Grace would relent and show signs of wanting to end the stalemate between them. To his increasing frustration, however, she appeared completely content with the situation, apparently happy as she engaged in the solitary activities with which she occupied herself each day.

As for himself, he'd read a lot of books, but not nearly as many as she must think. Instead, he spent most of each afternoon in the library, sleeping — often exhausted after spending a restless night lying next to her in bed, his body aroused to the point of near pain.

He supposed he was a fool not to simply take her as he wished. But even knowing he was capable of rousing her natural passions to the fore, he didn't want her accusing him of taking advantage of her when her defenses were down. No, he'd promised to give her time. It's just that he wasn't sure how much more time he could grant her.

Tossing back in a single gulp the brandy he'd poured, he set down the glass and strode out of the library. Opening the bedroom door across the hall, he slipped into the darkened room on silent feet. As he had every night before, he expected to find Grace curled up in the armchair in front of the fire. But for once the chair was empty and she was asleep in their bed.

His stomach tightened in surprise, even as his shaft stiffened with approval. Walking close, he stopped and gazed down at her.

How lovely she was, her fair skin flushed from sleep, her fiery hair tousled around her head. She slept deeply on her side, her lips relaxed and slightly open, as though she was waiting to be kissed.

And perhaps she is, he mused.

With his throat already bare from having removed his cravat earlier, he reached for his shirt and pulled it off over his head. Slipping out of his shoes and trousers, he left them where they fell, then crawled between the sheets.

Sliding near, he wrapped his arms around Grace so that he was settled behind her, his knees tucked in close to hers. Letting his hand rest where it seemed most natural, he cupped one full, luscious breast in his palm. His eyes closed in acute pleasure.

He sucked in a harsh breath as she shifted against him in her slumber, her bottom rubbing briefly against his throbbing shaft. Good thing he'd left on his drawers, or else he wouldn't have been able to stop himself from opening her thighs and thrusting into her right then and there.

Instead he kept a tight leash on his needs, willing himself to do nothing more than hold her for the present. He would let her decide what came next. If she awakened, he would make love to her. If she didn't, he would let her sleep.

For now.

Grace came slowly awake, cradled in a blissful cocoon of warmth and relaxation. Sighing contentedly, she snuggled closer to the wondrous source of heat, pressing her face more fully into the pillow beneath her cheek. Strangely enough, though, the goose feathers didn't dip but remained smooth and firm in a way that wasn't pillowlike at all.

Her nose twitched as something soft tickled it. Reaching up, she rubbed the itch, then settled back. As she did, she became aware of two things at once — that the solid warmth beneath her thigh was shaped a great deal like a leg, and that her pillow was breathing.

Her sleepiness fell away, her eyes opening to find a shadowy, dawn light just beginning to filter into the room. She leaned upright — or at least she tried to lean upright — but found herself unable to move more than a single inch due to the long, muscular, male arm draped across her shoulders.

Tipping back her head, she encountered Jack's heavy-lidded, blue-eyed gaze.

Shock radiated through her in an electrical tingle as she realized that he was awake and watching her. Even worse was the fact that the two of them were literally entwined, her breasts and stomach pressed against his side, while one of her legs rode his thigh, her calf trapped beneath his own hair-roughened one. As for her nightgown, the material had ridden up so that the hem barely covered her naked bottom.

Somehow, without her awareness, she'd obviously sought him out during the night, curling around him like a vine while she'd slumbered. Mortified, she tried to pull away. "I-I'm sorry. I didn't realize . . . that is, I didn't mean to . . . to . . ."

"Sleep on me?" he drawled, his words slow and husky.

Opening her mouth, she tried to speak, but nothing came out. She nodded instead.

"Don't worry." He smiled. "You make a very nice blanket."

Shifting again, she waited for him to release her.

Instead, he kept his arm looped over her shoulders. "Go back to sleep. It's barely dawn."

Sleep? There was no possible way she could sleep now, even if it was too early to begin the day. "I . . . I'm not tired."

"Are you not?" His palm settled on the back of her bare thigh and stroked in an easy circle. "I'm not either."

Her pulse pounded in a heavy rhythm. "You should let me go."

"Should I?" His hand moved higher, fingers gliding just under the edge of her nightgown. "Are you sure?"

For a long moment she couldn't answer, a lassitude stealing through her that made it hard to remember exactly why it was wrong for her to lie here with him like this. "Y-yes."

"You don't sound terribly sure. Maybe you need to reconsider."

Spearing the fingers of his other hand into her hair, he held her steady as he used gentle pressure to lower her head and claim her mouth. With a finesse that made her shiver, he parted her lips and eased his tongue inside. Hot, wet, and silky, he led her into a realm of dark temptation, as he ravished her mouth with a lazy thoroughness that sent her thoughts spinning out of control. Enthralled, she could do nothing but hold on, helpless against the stunning bliss of his touch. Then his palm slid higher to caress her naked bottom.

On a breathless gasp, she tore herself away. "Stop."

"Stop what?" His words were slurred with passion.

"This. Now l-let me go."

"Why?"

She stared at him for a long moment. "You know why."

"Actually, I don't," he said in a reflective tone. "Since I know you used to enjoy" — he gave her buttocks a very light squeeze and smiled — *"this."*

"That was before," she admonished, pressing her palms against his chest in an effort to break away.

Stronger by far, he kept her easily anchored in place. "Ah, yes. *Before.* Then again, given the fact that we are married now, it seems to me we're free to do anything we like in this bed."

"Anything *you* like, you mean," she retorted. "I told you not to touch me, and I haven't changed my mind. You got what you wanted the day we wed. I refuse to be your plaything again simply because you've decided you're randy and I'm convenient."

"Convenient! Is that what you are?" He let out a hollow laugh. "It seems to me you've been deuced *inconvenient,* madam. I'd have gotten as much satisfaction from squeezing a stone as I've had from you this past week."

Her mouth thinned. "I don't know why you're complaining. It's not as if you really want me. Any female would do."

He arched a brow. "Is that right? Then I guess I've been denying myself for nothing. By your measure, I should have ridden into the village and availed myself of one of the local girls by now. I'm sure there must be one or two willing to service me. Maybe I ought to go now and see if I can find a milkmaid who wouldn't mind providing an extra bit of cream with her morning chores."

She restrained a gasp at his deliberate crudeness, her chest aching at the idea of him with another woman. "Yes, perhaps you should." Refusing to lower her gaze, she waited for him to set her aside and leave.

Instead, he kept her locked in his arms. "Unfortunately, I don't want a milkmaid, or any other woman. I want you."

"No, you don't," she said with patent skepticism.

"Do I not?" He drew his palm over the curve of her bottom, then along the top half of her thigh.

She trembled but held herself resolute against him. "Attraction isn't the reason you pursued me. If not for the debt you owed my father, you would never have sought me out. You would never have given me so much as an extra glance."

His gaze turned rueful, but he didn't look away. "It's true that I might not have sought you out, but I would definitely have given you more than one look. From our very first meeting that day at Hatchard's, I knew I had to have you. I desired you, Grace, and my interest was never feigned. I tried to tell you as much before, but you wouldn't listen."

No, she hadn't been much for listening then, not after she'd learned the truth about everything. Nor had she been inclined to believe a great deal of what he'd had to say since then. And yet, against her better judgment, she did think he was being sincere now. Even so, could she afford to trust him? Or was this just another one of his devious games?

"We'll be living together for the next few months while we act like contented newlyweds," he continued. "Given that, things are likely to get awfully wearisome if we're constantly at daggers drawn. Why not make the best of the situation and call a truce?"

She lifted an eyebrow. "You want a truce, do you?"

"Yes. Most particularly in the bedroom." His fingers inched toward the small of her back, pausing to draw clever little circles over a spot where she was extremely sensitive.

Damn him for knowing about that spot, she thought as she arched involuntarily beneath his touch. Her heart hammered, telltale moisture gathering between her thighs.

"It's not as if we'd be breaking any rules," he pointed out with husky persuasion. "Quite the contrary, in fact, since our union is sanctioned by the laws of both God and man. So why deny ourselves? Why not enjoy what pleasure we can find?"

She stared at him, considering. "So, you want to be lovers?"

His blue eyes darkened. "Don't you?"

A shiver went through her at the idea. To her chagrin, she realized that she was tempted. "For how long?"

One brow arched upward. "For as long as the arrangement suits us both."

"And when I decide to leave? When I no longer want to be your wife or your lover, what then?"

His hand stilled. "You'll be free to go,

exactly as promised."

"So this . . . *arrangement* will really just involve sex?" she challenged.

A small silence fell. "That's right. Just sex."

She swallowed and glanced away.

Should I do it? she wondered.

More to the point, could she do it? Could she be his paramour and nothing else? If she agreed, she had no doubt he would bring her exquisite pleasure. He was a superb lover — a powerful, virile man with a strong sexual appetite. She would have no cause for complaint in his bed. But if she said yes, would she merely be giving in to his will? Allowing him to find yet another means of controlling and using her?

On the other hand, if this was strictly about sex, then maybe she would be gaining as much as she gave. Maybe she would be using *him,* taking advantage of *him* for her own physical gratification. As he said, they were married, so why not indulge? Why not get something out of this cold-blooded union other than an empty bed and an endless string of lonely nights?

But what about her feelings?

What feelings? she scolded herself, brutally casting aside the question. The instant she'd read those settlement papers, her love for him had died.

In fact, she was ashamed now to think of how she'd felt then, to know what a gullible, innocent simpleton she'd been to fall so easily for his blandishments and his lies.

Well, she wasn't innocent anymore. Her eyes were fully open now, and she saw him for precisely what he was. A gorgeous, charming, heartless rake, who liked to play cards and pleasure women.

Should I let him pleasure me?

"So?" he drawled. "What do you say?"

Slowly, she met his gaze, wavering on the thin edge of indecision. Then, before she gave herself too much time to think, she plunged ahead. "Yes," she said, casting herself into passion's abyss.

He grinned, his smile wide and wicked.

"This changes nothing, though," she stated in a deliberate voice. "I want there to be no misunderstanding about the fact that I still hate you."

His grin fell away, his eyes turning hard. "Hate me all you want, but don't ever try to deny that you love doing this with me."

In a devastating move, he stroked his hand over her naked bottom, then slid a pair of fingers deep into her aching core. Her spine arched, instant bliss flooding her system.

Cupping the back of her head, he drew

her down for a torrid kiss, ravishing her mouth without mercy as he drove her passion high. Her breath came in panting little gasps, her body shuddering as he pushed her relentlessly closer to her peak. She waited, needing the release she knew he could give her, hungry for the oblivion only he could provide.

And suddenly she was flying, shattering into a million tiny pieces as rapture spread through her in a hot molten flow. She moaned and shook, pleasured beyond any coherent form of expression.

She'd barely begun to recover when he started again, driving her up in a way that was just short of agony. Biting her lip, she fought to retain some faint sense of control, struggled not to lose herself completely beneath the mastery of his touch.

He scattered a line of kisses across her cheek, then paused to catch her earlobe between his teeth. "Tell me, Grace."

"What?" she panted, half-dazed.

"Tell me how much you love this," he demanded, as he continued pleasuring her with unrelenting intensity. "Admit that you adore every wild, wanton thing I make you feel. That you couldn't bear it if I stopped."

And he was right, she did love it. And she would be devastated if he stopped. But he had to know that already, since her body was quite literally weeping from the ecstasy he'd given her, and was giving her still. Yet pride demanded she not say the words, no matter how true they might be. Clamping her lips shut, she closed her eyes.

"No answer, hmm?" he said. "Let's see just how long that lasts."

Suddenly and without warning, he withdrew his fingers.

For a terrible moment, she feared he really was going to stop. Instead, he rolled her over on her back and shoved her nightgown to her waist. Sliding his palms under her buttocks, he spread her legs open and settled his broad shoulders in between.

Quivering with relief, she waited in eager anticipation for him to take her.

Instead, he bent low, sliding down her body so that his head was positioned between her thighs. And then, he kissed her where she'd never imagined she could be kissed.

Her hips arched off the mattress, as though she'd been struck by a bolt of lightning. Acting on instinct, she tried to shift away, but his powerful hands held her in place, forcing her to accept his shocking, astonishing embrace.

Reaching down, she tried to push him

aside, her entire body suffused with heat and mortification. But he wouldn't let her go, instead opening her wider as she squirmed against him. Only then did she realize that he'd positioned her for maximum access, leaving her helpless to resist whatever it was he had planned.

Her heart hammered in violent beats as he licked her, sweeping his tongue over her swollen flesh in a way that made her writhe. She shuddered and moaned, unable to keep herself from responding. Then he began to suckle too, pausing to kiss and lave her in between, employing a merciless rhythm that made her burn hotter than she'd ever burned before.

Held in complete thrall, she surrendered abruptly, her need too profound to deny. Instead of resisting, she began to urge him on, no longer the least bit interested in having him stop.

Flinging her arms over her head, she gripped the headboard. The wood creaked beneath her grasp, moans coming from her throat that she was helpless to control.

With each caress, he brought her higher. With every new sensation, he forced her closer to the edge. Yet every time she thought she was on the brink, sure that the very next touch would be one that sent her toppling over, he would let her slide back, easing off just enough to deny her. Then he would begin again, tormenting her until she feared she was close to madness.

And that's when she realized what he was doing.

That's when she knew he was going to make her beg.

She whimpered as he forced another helpless moan from her lips.

Moments later, he paused and raised his head, meeting her gaze across her recumbent form. "Did you say something?"

"N-no," she whispered, shuddering at the cessation of his caresses.

"Oh. My mistake. Shall I continue?"

Continue tormenting her, he meant. Still, how could she say no?

"Please, Jack."

"Please what?"

Despite their intimacy, she felt her cheeks flush. "Y-you know."

"I'm sorry. I'm afraid you'll have to be more specific."

She blushed more and groaned. "Don't do this."

"Do what?"

"T-torment me."

"Is that what I'm doing? I thought I was pleasuring you."

"You are, but you're not letting me —"

"Letting you what?" he drawled in a devil's voice.

"God, I don't know how much more I can take."

His eyes darkened. "Oh, you can take more. A lot more. Then again, just say the words and I'll give you what you want. Tell me how much you need this from me. Tell me how much you love this from me."

Still, even aching and desperate as she was, the words didn't want to come.

His jaw tightened. "Perhaps you need a bit more incentive."

Before she could react, he leaned down and located a particularly delicate bit of flesh with his tongue. Drawing it farther into his mouth, he suckled intently. She shuddered, bucking in his hold, only seconds away from completion.

Then, as suddenly as he'd begun, he drew away.

"Aaaaagh," she cried. "God, don't stop."

"Why not? Is it because you like it?"

"Y-yes," she whimpered.

"Is it because you love it?"

"Y-yes," she admitted, her voice and willpower breaking beneath the strain. "Yes, I love it. I absolutely adore it. Now, I swear to God if you don't tup me, Jack Byron,

I'm going to do something diabolical to *you.*"

"Diabolical, hmm?" he said with a devilish grin. "Maybe I'll let you try that later. For now, I believe you have a reward coming. Or should I say, you'll get your reward *by* coming."

Diving low again, he used his mouth to send her senses whirling like a maelstrom. Her blood beat hot and fierce, passion crashing through her in wild, heady draughts that made her half mad with longing.

She started to worry that he was toying with her again, when suddenly he did something with his teeth and tongue that was so utterly shattering her mind went completely blank for a brief while. Rapture exploded inside her, bliss pouring into every nerve ending and sinew in her body. Moaning loudly, she shook violently within his grasp. Then she plummeted back to earth, lying limp and breathless as she floated on a sea of pure delight.

Jack didn't give her long to recover. Rising up on his knees, he pulled her closer.

"My turn now," he murmured in a velvety rasp.

Hooking her legs high around his waist, he took a moment to position her before thrusting inside her in one long, deep stroke. A harsh gasp sighed from her mouth, as his powerful penetration filled her completely, his shaft stretching her nearly to her limits.

But her body didn't seem to mind, responding with an instant, yearning surge of hunger that surprised her with its strength. As improbable as it seemed, she wanted him again.

Desperately.

Dark need claimed her as he began to thrust, his powerful rhythm setting up an almost frantic ache inside her. Reaching up, she caught his head in her hands and pulled him down for a wet, rapacious kiss. The move pushed him deeper, making both of them groan with delight.

He seemed to go a little wild then, clutching her hips more firmly to take her with fast, deep, unbridled strokes. She held on, held him, taking his mouth with more fervid, open-mouthed kisses, whose frenzy he seemed quite happy to match.

This time, when she screamed out her release, the sound was muffled against his lips, her body trembling still as he poured himself inside her less than a minute later.

Together, they sank backward, the mattress bouncing a little as they settled into a tangle of warm, damp flesh and utter satisfaction. For long minutes, she couldn't speak, content to do nothing but drift, too peaceful to move even so much as an inch.

At length, he raised his head and met her gaze. Bending close, he gave her a kiss that was soft, slow and sweet.

Before she could decide how to respond, he eased away, a wave of cool air rushing in to take his place. Shivering, she reached for the covers, only then realizing that her nightgown was bunched up around her breasts.

Pushing the material down over her hips and legs, she sat up. As she did, she cast a glance over her shoulder and saw him lying on his back, asleep.

Dismissed already and so quickly too. Then again, perhaps she was being too harsh and he was merely tired.

Either way, though, a new chill burrowed into her bones.

Turning her back on him, she curled into a ball on her side and pulled the covers high. Nearly an hour passed before she finally found her own rest.

Chapter 20

For Grace, the next three weeks passed by with an odd sense of duality. Much as they had during their first week of residence at the honeymoon cottage, she and Jack shared formal meals in the dining room. Their conversation improved in frequency, but it remained confined to innocuous small talk and a range of impersonal topics that never seemed to delve much below the surface.

During the day, the two of them separated to engage in a variety of solitary pastimes — Jack often riding out on a swift-footed roan gelding he'd received as a wedding gift from Edward, while she painted, read, or sewed. Occasionally, they shared a long walk around the grounds or drove into the nearby village to do a bit of sightseeing and visit the shops. But the weather was frequently dreary and cold, encouraging them to spend a great deal of their time tucked warm and snug inside.

Otherwise when they weren't sleeping, they had sex — and lots of it.

After that first coupling, they'd wiled away the next day separately. But when bedtime arrived, so did Jack, yanking off the nightgown her maid had just helped her into before tumbling her down onto the mattress. Near dawn, he awakened her again for another energetic bout that left her exhausted and sleeping until almost noon.

And thus began a pattern of sorts, since she could count on him to take her each morning and at least once every night.

He wasn't always content with just those encounters, however, surprising her at unusual times to sweep her off her feet and into bed.

And then there were the occasions when he didn't even bother with a bed, instead finding inventive ways to try out various pieces of furniture around the house.

He took her in a chair in the study one afternoon, and another time on the chaise. Once he came upon her in the main room and bent her over the sofa, tossing her skirts up around her shoulders so that he could thrust himself into her from behind.

But the occasion that remained most vivid in her memory was the morning after breakfast when he locked the door and laid her atop the dining table. There, among the uncleared pots of tea and jam, he proceeded to enjoy a "second repast," as he dubbed it. Stripping her bare, he'd anointed her skin with dollops of honey and preserves before eating them off her quivering flesh with agonizing slowness. In the end, he'd left her lax and glowing, her body sticky but thoroughly satisfied.

No matter how often he came to her though, she never denied him. Nor did she wish to, thrilling to his every kiss and caress, grateful that he never left her anything but completely fulfilled.

Still, she never sought him out of her own volition, nor initiated any of their couplings, even though she had no doubt he would have welcomed her advances. And although she gave him free access to her body, she refused to let him back into her heart, closing off that part of herself with an implacable firmness.

But their honeymoon was nearly done now, and her maid was busy packing the last of her belongings for the journey home to London.

Dressed this morning in a soft, dark blue woolen traveling gown, Grace stood at the bedchamber window and gazed out at fields turned white from an overnight dusting of snow.

Not far in the distance, a small flock of brown sparrows had landed and were hopping to and fro in search of hidden seed. With only partial attention, she noted their efforts, until some noise startled them and off they flew in a rush.

"That's the rest of it, milady," her maid announced as she closed the fastenings on Grace's valise. "Will there be anything else yer needing?"

Needing? Yes, a great many things, Grace thought, but nothing this girl could possibly provide. "No, thank you," Grace said with a quick glance. "Carry that below, please, and I shall be down in a minute." Bobbing a curtsey, the servant gathered the case and left. Not long after, Grace heard a set of footfalls in the hallway and thought perhaps her maid had returned.

Instead, a glance showed her that it was Jack who stood in the doorway, looking tall and resplendent in his dark, many-caped greatcoat. Moving with the lean stride of a cat, he walked into the room, his booted feet making barely a sound on the wooden floors. "I came to see if you're set to leave?" he stated. "The coach is in the drive with the horses standing at the ready."

She took a few last moments to gaze out the window before turning around. Crossing to the dresser, she picked up her gloves and drew them on. "We can depart whenever you choose. Just let me don my pelisse and we'll go."

He waited quietly while she retrieved the garment. Before she could put it on, though, he stepped close and took it from her.

"Allow me," he said, holding up the long, emerald green wrap.

After the faintest hesitation, she let him assist her into the pelisse. When he was done, he turned her around to face him, his fingers moving to fasten the buttons.

"I can do it," she said, trying to brush his hands aside.

But he refused to let her, working the second button through its corresponding buttonhole before she gave up trying to prevent him from doing so.

"You look beautiful this morning," he said. "These colors become you. They make your cheeks glow."

Once she would have melted to hear him say such things. Now, they only turned her cold.

"Must you do that?" she said before she could stop herself.

One mahogany brow winged upward. "Do what?"

She paused before continuing. "*That.* Attempt to flatter me. I'd rather you didn't. If you want something, you have only to ask."

His brows creased into a scowl. "I don't *want* anything at the moment. I was merely making an observation."

"Well, you needn't bother. As I've told you before, I have no use for false praise and am quite familiar with my own shortcomings. Pray don't feel that you need to cajole me."

"I am not *cajoling* you. And I resent the implication that I'm trying to manipulate you for some nefarious purpose." His face turned stiff, his eyes flashing a bright, infuriated blue. "And if I say you're beautiful, then by God, that's exactly what you are."

She locked gazes with him for a long moment before looking away. A sharp quiet fell between them.

"You don't believe me, do you?" he said.

"Whether I do or not, I scarcely see how that matters. Now, we should be going." Edging around him, she moved toward the door.

He moved faster and shut it before she could pass through, then leaned back against the painted wood. "I thought we'd ceased hostilities on this subject and that you understood I never deceived you —"

Her eyes narrowed.

"— that I never *misled* you about anything other than the situation with your father and the motivation for our marriage."

"Do not start this again, Jack."

"And have you imagining that every other word I utter is an untruth? That you can't even believe me when I give you a simple compliment? What has become of our truce?"

"Our truce remains intact. However, that's all it is — a truce, not a surrender. You ask too much of me if you think otherwise."

"And you ask too little of yourself if you assume any praise I might offer you to be false. What reason would I have to lie about such a thing? What could I possibly hope to gain when, by your measure, I already have everything I want?"

His words sank in as she considered them, realizing that he *did* have everything he wanted. He even had her in his bed, as often as he liked, so why would he need to compliment her out of hand?

In the next moment, she acknowledged the underlying problem. She realized that learning of his bargain with her father had destroyed more than her trust in him; it had undermined her faith in herself as well. For a time, when she'd been happy during their engagement, she'd let her old insecurities go. But they'd come back more strongly than ever once she'd discovered the truth. Yet maybe he was right and she was being unkind to herself. Maybe it was time to lay those particular demons to rest once and for all.

"Very well," she conceded. "In future, I shall attempt not to ascribe ulterior motives to any compliment you may choose to give me. If you say I look pretty in a particular color, then I look pretty."

"Beautiful," he murmured gently. "You look beautiful."

Her skin warmed, finding herself pleased in spite of her best efforts not to be.

"Now, was that so dreadful?" he asked, stepping forward to take her in his arms.

"Only somewhat dreadful," she replied.

A laugh rumbled from his chest. Still laughing, he bent his head and kissed her.

Sighing with a delight she couldn't deny, she closed her eyes and let him take her deeper. Before she knew it, he was waltzing her backward toward the bed. They came down on the mattress swathed in a mass of winter wool.

Still plundering her mouth in a way that made her pulse race, he began unfastening the buttons of the pelisse he'd only recently fastened with such dedication.

"Didn't you say the coach is waiting?" she asked with a breathless catch in her voice.

"Let it wait."

"What about the horses? Won't they be awfully restive?"

"Not as restive as I will be if I don't have you." The garment now open, he went to work on her skirts, pushing her heavy traveling gown and petticoats to her waist. "Now, you were saying?" he asked, as he stroked a hand up her inner thigh.

Reaching down to help him unbutton his falls, she smiled. "Nothing. I wasn't saying a thing."

London was the same, and yet to Grace the city felt completely different, strangely askew and just a bit foreign. During her first month's residency at the town house on Upper Brook Street, she attributed the sensation to the fact that everything was new.

New house.

New neighborhood.

New servants.

Not to mention a new husband with whom she was trying to find a tolerable balance.

But as she gradually began to adjust, she realized that her discomfort stemmed from more than ordinary change and the tenuous nature of her relationship with Jack. Instead, it came from the fact that her entire life was different now. Her old existence, for good or ill, was gone forever. She was alone in a new world, and striving each day to make it her own.

Huffing out a breath, she gazed at the small cluster of cards Jack's butler — *her* butler — had carried into the drawing room for her perusal. The cards had started arriving by messenger a few days ago — invitations that she had no real idea how to answer.

Jack was little help, telling her to accept the ones she liked and toss the rest into the fire. But therein lay her dilemma. She didn't know one from the other, since the invitations were all from strangers. Strangers, at least, to her.

She'd just finished opening the newest arrivals and was preparing to add them to the growing stack of unanswered invitations she kept in a box on her writing desk when she heard someone enter the room.

"I told Appleton not to bother announcing us," declared Mallory Byron's lilting voice. "It would be silly, I thought, considering we're family. Poor man seemed so vastly disappointed, though, that I almost let him do it. But in the end, I just couldn't bear the formality."

Grace spun around, a smile spreading instantly over her lips. "Mallory! Your Grace! . . . I mean Mama! And Esme!" she added, noticing the willowy young girl standing just behind her mother. "What are you doing here? I had no idea you were even in the city."

"We weren't, not until last night." The dowager duchess walked forward, as elegant and lovely as always in an afternoon gown of puce silk. "We'd had enough of the country and decided to come to Town. I hope we're not intruding on you newlyweds too soon. We don't want to be a bother."

Grace shook her head. "Of course you're not a bother. Any of you."

"Then come and give me a hug."

Hurrying forward, Grace let herself be wrapped in the dowager's maternal arms, gladder to see her than she would have imagined possible. She and Mallory shared an embrace next, then Esme, all of them smiling at each other once they were done.

"Oh, it's so good to see you," Grace said. "Let me ring for tea."

"That would be lovely, dear," the dowager

said, as she crossed to take a seat on the sofa. Mallory followed to do the same, while Esme ran in a flash of skirts to the far side of the room, where she perched on the window seat in a patch of sun. Grace smiled as she saw her withdraw a piece of paper and a pencil from her pocket and begin to sketch.

"So, is Jack home?" Ava said, drawing Grace's attention back to her and Mallory.

"Um, no," Grace replied. "I'm afraid he's out."

She decided not to say more, hoping they wouldn't ask where he was, since she hadn't the faintest idea. Jack shared little information about his activities outside the house, and she made a point not to ask.

"Ah, well, I'm sure we shall see him soon," the dowager continued. "Besides, his absence will give us ladies more time to talk. Are those invitations, I see?"

"Yes, ma'am."

"You'd think they could give you and Jack a little more time alone before importuning you both, especially considering the fact that the Season doesn't begin for some weeks yet. Still, I'm sure every Society matron worth her salt is dying to make your acquaintance."

Grace felt tiny lines gather on her forehead. "You mean Jack's acquaintance."

Her mother-in-law smiled. "No, I mean *yours,* dear. Everyone already knows Jack."

Oh, mercy.

Grace gulped, her nerves tightening into a knot in her stomach.

Just then, a housemaid arrived with the tea, momentarily diverting everyone's attention. The dowager poured, while Grace handed around plates of biscuits. She took a moment to add an extra gingersnap to Esme's portion, since she knew the girl had a fondness for the spicy treat. Esme's eyes twinkled, her smile wide as she took the plate.

The four of them ate and sipped for a few minutes, talking of mostly inconsequential subjects.

At length, the dowager set her cup aside, while her youngest daughter drifted back across the room. "So which ones have you answered?"

"Which ones — ? Oh, of the invitations."

Ava cast an idle glance toward the little stack of cards on the side table, her gaze pausing for a long moment on a cream-colored vellum card with several lines of the spidery black handwriting scratched across its surface. "Hmm."

Grace noted the sound. "Your pardon, is

there something wrong with that one?"

The dowager gave a little shake of her head. "No, of course not, child. These matters are up to you to decide as Jack's wife. I don't wish to interfere."

For a moment, Grace worried a fingernail between her teeth, then plunged ahead. "Actually, I'd really rather that you did interfere," she said, sending a hopeful look toward the dowager and Mallory. "These have been arriving for days now, and I haven't the faintest clue how to respond."

Ava looked momentarily surprised, then her face relaxed. "I would be delighted to aid you, but only if you're sure."

"I'm very sure," Grace sighed, relief sweeping through her. "Here, let me get the rest."

The dowager and Mallory laughed when they saw the stack she retrieved. "Good heavens, all those? You poor dear, no wonder you're overwhelmed. Here, lay them all down and we'll be through them in two shakes of a lamb's tail."

And so the sorting began, Ava dividing the cards into "yes's," "no's" and "probably no's."

The dowager was down to the last of two invitations when she stiffened, her fingers tightening briefly against a card written in an elegant, flowing and obviously feminine hand. "Of all the nerve," she muttered under her breath. Firmly and without hesitation, she transferred the card into the "no" pile.

Curious now, Grace couldn't help but glance at the name, reading it upside down.

Philipa, Lady Stockton

"Why does Lady Stockton go in the 'no' pile?" she asked.

Her mother-in-law met her gaze for a long moment before looking away. "Because that is where she belongs. Now, don't concern yourself over her further. Although should you happen to encounter her over the course of the Season, I suggest you avoid her — politely, of course."

"I see." But Grace didn't see, not at all. "Is she so very dreadful then?"

The dowager paused. "No, not in the way you mean. She is good Ton. A very beautiful widow, who's received in all the best houses. It's just that . . . well, I've said more than enough."

But she hasn't said enough at all.

"Perhaps it would help if I knew *why* I should avoid her," Grace suggested. Ava paused again and said nothing. Mallory met

Grace's gaze, knowledge alive in her eyes. With a quick glance toward her little sister, who was occupied sketching across the room, she leaned forward. "It's because she and Jack used to be involved," she whispered.

"Mallory!" her mother scolded.

"Well, you've gotten her all curious now," Mallory replied, turning toward the dowager. "Besides, someone is bound to tell her. Better she hear it from us rather than letting some mean-spirited tattlemonger take delight."

Her mother scowled. "You, young lady, aren't even supposed to know about such matters."

"There are a great many things I am not supposed to know. Even so, I have ears and a brain, do I not?"

"Obviously too many of both," remarked her aggrieved mother. "So when you say involved," Grace interrupted, "you mean she is his —"

"*Mistress*, yes," Mallory whispered. "Oh, but she's not anymore. Jack ended it with her before he began courting you. So you mustn't be angry with him."

Mustn't? she thought.

Still, she had so many things to be angry with Jack over these days, what was one more? Actually, the fact that he'd had a beautiful widow for his mistress didn't surprise her. Grace was well aware that she was far from the first woman to be his lover. Why, knowing Jack, the city was probably littered with his former bedmates.

Her stomach rolled suddenly, making her wish she hadn't eaten that last biscuit with her tea. The reaction had nothing to do with what she'd just discovered, though, she assured herself. It's not that she minded his having former mistresses, it's just that she didn't particularly want to know about them. Certainly not by name!

Mallory and Ava sent her suddenly concerned looks.

She forced a smile. "Don't worry. I shan't be angry. With either of you or Jack."

Both women visibly relaxed.

"You know, I rather suspect Philipa Stockton is only curious about you," Ava stated in a soothing tone, "despite her astonishing audacity in issuing the invitation in the first place."

"Well, she can stay curious." Leaning over, Grace picked up the card. With an efficient movement, she ripped the fancy paper neatly in two. "This one is most definitely a 'no.' Now, are we back to the 'probably no's?' How shall we decide?"

Chapter 21

"My apologies, gentlemen, but I'm afraid I cannot stay." Jack set down his half-filled whiskey glass and prepared to rise from the eminently comfortable chair in which he'd been relaxing for the past two hours. Arranged around him in various other chairs inside the male-only environs of Brooks's Club sat a few of his friends.

A roar of complaint issued from their ranks at his pronouncement. "Come now, Jack," Niall Faversham said. "Surely you can spare a bit more time. It's barely evening."

"Exactly. It *is* evening and I need to get home."

"What he means," quipped Lord Howland as he slung a leisurely arm over the back of his chair, "is that he's *expected* home. Scarcely two months married and already he's been trained to obey the cat's paw."

Scowling, Jack rose to his feet. "Don't be stupid. I have a hot dinner and a warm fire waiting for me. I plan to enjoy them both in the comfort of my own residence."

"You can enjoy a hot dinner and a warm fire right here," drawled Tony Black, Duke of Wyvern. "You don't need to go home for either of those."

Adam, Lord Gresham, broke his silence. "Ah, but Brooks's Club doesn't offer the companionship of a lovely wife, now, does it? Nor the opportunity to take her upstairs after that hot supper is done. If I had what Byron does, I'd be going home now too."

Since none of the men could disagree, they gave up their attempts at further persuasion.

Jack accepted the easy escape and said his good-byes.

Leaving the club, he climbed into his coach and told the driver to take him home. As Gresham had pointed out, he did have a lovely wife at home. What he didn't know is whether she would be joining him for dinner or not.

Since arriving in Town, a new distance had arisen between them. At first he'd made an effort to escort her out for a few amusements. But she'd lived her entire life in London, so the customary diversions seemed largely to fall flat. They still took the occasional meal together, but during the day she was usually busy establishing the domestic routine of the house, while he occupied himself much as he had always done, with one important exception. He'd stopped playing cards for profit.

The money from Grace's father had given him the kind of financial stability he'd never known before. True, he hadn't lacked for the necessities, even without his gaming money, but now he no longer had to worry over every gold guinea that came and went from his pocket.

Even better, he was able to invest. If he listened to the sound advice of men like his father-in-law, and applied a measure of prudent management, his income should remain steady — or even increase — in the years to come.

And so ended the necessity of gaming for extra funds. Now when he played cards, it was strictly for fun, and never for anything but modest stakes. If the rumor was spreading that marriage was turning "Bad Jack Byron" dull, well, he could tolerate the remarks.

Of course there would be far more negative rumors and remarks if Grace went through with her plan to leave him at the end of the Season. Determined, however, to honor their agreement, he'd taken action to fulfill the terms of their secret addendum to the settlement not long after reaching Town.

Tucked safely now into a separate account at the Bank of England was Grace's promised sixty thousand pounds — structured so that only she would have control of the funds. And tomorrow he had an appointment to meet with a land agent who would search for a comfortable house in the country that he hoped would meet all of Grace's requirements.

As for her decision to separate permanently? Well, he would see how she felt a few months from now. He supposed he would see how he felt as well.

Arriving at the town house, he strode up the front steps, then inside.

"Good evening, your lordship," Appleton greeted, accepting Jack's coat and hat. "Raw night outside, if I may say."

"It is indeed," Jack agreed, thinking not only of the cold, damp night air but of the atmosphere inside the house as well. Depending on what Appleton revealed, he would see exactly how chilly it was bound to be.

"Is her ladyship about?" he asked.

"Milady is abovestairs. I believe she called

for a tray in her room about an hour since. Shall I send word to her of your arrival?"

Jack restrained a sigh. "No. Have a meal brought to my study, along with a bottle of burgundy. The '92, I believe."

"Right away, my lord."

Jack strode away, releasing the sigh still trapped in his chest the moment the servant was too far away to hear. Entering his study, he took care not to slam the door.

Grace awakened to the sensation of the mattress dipping at her back. Only partially conscious, she knew Jack had joined her, his warmth and the wonderful scent of his skin enveloping her only seconds before his arms did the same.

Lying on her side, too drowsy to speak, she didn't bother to open her eyes. Used now to the frequency of his possessions, she let him touch her as he pleased, his broad hands sliding beneath her nightgown to caress her with long, sweeping strokes that soon pulled a moan from her lips.

No matter how often he took her, she never got used to the sheer beauty of his touch — each time a new first, every encounter better than the one that had come before.

She tried to turn then, wanting his mouth

on hers. Instead he held her in place with an arm draped across her stomach, one of her breasts cradled in his palm. Finessing the tip until it drew up into a tight, aching peak, he moved on to her other breast to play there with tantalizing purpose.

Restless and abruptly needy, her breath quickened, her skin sizzling as he scattered hot kisses over her throat and cheek and ear. Closing his lips around her earlobe, he gave her a shiver-inducing bite before soothing her throbbing flesh with a warm, wet lick.

Shoving her nightgown higher, he inserted a heavy, masculine thigh between her legs. Then, holding her steady with his arm still cradled against her belly, he penetrated her in a long, deep thrust.

She groaned, their position making her exquisitely sensitive, as he rocked them together with increasingly harder, deeper strokes. Nudging her knee slightly upward, he thrust again and gained total possession, the move taking him as far as he could possibly go. He took her with a relentless rhythm, building the ache until she thought she might go mad.

Without warning, the fever broke, rapture claiming her in a sweeping torrent of delight. She clung, aware of him still thrusting fast and deep within her until he found his pleasure as well.

Skin damp beneath her tangled nightgown, she lay quivering and waited for her sanity to return.

He held her for a long while, until their flesh cooled and their breathing returned to normal. Sliding from her, he rolled away, turning onto his back so he could go to sleep.

Relaxed and drowsy again, she waited for sleep to embrace her too. It was only as she was drifting off that she realized neither of them had said a word through the whole of their coupling. Maybe in this one place, though, it was because no words were needed.

"Don't be nervous," Mallory whispered to Grace nearly seven weeks later, as they stood together in the marble-tiled entrance to the Clybourne House ballroom. "You're going to be brilliant."

"If you say so," Grace replied in an equally restrained tone.

The guests were due to arrive any minute now, the family gathered in preparation of their welcome. Grace only hoped her tongue didn't seize up when it came time to make the actual greetings.

Hosted by Edward and her mother-in-law, tonight's ball was being held in her honor as a dual celebration of the start of the new Season and her introduction to the Ton. As Jack's wife, she was expected to take a place beside him in the receiving line.

Glancing across the room, she found him talking with Edward and Cade. The three Byron men were all handsome, but to her, Jack far outshone his siblings. He was the epitome of masculine beauty, standing tall, dark, and dynamic in his stark black and white evening attire, his neatly combed hair already showing a charmingly rebellious bit of wave.

Her chest grew uncomfortably tight and she looked away.

"Of course I say so," Mallory reassured her, returning Grace's attention to the conversation at hand. "You look absolutely gorgeous in that gown. I only wish I were allowed to wear such a strikingly deep shade of green. But until Michael and I are wed, I shall have to content myself with the same old maidenly whites and pale pastels."

As soon as the words were out of her mouth, Mallory's smile faded, a wistful expression clouding her lovely aquamarine eyes.

Fully aware of the source of her discontent, Grace reached out and squeezed her gloved hand. "He'll be back soon, and you'll hear from him often. I'm sure he'll try to write you every day while he's gone."

"Exactly," Meg Byron stated, entering the conversation. "The military is generally very good about delivering the mail. No matter where Papa used to be assigned, his letters never failed to reach us. Often more reliably than the domestic post."

Mallory gave them both a weak smile. "I know you're right. It's just that I worry so about him down there in Spain." For a moment, the girl's gaze strayed to Cade. Grace and Meg were aware in which direction Mallory's thoughts had taken her, since her brother had nearly died of his war wounds. His limp served as a permanent reminder of the price he'd paid in service to his nation. It was only natural that she would be afraid for her fiancé.

As for Michael Hargreaves's departure, the major had received his orders shortly after he and Mallory had announced their engagement. They'd barely had time to celebrate their coming nuptials, when he'd been packing his kit and kissing her goodbye.

"The major is wise and won't take any unnecessary chances," Meg counseled.

"He'll come through just fine."

"Of course he will." Mallory forced another smile and nodded. "Still, my spirits are going to need buoying until he comes home. Until the last of this dreadful war is over and done."

"I shall cheer you at every possible opportunity," Grace pledged. Meg seconded her promise.

Lowering her gaze, Grace took a few seconds to collect her own suddenly scattered emotions, wishing she could ask for the same pledge.

Lord knows, I could use a measure of cheering myself these days. But since she was supposed to make everyone, including her new family, believe she was happy in her marriage, she had no one in whom she could confide her troubles.

With any luck, the busy pace of the Season would keep her mind occupied and her spirits out of the doldrums. And based on the way the last several weeks had flown by, she had good reason to hope.

A tingle traced over her skin just then, her body recognizing Jack's presence at her side, even before her mind did. Glancing up, she met her husband's gaze.

"Apparently, the first guests have arrived," he said, addressing the remark to them all.

"Mama says we are to take our places now." Offering his arm, he waited.

Grace accepted in silence, while Mallory moved to his opposite side. Cade appeared, bending to kiss his wife with visible affection before the pair started across the room. Seconds later, the rest of them followed.

The next hour went better than she'd imagined it might, her initial nerves quickly dissipating beneath the steady succession of curtseying, smiles, and banal chitchat. The exercise had become so routine by the end that she was almost relaxed.

Then Jack asked her to dance and her muscles drew up tight again.

"It's the expected thing for me to lead you out for the first set," he explained on a murmur only she could hear. "Never fear, I'll be careful not to step on your toes."

But her toes were the least of her worries. Spending the next half hour with him while the whole room looked on — that's what worried her.

"Maybe you're the one who should worry about getting stepped on, my lord," she said with a sudden spark of defiance.

Jack laughed, his smile so warm that anyone watching would have mistaken the expression for devotion.

Oh, how deceptive looks can be, she mused.

Allowing herself to be escorted into the ballroom, she and Jack mingled for a few minutes, furthering her acquaintance with several of the people she'd met earlier in the receiving line.

Then the first dance was called, and couples moved onto the dance floor to form a line for a contra dance. Facing Jack, Grace waited for the first notes to be struck.

True to his word, he didn't come close to stepping on her feet, his movements light and agile. But then she already knew what a superb dancer he was from the times they'd stood up together in Bath.

Memories of Bath curdled in her stomach, making it suddenly hard for her to maintain her happy expression.

"If you're not careful," he whispered to her during a turn, "people will think you're in pain."

"I'm smiling," she defended.

"Like a cadaver. Try something a bit less forced."

Glaring, she showed him her teeth.

He laughed again, then deliberately bobbled his step so that she tripped against him. Her eyes widened only seconds before he clutched her tight and pressed his mouth to hers. Her thoughts scattered in an instant, the music fading to a low hum as the pleasure of his kiss surged through her.

But just as abruptly as he'd drawn her to him, he released her again. "There," he stated, "that should set them all agog." Barely missing a beat, he resumed the intricate steps of the dance, while she struggled to do the same.

Heart fluttering, she realized she was rather agog herself. Hot color crept into her cheeks, embarrassment working to mask the other emotions churning inside her.

Recovering enough that she was able to continue dancing without shaming herself, she realized that his ploy had achieved its intended goal. No matter how she might appear to others at present, everyone would attribute her reaction to his audacious kiss. And they would not be far wrong.

When the music ended, she found the entire room watching them. But instead of disapproval, she discovered indulgent smiles and twinkling eyes. As he led her from the dance floor, she overheard someone whisper their astonishment over the fact that Lord Jack's marriage was clearly a love match, after all.

How foolish they would surely feel if only they knew the truth.

Jack escorted her to a quiet spot on the far side of the room. Grateful for the respite, she opened her fan and applied it to her still burning cheeks.

She was about to suggest that Jack go do something useful — like procure her a glass of punch, or perhaps soak his head in a bucket — when her father strolled into view.

"Well, aren't you two a sight!" Ezra Danvers declared with a toothy smile. "A right pair 'o lovebirds, if ever I did see."

Her fingers tightened against the delicate staves of her fan, but she mustered a smile nonetheless. "Papa."

Inviting her father to tonight's ball had been Ava's idea, a suggestion Grace had naturally had to support in spite of the resentment that still brewed inside her over his underhanded bargain with Jack.

Since returning to London, she'd seen little of her father, and not once had she visited the house on St. Martin's Lane. She'd used the excuse of being too busy in her new life to make the trip across Town. But in truth, she'd been afraid to go, fearing the welter of emotions that might rise up and spill over once she was surrounded again by old memories and familiar surroundings. She worried too that her unhappiness would show. Or that her simmering temper might cause her to reveal that she knew the whole of his and Jack's scheme.

Perhaps such revelations wouldn't matter at this point, but pride was a strange thing. Pride and the fact that she refused to give her father the opportunity to ever again interfere in her life.

To maintain the appearance of family harmony, she'd twice invited Papa to dinner at the town house, where he'd been one of a larger group of family and a few intimate friends. But he never stayed long, too "uncomfortable" around the Quality to be at his ease. So her real feelings and the truth about her marriage remained easy to conceal from him.

Actually, she was surprised he was even here tonight, considering his discomfort around members of the Ton. But apparently his puffed-up conceit at seeing her so well-placed in Society had overcome his reluctance to be in their exalted midst.

Striving to push aside such unkind musings, she waved her fan in languid arcs before her face, using it to distract both her father's attention and her own.

As though sensing her agitation, Jack laid a hand against her waist. Rather than pull away, she leaned into his touch, strangely glad of his support.

"If you aren't careful, yer going to get my girl talked about in the papers, my lord," her father admonished in a cheerful tone. "But it does my heart good to see the both of you so wild for each other. Why even now, you can hardly keep your hands off my Gracie. As for that spectacle on the dance floor . . .. well, I suppose there's no harm done, seeing yer married and all."

She continued waving her fan, by no means trusting herself to speak.

Luckily, Jack stepped into the breach. "You are most understanding, Mr. Danvers, since Grace is simply too sweet to resist. No man could wish for a better wife."

She lowered her gaze, an ache forming beneath her ribs to hear him utter such charming lies.

"Moment I laid eyes on you, Byron, I knew you were the one for my girl," her father continued. "It's good to be proven right. Now, I just need a few grandchildren."

Jack eased her even closer and smiled. "Not to worry. We are applying ourselves to the matter with great diligence."

Her father let out a booming laugh. "From what I've witnessed tonight, I can be assured of that."

Jack gave a reciprocating laugh. But even knowing she should, Grace couldn't bring herself to join them.

A couple of moments later, a tall, older gentleman joined them. If Grace remembered right, the man was one of Jack's paternal uncles. They all conversed for a brief time before his uncle asked if he could "steal" Jack away for a minute or two, leaving Grace alone with her father.

Waving her fan a little faster, she wondered how much longer it would be until dinner — not that she was hungry, but at least the meal would give her an excuse for new company. Something of her displeasure must have shown as her father met her gaze.

"Come now, don't poker up so," he said. "We were just teasing before. Never knew you to be so sensitive."

At first, she wasn't sure what he meant. Then she realized he was talking about his and Jack's recent conversation. Grabbing onto the topic, she used it as cover for her uncertain mood.

"I am not sensitive. I just don't think a ball is the place to discuss the subject of making grandchildren."

"Don't see why not," he chortled. "But if it discomposes you, then I won't say another word."

She gave him what she hoped was an appreciative smile.

Music filled the room as a new set began, couples moving with elegant form to the melody. She and her father watched in silence for a short time.

"Yer happy, aren't ye, Gracie?" he asked, thumbs tucked into his waistcoat as he rocked back and forth on his heels.

Her gaze shot to his. "Yes. Of course I'm happy."

He studied her for a moment before he relaxed. "Good, good. Because you know, I've never wanted anything but the best for you."

"Yes, Papa. I know."

"And I've never done anything that I didn't think would lead to your happiness."

Why is he saying this? Is he feeling guilty? she wondered.

"But I'm glad you're so happy. And I know ye are. Doesn't take a genius to see how much you love Byron. And he's clearly besotted with you. I'm just pleased it's all worked out so well."

And she realized that in his own opinionated, overbearing, high-handed way, he meant what he said. As wrong as his methods might be, in his mind what he'd done had been for her benefit. She would never be able to condone his actions, but she understood them. Perhaps she could even forgive them in time.

Suddenly, her anger fell away.

This time when she smiled, it wasn't forced. "You're right. It's all worked out as planned. Frightening as it may seem at times, this is my world now, the world to which you've always wanted me to belong. And now I do because of you and Jack. How could I possibly be anything but ecstatic?"

Yes, she thought sadly. *How indeed?*

Chapter 22

Grace had thought herself busy in the weeks leading up to Easter, but as she rapidly discovered, those days had been a leisurely rehearsal compared to the whirlwind that was *The London Season.*

From morning to night, her schedule was full, whether she was promised to attend a breakfast fête, an afternoon picnic, or an elegant evening soirée. In between, there were social calls and shopping expeditions, carriage rides and promenades in the park, and an occasional night at the theater or opera.

Having been taken beneath the collective wing of Ava, Meg and Mallory, Grace was content to abdicate the responsibility of deciding which invitations she would accept, while she learned to navigate the sometimes treacherous shoals of the Haut Ton.

To her great surprise, she found herself

warmly received by Society — although with the Byrons standing guard over her, most people would have been hard-pressed to attempt a cut, especially with Jack being her husband.

As for Jack himself, there were days when she saw a great deal of him, others when she saw almost nothing.

An excellent escort, he was always available to accompany her to whatever entertainment she chose. At balls, they would frequently share a dance before taking a walk around the room to converse with various acquaintances and friends. Afterward, they parted as expected, since even couples who'd supposedly married for love were frowned upon if they spent too much time "in each other's pockets," as the saying went.

As for her own obligation to play hostess and entertain at home, she was relieved when Jack made no such demands on her time. And given her newness to Society, as well as her status as a newlywed, no one seemed to mind the lapse. Next year, they all agreed, would be soon enough for such polite duties — except there would be no next year, she knew, only the remains of the one presently at hand.

With June now upon them and the Season

entering its final weeks, she realized she'd grown almost used to the constant rush. And as she often told herself, the frantic pace kept her mind off her troubles and her body weary enough for sleep.

Awake and attired in a light silk dressing gown, she smothered a yawn as she took a seat at the small table in her sitting room. Breakfast was spread there courtesy of her very efficient lady's maid.

Reaching first for her tea, she took a sip, pleased to find the brew hot and strong, exactly the way she liked it. Across on the fireplace mantel, the flower-covered porcelain Meissen clock pinged out the hour in dulcet, high-pitched strokes.

Noon. Late even for her.

But then she had good reason to have overslept, considering the fact that it had been nearly three in the morning when she'd taken to her bed. And not much past five when Jack had joined her beneath the sheets to take her in another way entirely.

Her skin warmed at the memory, remembered pleasure curling like an opiate through her veins. And he was rather like a drug, she decided, addictive and dangerous. She only hoped that when the time came, she would be capable of weaning herself away. Frowning over the thought, she picked up a buttered toast square and bit in with savage purpose.

She was finishing off a small dish of fresh strawberries when a brief knock sounded on the door that connected her bedchamber to Jack's. Before she could answer, the door opened and he walked inside.

Striding across, he dropped into the chair opposite and poured himself some tea. Her maid always provided an extra cup for just such an occurrence, even if he'd never before put one of them to use. But there was a first time for everything, she supposed. "Please, help yourself," she invited with a tinge of sarcasm.

His lips curved as he reached for a slice of toast. "I wasn't sure if I'd find you awake. I thought perhaps you might sleep longer."

"No. I have things to do today. Can't lie abed indefinitely."

His eyes twinkled, as though he were thinking about disagreeing with the remark, but he let it pass. Silently, he ate his toast. Finished, he reached across and liberated the remaining rasher of bacon from her plate, devouring the fried meat in a few quick bites.

"Would you like me to ring and have another breakfast brought up?" she asked, curious to find him demolishing what was left of hers.

He shook his head. "This will do." Using his napkin to wipe his hands free of crumbs and bacon grease, he poured more tea, then relaxed back in his chair. "So," he asked at length, "what's on your schedule for today?"

Her brows arched. "Afternoon calls, I believe. Followed by the park, then the Putnams' dinner party tonight."

"That's right. I'd forgotten about the Putnams. Pleasant people, though a tad on the stuffy side." He paused, tapping a finger against his lips. "What would you think about sending our regrets and doing something else entirely?"

Her brows arched even higher. "I'd think you'd put something stronger than tea in that cup, that's what."

He chuckled. "The day is beautiful, excellent for a drive to Richmond."

She stared. "For whom?"

"For us."

"You want me to accompany you to Richmond? Why?"

"Must there be a reason?"

"Yes, I rather think there must."

Spinning his teacup in a circle against its saucer, he took a long moment before responding. "I just thought it might be nice to lay down the gauntlets for a day. Our truce is rather untruce-like most of the time. I think both of us could use a brief armistice."

"You make it sound as if we're at war," she defended.

His piercing gaze met hers. "Are we not? What do you say, Grace?"

What she should say was a firm and unequivocal no. Instead she found herself longing to throw off the yoke of tension between them, even if it was only for a day. Perhaps that's how he felt too.

"I ought to refuse. But yes, all right."

He grinned, his good humor and charm pouring over her like a warm breeze.

I know I'm going to regret this, she thought.

Shooing him out of the room, she rang for her maid.

Jack honestly didn't know why he'd dreamed up this excursion, but gazing over at Grace now, where she sat beside him in the phaeton, he was glad he had.

She looked lovely, dressed in a lilac-and-white-striped gown, a chipstraw bonnet perched at a saucy angle on her upswept, fiery locks. She'd always been pretty, but over the last few months, she'd blossomed into a truly irresistible beauty.

Perhaps the credit should be given to her

stylish new wardrobe, since, with the assistance of his mother and sisters, she never appeared in less than the latest fashions. There were many days, in fact, that she could have stepped off the pages of *La Belle Assemble* itself.

But he also knew that her increased loveliness stemmed from a newfound source of inner confidence — her outer beauty growing in tandem with an ever-deepening ability to hold her own in Society. No longer did she try to conceal her height as she used to; the days of sitting in the back of the room were gone for good. Now, when she met people, she did so with aplomb, her shoulders square, her chin held high.

Of course, there was also her sensuality — and mayhap therein lay the true wellspring of her beauty. She'd come a long way from the shy young woman who'd once trembled at the thought of a stolen kiss.

Now when he came to her bed, she met him with bold assurance, accepting his caresses and returning them with inventive ones of her own. She'd taken him by surprise the first time she'd initiated their lovemaking — pleasing him more than he could imagine. Since then . . . well, she never left him any cause for complaint.

Without his quite knowing how or when,

Grace had become a mature, sensual, alluring woman — one who would surely tempt any man.

He frowned at the thought, his hands tightening slightly against the reins as the horses gamboled along the turnpike.

For weeks, he'd been waiting to tire of her. Every day he awakened expecting to find some lessening of his interest, to discover the seeds of disillusionment and ennui growing inside him. But then night would arrive and he'd want her all over again. If anything, he desired her more now than when he'd first taken her — although frankly he didn't know how that was physically possible. And the emotional distance between them was no deterrent. In some ways, it merely encouraged his needs, leaving him craving more than her body but her heart as well.

He'd possessed it once under false pretenses. Was it wrong of him to want it back? Perhaps that was the reason he'd suggested today's outing, so he could see how she felt when they weren't in company, or in bed.

Glancing over again, he saw her lift her face to the sun, a slow smile moving over her cherry red lips. His heart took an extra beat, a swell of longing pumping in his chest. Shunting the sensation away, he forced his gaze ahead.

"This *is* nice," she said.

He smiled and darted another glance her way. "As I said, perfect weather." A light wind teased the ribbons tied under her chin, making him want to give them a tug and set the little hat free. "Shall we go faster?"

"Faster than this? Is that wise?"

A grin creased his face. "Of course not, which is exactly the reason we should."

With a smart flick of the reins, he urged the team into a run.

Crying out in surprise, she grabbed the side of the phaeton. And then she laughed. High and light and adorably girlish. When their gazes met, he saw that her eyes had turned a vibrant, bluish-grey — a shade he realized he hadn't seen in ages.

Several hours later, Grace was laughing still, as she and Jack strolled along one of the many paths that led through Richmond Park.

In every direction, nature thrived; the grounds were composed of majestic hills with breathtaking views, serene ponds and woods full of magnificent old trees bedecked in regal cloaks of verdant green. But it was the wildflowers she loved best, their colorful heads dotting the landscape like thousands of tiny jewels.

Obviously, Jack had known she would enjoy the park — which, to her begrudging delight, she had. Just as she'd enjoyed the phaeton ride and a brief exploration of the shops and businesses that lined the Thames-side of Richmond itself. Despite her initial hesitation over the excursion, the day had turned out to be one of the best she'd known in recent memory.

If only we could remain here like this indefinitely, she thought. *If only this day away could last forever.*

Brought back to reality by her foolish, wistful musings, her humor dimmed a bit. She repressed a sigh. "I suppose we ought to be getting back."

"Oh, surely not," he said. Slipping his pocket watch from his waistcoat, he opened the gold lid to check the hour. "Why, it's barely six. Plenty of time left yet to explore. In fact, why don't we walk around a little more, then have an early dinner here in Richmond? I know just the inn."

"I suppose we could, but I —"

"— will be absolutely famished if you insist on waiting until we return home," he interrupted.

"I'm used to dining late. Town hours, remember?"

"Yes, but we usually have nuncheon and we missed ours today. As a result, I fear I'm coming down peaked."

She gazed into his healthy, youthful face. "You don't look peaked."

"I am. *Inside.* You should hear my stomach crying out in agony even as we speak." A roguish smile spread across his mouth.

She laughed again, her resolve crumbling.

As oddly malleable today as a handful of clay, she soon found herself falling in with his plan. Strolling at a leisurely pace, they spent another half hour in the park before returning to their carriage. In peaceable harmony, he drove them toward the inn.

When they arrived, the innkeeper showered them with a voluble welcome, the round-bellied proprietor with his toothsome smile and tufted grey eyebrows doing everything in his power to make them feel at their ease. Puffing out his massive chest with pride, he showed them to his "best private parlor." Promising to return soon with a bottle of his finest wine and most delectable hot repast, he withdrew, closing the door at his back.

The moment he departed, Grace became abruptly aware of the fact that she and Jack were alone — a curious sensation, given the fact that they'd been alone together all day.

Not to mention the fact that they were married and shared both a house and a bed.

Preposterous.

Still, until now, their day had been spent in public settings, the world's watchful gaze conferring an unspoken restraint of sorts. Now that restraint was gone.

Suddenly in need of space, she crossed to the window and peered down into the inn yard below. As she watched, nimble-footed hostlers ran to and fro, while off in the distance the mighty Thames curved in a steady, relentless flow.

Determined, unchangeable, unforgiving.

Am I those things as well? she wondered.

A tremor skipped across her skin as Jack drew to a halt at her side, then again when he curved a palm over her shoulder. Bending, he pressed his mouth against her neck. Her lips parted, eyelids falling closed, while pleasure sang a sweet song in her blood.

Suddenly, a brisk knock came at the door, followed by a click of the lock, as the innkeeper and a pair of maids bustled inside. Immediately, she pulled away from Jack, relieved by the interruption.

He cast her an inquiring glance but made no comment while the table was prepared for their meal. He and the innkeeper carried on a lively conversation, Jack pronouncing the wine an excellent choice, much to the beaming approval of the other man.

And then they were alone once more, the table nearly groaning beneath the plentitude of the offerings before them.

Sliding into a seat opposite, Jack took up a plate and served her first. She couldn't help but notice that he chose only her favorites, including a large spoonful of cheesy scalloped potatoes that made her mouth water in anticipation.

He served himself next, carving from both a rare roast beef and a tender boiled ham, adding dollops of coarse grain mustard and freshly grated horseradish alongside. With a selection of accompaniments taking up the remainder of the space on his plate, he poured wine for them both, then dug into the meal.

She half expected him to mention the embrace they'd shared at the window. Instead, he launched into an amusing tale about a boyhood prank he and Cade had once perpetrated in church that soon had her relaxed and laughing again.

While they talked, food disappeared from her plate and wine from her glass, which he kept replenishing at regular intervals.

Finally she stopped him with a hand over the top of her goblet, giving him a firm shake of her head. "No more. I've had too much as it is."

He peered at the bottle and the two inches of wine left inside. "A shame not to finish this, seeing it's our host's best vintage and all."

"You drink it," she said, holding firm to her decision. "Besides, I remember all too well what happened the last time you plied me with alcohol and the sore head I got the next morning. I have no interest in repeating the experience."

"That was brandy, a far more potent spirit. But if you're sure . . ."

After a last questioning look, he tipped the remainder of the Bordeaux into his glass, filling it nearly to the rim. Lifting the beverage, he took a long swallow. "As I recall, you seemed to enjoy that night — and the next morning as well, once you got over your initial discomfort."

For a moment, she didn't know if he was referring to the loss of her virginity on their first night together or the results of all the liquor she'd consumed that evening. Either way, his statement was unerringly accurate. In spite of her trepidation then, she'd more than enjoyed that first night. She'd love it and him. She'd been so happy. So innocently full of hope, and the joy of simply being together.

But now she knew his actions for the lies they'd been.

Only his touch hadn't been a lie, she realized. In that, he'd never deceived her.

"Yes, well, those days are long gone," she said, laying down her fork.

Reaching over, he captured her hand. "They don't have to be."

Her gaze went to his. "What is that supposed to mean?"

"Just that we have the power to do anything we want, to be the people we each wish to be. I'm tired of this estrangement, Grace. Are you not weary of it too?"

Is that what today has been about? Suddenly it all made sense.

She looked away. "But I thought you were content with things as they are."

"I'm content having you in my bed, though content hardly seems an adequate description for the passion we share. I want more. I want *you.* Can you not find some way to forgive me? Even a little?"

Her heart boomed in her chest, blood throbbing with near pain between her temples. "You want my forgiveness?"

"Yes. And I want you as my wife. My real wife. Can we not try again? Start over anew?"

For a long moment, she stared, not quite comprehending what he'd just said. Yanking her hand from his grasp, she shoved back her chair and stood up. Hugging her arms around her waist, she paced several steps away.

She didn't know how to respond or what to do, stunned by the declaration he'd just made. She'd assumed he would be glad to see her leave when the Season came to an end. That he would savor the freedom of their separation, since it would allow him to return to his bachelor life and his bachelor ways. Instead, he was telling her the exact opposite. That he wanted her to remain. That he wanted to make their marriage work.

I hate him, don't I? she thought wildly. All she needed to do was say those words aloud, and it would all be over. But did she want it to be over? And did she still truly wish to leave?

A shiver racked her frame despite the summertime warmth inside the room. He'd already destroyed her faith in him once, crushing her hopes and her heart so that she'd had to close off a piece of herself in order to survive. Could she afford to lower her defenses again? Did she dare risk letting him in? Of trusting him despite his past deceits?

With conflict warring in her breast, she paced forward and away. Forward and away again.

On one of her passes, he reached out and caught her hand, drawing her to a halt. Their gazes met, his eyes a deep, percipient blue.

Silence beat like wings between them.

"I just don't know," she whispered, her voice tight with uncertainty.

Long seconds passed, then he nodded. "Well, while you're deciding, why don't you do it over here?" With a gentle tug, he began towing her forward.

"Jack," she reproached in a soft voice. "This won't resolve anything."

"Maybe not," he stated as he settled her onto his lap, "but we'll both enjoy ourselves in the meantime."

His mouth met hers in a languid mating, fervid and fresh, the power of his kiss never failing to steal her breath and ignite her desire. She could have put up some token effort to resist, but what was the point? He would have her eventually, and she would be eager to let him. In this there were no denials and no regrets.

Suddenly aching to make love, she kissed

him harder, sinking her fingers into his hair so she could hold his head steady for her own intense, carnal claiming.

He was panting when they came up for air. "We may have our share of troubles," he said, fitting his palm over her breast for a tantalizing massage. "But we always get along perfectly in bed. What do you say we go find one?"

"Y-you mean now? *Here?*" she gasped, her own breath far from steady.

His fingers found her nipple and stroked her flesh, so that it beaded into a sharp, aching peak. "I'm sure the innkeeper would be happy to oblige us with his best accommodation."

"B-but what about d-driving back to Town? Won't our absence be noticed?"

"Let them notice. It's not as if there's anything wrong with Lord and Lady John Byron spending a night away."

Realizing he was right, she nodded her agreement and kissed him hard again.

In reply, he ravished her mouth, opening her lips to take her with his tongue the way he would soon be taking her with his body.

Suddenly, he pulled back. "I'd better go see about that room while I still have enough blood left in my brain to think."

In answer, she skimmed her lips over his

cheek and temple, pausing to kiss him behind his ear in a spot she knew drove him mad.

"Stop that," he admonished in a stern voice. "Or I'll be taking you right here in this chair."

Smiling, she swirled her tongue over the area, feeling him stiffen beneath her as she parted her lips for a kiss that would likely leave a mark. After suckling for a long moment, she pulled away just enough to blow against the wet skin, while below her fingers went to the hard bulge of his erection and gave a gliding stroke.

His hips arched, hands lowering to lift her off his lap. "Then again, maybe you *want* me to take you in this chair."

Pushing her skirts up, he spread her legs apart so she straddled his thighs. Tearing open the buttons on his falls, he slid his knees wider and her as well.

She moaned, wet heat throbbing in her core. Afraid of overbalancing, she gripped his shoulders. But she needn't have worried; Jack's hold was strong and steady. And then without further hesitation, he brought her down, impaling her fully on his rampant shaft.

"Don't say you weren't warned," he told her on a harsh rasp, as he began thrusting deeply inside her.

She groaned and matched his pace. "Don't s-say you w-weren't either."

And then she plundered his lips with long, torrid kisses, riding him with abandon until they both claimed their bliss.

She came awake slowly with her head pillowed on Jack's chest, their naked limbs tangled together. He was soundly asleep in the bed, one arm draped over her back, while the other lay bent above his head.

After the last few months together, she knew it was his preferred posture. That and spooned in behind her so he could take her in the morning before either of them was completely awake. He seemed to enjoy that position the best — as well as their early morning couplings. She did too, if only because she didn't have to think or try to raise her emotional armor against him. They were simply two people, drawn together by mutual need.

Opening her eyes, she gazed into the darkness, not immediately recognizing the room. Then her memory snapped back into place.

The inn. Of course.

Somehow, after their impetuous lovemaking in the private parlor, they managed to rearrange their clothing and smooth their hair long enough for Jack to request a room for the night. Once inside, they'd said little, stripping to the skin before falling into the bed to pleasure each other again. This time, however, the loving had been slow, easy, almost poignant. Jack kissing and caressing her with a tenderness that had left her shaken. When it was over, she'd lain in his arms, wondering again what she should do, no closer to an answer than before.

At length, she'd fallen asleep.

So now here she was again, undecided and unsure.

He wanted them to have a real marriage, he claimed. To end their estrangement and have her stay permanently as his wife. Yet, despite his declaration, there had still been no mention of love.

Only want. Only need. And a desire to try again.

Is it enough?

She just didn't know.

Part of her longed to say yes, to give up her struggles and worries, and accept her life at his side. But by doing so, she would be leaving herself vulnerable to him once again. And still more terrifying was the risk she took of falling in love with him all over again.

As suddenly as the thought occurred,

though, she knew that it was already too late.

Oh, God, I do love him. Did I ever really stop?

In spite of admitting the truth to herself, she wasn't sure she was ready to commit. She didn't know if she could ever again give herself to him in the same unreservedly trusting way she once had. What if she opened her heart again and he betrayed her? What if she gave him everything only to awaken one morning to see regret in his eyes? Or, worse, disinterest and boredom?

The very idea made her shrivel inside. If she let him in and he hurt her again, she didn't know if she could recover.

And yet, he wanted an answer.

Yes or no?

Lying in the dark with her head pillowed on the warm plane of his chest, she listened to the quiet, even susurration of his breathing. She took comfort in the sound and the faint movement as her thoughts tumbled in endless circles.

Still considering, she fell asleep.

CHAPTER 23

The next morning Grace was no closer to making a decision than she had been the night before.

To her relief, Jack didn't bring up the issue, and neither did she. Talking about practically everything else, they shared a companionable breakfast at the inn, then returned to London.

The instant they walked through the town house's front door, the Season and all its attendant obligations came rushing back upon them. Wading straight into the thick of things, she changed her gown, then hurried off to a promised garden party, while Jack drove to Tattersalls to meet friends and inspect the newest horses arrived for sale.

That night, she and Jack attended a ball, dancing twice before sharing a midnight supper at an intimate table for two. After arriving home, they went to bed, where he made exquisite love to her. She fell into a dreamless sleep, locked again inside the comfort of his arms.

The following morning, she expected him to once again press her for an answer. Especially when he joined her for breakfast at the little table in her bedroom. But in spite of sharing a cheerful meal, nothing more was said on the subject.

And nothing would be, she began to realize, as one day flowed smoothly into another. The next move was up to her, and clearly he was letting her choose when and how to make it.

Secure in that knowledge, she relaxed, deciding *not* to decide for the present and to let their time together during the last weeks of the Season help her make the right choice.

On the surface, their lives were very much as they'd been before their night at the inn, with endless rounds of parties and social obligations that frequently took them out of each other's company. And yet underneath, nothing was the same, a subtle connection forming between them that she couldn't entirely describe. He'd always been attentive in the past, but now he was especially gentle with her. He anticipated her needs in small ways without her ever having to say a word, whether it was making sure she'd remembered to bring her fan to a rout or suggesting they depart early if she seemed tired.

He touched her more too, and not just in bed. While chatting with others at a party, he might lay his hand against her waist. Or when visiting with his family, she often found his fingers playing absently over the warm gold of her wedding band and across the center of her palm. Many times, she didn't think he was even aware he was doing it, his actions seeming unconscious and automatic. And because they were, she began to wonder. Began to nurse the fragile hope that he was actually falling in love with her.

But as much as she longed to ask him, she could not. She would not. She had to have the words from him, freely given and honestly expressed.

As for their marriage — she was starting to believe there might be hope for it too. They'd been . . . dare she say it? . . . happy of late. Perhaps she should give them — give *him* — the second chance he wanted and find out if they could have a life together, after all.

She was pondering that precise question five weeks later, during a quiet moment at the Pettigrews' ball, when Meg unexpectedly appeared at her side.

"Here you are," her sister-in-law stated, slipping into an empty seat next to her. "I never thought you'd stop dancing. You've had a partner for every set this evening."

"All but this one, and I'm glad for the respite."

Smiling, Meg nodded her lovely blond head with understanding. Since joining the ranks of the Ton last year, she'd become a favorite among Society's elegantly dressed men and women — half of whom seemed to be crowded at present into the overly warm ballroom.

"Where is Jack, by the way?" Meg asked. "I was sure he'd be at your side the moment he noticed you were alone."

"He mentioned something about port and political talk with several of the men, then told me to enjoy myself until the supper dance. I am forbidden to entertain invitations for it from anyone else."

"Jack is so possessive these days. I'm surprised he left you alone at all."

"It's not possessiveness. He just doesn't want to have to make small talk with some other lady over supper," she said with humorous dismissal. "He knows with me he can eat in complete silence and I won't take offense."

Meg waved a hand. "As though he would. You two are always talking, even when you think yourselves alone."

"I could say the same of you and Cade. I've never seen a happier couple."

Meg gave her an almost shy smile, an interesting glow rushing to her cheeks. "I was going to wait a bit longer, but I'm just bursting to tell someone. Besides Cade, of course. He's the only one who knows."

"Knows what?"

Glancing around to make sure no one else was listening, Meg leaned forward. "I'm with child! The doctor was by just yesterday and confirmed what I already suspected. There's going to be a new Byron in the family come the New Year."

Giving a small shout, Grace flung her arms around her friend. "Oh, Meg, I'm so happy for you! No wonder you're bursting to tell. If it were me, I'd be telling everyone I met."

Meg laughed and returned her hug. "You'll have your chance soon, I've no doubt. By next year, we'll both be mothers. Mark my words."

In that moment Grace realized that she wanted her sister-in-law to be right. She longed for a baby — a son who looked exactly like Jack. Thinking of Jack, she knew she had to share Meg's secret with him. Assuming she could gain her approval first.

"Oh, I must go find Jack and tell him the good news," she said. "If you'll let me, that is?"

Meg paused briefly. "I suppose it's fine. Cade won't be able to keep his mouth shut for long either. We were going to wait and tell his mother tomorrow, then announce it to everyone else afterwards. But since you already know, I can't see the harm if Jack does too."

"Oh, he'll be so excited to hear he's going to be an uncle!" Giving the other woman a second hug, Grace sprang to her feet and left the ballroom.

". . . excellent chap for finance. If you're looking for some sound investment advice, you can't go wrong with him."

"Rafe Pendragon, you say," Jack remarked, taking Lord Pettigrew's calling card with the other man's name penciled on the back. "My thanks. I'll consider the suggestion."

"If you're smart, you'll do more than consider. I'm telling you everything that fellow touches turns to gold. If you don't believe me, talk to Wyvern. The duke's known him for years. Went to Harrow together, if rumors are to be believed. Don't know if I do, considering Pendragon's street-hardened reputation. Then again, I hear he's some lord's by-blow, so who knows for sure. Anyway, next time you see Tony Wyvern, mention that name. He'll tell you what's what."

Jack gazed at the card once more, then slipped it into his coat pocket. With a nod, he watched as Pettigrew left the study.

Glancing around, Jack noticed he was alone, the rest of the gentlemen who'd gathered earlier for drinks and discussion having left already to return to the party. He would have done the same himself a good twenty minutes ago if Lord Pettigrew hadn't kept him talking so long.

Tossing back the last of his brandy, he set down the snifter and turned to go in search of Grace. Hopefully she wouldn't be dancing with some popinjay who was eager for a chance to become her cicisbeo. If so, he'd just have to cut in and send the scoundrel on his way. Smiling to himself, he started toward the door.

He stopped short seconds later, eyebrows arching upward as a woman glided into the room, the diaphanous red skirts of her gown swirling around her legs. "Philipa," he said in surprise.

Her mouth curved into a sensuous smile,

her beautiful green eyes gleaming like a cat's. "Jack. I thought I heard you in here."

"Did you now?" he drawled in amused disbelief. "Odd, but I wasn't talking, being that I'm alone as you can see."

"Yes, I *can* see." On a graceful step, she sauntered deeper into the room. "But up until a minute ago, Lord Pettigrew was bombarding you with one pontification after another. I never did think he'd cease his endless prattle."

He decided not to counter the remark. "So, you've been waiting for me, then?"

"Well, not waiting exactly. And certainly not in the hallway, if that's what you're implying. The little ante-room next door has amazingly good acoustics. A cozy seat next to the grate and voices carry like bells. Besides, I brought a friend along for company. He kept me . . . entertained, shall we say."

"*Entertained,* was it?"

She shrugged, eyes twinkling slyly. "A girl gets bored, you know. He proved to be a deliciously meaty appetizer, but I shooed him off back to the party before I came to find you."

A laugh rumbled from his lips. "You are the most unabashedly decadent woman I've ever known."

"And you adore it. Or at least you used to when we were together. Why haven't you come to see me, darling?" she said, thrusting out her full, lower lip in a sultry pout. "You've been in Town for weeks and weeks, and not so much as a word."

"We've spoken a time or two, as I recall. We seem to attend many of the same social functions."

"Same circles, same balls. Yes, yes, I know," she said, gliding closer. "But that was just insignificant small talk. I meant that we haven't talked *in private.*"

"That's because I'm married now."

"Yes, I know," she sighed. "Your bride is invited everywhere these days, and considering her height and hair color, she's rather hard to miss."

His eyebrows furrowed.

"Not that she isn't pretty," she amended quickly. "She's very striking in an Amazonian kind of way. I was merely pointing out the obvious."

He crossed his arms over his chest.

"And I'm sure she's proved amusing," she continued. "Those legs of hers must wrap around you like sailors' knots."

"That's quite enough, Lady Stockton," he said, his words low and hard.

"Oh, don't fly up the boughs. I was only

having a bit of fun. Where's your sense of humor?"

He stayed silent, not trusting what might come out of his mouth.

"I was simply testing you," she went on. "I had to know if the rumors are really true."

"What rumors?"

"The ones that claim you're desperately in love with her." Her shoulders sank, a measure of her bravado falling away. "I've seen the two of you together, but I didn't want to believe it. I had to find out for myself."

This time when he scowled, it wasn't in anger but rather in confusion.

"But I can see now that she's captured your heart," she continued. "Remarkable, considering what you told me about how you had to marry her for her money."

"I never said that," he shot back.

"Didn't you? As I recall, you told me you got stuck with her as the result of a bad run of luck at the tables."

He cringed inside, hating to hear what he'd once said. Had he really been so callous? So thoughtless and cruel? But he hadn't known Grace then. Not the way he knew her now.

Stepping closer, Philipa laid a hand on his sleeve. "There's no chance you'll come back to me, then? No hope you'll grow tired of her and seek my bed again?"

Gazing down, he met her eyes, acknowledging the magnetism of her personality. Without even trying, Philipa Stockton fairly smoldered sexuality. And yet despite her undeniable physical beauty and admitted talent in all things amorous, he wasn't tempted.

Not in the least.

He didn't want her. He wanted Grace.

He didn't love her. He loved Grace.

And by simply thinking the words, he knew them to be true. *Lord, how could I have been so blind for so long? Of course I love Grace. She's everything I want.*

"I'm sorry," he said. "But whatever you and I once were in the past, it's over. My life, and yes, my heart, belong to my wife."

She trembled, her hand tightening on his sleeve. "Well then, I see I should wish you happy." A forced smile came to her lips. Instead of stepping away, however, she pressed nearer, sliding a hand up his chest. "One last kiss? What do you say? One final embrace for old time's sake?"

He stared down at her. "Philipa, I don't think that's a good idea."

"What harm is there in a little kiss? It's nothing we haven't done before. One short embrace, then never again."

Instead of waiting to see if he was going to refuse her, she wrapped her arms around his neck and pulled him down. "Just one," she breathed.

And then, without his consent, her lips were on his, kissing him with everything in her sexual arsenal. He knew he should pull away immediately, put her from him with force, if needed. Instead, he hesitated, curious in spite of his revelation about Grace to see what he would feel.

To his relief, to his joy, he experienced nothing more than an interesting sense of detachment, as though he were observing the kiss rather than being an active participant in it.

She isn't Grace, he thought. *Her lips aren't as soft. Her flavor isn't as sweet. She's not the woman I love and she never will be.*

Satisfied with the results of his brief experiment, he prepared to set her aside, sliding his hands upward to unlock her arms from around his neck.

Suddenly, a muffled thump came from the vicinity of the doorway. Breaking the kiss, he turned his head and glanced toward the sound. In an instant, his lungs stopped functioning, his heart missing a necessary beat as he met Grace's horrified stare.

Chapter 24

Grace stood mute, her gaze fixed on the couple kissing in the center of the Pettigrews' study.

At first, the scene made no sense to her. Unmistakably, the dark-haired woman was Philipa Stockton. Grace knew her identity, since she'd long ago made a point of finding out just what her husband's former mistress looked like.

But the man . . . no, the man couldn't be who she thought he was.

Seconds later, he slid his palms up Lady Stockton's arms and she knew it was Jack. *Her Jack.* Gooseflesh popped out all over her skin, bile rising into her throat with a burning sting. Taking a pair of steps backward, she stumbled against the door, desperate to look away, yet somehow incapable of the act.

Then, sensing her presence, Jack's head came up and his gaze locked on hers.

The shock broke her free, her limbs suddenly functional again. Wheeling around, she ran from the room. Behind her, Jack called out her name, but she didn't stop, knowing only that she had to get away.

Perhaps running was a cowardly act. Maybe if she were another woman, she would have stayed and confronted the pair. Flown at them with fists and fingernails and screams of outrage.

But such violence wasn't in her nature, and she'd already seen more than enough. She couldn't bear the idea of staying to listen to their excuses.

Slippers flying, she sped toward the entrance, uncaring who might see her along the way. A few eyes did follow her, but she barely noticed, intent as she was on escape. She was just hurrying past the ballroom when a man stepped into her path. For the faintest instant she thought it was Jack, that somehow he'd managed to catch up. But then she realized it was Cade instead.

"Easy there," he said. "Where are you going so fast?"

Before she could answer, Meg appeared at his side. "So? Did you tell him?" she asked Grace with a bright, conspiratorial smile.

Grace stared back, uncomprehending.

"Tell who, what?" Cade demanded.

"You know. About the *baby,*" Meg said, lowering her voice to a near whisper. "I just couldn't keep it secret and told Grace. She was going to share the news with Jack, but . . ." She broke off, an expression of unease replacing her happy smile. "What is it, Grace? You don't look well. Forgive me for not noticing right away."

"It-it's fine," Grace muttered. "And n-no, I d-didn't have a chance to tell him. I'm sorry."

"Are you ill?" Meg asked with clear concern. "What has happened?"

"Yes," Cade said, stepping closer to take hold of her elbow as though he were worried she might fall. "You look quite pale. Why don't you have a seat and I'll go find Jack."

"No!" she cried.

Cade lifted a brow.

Modulating her tone, she continued. "No, d-don't bother him. All I want is the coach to take me home."

"Well, of course, but we should still tell him. He'll be worried."

But he won't be, she thought with dismal certainty. And even if he were, she didn't care. Not anymore. Still, all this talk of Jack made her realize that he might find her at any second. Recoiling at the thought, she pulled away from Cade.

"I n-need to go home. I shall see both of you later."

"But Grace," Meg called. "Where are you g— ?"

Grace didn't stay long enough to hear the rest, hurrying away again as fast as her feet would carry her. Knowing there wasn't time to call for the coach, she sought out a footman.

"A hackney, please. As quickly as possible." She found a coin large enough to ensure his immediate compliance.

Less than two minutes later, she was inside the hackney cab. For a few seconds, she considered telling the driver to take her to her father's house. But Papa would be full of questions and demands she didn't wish to answer. Knowing she had nowhere else to go, she gave the address for Upper Brook Street.

Jack walked into the town house half an hour later, relieved to hear from Appleton that her ladyship had arrived only minutes before.

He would have been there sooner himself, but first he'd had to extract himself from a surprisingly contrite Philipa. After escaping her, he'd hurried off in search of Grace, only to be set upon by a concerned Cade and Meg. They had proceeded to inform him that Grace was greatly distressed, had refused their offer of assistance, and fled the party on her own.

Noticing their hushed conversation, Mallory, Mama and Edward had joined in as well, demanding to know what was wrong. Only the arrival of his coach allowed him to make his exit.

Now finally he was home. Now he could talk to Grace and straighten out this mess.

Taking the stairs two at a time, he strode down the hallway to her bedchamber. Pausing for a moment, he gave a quiet tap on the door and waited — not surprised when the only reply was silence. He tried the door latch and — also not surprisingly — found it locked.

"Grace? It's me. Would you open the door, please?"

Silence.

"We need to talk about this."

More silence.

"I'm not leaving until we've had this out. Now, let me in."

Something hard hit the inside of the door, making him jump. Moments later, a second something rapped against the wood with a resounding *whack!*

Is she throwing her shoes at me? Or is it books?

Either way, the gesture boded ill.

"Now you're just being childish," he said. "Open the door so we can discuss this like adults."

From inside the room, he heard movement. There was a long pause, then footsteps. A note came sliding out from underneath the door.

After a faint hesitation, he bent down and retrieved it.

Go away!

"Grace, I realize you're upset, but it's not how it looks. Give me a chance to explain."

Quiet fell, then more footsteps. Not long after, another note came shooting out at him, twirling in a circle in front of his feet this time.

No!

A measure of his patience fell away. "Enough of this," he stated in a firm voice. "Open this door."

She didn't repond.

"Now!" he demanded.

Something struck the wood hard again,

quickly followed by another violent rap.

"All right," he said. "If that's the way you want to do this, then that's how it will be."

Turning, he strode away.

On the opposite side of the door, Grace stood trembling, the shoes she'd thrown scattered in haphazard disarray around her.

Good, she thought; he'd taken her none-too-subtle "hint" and left. Although, to be strictly honest, she was rather surprised he'd withdrawn so easily. Jack wasn't the kind to give up without waging a worthwhile fight, and his attempt had been little more than average.

Perhaps his talk of explanations had only been for show, a halfhearted effort to mollify and pacify her yet again. Perhaps too he'd assumed he could cozen her with another creative string of falsehoods and had withdrawn when he realized his ploy wasn't working.

Well, he could try again tomorrow — as he was certain to do — but his efforts would still be for naught. She knew what she'd seen. God knows, she couldn't get it out of her mind — the memory of him and Philipa Stockton entwined together, kissing, seared like a brand inside her brain. Pressing her hands to her eyes, she willed away the image. She battled back the flood of tears that threatened to start as well.

I've cried enough over him already. I will shed no more tears, she swore to herself. *Heaven knows he doesn't deserve them. Not after this!*

On a shuddering sigh, she crossed to a chair and sank onto it, feeling as weary as an old woman. Gazing down, she realized she was still in her evening gown.

She'd been too distressed when she'd arrived home to bear any scrutiny, so rather than have to put on a brave face, she'd sent her maid off to bed. Stupid, she supposed, given the fact that she would likely end up sleeping in her ball dress.

Assuming she *could* sleep. She rather doubted she would get any rest tonight at all.

She was contemplating possible ways to unfasten a few of the buttons on the back of her gown when she heard the brass knob turn on the connecting door.

Her exhaustion vanished.

Trying to get in that way, is he?

Well, he would have no more luck opening that door than he had the other one. Not only had she made sure it was securely locked but she'd also taken the precaution of collecting all the keys, including the spare one she knew he kept in his shaving stand.

The knob rattled again, then he rapped on the wood three sharp times. "Open the door, Grace," he ordered in a quiet, yet forceful, tone.

She considered writing him another note but decided a repetition of that particular tactic wouldn't have as much impact now. Besides, it took too long.

Standing, she moved forward and crossed her arms. "No!" she called.

Silence followed, energy fairly crackling in the air. She imagined him on the other side of the door, his fists squeezed tight, a pugnacious tilt to his mouth.

"You and I are going to talk tonight," he said. "So I'm going to give you one more opportunity to *open-the-God-damned-door!*"

"Don't you dare swear at me! You can have nothing to say that I could possibly want to hear, you lying, adulterous bastard!"

"I barely touched her and you know it. Now open the bloody door this instant. I mean it, Grace."

Clutching her arms more tightly against her middle, she shivered. "Go to perdition!"

Another silence fell, long moments of stark quiet that were unnerving in their magnitude.

Then with a violence that made her jump,

noise exploded into the room. The door shook in its frame, lock rattling, as he began hammering it with blows.

Her hands went to her throat, utterly mute. Completely shocked. *What is he doing?* He wasn't actually trying to kick down the door, was he?

But apparently he was, she realized, as the wood began to weaken under his powerful assault.

Suddenly, it gave way with a tremendous splintering groan, what remained of the door hanging at a drunken angle on its hinges. Using his shoulder, he applied a last pair of blows, then shoved his way through the opening. Stalking into the room, he halted a couple feet away, lungs working as he planted his fists on his hips. "Now," he declared. "We're going to talk and you're going to listen. So, sit!"

But in spite of her astonishment, she wasn't afraid. She planted her fists on her hips in a mirror image of him and raised her chin in a clearly pugnacious refusal.

"God, you're stubborn," he said after a long moment. "Fine, then, *stand* and listen."

"To what? I can't imagine what there is to say."

"There's plenty to say. What you saw tonight, it isn't what you think."

"Oh, isn't it? So you're going to claim I didn't see you kissing that . . . that . . . woman?"

"Yes. What you saw was *her* kissing *me.*"

She gave a hollow laugh. "Kissing *you?* Hah! And that's supposed to make all the difference, is it?"

"It should, since I didn't ask her to kiss me and didn't want her to continue. I was about to set her away when you came in. It was nothing, Grace. It meant nothing."

Her fingers clenched together so hard they hurt. "Well, it certainly looked like something to me. For a man being kissed against his will, you certainly didn't look as though you were fighting off her advances. From what I observed, you seemed to be enjoying them. So just how long have you been carrying on with your mistress behind my back?"

"*Carrying on?* Good Lord, considering the number of times I have you every day, where would I get the time? Or the energy! And Lady Stockton is *not* my mistress."

She shot him a look of pure disdain.

"Fine. She *was* my mistress, but she isn't anymore, and hasn't been for a very long while. Not since I began courting you in Bath." Pausing, he raked his fingers through his hair. "Grace, I don't have a mistress.

You are my one and only lover. The only woman I want."

Maybe now. But for how much longer? she thought, as sorrow swept through her like an icy wind.

In her heart, she knew he wasn't having an affair, despite her having caught him kissing Philipa Stockton tonight. Even so, the shock of it served as a kind of precursor to the future. And of what she feared she would witness again eventually, only then for real.

How long before he decided she didn't please him anymore?

How many weeks or months remained before he really did stray?

How many other Philipa Stocktons would there be in his life? And, as his wife, in her own, as well?

He gave her an imploring look. "Grace, surely you believe me. Tell me you know nothing is going on between Philipa and me. My God, the two of us were saying goodbye. Permanently. And she kissed me before I knew what she was planning. I really was trying to pull her off when you came in."

She glanced away, an ache radiating between her ribs.

"Grace?"

Slowly she lifted her gaze. "Yes, I believe you."

Voluble tension eased from his shoulders. Holding out his arms, he stepped forward.

She stepped back.

His arms fell to his sides. "What? What is it?"

"Us. It's us. This . . . arrangement we have isn't going to work."

"What did you say?" he asked in clear disbelief.

She couldn't look at him, so she stared across at a painting on the wall. But the colors and brushstrokes bled together into an indistinct blur, her senses too consumed by the sensation of her heart breaking to see the image before her eyes.

"Our marriage," she said quietly. "I don't think it's going to work. You said you'd buy me a house. Did you?"

"A house?" he repeated, as though he didn't understand the word.

"Yes. As part of the agreement between us, you promised me a house in the country and half the money my father paid you in the settlement. Have you . . . have you followed through on your promise?"

He paused before answering. "Yes . . .. um . . . actually, I have, some while ago. But I didn't think you would be making use of either of them, given how well we've been doing these past weeks. I thought you seemed happy."

She blinked away the moisture in her eyes. "Appearances can often be deceiving. The Season is nearly done and I've more than fulfilled my side of the bargain. It's your turn to reciprocate now."

A long silence descended, every bit of expression leaving his face. "You want to proceed with the separation?"

No! Tell me to stop talking and make me take it all back.

"I think it's for the best," she heard herself say.

"For the best?" he retorted, his voice taking on a harsh cast. "So because of what happened tonight, because of one meaningless kiss with Philipa Stockton, you're going to throw it all away? Throw us away?"

"I don't think there is an us, not in the way you mean. We're admittedly very compatible in bed and enjoy each other's company on occasion. But as for a sustainable relationship, I don't think we have one. Tonight merely served to illustrate that fact."

Don't let me go. Tell me you won't hear of it and that you absolutely refuse to let me leave.

He folded his arms across his chest. "So

you want to live apart?"

No! I don't want to ever be apart. Tell me you don't either. Tell me you can't bear to be without me. Say you love me!

But he didn't say anything. And she didn't express the wishes tumbling through her mind and screaming inside her heart.

At length, she drew a breath, her tone listless with resignation. "Yes, it's what I want."

He gazed at her then, his eyes cold and remote. "It will be as you wish then. I'll send word to have the house prepared for your arrival. The money is already in an account, established in your name alone. My solicitor will see to it you have all the particulars. Is there anything else you require?"

"No," she whispered.

Nothing else. Everything is over and done with now.

Straightening, he gave a curt bow, as though she were a stranger instead of his wife, then turned and walked to the doorless threshold that connected their rooms. "I'll have this repaired in the morning," he said.

Hefting the battered door, he stepped backward through the opening into his room, moving to prop the wood so that it covered the majority of the opening. "If you have need of me this evening, I'll be in my study," he stated in an unnaturally soft voice.

And that's when she realized he would not be coming to her bed tonight. He would never be coming to her bed again.

Standing still and silent, she listened to his footsteps as he made his way through his sitting room, then out into the corridor beyond. Once she couldn't hear him any longer, she walked to her bed, clutching her chest as though she feared her heart would cease to beat.

Perhaps it already has, she thought as she lay across the counterpane. *I'm broken and will never mend again.*

Hot tears slid over her cheeks, soundless and devastating. And as she'd feared, she didn't sleep the rest of the night.

Chapter 25

A week later, he and Grace left London.

Rather than set rumors swirling among the Ton, they'd agreed that it would be easier to depart together, then go their separate ways once they were away from Town. The plan served a second purpose as well, since it would help deflect difficult questions from their families — at least for a short while.

They'd already answered enough awkward questions as it was, starting the morning after the Pettigrews' ball. Concerned about Grace and her uncharacteristic behavior, the Byrons had descended to make sure she was well. Rather than admit the truth, Grace had fallen back on the excuse of illness and pleaded overexertion and fatigue. Jack had seconded her claim, saying a physician had already been called and that Grace just needed some extra rest.

He could tell that his family — his mother

in particular — wasn't sure whether to believe them or not, but in the end, nothing more was said and the explanation was accepted.

Luckily, news of Meg's pregnancy helped circumvent further speculation — everyone was too cheerful over the prospect of a new baby to pay much attention to the tension between him and Grace.

He used the same explanation a few days later when he informed everyone that he and Grace would be leaving for the countryside a few weeks earlier than originally planned. It was late enough in the Season that many families were already shaking off the heat of the city for cooler country climes, so their early departure would cause little comment.

So here he and Grace were now, traveling into Kent. The journey to the house he'd chosen for her wouldn't take more than a few hours. Once there, he would see to it that she was comfortably settled, then he would depart.

For where, he still wasn't certain.

As he well knew, he couldn't go back to London — not for several weeks, anyway. And even if he were so inclined — which he most certainly was not — Braebourne was out of the question as well, since his family would be returning home before too long.

There was always Adam Gresham's hunting box in Scotland, he supposed. Perhaps a trip into the northern wilds would be just the thing. And Gresham was a generous sort, so Jack knew he wouldn't object to letting him open up the place for a few weeks.

Then again, he didn't know if he wanted to risk the possibility of company should Gresham and some of his friends decide to join him there. Naturally, they would inquire after Grace, and he had no stomach for their questions and speculation.

From the corner of his eye, he saw her shift slightly on the upholstered seat, her lovely profile in view as she gazed out the window at the passing scenery.

For a moment, he couldn't help but stare, tracing the familiar contours of her face, aware exactly how soft her skin would feel and how sweet her mouth would taste were he to lean across for a kiss.

Abruptly, he turned away, his chest tight with an anger that had consumed him ever since that dreadful night at the Pettigrews' ball. Even now, he couldn't believe she was leaving him. And part of him couldn't believe he was letting her go.

He'd thought about confronting her again, declaring himself and his love for her. But she'd made it clear that whatever tender feelings she might once have held no longer existed. She'd made her choice.

She wanted her freedom.

She didn't want him.

At length, the coach rolled to a stop in front of the house.

Her house.

After letting the footman help her down, he followed, casting an idle glance at the stately Georgian manse, with its red brick exterior and multitude of windows. She'd wanted lots of light and sunshine for her painting. She would find it here in this dwelling. And also in the big garden, where she could carry her easel and draw to her heart's content.

He waited in the front parlor, refusing to do more than take off his hat, while the housekeeper took Grace on a tour. Only a few minutes later, she returned.

"Does the house meet with your approval?" he asked.

"Yes. Even more so than I expected," she said in a quiet voice. "It's absolutely lovely."

Unable to look at her, he set his hat on his head. "If you have everything you require, I shall take my leave. You need only write should you find anything that is not to your liking."

"I am certain I shall be more than comfortable."

"Well then, I bid you adieu."

He strode to the doorway, intending to walk through without another word or glance.

Instead he stopped on the threshold, one hand curled against the frame as he looked back. "Grace?"

She met his gaze, her eyes looking very grey.

And for a moment, he very nearly poured out his heart, very nearly begged.

"Enjoy your independence, Grace," he said instead.

Then, before he could disgrace himself, he turned on his heel and strode into the hallway and out the door. Stepping into the coach, he gave the order to drive on. To where, he still had no idea.

From inside the parlor, Grace stood motionless. Part of her wanted to run after him. Another part told her to let him leave.

Then suddenly it was too late, as Jack's coachman gave a shout that set the horses in motion. Running to the window, she watched until the coach vanished from sight. Even then, she stood, one hand on the glass, as if she could call him back.

She didn't know how long she waited there, time slowing to an indistinct beat. The sun shifted in the sky, but she noticed it only as a change in the light and not as an indication of the waning day.

A brief knock came at the parlor door. "Excuse the interruption, my lady," the housekeeper said. "But will you be wanting dinner soon? We can serve it in the dining room, if you'd like?"

Dinner? No, she wouldn't be able to eat a bite. In fact, the very idea of food made her queasy.

"Just tea, I think," she told the servant. "And a bath. I'm very tired from the journey."

The housekeeper paused for a moment, then gave a nod. "You go on upstairs, your ladyship, and we'll see to you right and tight. Don't you worry about a thing."

Following the woman's suggestion, she did as she was bade.

Nearly a month later, Grace slid her paintbrush into a water-filled pottery jug set on the small table next to her painting. Leaning back in the cane-backed chair the footman had also carried out into the garden for her earlier that morning, she studied her latest efforts.

Lackluster, she thought. *And dull.* With none of her usual creative spark.

But then she supposed her artistic endeavors were merely a reflection of her mood of late, which was also lackluster, dull — and if she were being brutally honest — relentlessly melancholy.

Yet she couldn't assign any of the blame for her sad disposition on her new place of residence.

The house was beautiful, with comfortable, well-appointed rooms and gracious amenities. The servants were uniformly cheerful and exceptionally well-trained. The nearby village was comprised of charming shops, thriving townsfolk, and a fine old Anglican church that tried to keep everyone's sins in check, especially on Sundays. Her neighbors were a friendly lot, but respectful — seeming to understand her need for solitude without ever being asked to provide it.

And then there was the expansive garden that ran the length of the rear of the house — lush with color and fragrances that seemed to burst from every branch and bloom. Whoever had designed it possessed a keen eye for beauty, each plant chosen with obvious care and an affinity for nature.

She'd even acquired a new cat from its

depths, a stray orange tom she found wandering among the hydrangea bushes one morning. An offered dish of milk and he'd been her bosom beau ever since. She'd decided to call him Ranunculus because Buttercup was far too feminine a name for such a large and impressive male. She gazed at him now where he slept in the sunshine, basking like a small potentate in the heat of the day.

If only she could take the same delight. Instead, the humid, mid-August air pressed upon her like a wet, woolen blanket. Mayhap that was the cause of her blue devils.

That and Jack. But she refused to dwell on him.

Her hands squeezed into fists on her lap as she willed away the ache in her breast.

Since the day they'd parted, she'd heard nothing from him. Her only contact had been a few letters forwarded by his man of business — and all those had been from friends and family, including Meg, Mallory and Ava.

So far, she hadn't been able to bring herself to divulge the details of her separation from Jack. And from the tenor of the missives she'd received, she gleaned that he hadn't either.

The news would have to be shared soon

though, she knew, but for the time being, she'd glossed over such particulars in her letters of reply in favor of more cheerful subjects.

As for Jack, the only thing she knew for certain was that he had not returned to London. Otherwise, she had no knowledge of his whereabouts.

Probably at a party in the country. Drinking, gaming and wenching with nary a thought for me.

Her stomach churned at the notion. But such circumstances were inevitable now. They'd said their good-byes. Their lives were now their own and she would be well-advised to get on with hers.

If only I could, she mused, casting another glance at her currently dismal painting. She was debating whether to forge onward with another attempt when a wave of exhaustion swept through her.

Sighing, she closed her eyes and prayed it would pass.

Over the past several days, she'd been struggling with what seemed like a case of the summer ague. Yet oddly enough, she had no fever, and her symptoms seemed to come and go with no apparent rhyme or reason.

In general, the worst of her malaise struck in the morning, when she would wake and be forced to fly from the bed in search of the nearest basin. Once she'd emptied her stomach in great shuddering heaves, she would crawl back into bed, then sleep like the dead. Usually, by the time she awakened, her queasiness would be gone, in its place a ravenous hunger that demanded immediate appeasement.

Then there was her weariness, bouts of irresistible sleepiness that would come over her at the most unlikely and inconvenient times of the day. One noontime, in fact, she'd gone into the library to get a book and ended up spending the whole afternoon curled up asleep on the sofa.

She supposed she ought to consult a physician, but she hated the bother of it, telling herself her present affliction would soon pass.

Only it didn't seem to be going away, not given her current tiredness.

Laying down her paintbrush, she wiped her fingers on a handkerchief, then stood.

Her head swam in a sudden, dizzying circle, blood thrumming in audible beats between her ears. Reaching out, she gripped the table edge and held on, fighting the blackness that threatened to engulf her. Swaying, she willed the vertigo to pass lest she crumple into an unconscious heap.

Stars above, what kind of malady do I have? she wondered as the worst of her dizziness began to fade. Not only was she periodically sick to her stomach and incredibly fatigued but now she was dizzy too!

For some reason, the thought of being dizzy triggered a memory of a comment Meg had made in one of her last letters.

> . . . I'm so dizzy these days with the baby that poor Cade has taken to hovering around me, terrified I may fall at any moment. He needn't worry though, since I spend half my time veering toward the nearest piece of furniture, so I can take a nap.

Dizziness. Naps. The only thing Meg hadn't mentioned was being sick in the morning. Or put another way, she hadn't complained of *morning sickness!* And now that Grace considered it, her menses was late. Very, very late!

Oh, dear heavens, Grace realized, as she let out a whooshing breath and sat down hard on the chair.

I'm with child!

Jack came awake with a start and gazed bleary-eyed across the room, with its shelves of leather-bound books and glass-fronted cabinets full of knickknacks and antiquarian items.

For a few moments, his mind stayed blank. But then recognition set in.

The cottage, he thought.

He was in the cottage where he and Grace had spent their honeymoon. Inside the library where he'd passed so much time during that first dreadful week.

What insanity ever possessed me to come back here? he wondered for the hundredth time. *I really should be carted off to Bedlam for such a stupid idea.*

But after leaving Grace nearly a month ago, he'd been like a ship without a rudder, floundering and cast adrift. And so he'd come to the only place that made sense at the time. The only place he could be at peace.

Only he wasn't at peace.

He was in hell.

Every room overflowed with memories of Grace, as though she were a ghost who haunted him wherever he went. Everywhere, that is, but here in this library. During her brief residence, she'd rarely been in this room, so the memories weren't as strong. Because of that, he used the space as a refuge.

He supposed he ought to have packed his luggage and departed by now, but where would he go? He had no interest in staying at an inn. And even less in staying with friends. Unlike Cade, he'd never acquired an estate of his own, and he couldn't set foot in London for a couple more weeks. Besides, the town house would be even worse than this cottage, with far more memories of Grace to be endured.

Yawning, he rubbed a hand over the heavy growth of bristle lining his throat and cheeks. He hadn't shaved in days. He hadn't felt like it, spending most of his time wallowing in cheroots, long walks and solitude.

As for sleep, he got very little.

Each night he stubbornly forced himself to lie down on the mattress in the bedroom. But every time he closed his eyes, Grace was there. And once he started thinking about her, he couldn't stop, until finally he would come here to the library and sleep in the armchair.

Another man might have drowned his misery in the bottom of a brandy decanter. But after a brief infatuation with that particular poison, he'd given it up, realizing he felt worse rather than better. The only thing the alcohol did was give him a sore head, a churning gut and no real comfort at all.

Reaching into his pocket, he searched for his watch to see just how late the hour really was. Instead of the timepiece, however, his fingers brushed against a now familiar piece of jewelry that he'd taken to carrying.

He'd discovered it among some of his things before leaving London, and had slipped it into his pocket. Why he'd done it, he still didn't know. Maybe he'd hoped to give it to her when they parted. Maybe he'd needed to carry a piece of her with him after she was gone.

Drawing it out, he gazed at the heart-shaped amethyst pendant, running his thumb over the tiny miniature garden in the center.

He wondered if she liked her garden at her new house in Kent. He wondered if she liked living there. Did she miss her old life? Did she miss him?

Christ, what a pitiful idiot I've become.

If he had any sense, he'd leave this room, ride to the nearest tavern, find a willing woman and tup her until he couldn't think straight. Tup her, and as many more nameless females as it took to drive one long-legged redhead out of his mind.

And what about his heart?

Eventually, he would cut her out of that as well, he assured himself. He just needed time and the right sharp implement to do the job.

He was considering taking another one of his long, rambling walks through the nearby woods and fields when a rap sounded at the door.

His first instinct was to ignore it. Frankly, he was surprised that any of the servants had the nerve to disturb him. His humor was so foul most of the time that he'd scared off all the maids; none of them would come near any more. Only the housekeeper remained to see to his meals and tend to the necessary cleaning. And the one remaining footman wasn't too keen on him either — not after he'd thrown a plate of fried eggs at the fellow's head one particularly bad morning.

The knock came again.

He grumbled under his breath, tucking the pendant back into his pocket before he called out. "Yes. What is it?"

The door opened, but the man who entered wasn't the footman, as Jack expected. In fact, he didn't even recognize the stranger at first. But then, as the slender, sandy-haired man moved farther into the room, his identity came clear.

It was Terrence Cooke, Grace's friend and publisher.

"What the deuce are you doing here?" Jack said, making no effort to rise from his chair.

Cooke straightened his shoulders and walked all the way inside. "Well, hallo to you too, your lordship. Not that I'd call that remark much of a greeting, particularly given the trouble I've endured traveling here from London." He doffed his hat and placed it on a small table. "You're a hard man to locate, did you know that?"

"Obviously not hard enough, since you found me."

"A friend of mine who knows your solicitor put me in touch," Cooke continued in a conversational tone, clearly not put off by Jack's less than warm reception. "He thought you might be here in Oxfordshire."

"Next time I'm in Town, I'll have to remember to get a new solicitor. What do you want?"

"Not *what* actually, but *who*. I've come to see Grace. Is she here?"

Jack's upper lip curled in a sneer. "Does it look like she's here?"

Cooke paused, his brows furrowing slightly. "No. If it weren't for your redoubtable housekeeper, I'd wonder if anyone were here, the place is so unrelentingly grim. Reminds me a bit of a hermit's den."

Jack sent him a fresh glare.

Cooke glanced around the room, wrinkling his nose, no doubt in offense over the acrid scent of the cheroots Jack had been smoking by the dozen. That and the stale remains of last night's mostly untouched supper, which had yet to be cleared away.

"If Grace isn't here, then where is she?" Cooke persisted.

Jack sent the other man a deliberately menacing look. "Worried I've done away with her?"

Cooke studied him for a long moment. "If anything I'd say she's done away with you. What's happened? You look like the very devil, Byron."

Jack clenched his teeth so hard they hurt. "Get out."

"Rumor in Town has it that the pair of you are like cooing lovebirds. Apparently, that's not the case."

"I said *get out,*" Jack ordered in a low growl.

"As you choose. I suppose I'll have to find another method of getting this book to Grace."

Jack stilled. "Book? What book?"

Only then did he notice the rectangular

volume the other man had set on the table beneath his hat when he'd first come in.

"It's the new edition of Grace's latest book. Rather than entrust it to the vagaries of the post, I thought I would give it to her personally."

"I'll give it to her," Jack said, without taking the time to consider his response.

"Pardon?"

"I said you are to leave it with me. I'll make certain she receives it."

What am I saying? he wondered. *I have no plans to see Grace, so why take on the burden of delivering this book to her?* Yet he realized that's exactly what he wanted. An excuse, anything that gave him the chance to see her again.

After a moment, Cooke picked up his hat — and only his hat. "Thank you, my lord. It'll save me a trip into Kent."

"What? Then you already knew?"

Cooke shrugged. "More rumors. I wanted the truth."

"About her location?"

"No, about you and whether or not you love her. I can see that you do. She loves you too, so why are the two of you living apart?"

Jack's chest tightened with a familiar ache. "Grace doesn't love me."

Cooke gave a humorless laugh. "In that, you are wrong. I've known her a lot longer than you. Years, in fact, while I tried to win her affection. Never once did she look at me — or any other man for that matter — the way she looks at you. I saw it that day in Bath when we met. Why else do you think I tried so hard to prize her away?"

"Her money perhaps, since I understand you have different . . . interests, shall we say?"

"Whatever other *interests* I have doesn't mean I don't love her. And I never cared about her money. But in the last few months, I've realized that Grace was right. I'm being true to myself now and I'm happier for it. Tell her I've met someone. A new business partner with whom I hope to share my life as well. Grace has my thanks for that. In appreciation, I want her to be happy too, and for that she needs you."

"You can see how much she *needs* me. She wants her independence. That's why she's living in Kent."

"Take that book to her and see if she's really content. Unless you're happier without her? If so, then send it by messenger."

But Jack knew he would take the volume to her himself. As for Cooke's assertions about Grace's feelings, well, he couldn't afford to let himself hope on that front. But he would visit. Suddenly, he knew he could do nothing else.

CHAPTER 26

~~Dear Jack,~~
~~Dear Lord Jack,~~
~~My Lord,~~
~~Husband,~~

"Aghh!" Grace cried as she grabbed up the piece of stationery and crumpled it into a ball.

If I can't even write something as simple as a salutation, she berated herself, *how am I ever going to find the right way to tell Jack that I'm expecting his child?*

Cursing under her breath, she tossed the wadded paper onto the pile along with all her other unsuccessful attempts. So far, she wasn't having much luck drafting a letter, despite the fact that she'd had nearly a week to contemplate the best way to break the news.

After the revelation she'd had concerning her health that morning in the garden, she'd decided to confirm her suspicions and consult a physician.

Less than an hour after his arrival, the doctor told her what she already knew. She was with child. About nine weeks was his best guess given the information she'd provided and the physical examination he'd performed.

After thanking him and sending him on his way, she'd sat on the chaise in her bedroom for a very long time, faintly stunned despite her prior knowledge.

I'm going to be a mother, she'd thought, a smile spreading over her face.

But in the next second, her smile disappeared, as she realized she would have to tell Jack.

But how?

And when?

More importantly, what would his reaction be to the news? Would he greet it with happiness — or not?

Doubt weighed on her over the next several days, leaving her no closer to a decision than before. Finally this morning, she'd forced herself to act, reasoning that a letter would be the easiest and most straightforward way of telling him. But so far the missive was proving much more problematic than she'd anticipated.

Sighing, she drew out a fresh sheet of writing paper and picked up her pen, determined to begin anew. She hadn't put so much as a mark on the page when she heard the muffled sound of voices coming from outside.

Had visitors arrived? she wondered. She certainly wasn't expecting anyone. Curious, she crossed to the window and gazed out at the front drive. Her lips parted on a sudden inhalation when she saw a familiar black phaeton — and the man standing beside it, conversing with her footman.

Jack!

Stars above, what's he doing here?

Then he strolled toward the house and disappeared from view. Seconds later, she heard the front door being opened and closed.

A quiver traced over her skin at the sound of his strong, silvery voice, as he exchanged greetings with her housekeeper. His words were indistinct, but not the rhythm or the tone. He sounded . . . serious.

Brushing a hand over her skirt, she prepared herself for his entrance. As she did, she caught sight of the wadded-up balls of discarded stationery lying all over the top of her writing desk. Rushing forward, she gathered them up and hurried over to stuff them inside the first convenient hiding place she could find — a brass ash pail on the fireplace hearth. She set the lid on the pail and raced back to her desk.

Swaying, she gripped the back of her desk chair and hung on, hoping she didn't disgrace herself by fainting at his feet. Heart pounding hard, she arranged her features into what she prayed would seem a serene expression. Only then did she glance across to watch him stride into the room.

Her knees weakened at the sight, her hand tightening painfully against the wood of the chair. He was so handsome that it hurt to look at him — his mahogany hair attractively tousled from his journey, his eyes the same pure, clear azure blue that still had the power to make her melt. Tall and powerfully male, his presence instantly filled the room. Even so, as he walked closer, she couldn't help but notice that the bones in his face seemed slightly more prominent, as if he'd lost weight.

Then she had no more time to consider the matter as he stopped and made her an elegant bow. "Hello, madam," he said. "How do you do?"

Responding in kind, she curtseyed, careful not to release her grip on the chair. "My lord." Not trusting her knees to continue holding her up, she let go of the chair long enough to sink onto its seat.

Crossing to a nearby side chair, he took a seat as well. As he did, she saw him set a paper-wrapped parcel onto a small nearby table.

"Forgive the unexpected nature of my call," he began. "I was . . . traveling and thought I would stop to see how you are faring. How are you finding the house?"

Traveling? Yes, she supposed he'd had occasion to travel recently. *Probably departing one house party and making his way to the next.*

"T-the house?" she answered. "The house is everything to be desired, extremely comfortable and pleasant."

"Good." He paused, a quiet descending that was both awkward and pronounced. "And the servants?" he continued. "They're to your liking, as well?"

"Oh, yes," she replied. "They take excellent care of me. I have only to make a comment, however offhand, and my wishes are seen to in an instant."

"They were hired for their efficiency. I would expect no less."

"You chose well, my lord."

Assuming he'd chosen at all. More likely,

his estate agent had made all the arrangements.

But what did it matter? What did any of it matter now? she thought, ruefully aware how stiff and formal everything was between her and Jack. It was as though they were little more than passing acquaintances. But perhaps that was all they were to each other now. What did she expect though, since they were separated? What is it she wanted?

"So, you're happy here then?" he ventured.

"Yes, I'm very happy with the residence."

His brows drew together a fraction of an inch, and he cleared his throat. "And what of you? Are *you* happy?"

Her pulse thudded in her throat and wrists as she lowered her gaze.

Happy?

Happy wasn't a word she used anymore, at least not in relation to herself.

Comfortable? Yes.

Surviving? Obviously.

But happy? No, she couldn't say she was happy.

Except when she thought of the baby. The promise of the child, and all the love she would shower on him or her, brought her immeasurable joy. Even so, she wasn't sure whether that was the sort of happiness Jack meant.

Clearly, he wanted to make sure she was well-settled. That way, he wouldn't have to concern himself over her any further. He could continue on to his party and not spare her another thought.

Forcing her lips upward, she put on a falsely cheerful smile. "Of course, I'm happy."

His face grew very calm and even, almost devoid of expression. And she knew she'd been right in her assumptions about his motivation for this visit. In a few minutes, he would leave and who knows how much time would pass before she saw him again. *If* she saw him again.

A fluttering erupted in her chest, a sensation not unlike panic. Tamping it down, she thought again of the baby, and let the knowledge bring her comfort. But with it came a reminder that she needed to share the news with Jack. All she had to do was open her mouth and say the words, and her duty would be absolved.

My lord, you're going to be a father.

How easy and simple the statement. And yet, how impossible the words seemed given the distance between them.

As though the baby agreed, her stomach

lurched, churning with a queasy dip that had grown almost familiar over the past few weeks. Ignoring it, she gathered her nerve.

Before she could speak though, he did.

"I brought you something." Reaching over, he picked up the parcel from the table and held it out. "Or rather I should say Terrence Cooke brought you something. He asked me to deliver this."

She let him press the package into her hands. "You saw Terrence? When?"

"A couple days ago. That's your book, the latest one. He wanted you to have it."

She smoothed a hand over the paper. "My book?" she said blankly. "Oh, of the birds. Of course."

She'd almost forgotten about the publication in the whirlwind of the last several months. How amazing to think that nearly a year had passed since that long ago day when she'd first met Jack in Hatchard's. How had everything that had once seemed so right, gone so very wrong?

Her stomach lurched again, more insistently this time.

Please God, she prayed, *not now!*

Laying the book aside without unwrapping it, she drew a few shallow breaths in hopes that it would stave off the need to be sick. "Well, thank you for bringing the g-gift to me. I shall have to write and thank Terrence as well."

"Yes, do that," Jack said in a low voice. "I'm sure he would appreciate hearing from you."

She nodded and concentrated on keeping her breathing slow and steady, hoping he didn't notice the perspiration beginning to dampen her skin.

"I suppose I should take my leave," he said.

"If you must, I won't keep you. It was good of you to call."

She thought she saw his jaw tense, but she wasn't sure, too consumed with her own inner turmoil to pay careful attention.

Perhaps she was being idiotic, but she couldn't bear the idea of being ill in front of him. She hated the notion of letting him see her at her worst — weak and vulnerable and stripped of her control. But what of her obligation to tell him about the baby?

She would do it later, she decided. She'd write him a letter, after all. Besides, given the awkwardness between them, he would probably prefer it if she shared the news in writing.

Her stomach lurched again. *He really does need to leave now.*

Relief poured through her when he stood.

But instead of moving away, he hesitated. "You will let me know if there is anything you require?"

She nodded and clamped her lips tight.

"I may be going north for a while," he said, gazing toward the window. "I'm not sure of my plans. As I told you before, you may reach me through my solicitor. Or Edward. My brother will always know where I may be found."

"T-thank you, my lord," she whispered. "You are most solicitous."

"Being solicitous has nothing to do with it," he said in a rough tone. "No matter our situation, you are, and shall always be, my wife."

Her gaze went to his, lingering for a long moment.

Then her stomach rebelled again and scattered every thought in her brain. Blood drained from her cheeks, as she shot to her feet.

"Grace?" he asked. "You don't look well. Are you all right?"

But she didn't have time to answer, her feet already moving as fast as they could carry her toward a stand on the far side of the room.

Thank heavens for her housekeeper, who'd quietly seen to it that a plentiful array of bowls and basins were set throughout the house for just such a circumstance. Otherwise, Grace knew she would have thoroughly shamed herself by being ill in the most inappropriate of ways and places.

As it was, she managed to grab the bowl just in time, sinking to her knees as she emptied her stomach in great, aching heaves. She sensed Jack standing somewhere behind her in the room. But he didn't come near. He was probably too disgusted.

Finally, the worst was over — her stomach calmed, her face streaked with tears. She huddled there, trying to find the strength to struggle to her feet, when a hand reached down to help her.

With efficient ease, he set the bowl away, then knelt beside her. Tipping up her chin, he stroked a dampened handkerchief against her hot, perspiring cheeks and across her trembling lips. She closed her eyes in gratitude, the refreshing coolness wafting over her like a benediction. Refolding the handkerchief, he slid the linen over her neck as well, then drew it away to offer her a glass of water.

Gratefully, she drank.

"Slowly now," he admonished, as she swallowed too fast. "Just a few sips."

Nodding, she took the glass again, careful

to sip this time.

"Why didn't you tell me you were ill?" he asked in a thick voice.

"It . . . it just came on me. I'm sorry."

"Sorry for what? It's not your fault you're sick." He stood, then reached down to help her do the same.

She'd barely gotten to her feet when she found herself off them once more, as Jack swung her up into his arms. "Put me down," she said. "I'm too heavy."

He made a dismissive noise and strode with her toward the door. "I'm going to put you to bed, then call for the doctor. You've obviously taken ill with a stomach flux of some kind."

"It's not a flux and I don't need the doctor."

"Of course you do. If you're worried about him bleeding you, I'll make sure he doesn't."

"No, it's not that, it's . . ."

"You, there," he said to her footman, who was standing wide-eyed in the hall, watching them. "Send for the physician immediately."

"No, don't," she countered, glancing over Jack's shoulder at the other man. "You are to ignore that order."

"You're too stubborn by half, do you know that?" Jack said to her through his teeth. "Well, it shall make no difference in the end."

Taking the stairs, he carried her up them with an ease that left her feeling as small and dainty as the tiniest of females. Leaning her head against his coat, she closed her eyes for a moment and let herself relish his familiar warmth and clean, male scent.

Without asking for directions, he took her straight to her bedchamber, then strode across the sun-filled room to lay her gently against the mattress. She nearly reached for him as he drew away, but she forced herself to allow him to let her go.

To her surprise, he smoothed a hand over her hair, brushing a few loose strands away from her forehead the way he might do for a child. "I'll go send for that quack now," he told her in a gruff voice.

Reaching up, she caught hold of his wrist. "No, truly, there's no need. He's already been here to see me."

Jack's brows drew together in a sharp arch. "What do you mean? Already been here? Have you been ill like this before?"

A bit of color seemed to drain from his cheeks, as though he were quite alarmed, but she supposed it must be her imagination. "It's nothing," she told him, lowering her gaze. "At least nothing unusual for a woman in my condition."

His fingers tipped her chin upward, forcing her to look him in the eye. "What condition, Grace? Why are you sick?"

She drew a quick breath. "I was going to tell you, but —"

"But?"

"I wasn't sure how you'd feel." Drawing a deep breath, she plunged ahead. "I'm with child, Jack. I'm going to have a baby."

For the space of several heartbeats, Jack just stared, not certain if he'd heard her right.

Did she say she was expecting a baby? My baby!

Without thinking, he sat down on the bed next to her. "Are you sure?"

"Quite sure," she assured him. "I had my suspicions, and the doctor confirmed them a few days ago."

"When?"

"When what? When is the baby due, you mean?"

He gave a clipped nod.

"This spring. March, the doctor estimates, since I'm only a couple months along. It's still early yet in the pregnancy."

And it is, he thought, realizing that she must have conceived only a few weeks before she'd left him. Before that dreadful night at the Pettigrews' ball when everything between them had changed. To think she'd been pregnant then. If only he'd known, could he have found a way to stop her? Could he find a way to stop her from sending him away again now?

A small frown settled above her nose. "What are you thinking, my lord?" she murmured. "You aren't . . . you aren't sorry, are you?"

"No," he declared in a firm tone. "I'm not sorry at all." He paused. "I'm glad. Very, very glad."

She sent him a tremulous smile. "I am too. So very happy."

And abruptly the anger he'd been nursing these past weeks fell away, along with the misery that had left him numb and only half-alive. Warmth seeped slowly into his veins, the faintest sliver of hope stealing in behind it. He had no right to hope, he knew, but he couldn't seem to prevent the impulse, or the desire, however futile it might seem.

Reaching out, he drew her up and enfolded her in his arms to press her gently to his chest. She stiffened at first but then gave a weary little sigh and leaned her head against his shoulder, relaxing.

They sat that way without speaking, time passing with no real awareness. She relaxed even more in his embrace, and, to his surprise, he realized she was falling asleep. Tenderly, he lay her back against the pillows.

"Forgive me," she murmured. "I get so . . . sleepy these days. It's because of . . . the baby. Sometimes I can . . . barely . . . keep my eyes . . . open."

"Then don't." Standing, he picked up the light cotton blanket folded at the foot of the bed and spread it over her.

She sighed and snuggled into the warmth, her eyes closed, her breath becoming slow and even.

Using the lightest of touches, he brushed his fingertips across her cheek, then bent to press his lips to her forehead. "I love you, Grace," he whispered, too softly for her to possibly hear.

Straightening, he gazed at her for another long moment, then turned toward the door.

"Are you . . . leaving?" she mumbled in a drowsy voice.

"You need to sleep."

"Don't go, Jack," she said, clearly caught in a state halfway between consciousness and dreams. "Don't go away."

The warmth and the hope curled inside him again. "Not to worry. I'll be here when you wake."

And I will be, he vowed.

This time he was staying, whether she wanted him to or not.

She came awake in slow stages, stretching as sleep fell gradually away. Turning her head, she gazed into the waning light and realized that she must have slept nearly the whole of the afternoon. At least her nausea was gone, along with her tiredness. Obviously, she'd needed the rest.

Jack.

Had he really come for a visit, or had it all just been a dream?

She remembered bits, like puzzle pieces falling into place. They'd talked for a while. Their conversation had been awkward and uncomfortable. Then he'd given her a book . . . from Terrence . . . *her* book with the birds she'd painted.

He'd been about to depart when she'd taken ill.

How kind he'd been afterward, carrying her up the stairs and here to her room.

She knew she'd told him about the baby, remembering how her heart had pounded while she waited for his reaction, and the rush of relief and happiness when he'd told her he was glad.

Her relief had turned to surprise, though,

when he'd taken her in his arms — and then to profound pleasure as he'd cradled her against him with a tenderness that had proven her complete undoing.

After that, everything grew hazy, drowsiness claiming her with a strength she'd been unable to resist. She thought she remembered him promising to be there when she awakened.

Was he? Or had that been nothing more than some somnolent fantasy? Her hopes manifesting themselves in the world of dreams? She supposed she would find out the answer soon enough.

Sighing, she sat up and pushed the blanket off her lap.

Walking quickly to the washstand, she bathed her face and brushed her teeth, then hastily tidied the strands of hair that had come loose from her coiffure while she'd slept. She could have rung for her maid, but she didn't want to wait. She had to know.

Is Jack still here?

She beat a hand against a wrinkle in her skirt, then drew a steadying breath and went out into the hallway. By the time she reached the ground floor, she'd convinced herself he was gone.

Very likely, she would find a note informing her that he'd been unable to stay, after all. His missive would go on to say that she should keep him apprised of her needs regarding the baby and her health, and to let him know when she was brought to childbed.

Spirits dashed, she walked into the drawing room, expecting to find it empty. Instead, she discovered Jack, settled into a comfortable corner of the sofa with a book on his lap.

The sight of him brought her to an abrupt halt. "You're here."

Glancing up from his reading, he gave her a smile. "Of course. I told you I would stay. So, how are you feeling? Are you sure you should be up?"

"I . . . I am much better, thank you."

"Still queasy?"

"No, not a bit. Luckily, the nausea seems to disappear nearly as quickly as it comes upon me."

"Here now," he said, jumping to his feet. "You shouldn't be standing there like that."

In seconds, she found herself ferried with a few gentle steps to the nearest armchair. A laugh escaped her as she sank down onto the comfortable cushions. "I'm perfectly capable of standing, you know. I'm enceinte, not an invalid."

"Perhaps so," he said as he released his hold on her elbow, "but I'd feel better if you rested a while more, just in case."

"Just in case of what?"

"I don't want you fainting. Your housekeeper's been telling me you have bouts of vertigo in addition to your nausea and tiredness."

Her lips pursed. "I hadn't realized what a very big mouth Mrs. Mackie has."

"Don't worry. She hasn't been unduly forthcoming. Just sharing a few interesting details here and there."

Yes, she thought — knowing Jack, she was sure he'd had no trouble wheedling information out of the servant. Mrs. Mackie might be middle-aged, but she was still female. And as Grace knew all too well, females of any age were susceptible to Jack Byron's charming ways.

Sobered by the thought, her smile fell away.

Jack, however, seemed to take no notice as he slipped a pillow behind her back. "Comfortable?" he asked.

"Yes, most comfortable."

Ranunculus chose that moment to saunter inside, the big orange cat going straight across to Jack to rub against his trouser legs. Clearly unconcerned about any hair the feline might be leaving behind, Jack bent to stroke the cat's striped head and back.

"I see the two of you have already met," she remarked, observing the friendly byplay.

Soft purrs issued from the cat, his eyes closing with contentment as Jack scratched him under the chin. "Indeed," Jack said. "This big fellow introduced himself to me while you were sleeping. He's quite expert at hogging the sofa." His gaze moved to the cat. "Aren't you . . . Ranunculus, is it not?"

"That's right," she confirmed. Obviously Jack had gleaned additional "interesting details" from the servants.

He stroked the cat's head, his voice lowering. "At least she didn't call you Buttercup, old man."

"You know what ranunculus means?" she said, surprised.

His gaze swung up to meet hers. "I know a great deal more on that subject than you might imagine. Let's just say you . . . inspired me to learn."

Before she had time to respond, he returned to his seat on the couch. "So, what shall we do?"

"Do?" she repeated as the cat jumped into her lap. Automatically, she began to pet him.

"Tonight. It's still a little early for dinner, assuming you're up to eating dinner. Until then, I thought we could play a game perhaps. Or I could read a story or some poetry aloud so that all you need do is relax and listen. Which would you prefer?"

Either, she thought, *or both,* realizing that his suggestions sounded delightful. But she couldn't afford to delight in them, or in his company. She couldn't get used to having him around, couldn't risk everything that meant.

As though aware of her mercurial mood, the cat gave a meow and leapt to the ground. Padding on quick feet, he left the room.

Exactly as Jack will do.

"I didn't realize you were staying the night," she said in a brisk tone. "Your trip north and all. I believe you mentioned you needed to be on your way."

His brows drew together for a few seconds before relaxing again. "I also said that I wasn't certain of my plans. I have no pressing engagements, so I can afford to be flexible."

"I don't want to be a bother —"

"You aren't. I'll sleep in the guest room tonight, shall I?"

She hesitated. Was it wise to let him stay, even in the guest room? On the other hand, it wasn't as if she could throw him out. They might be estranged, but in the end, he was still her husband.

"I'll let Mrs. Mackie know to prepare the room," she said with a nod. "And lay out another place setting for dinner."

His mouth curved in a faint smile. "Thank you, Grace."

She didn't answer, too aware of how fast her heart was suddenly beating.

"Well then," he prompted. "What's it to be? Games or a story? I found a Maria Edgeworth novel in the library that you might enjoy. *Ennui,* I believe."

"Oh, I haven't read that one," she said, more tempted than she ought to admit.

"Or we could play chess. There's a board I can bring in."

She paused, knowing she shouldn't choose either option. "The story, please," she told him in a rush. "If you don't hate Mrs. Edgeworth, that is?"

A chuckle rumbled from his throat as he rose to retrieve the volume. "I trust I shall survive."

He's only here for tonight, she told herself, settling back in her chair. *Tonight and then he'll be gone, so enjoy the moment.*

Jack returned and took his seat again. Opening the book, he began to read.

The deep cadence of his voice stole over

her, the words like music. Closing her eyes, she gave in to the pleasure.

CHAPTER 27

Six weeks later, Jack was still there.

Each day, when she came downstairs, she expected to find him packed and ready to depart, anxious to finally be on his way. But then he would smile and ask how her night had been and before she knew it, half the day would be gone. Afternoon would amble past at a lazy pace, then Mrs. Mackie would be at the doorway announcing that dinner was served. By the time Grace glanced at a clock again, she would find the hour far too advanced for him to leave that night.

She supposed she could have asked him to depart, but selfishly — and stupidly — she found herself hoping he would stay just one more day. Equally as foolish was the way she began to depend upon him, especially when it came to her pregnancy.

Instinctively, he seemed to know exactly what she needed — coaxing her to sleep when she was drowsy, making sure she drank enough fluids and got enough to eat, ready with a basin and a comforting hand when the nausea struck and nothing would stay down.

He comforted her when she felt so dreadful she could barely lift her head, and he kept her relaxed and entertained the rest of the time — and all without making a single demand upon her.

As she well knew, Jack was a man of strong appetites — particularly of the passionate variety — so the lack of sex must surely have been wearing on him.

And yet he gave no indication of being displeased. Nor did he appear bored or distracted, as she'd assumed he would be without a constant round of parties and entertainments to keep him amused. In fact, if she didn't know better, she would almost believe he was . . . content.

But how could he possibly be satisfied living in a sexless union with his frequently ill, pregnant wife? Surely he must be chafing under the burden, anxious to send for his carriage and drive away with as much speed as he could muster. She was certain it was only a matter of time until he did.

Nonetheless, he remained — for reasons she couldn't possibly begin to fathom. But rather than make the attempt, she abdicated the responsibility, knowing he would tell her when he'd finally had enough and wanted to leave.

The last days of September drew to a close, and with them came not only cooler temperatures but also an end to the worst of her symptoms. As her pregnancy grew more advanced, her morning sickness disappeared, her energy rebounding as her body began to develop a new roundness.

She wasn't showing yet — at least not through her clothes — but now, as she lay in bed, she couldn't help but notice the slight bulge beneath her nightgown where her belly used to be flat. On a whim, she tried to suck in her stomach. It wouldn't budge.

Definitely the baby.

Running a hand over the new curve, she smiled.

She was woolgathering when the oddest sensation, like the fluttering of faerie's wings, made the breath catch in her lungs.

Oh, stars, did the baby just move?

Then it happened again, causing a laugh to bubble from her throat.

Abruptly she was overwhelmed with the need to tell someone. To share this small, yet miraculous, occurrence.

Flinging back the sheets, she hurried

across to the door that connected her bedchamber with Jack's — a door neither of them had ever attempted to open before. Without thinking, she pulled it wide and raced inside.

Standing in front of his shaving stand, Jack turned at her entrance, his razor poised less than an inch from his soap-covered, half-shaven face. He was dressed in a pair of fawn trousers and nothing else, his bare, muscular chest and broad shoulders a glorious sight to behold. Even so, she was too exhilarated over her news to pay more than momentary heed.

"Grace, what is it?" he demanded in clear concern, setting down his razor. "What's wrong? Are you ill?"

"No, not at all. I'm . . . oh, I don't know how to describe what I am. Just come here and feel."

His brows rose. "Feel what?"

"You'll see. Just give me your hand."

A peculiar expression flashed across his face before he reached for a towel to quickly dry his cheeks. Approaching, he stopped about a foot away from her.

"Closer," she urged. "You'll never be able to feel it from there." Caught up in her excitement, she reached out and took his hand, then placed his palm flat against her belly over the spot where she'd felt the fluttering sensation.

"What are we doing?" he questioned. "What is it I'm supposed to feel?"

"The baby!" she whispered.

Some of her excitement transferred to him. "You mean it moved?"

She nodded. "Yes. At least I think he did. Now, be quiet and let's see if he'll do it again."

Jack edged closer, sliding an arm behind her back while he positioned his palm more fully across her nightgown-clad stomach.

Together, they waited.

And waited.

"I don't feel anything," he said in a low voice.

"Give it another minute," she hushed. "Surely he'll move again."

Just as she was on the verge of conceding defeat, when the fluttering came once more, a gossamer quiver that made her inhale with awe.

"Well, I'll be," he murmured. "I did feel something. At least I think I did. Will he do it again, do you imagine?"

"I'm not sure. I can barely feel it myself, but it's there. Our baby is really there."

She sent him a smile, buoyant and without barriers.

Something in his eyes changed, his pupils dilating inside rings of peerless blue, as he gazed deep into her own.

Her lips parted, her breath coming faster for reasons that had nothing to do with her excitement over their child. He bent nearer, pausing for an instant, as though he were giving her a chance to retreat. When she didn't, his mouth met hers — warm and slow and astonishingly sweet.

Her eyelids slid closed and she held herself utterly still, as if she were afraid even the smallest movement would shatter the moment. Instead, she let herself float, giving herself permission to indulge — if only for a few precious seconds — in the perfect beauty of his touch. Breathing deeply, she drew in his scent — a delectable combination of shaving soap, warm skin and man that swirled like an elixir in her head.

Then, before she had time to make a clear choice about whether to step out of his hold or move deeper into it, he took the decision out of her hands. Gentle as a sigh, he broke their kiss, easing his lips ever so gradually away.

He left his arm looped in an undemanding circle around her waist, as if he couldn't quite bring himself to release her entirely. "I've missed that. I've missed *you.*"

"What do you mean? I've been right here."

"You're here, but not always with me. You keep me . . . separate."

As she considered, she realized he was right. In spite of all his support and companionship these past few weeks, and in spite of her undeniable pleasure in his company, she did keep him at a distance. To protect herself, she'd put up an emotional shield, an invisible wall that no one — most especially Jack — could possibly penetrate. But during the past few minutes, she'd let that wall drop. She'd let him in.

Breaking eye contact, he glanced away. "There's something I've been meaning to tell you. Something I ought to have said long ago."

She froze, unable to believe he would do this here and now. But she'd known from the day he arrived that this moment would come, that he would leave as abruptly as he'd arrived.

Muscles suddenly rigid, she tried to step out of his grasp. When he wouldn't let her, she forced herself to relax and wait.

It would all be over soon. He would set her free, then he would leave, finally and for good.

"Grace, I love you."

Her gaze flew to his, confusion drowning

out the fabrication she'd prepared in order to show just how little she supposedly cared. "What did you say?" she whispered in a faint voice.

His eyes locked on hers. "I said, I love you."

She blinked and gave her head a tiny shake. *No, you don't,* she thought.

"But I do," he stated, as though he'd heard her silent denial. "And what's more, I'm not leaving. I know you're waiting for me to, I can see it in your eyes. But you're not getting rid of me so easily this time. I'm staying, whether you like it or not."

Blood throbbed between her temples, her heart hammering violently in her chest.

"I know you still don't trust me," he continued. "I realize you believe you have good reason not to. Perhaps your doubts were valid in the beginning, but no longer."

She couldn't move, couldn't speak.

Reaching up, he stroked the back of his fingers over her cheek. "You're the only woman I want, the only woman I will *ever* want. Despite what you think you saw that night with Philipa Stockton, I've been faithful and I'll continue to be. I can't prove it with words, only in deed. Just as I can't prove the strength of my love, I can only show you, day by day by day. And I will, even if it takes the rest of my life to make you believe me."

Taking a breath, she worked to form a response, so conflicted she scarcely knew how to react. But before she could, he moved his fingers to cover her lips.

"It's all right," he reassured her. "You don't have to say anything right now. I just wanted you to know how I felt. How I feel. And that I'm going to fight for you, Grace. You loved me once. I can wait and hope you will again."

Leaning close, he pressed his mouth to hers — quickly, gently.

"In the meantime," he said, his tone thick as he pulled away, "I'll be here for you and the baby. We'll live wherever you want. The choice will be entirely up to you. Just don't ask me to go away. I tried that once and it nearly killed me. I'd rather live with your indifference than not live with you at all."

Stepping back, he went to his bedside table. He returned carrying something. Opening his palm, he revealed the heart-shaped pendant he'd given her so many months ago.

"I've kept this," he explained. "You might say it's become a talisman of sorts. I . . . I carry it everywhere. But I'm going to give it to you again, if you'll take it. Whether you decide ever to wear it or not is up to you."

"Jack," she murmured, as she let him press the jewelry into her hand.

Smiling gently, he kissed her forehead. "Now, enough of such syrupy talk. Why don't you get dressed and I'll finish doing the same. We can have breakfast together. Then I'm off for an appointment with a couple of the local farmers."

"Farmers?" she repeated, nonplussed at the abrupt change of subject.

"I have an idea for planting an orchard in the fallow field that lies south of the house. You may not realize, but a couple hundred acres are attached to this property. I thought it might provide us with some extra income, while also giving the people around here a new source of employment."

"You're right. It would," she agreed. "It's an excellent notion."

He smiled again. "I'm glad you approve. Well, go on now and get dressed, sweetheart. The rest of the day awaits."

They met in the breakfast room three-quarters of an hour later, sharing a meal and friendly conversation during which neither of them remarked in any way on Jack's unexpected declaration. Nor did they discuss the fact that she hadn't said anything in reply.

Once breakfast was finished, he bid her a warm goodbye, then departed for his meeting. Meanwhile, she was left to do as she wished for the remainder of the morning.

Deciding she would enjoy some fresh air, she donned her most comfortable walking boots and a bonnet, then set off along the tree-lined path that led toward the village. She told Mrs. Mackie she wouldn't go far or be away too long, promising to turn back immediately should she experience the least hint of vertigo or nausea.

But she felt well. Excellent, in fact. The best she had in weeks. Physically, at least.

As for her emotional state . . .

She listened to her boots slap softly against the packed earthen path and to the random call of birds perched in various tree branches above her.

I love you, Grace.

His words echoed in a dulcet whisper through her mind.

Without realizing, her step slowed, her thoughts turning inward.

I love you, Grace.

Yes, but did he really mean what he said?

And if he did, why had he waited until now to tell her? Why today and not yesterday? Why not last week or last month or last year?

Maybe because he hadn't realized his true feelings until recently, the emotion coming on him so gradually that he hadn't seen it for what it was?

Or perhaps he'd known for ages that he loved her but had been hesitant to reveal himself and risk rejection.

Then there was another possibility — one she found the most likely and the least satisfactory. He didn't really love her but only said he did because of the baby.

Her hand went to her stomach, thinking of the life inside. Was it this little baby he actually loved — and through a sort of benign default, her too?

Lowering her hand again, she walked on.

If she were the same person she'd been a year ago, she would have been dancing on air to hear him speak such words, never questioning his truthfulness. But she wasn't that woman anymore — that naïve girl — and to her chagrin, she realized she did need more from him than words. He'd hurt her too deeply in the past for her to blithely accept his declaration of love on its face.

But as he'd pointed out himself, what other proof could he provide, if words weren't enough? What could he do, except show her each and every day that he meant what he said, that he honestly and truly loved her?

Still, that would take time.

Should she give it to him? Dare she take the risk again? Yet how could she not when he was her husband and the father of her child? How could she turn her back on a chance at happiness when she loved him and always would?

Could she trust him, though? Could she ever give her whole heart to him again?

Unsure, but knowing her path led back to the house and to Jack, she stopped and turned around to retrace her steps.

CHAPTER 28

The next ten days passed in much the same way as the ten before them — with a few very important differences.

Each morning when Jack greeted her, he now also said those three important words.

I love you.

And every night at her bedroom door, he told her again. Often giving her a sweet, soft kiss that lingered on her lips long after he'd sought his own solitary bed.

He spoiled and cosseted her, bringing her interesting little gifts that ran the gamut from a new set of sable-tipped paintbrushes to a trio of smooth stones he said would be perfect for skipping on the little pond not too far from the house.

Every day brought a new delight and a new experience as her body continued to change. When she complained about putting on weight, he told her the extra pounds only made her more beautiful. Expectant women were supposed to glow, he informed her, and she was more radiant now than the sun itself.

After a few days, she realized that it was almost as if he were courting her, seducing her all over again, as he had during those halcyon days in Bath.

Only this time was he courting her for real? she found herself wondering more and more often. Or was she only imagining what she wanted to believe?

She was no closer to knowing the answer, as October moved into its second week. So far the temperatures had been unusually warm for fall, allowing the plants and flowers to bloom long past their usual growing season, as if nature had given them all a reprieve.

Deciding to take advantage of the clement weather, Grace gathered her art supplies, and with the help of a footman, set up a table and chair so she could paint in the garden. If Mother Nature changed her mind and brought cold temperatures tonight, this might well be her last chance until next spring to capture the colorful blossoms. And with Jack away in the village for a few hours, painting seemed an excellent occupation.

Actually she'd been doing a great deal more painting lately, resuming her work on the flower folio at Jack's urging — and Terrence's, as well.

She'd had a lovely letter from Terrence about three weeks ago, in which he'd expressed his delight at learning of her pregnancy. He shared the latest goings-on in London. Then he went on to tell her about his efforts to expand the business with his new partner and how much happier he was of late. In closing, he assured her that her artwork would always be welcome at Cooke and Jones Publishers and to send word when her next set of paintings was complete.

Later, when she'd mentioned Terrence's comment to Jack, he instantly agreed.

"Of course you must paint!" he stated with an emphatic tilt of his chin. "It would be nothing short of a crime if you did not."

And so with lighter spirits and a renewed enthusiasm for her creative endeavors, she'd pulled out the partially completed folio and set to work.

Seated now in the garden, she swished her brush clean before twirling the soft bristles over a small block of yellow paint. Humming under her breath, she mixed it with a little blue and watched a compelling, muted shade of green spring to life. She smiled and feathered the new shade in light strokes over the watercolor paper.

Pausing, she took a moment to study the results.

" 'Tis a right fine 'un, that picture, if you don't mind me sayin' so," declared a wizened voice from somewhere over her right shoulder.

Glancing around, she saw the gardener standing a few feet distant, his squat body and nearly bald pate always putting her in mind of a monk. But the old man, with his twelve children and twenty-two grandchildren, was far from a somber or celibate holy man. Although, as she'd long ago noted, he did seem to have an almost miraculous ability with plants. Everything he touched seemed to thrive.

"Good afternoon, Mr. Potsley. Come to tend the grounds?"

"Right y'are, missus . . . I mean your ladyship. Although I'd have likely been here sooner if I'd known ye were going to be outside. Prettiest flower in the garden, ye are," he said, giving her a friendly wink.

She laughed, not the least offended, since Mr. Potsley was not only married but had just celebrated his seventy-fifth birthday last month. Despite the impropriety of a servant addressing his employer in such a casual manner, she didn't mind his harmless banter. Lighthearted conversation was simply part of who he was, in the same sort of way that charm was an intrinsic part of Jack. Neither could help who they were.

Nor would I want them to, she realized.

Pushing aside the thought, she swished her paintbrush clean again. "Well, I shan't keep you from your work. I'm sure you're anxious to take advantage of this beautiful day."

He nodded. "Exactly so. And ye as well. These blossoms won't keep past the first frost. I see ye're paintin' them pinks."

"The dianthus, yes."

"I just know 'em as pinks," he said with a shrug. "Same as I know the marigolds, the honeysuckle, and the hollyhocks. Now, that'll be the last of those 'til next year, since they're not so hardy as the others. 'Tis a wonder they've lasted as long as they have. Mebbe ye ought te paint them first."

"Yes, well, luckily I have already finished a rendering of that particular variety."

He grinned and shook his head again. "Ye sound jest like his lordship. He's always puffing on with them fancy names and fancy words."

Was he? How curious. But doubtless Jack was discussing something other than plants with Mr. Potsley. Though what else she couldn't easily imagine.

"Still," the old man stated in a proud tone, "I get things to grow whether I know their fancy name or not."

"That you do," she agreed with a smile. "And very ably, too, I might add."

"Thank ye, milady," he said, glancing away, as though he were embarrassed by the compliment. "I do my best."

"You've obviously put a great deal of care into this garden. I've rarely seen one so lovely and with such a thorough range of plantings. Sitting among so many gorgeous flowers always lifts my spirits, no matter what they might be. I expect the former owners of the house used to feel the same."

His grey brows drew tight. "No, ma'am. Least I don't suppose they did. But then I didn't tend to the property when the Chesters lived here."

This time her brows furrowed. "Oh, but I assumed you'd worked here for years."

He shook his head. "Just started a few months ago, right after his lordship bought the property. Until then, weren't all that much call for a gardener."

"Why not?"

"Cause there was hardly a garden to tend. Least not one worth mentioning. The trees were here and some of the shrubs, but the flower beds were thin and sad. The Chesters said nature should see to itself and whatever grew, nor didn't, was fine with them."

"So you cleaned up what was here?"

"Ripped out most of it, more like. His lordship told me he wanted this garden to be a showplace and that whatever I couldn't seed by summer, I was to find and transplant. Wanted it to look established-like with color for every one of the seasons. When I said it would cost him plenty, he told me he didn't care. No expense to be spared, he says."

She laid her paintbrush aside, hardly able to grasp what she was being told. "You designed the garden then?"

"Oh no, 'twasn't meself at all. His lordship did all the work. Had drawings and lists of every plant to be used and knew exactly where he wanted 'em put. Knew all the Latin names of 'em too. Saw that first plan meself with all his notes and jots before he gave me another copy with the common ones writ out so I could tell what they were. He asked me what I thought and if a lady would like it. Says as I thought the Queen herself would approve."

Breath grew thin in her lungs, her pulse speeding faster in confusion. Jack had done all this? Had arranged for the planting of this garden months ago before she'd even known about the house?

"Yup, even a Queen would like it, I says," she heard the gardener continue. "An' do ye know what he says back?"

"No," she whispered in a faint voice. "W-what did he say?"

He gave her a smile. "He says it don't matter if a Queen likes it, cause the only woman who matters is his wife. 'If this garden makes her smile,' he told me, 'then my efforts will have all been worthwhile.' "

Her hand shook as she realized that Jack had designed the garden.

For her!

"I said you must be a special woman," Mr. Potsley went on. "He said there was none finer. And he was right. Yer a sweet 'un, milady, and no mistake. I can see why his lordship is so smitten with ye. Fact is, ne'er seen a fellow so in love as that man o' yers. But then you must know that, way he dotes on you and that babe yer carrying."

And suddenly she knew the truth, knew the answer she'd been seeking. "Yes," she whispered. "I do know."

After a long minute, as if sensing her need to be alone, the old man turned away, ambling deeper into the garden.

As he did, a knot formed in her throat,

tears shimmering in her eyes.

Then she smiled.

It's not working, Jack thought as he rode his horse up the lane to Grace's house.

I've been here in Kent for weeks and I'm no closer to winning back her trust and love than I was at the start.

But those were two emotions that couldn't be forced; they had to be freely given and honestly earned. And considering his past actions, he'd given her good cause to do neither.

Even so, as he'd told her, he would do whatever it took, for however long it took, to win her back.

What if that day never comes? whispered a terrible voice in his head, bleakness stealing over him like a shadowy specter.

It will, he assured himself. *It must.*

What other choice was there, when he loved her so much he literally ached with it sometimes?

At least she'd given him some reason to hope, since she hadn't asked him to leave. He took comfort in the fact that they were living together again — even if it was in the most innocent and platonic of ways.

Lord only knew how many nights he'd lain awake, wanting her, knowing she was just in the next room. But until she invited him into her bed again, he would continue to sleep alone. Of course too, there was the baby to consider, so he might be in for many, many long months of doing without.

Yet, despite his desire, simply being with her was enough. Loving her, privilege enough.

The thought reminded him of his passionate declaration that morning in his bedroom. The way he'd poured out his heart to her as he'd never done before. Because he'd never been in love before.

Not truly. Not for always.

Which is why he would continue to wait — and pray — that someday she would do more than let him into her home: she would let him into her heart again, as well.

Arriving at the house, he dismounted, exchanging a brief good-evening with the groom before allowing the man to lead his bay gelding to the stable.

He entered through the front door, working to shake off the last of his blue devils as he handed his coat to the footman. He was about to go upstairs to change his clothes when one of the housemaids approached.

She gave him a timid smile as she curtseyed. "Her ladyship would l-like you t-to join her in the garden, my lord."

"The garden?" He paused for a moment, then nodded. "Very well. I'll join her now."

"Oh no, not now!" the girl stated. "At six. I-I was to tell you most expressly not to be there until six."

He frowned, a puzzled smile hovering over his lips. "Six, is it? What's this about, then?"

"Oh, I wouldn't know, milord. She just told me to give you the message and naught more. Beg pardon, but I've duties to attend, and Mrs. Mackie gets right peevish if I'm late."

"Heaven forfend you turn Mrs. Mackie peevish."

The servant stared, clearly not understanding his teasing.

"Go on," he said, taking pity.

Visibly relieved, she dropped another curtsey, then scurried off.

Crossing his arms, he stood still for a moment, wondering at this latest development. It was slightly past five o'clock now and the sun would be setting in the next hour, so what possible reason could Grace have for wanting to meet him in the garden at six?

His arms fell to his sides, though, as a sudden thought occurred, a memory forming of another meeting they'd had in another garden. The morning at Braebourne when she'd told him she would marry him, but only if he gave her this house and, later, a separation.

A lump formed in his throat. Had she finally made up her mind about them? And if so, had she decided to choose her freedom over making a life with him?

Chapter 29

The garden shimmered with candlelight from dozens of sweetly scented beeswax tapers set around to illuminate the space. In the center stood her painting table, now neatly draped in a crisp, white linen tablecloth and laid with her best china, crystal and silver.

More lighted candles were arranged on the table, a small vase of flowers set in the middle, tender petals of red, pink and ivory adding a pleasing burst of color. More color glowed in the sky, sunset turning the horizon a glorious golden apricot.

The clock inside the house chimed six. She hoped Jack wasn't late or he would miss the glorious show nature was performing.

Briefly, she considered sending one of the servants to find him, but the staff already thought she was acting oddly enough today with all her unusual requests. She didn't need to give them more grist for their mill.

Tugging her shawl more closely around her shoulders, she waited.

Soon, she heard footsteps and knew he'd arrived. Turning, she gave him a wide smile, excitement bubbling inside her like champagne.

"What's all this?" he demanded, his dark brows knitted together.

She paused at his tone but recovered quickly, too happy to let his less-than-enthusiastic greeting dim her giddy spirits. "Dinner," she announced with a wave of her arm. "I thought it might be fun to eat al fresco tonight with the sunset providing a beautiful tableau."

He studied the sky, painted now with brushstrokes of amber and pink. "The sun will be down soon, and then it'll be dark."

Her smile faltered slightly, but she recovered again. "The stars will take its place. Candlelight and stars are a heavenly combination."

"Not in October." He crossed his arms over his chest. "It's too cold to eat outside this time of year."

"I don't think so," she defended. "Not with the temperature as warm as it's been lately. Why, my guess is, we'll scarcely notice a little nip in the air."

He didn't reply, staring at the sunset as if

it were an offense to his eyes.

What is wrong with him? she wondered. *Why is he being so cross and disagreeable? Maybe he's simply hungry,* she told herself. *Perhaps all he needs is a good meal and his humor will improve.*

"Why do we not go ahead and start dinner?" she suggested, with an encouraging smile. "I thought soup would be the best way to begin."

He continued to stand with his arms crossed, a scowl on his face. For a moment she thought he was going to return inside the house, but then he walked forward. Or rather *stalked* forward.

Stopping, he pulled out one of the chairs and waited for her to take a seat. Moving to the one opposite, he took his place across from her.

At her signal, a pair of footmen emerged, trays in hand. The first man poured beverages — wine for Jack and lemonade for her — while the other served the soup. Then they withdrew.

Tendrils of steam drifted upward from each bowl, the pale broth gleaming faintly in the waning light. Dipping in her spoon, she took a sip.

"Hmm, delicious. Cream of potato. One of your favorites, is it not?"

He gave a soft grunt and ate a mouthful, and then another. His gaze moved to hers. "You'd better eat fast. This will be cold in the next two minutes."

Tightness spread through her chest. "Jack, you seem upset. Has something happened?"

"No. What could have happened?" He dipped his spoon in the soup again and ate another pair of bites, almost shoveling in the food.

"Your trip to the village. Nothing untoward occurred?"

"Of course not. The village was fine."

"Oh," she replied, utterly confused.

She stared at the soup before forcing herself to take another spoonful. After a single bite, she laid her spoon aside.

"Too cold already?" he asked, laying his own utensil into the empty bowl.

"No. I . . . am not in the mood for soup, after all. Shall we have the next course?"

His shoulders suddenly drooped. "Yes," he said in a resigned tone. "Let us proceed."

And so they did, the next course worse than the first. Not the food, of course. The food was delicious, even if she could barely eat a bite. But Jack . . . something was terribly amiss with him, only he wouldn't tell her what.

She endured another fifteen minutes of

his near silence before she'd finally had enough. Folding her napkin, she laid it aside. As she did, a quiver ran over her skin.

"You're shivering," he accused. "It's dark and chilly and you shouldn't be out in this weather. Not in your condition."

But her shivering had nothing to do with the cold or her pregnancy. "You're right," she said, tears rising in her eyes. "I-I'm going inside. I'm going to bed. This was a stupid, stupid idea."

"Then why did you do it?" he asked in a strange, dull voice. "Were you just trying to soften the blow?"

"Blow? What blow? You aren't making any sense. You haven't made sense all evening." She pushed her chair back and got clumsily to her feet. As she did, her control broke, tears raining down her face. "I-I was just t-trying to do s-something s-special, to c-celebrate and you've r-ruined it!"

"Ruined *what?* Celebrate *what?* God, Grace, are you crying?"

"No!" she wailed. Then she began to sob.

His arms came around her and pulled her close.

She struggled against him briefly before quieting as she continued to cry.

"Shh, I'm sorry. I'm sorry," he murmured, rubbing his palm over her back. "I'll leave if that's what you want. Just don't be unhappy. Please don't be sad."

"Leave?" she sniffed, her head coming up. "Why would I want you to leave?"

He met her gaze, his eyes stark in the candlelight. "Don't you? Isn't that what this was about tonight? A memorable last meal before you send me on my way?"

"No, I'm not sending you anywhere. Is that what you thought? Why you've been so h-horrible tonight?"

"I'm sorry. I guess I have been moody —"

"Moody! You've been abominable, and all for nothing. By God, Jack Byron, for an intelligent man you can be an idiot sometimes." She stepped back, wiping a palm against her wet face. "I did all of this tonight to tell you I love you! To say that I believe you really love me, that you have loved me. And that I forgive you for everything."

His lips parted. "You did? You do?"

"Yes. I thought it would be romantic to have dinner here in the garden. The garden you had p-planted just for me! Mr. Potsley told me what you did. He told me how you did all this so I would like it and I knew . . . I . . . knew you'd never have done so much if you didn't really care. If you didn't really love me! I was going to tell you after d-dinner but —"

"But I spoiled it," he said, reaching out to draw her back into his arms. "You're right, sweetheart. I am an idiot. A stupid dolt who jumps to ridiculous conclusions. Can you forgive me? Again?"

She sniffed. "I shouldn't. Not after tonight! But I will because I love you."

"Do you?" he murmured, a smile curving his lips. "I was afraid I'd killed off those feelings for good and that you'd never love me again."

"I've never stopped loving you," she confessed in a whisper. "Not even when I hated you. And for a while, I really *did* hate you!"

He laughed and hugged her tighter, then his expression grew serious. "And I really *do* love you. You are my dearest, most darling wife. My lover. My friend," he said, punctuating each declaration with a soft, sweet kiss.

She trembled and snuggled closer, drawing in his warmth.

"You *are* cold," he said, rubbing his hands over her arms. "Why don't we go inside in front of the fire and have our dessert."

"Actually, I'd rather postpone dessert and just go upstairs."

"Oh," he said, unable to hide the disappointment in his voice. "Of course, if you're tired, then you should rest."

"Who said anything about being tired?" she asked, sliding her arms around his waist. "I said I wanted to go upstairs. With you."

He met her gaze, a smile spreading slowly across his face. "Really?"

"Yes, really. So? What are you waiting for? Or have you lost your touch, my lord?" she added with an impish grin.

"*Lost my* — I'll show you all about my touch."

Claiming her mouth, he kissed her, heat rising to warm her skin from the inside out. By the time he let her come up for air, her pulse was throbbing, her toes curled in blissful delight inside her shoes.

"Now, what is it you were saying about my having lost something?" he drawled.

"Nothing," she sighed. "Absolutely nothing at all."

After another quick, hard kiss, he took her hand and pulled her into the house. Ignoring the curious glances of the footmen, they hurried up the stairs.

Without asking, he led her into his bedchamber. A small branch of lighted candles stood on a table near the window, a fire crackling pleasantly in the grate. Locking the door behind them, he crossed the room and drew the curtains closed.

"I've dreamt of having you here in my bed for weeks," he said, turning around. "Especially after your visit — your one and only visit. You have no idea all the fantasies I've spun about you in this room."

She smiled and draped her shawl over a chair. "Perhaps a few. You're not the only one whose bed has been lonely."

"You won't ever be lonely again." Taking her hands, he tugged her near for another long, sultry kiss. "Or alone."

That's when she saw his gaze drift downward, alighting on the heart-shaped pendant clasped around her neck.

"You're wearing it," he said, his words carrying a wondering tone.

Reaching up, she fingered the amethysts, then smoothed her thumb over the flat piece of porcelain in the center with its tiny painted garden. "Yes. Because I realize now that it was given in love."

"It was, even if I was too blind to know it at the time. Something else for which I must beg your forgiveness."

"It's yours." She laid her palm on his chest near his heart. "Did you really carry the pendant around with you when we were apart?"

"Constantly. It made me feel closer to you. Strange, I suppose, considering you wore it for such a brief time."

"Not so strange," she reassured. "I kept a handkerchief of yours, though I never planned to tell you that."

Leaning near, he pressed his lips to hers. "Besotted. The pair of us."

"Definitely."

"Now," he said, after another lingering kiss, "what do you say to getting naked?" He waggled his brows, eyes gleaming with wicked anticipation.

Giggling, she nodded, then let him help her undress.

It was only when she stood in her shift — the one thin garment all that separated her body from his gaze — that she felt herself grow shy.

"What's this now?" he asked, sliding a tender finger beneath her chin to tip up her face. "Are you turning bashful on me?"

"I've turned round with child," she said, confessing her qualms. "My shape is . . . fuller since the last time you saw me."

"Yes, and I can't wait to find out just how much lovelier you've become."

"But what if you . . ."

"Don't like the way you look? Impossible."

We'll see, she thought.

But her fears proved groundless, his eyes darkening with clear desire. Gently, reverently, his hands traced the shape of her new curves, careful of her breasts whose larger size he seemed to find particularly appealing.

"Lord above, Grace, you're magnificent."

Her muscles relaxed, her confidence returning. "I believe, my lord, that you're a bit overdressed at the moment."

He glanced at his fully clothed body. "I believe you're right."

While she stretched out across the sheets, she watched him undress, smiling at his haste.

He joined her, settling his long, powerful body against her own. But he was infinitely tender as his mouth took hers again, his hands wandering over her sensitive flesh in ways that literally stole her breath. Trembling, yearning, she waited for his possession, needing him, loving him, finally secure in the knowledge that he loved her too.

"Heavens, Jack, I've missed being like this with you."

"Not half as much as I have, I'll wager."

Winding her arms around his neck, she gave him a long, passionate kiss. "Perhaps we should bet on that?" she said. "After all, isn't that what started all this between us? A bet?"

"Indeed it is. And so long as you're the

prize, my love, then it's a wager I'll gladly make over and over and over again. But perhaps you need a demonstration?"

"Hmm, perhaps I do," she purred.

And to her ecstatic delight, he proceeded to show her that when it came to love, both of them were on the winning side.

EPILOGUE

Kent, England
Late February 1811

"Do you need anything?" Jack asked from his seat in the second-floor family drawing room.

Ensconced in a plump armchair opposite, Grace glanced up from her embroidery and met his gaze. "I'm fine, darling, but you're sweet to ask."

"Another blanket? I don't want you taking a chill."

"I think there's little likelihood of that," she replied, hiding a gentle grin.

Despite the snow-covered fields outside and the watery winter sunlight that was doing its best to filter through the windowpanes, the room was warm and cozy. A hearty fire blazed in the grate, Ranunculus curled up in a contented circle on a nearby side chair, his fur nearly as orange as the flames.

"What about food? Are you hungry?"

"Not after that huge plate of cakes and sandwiches I had just an hour ago. No wonder I'm as wide and round as one of those hot-air balloons Drake was talking about over the holidays. If I eat any more right now, I'll probably ascend. Or else pop."

He sent her a reproving look. "Don't be absurd. You're eight months pregnant, you're supposed to be round. As for your appetite, you're eating for two. So, no worrying about your figure — which is beautiful, I might add. Every morning, when I wake up and see you beside me, I ask myself how I ever got so lucky."

Joy burst inside her, turning her as gooey as melted sugar. "You really don't mind me keeping you up all night with my tossing and turning, or my having to get up every hour to use the commode?"

"No," he said in a serious tone. "I really do not."

"You could sleep in your old bedroom —"

"I'm not sleeping in my old bedroom. Never, ever again. Besides, you need me."

He was right. She did need him, and loved him so very deeply.

"Now, can you use another pillow?" he continued. "Your ankles are swollen. Do you have them propped up enough?"

With a little tug on her skirt, she showed him the pile of pillows under her feet. "I'm wonderful. Pampered as a pasha."

"Well, then, if there's nothing I can bring you, could you do with a kiss?"

A smile teased her lips. "I can always do with a kiss."

Standing, he moved close and bent down, bracing his hands on the chair arms on either side of her. Her eyelids floated downward, her heart thrumming with a quiet rapture as his lips met hers. Delight poured through her in a honeyed wave, a pleasure of which she knew she would never get enough. Every kiss was always as deliriously wonderful as the first, each touch somehow new and uniquely special.

Her senses were tingling, her skin flushed when he pulled away, carefully banked desire in his azure eyes.

Then their child kicked from within her with a force strong enough to draw Jack's gaze.

"Was that the baby?" he asked.

She nodded. "He's at it again. At least he's not pummeling me under my ribs like he was last night."

"She's strong-willed, like her mama. Has a definite mind of her own."

"What makes you so sure this is a girl?

Don't you want a son?"

He laid a wide palm over her belly and rubbed in a soothing motion. "Honestly, I don't care. Either will do fine by me."

"So, you won't object if I give you nothing but daughters?"

"I can't think of anything more delightful than spending my days surrounded by a flock of lovely Byron ladies."

"A flock, hmm? I haven't consented to producing a flock."

"You will," he murmured, dropping another long kiss on her mouth. "I'll persuade you somehow."

She knew he would, and that she'd delight in every moment.

A knock came at the door. "Pardon me, your lordship. Your ladyship," said a housemaid as she bobbed a curtsey. "I'm ever so sorry to interrupt, but the post just come. And a messenger as well."

"Put it over there on the table, would you?" Jack told the girl without looking around.

Grace rolled her eyes at him and bit her lip to keep from laughing.

"Now, where were we?" he asked as soon as the servant had gone.

"At a point where we should probably stop," she said ruefully.

He sighed and straightened. "I suspect you're right. Unfortunately. Shall I see what's in the mail?"

"Yes. Maybe the messenger has brought word from Cade. I wonder if Meg's had the baby yet? She's due any day now."

"Exactly," he agreed. "And she's safe and sound at Braebourne, where you should likely have stayed for your confinement, as well."

She laid a hand over her stomach. "The circumstances weren't the same at all. She and Cade live in Northumberland, and they were worried about finding themselves caught in a snowstorm during the birth. Or at least Cade was. Meg told me over Christmas that she would have been willing to risk it, but she worried Cade wouldn't fare so well. Especially if the doctor couldn't make it there in time. So a few months at Braebourne, it was."

"I ought to have insisted too. You'd have had family around to help you."

"I *have* family. I have you."

"I meant female family."

"You and Mrs. Mackie will be here, and the midwife. I know men aren't supposed to attend the birth, but I want you with me."

"Don't worry. I'll be there, though I doubt I'll be much help."

"I can hold your hand."

"And squeeze it as hard as you like, too."

She smiled, then returned to the previous topic. "As nice as Braebourne is, I want our child to be born here at home. *Our* home, that you chose for me."

"Well, I just want you to be happy. And while I like this house, the place isn't important. Wherever you are, whether it's here in Kent or London or anywhere else you may decide you wish to live, that's home to me."

His gaze met hers, his eyes warm and full of love. After a long moment, he turned and went to retrieve the mail.

"So, is there a letter from Cade?" she asked. "Did Meg have the baby?"

Returning to his seat, he flipped through the correspondence. "There is a letter, but it's from Edward."

"Well, open it. Let's hear."

He read silently for a moment, then smiled. "She's had the baby. A boy, born on the twenty-first. They haven't named him yet, but they'll send word again as soon as they do. Apparently, Cade would have written to tell us the good news himself, but he was too exhausted. Meg's labor went on for nearly nineteen hours and Cade was frantic with worry. But mother and baby are doing fine, both of them hale and happy."

"Oh, I'm so glad. What else does he say?"

"Mama was a godsend, apparently. Kept everyone calm. She says to tell you that if you haven't delivered in the next two weeks and Meg and the baby are still doing well, that she would love to come here to help with your lying-in."

"Your mother is wonderful, and I would adore having her here for the birth. Of course you must write and say she is most welcome."

Jack dipped his head, but not before she saw a glint of relief in his eyes. She knew in her heart, though, that he had no cause to worry. Everything was going to go well, and next month they would bring a beautiful new baby into the world. On the other hand, she had to confess that it would be reassuring having his mother with them to give advice and lend her support.

Laying a hand on her rounded belly, she let herself daydream.

"What's this now!" he declared. "Good heavens, I don't believe it."

"Believe what?"

"He's really going to do it!"

"Do what?"

"Get married."

"Edward, you mean?"

He nodded. "He says the time has arrived for him to take a duchess."

"Well, if Edward wants to marry, I can't see the harm. I assume he's going to look for a wife during the Season."

"No, he's already found one. They've been betrothed for years."

Her jaw dropped open, stunned to silence.

"Exactly!" he said in complete agreement. "Ned says he hopes we'll be able to come to London this summer to meet her, if the baby is able to travel by then, of course."

She considered for a long moment. "Well, we'll have to go, since I'm sure my curiosity won't let me stay home."

Their gazes met and they both smiled. A yawn caught her a few seconds later, her eyes growing moist with sleepiness.

Folding the letter in half, Jack set it aside. "Nap time."

"I don't need a nap," she protested.

"You most certainly do, since you got barely a wink last night." Standing, he leaned down to help her out of her chair. "Come, my lady. It's off to bed with you."

"Now why does that sound so vastly improper when you say it?" she murmured, as he levered her to her feet.

"Because I'm a vastly improper sort of man." Enfolding her in his arms, which were long enough to reach around her, even with the baby between them, he drew her close for a kiss. "Aren't you glad?"

"Eternally." A radiant smile stole over her face. "I love you, Jack Byron."

He kissed her again. "I love you, too, Grace Byron."

"I know you do. You show me every day just how much. Now, take me to bed, my lord."

Tucking her against his side, Jack did exactly that.

We hope you have enjoyed this Large Print book. Other Thorndike, Wheeler, and Chivers Press Large Print books are available at your library or directly from the publishers.

For information about current and upcoming titles, please call or write, without obligation, to:

Publisher
Thorndike Press
295 Kennedy Memorial Drive
Waterville, ME 04901
Tel. (800) 223-1244

or visit our Web site at:

http://gale.cengage.com/thorndike

OR

Chivers Large Print
published by BBC Audiobooks Ltd
St James House, The Square
Lower Bristol Road
Bath BA2 3SB
England
Tel. +44(0) 800 136919
email: bbcaudiobooks@bbc.co.uk
www.bbcaudiobooks.co.uk

All our Large Print titles are designed for easy reading, and all our books are made to last.